Steve nodded gravely. "It was a set up, Maura. The tax records you needed were right next to the section of floor that collapsed. And I'm willing to bet that those floor joists suffered a lot more than simple earthquake damage."

"But . . . why would someone want to kill me?" Maura asked.

"For something you knew. Or something they thought you were about to remember. Someone knew your memory was coming back. Who did you tell?"

"No one. Just you, and Jan, and Nita. And Nita told Hank."

"Then one of them told someone. Or someone noticed. How about Liz? Did she know?"

Maura started to shake her head, but then stopped. "It's possible. She was wearing a necklace and I commented on how beautiful it was. I'm sure Liz mentioned it to Keith, and that means Keith would have known that my memory was coming back."

Steve nodded. "Okay. We'll add Keith and Liz to the list. And they might have told any number of people. How about Jan?"

Maura sighed. "She told me that David guessed."

"I'll add David. This is getting us nowhere, Maura. Too many people are involved already. I think we'd better approach it from another angle."

"What other angle?"

"It's time for you to remember everything," Steve said. "Think back, Maura. There's a reason someone's trying to kill you. Think back and try to remember that reason for me . . ."

**NOWHERE TO RUN . . . NOWHERE TO HIDE . . .
ZEBRA'S SUSPENSE WILL *GET* YOU —
AND WILL MAKE YOU BEG FOR MORE!**

NOWHERE TO HIDE   (4035, $4.50)
by Joan Hall Hovey

After Ellen Morgan's younger sister has been brutally murdered, the highly respected psychologist appears on the evening news and dares the killer to come after her. After a flood of leads that go nowhere, it happens. A note slipped under her windshield states, "YOU'RE IT." Ellen has woken the hunter from its lair . . . and she is his prey!

SHADOW VENGEANCE   (4097, $4.50)
by Wendy Haley

Recently widowed Maris learns that she was adopted. Desperate to find her birth parents, she places "personals" in all the Texas newspapers. She receives a horrible response: "You weren't wanted then, and you aren't wanted now." Not to be daunted, her search for her birth mother — and her only chance to save her dangerously ill child — brings her closer and closer to the truth . . . and to death!

RUN FOR YOUR LIFE   (4193, $4.50)
by Ann Brahms

Annik Miller is being stalked by Gibson Spencer, a man she once loved. When Annik inherits a wilderness cabin in Maine, she finally feels free from his constant threats. But then, a note under her windshield wiper, and shadowy form, and a horrific nighttime attack tell Annik that she is still the object of this lovesick madman's obsession . . .

EDGE OF TERROR   (4224, $4.50)
by Michael Hammonds

Jessie thought that moving to the peaceful Blue Ridge Mountains would help her recover from her bitter divorce. But instead of providing the tranquility she desires, they cast a shadow of terror. There is a madman out there — and he knows where Jessie lives — and what she has seen . . .

NOWHERE TO RUN   (4132, $4.50)
by Pat Warren

Socialite Carly Weston leads a charmed life. Then her father, a celebrated prosecutor, is murdered at the hands of a vengeance-seeking killer. Now he is after Carly . . . watching and waiting and planning. And Carly is running for her life from a crazed murderer who's become judge, jury — and executioner!

Available wherever paperbacks are sold, or order direct from the Publisher. Send cover price plus 50¢ per copy for mailing and handling to Penguin USA, P.O. Box 999, c/o Dept. 17109, Bergenfield, NJ 07621. Residents of New York and Tennessee must include sales tax. DO NOT SEND CASH.

DEADLY MEMORIES

JOANNE FLUKE

ZEBRA BOOKS
KENSINGTON PUBLISHING CORP.

ZEBRA BOOKS are published by

Kensington Publishing Corp.
850 Third Avenue
New York, NY 10022

Copyright © 1995 by Joanne Fluke

All rights reserved. No part of this book may be reproduced in any form or by any means without the prior written consent of the Publisher, excepting brief quotes used in reviews.

If you purchased this book without a cover you should be aware that this book is stolen property. It was reported as "unsold and destroyed" to the Publisher and neither the Author nor the Publisher has received any payment for this "stripped book."

Zebra and the Z logo Reg. U.S. Pat. & TM Off.

First Printing: February, 1995

Printed in the United States of America

This one's for you, Ruel.

And thank you to everyone who helped us out, during the earthquake.

Prologue

Hank Jensen smiled as he drove the white stretch limousine up the Sunset Boulevard on-ramp, and merged smoothly with the existing freeway traffic. It was a good hour for a trip to the airport, shortly past eight on a Thursday night. Rush hour was over, movies and plays had already begun, and the drunks were still in the bars. He signaled a lane change and eased over to the fast lane, dropping in behind the brown Mercedes he'd been following.

A champagne cork popped in the back of the limo, the second in less than ten miles. It was a damn good thing they were riding instead of driving! They'd already been stoned when he'd picked them up at the hotel, and now they were adding booze to the mix.

Hank glanced down at his clipboard. According to his call sheet, his passengers were called the Speed Streeters. They were dressed in identical silver jumpsuits, three skinny guys and a girl with kinky red hair who didn't look more than sixteen. At least rock groups were usually good tippers, unless they got so bent out of shape they forgot.

It was a hot summer night in Los Angeles, and Hank rolled down his window. The Speed Streeters had the air-conditioning cranked up so high, he was beginning to shiver. He preferred to drive with the window open anyway, a throwback to his teenage years in rural Texas. The family pickup truck hadn't been equipped with anything as fancy as air-conditioning, and he'd gotten used to driving around with the wind in his face.

Hank figured he would have been stuck in Texas forever, if his uncle hadn't moved to L.A. to start the LoneStar Limo Service. It had taken some fast talking on his mother's part, but finally Uncle Jimmy had caved in and put him on the payroll.

There were times when Hank missed the wide-open spaces of Texas, but L.A. was an exciting city. He'd been working for Uncle Jimmy almost five years now, and he'd met his share of celebrities. Most of them were nice, and some of them had been very generous, like the Academy Award-winning actress and her husband he'd driven last month.

Hank had picked them up at their home in Beverly Hills and taken them to Rex, L.A.'s most expensive restaurant. Then he'd settled down in the parking lot to wait for them to finish their supper, which was called dinner out here. He'd just kicked off his shoes, tuned in his favorite jazz station on the radio, and cracked open a book, when a waiter had tapped on the window. The actress and her husband had sent out a complete meal for him: appetizer, salad, entree and dessert, along with a silver carafe of coffee.

It still made Hank grin to think of that night. It had been a real treat to taste all those expensive things he couldn't afford, like caviar and lobster and hearts of palm. And to top matters off, at the end of the evening, the actress and her husband had slipped him an envelope with a crisp hundred dollar bill inside!

Hank took a big gulp of the air rushing past his open window, and smiled. The highway department had planted some night-blooming jasmine by the side of the Overland Avenue off-ramp, and the air smelled fresh and sweet. It was quite a change from the exhaust fumes that usually clogged the air. California had beautiful landscaping by its freeways. He was always seeing something unusual like a hill covered with pink oleanders, or a whole section of tall plants that looked like plumes.

The airport exit was about a mile ahead, and Hank changed lanes in tandem with the driver of the brown Mercedes. Now that he was following more closely, he could read its license plate, DPRESHE8.

"Depreciate." Hank grinned to acknowledge the clever plate. Someone had a good sense of humor. And then he pulled forward to pace the brown Mercedes. Just as he'd expected, the driver was a middle-aged man with neatly styled silver hair who looked like an accountant, but he wasn't adding up columns of figures right now. Mr. Accountant was very busy talking to his female passenger.

Just as Hank was about to ease up on his accelerator, the woman pulled down her visor to use the lighted make-up mirror. She was holding a carry-on airline bag in her lap, and she would have been beautiful if she hadn't been crying. A second look and Hank changed his mind. The tears made no difference; she was still a knockout with her shining red hair and bright green eyes. As Hank watched, she slipped on a pair of dark glasses and brushed back her hair with long, slender fingers. It was a totally feminine gesture, and Hank felt a tug of sympathy. He wished he could magically transport her to the front seat of his limo where he could dry her tears, and find out why she was so sad.

The airport exit was just ahead, and Hank slowed down

to drop in behind them. He was careful to leave plenty of room as he followed the Mercedes off the freeway. They were doing some new construction at the airport, and traffic had been re-routed up a steep ramp and then down in a series of dangerously sharp turns.

Flashing lights and caution signs flanked both sides of the ramp, and Hank dropped back another car length. This section of temporary roadway was extremely dangerous. He watched as the brown Mercedes crested the top of the hill and its brake lights flashed brightly. Mr. Accountant was a cautious driver. But instead of slowing, as the brake lights indicated, the brown Mercedes seemed to leap forward into the curves, picking up speed and swerving dangerously.

Tires squealed as the Mercedes fishtailed down the steep grade, and Hank hit his own brakes. Mr. Accountant was going to wipe out right in front of him!

Hank stomped hard on the brakes, and steered to a screeching halt. There were muffled curses from the back of the limo, but he didn't have time to worry about spilled champagne. He jumped out and watched as Mr. Accountant side-swiped the guard rail on the right side of the ramp.

Miraculously, the wooden barrier held. But the glancing impact sent the Mercedes careening across the full width of the ramp, heading straight for the opposite rail.

The beautiful woman screamed in terror. Hank could hear her clearly. And a split second later, the brown Mercedes plowed through the left barrier and tumbled end over end down the steep embankment.

Chapter One

Maura woke up to the sound of a voice. Someone was calling her name. Her head felt huge and fuzzy, as if someone had emptied out everything inside and filled it with fluffy cotton batten. If this was a hangover, she'd never drink again!

It took her a moment to remember the events of the preceding day. She'd taken her dreaded chemistry final and nailed it cold. Her roommate's tutoring had really paid off. Maura had been so grateful, she'd taken her roommate out to dinner, and they'd ended up at the campus pub. If her pounding headache was any indication, she must have had much more than her customary mug of beer.

The voice was still calling her, and Maura groaned. She'd told everyone that she was sleeping late this morning, and there was a DO NOT DISTURB sign on her door. Why wouldn't the voice leave her alone?

Maura groaned again and tried to shake her head, but it was just too heavy to move. If the voice would only go away, she could go back to sleep. Even ten minutes more might help to clear her head.

"Maura? Wake up, Maura. I want you to open your eyes."

It was no use. The voice was too persistent. She'd have to see what it wanted. But it was a man's voice, and men weren't allowed in the dorm unless they were family. What a lousy time for her father to drop in for a surprise visit!

She tried to open her eyes, but they felt as if they were glued shut. Then someone dabbed at her eyelids with something cold and wet. It felt good and she managed to gasp out a word, "Thanks."

"You're welcome." It was the man's voice again, but he no longer sounded like her father. "Try to open your eyes, Maura."

Maura tried, but nothing happened. Her eyelids were as heavy as the lead sinkers her father used on his fishing line.

"You can do it. Come on, Maura. Open your eyes."

Maura concentrated, and her eyelids lifted slightly. She doubled her efforts and they opened, slowly. She'd done it. Maybe he'd give her an "A" in Eye-Opening 101.

But the sight that greeted her was completely foreign! She was in a bed in a room with pale green walls. It was a sterile room, no paintings on the walls, no rugs on the floors. It certainly looked nothing like the dorm room she'd taken such pains to decorate.

Light flickered on the far wall, and Maura's eyes were drawn to a television set which was perched on a high ledge facing the bed. The volume was inaudible, but the picture was on. And it was in color!

For a moment Maura was sure that she was dreaming. Color television sets were terribly expensive. None of her friends could afford one. The set in her parents' living room was black and white, and so was the one in the rec room at the dorm.

Maura was so startled to see Dan Rather in color, she almost didn't notice how awful he looked. It hadn't been in the papers, but he must have terribly ill. He'd aged dreadfully since the last time she'd switched on the news.

As she watched, Dan Rather's face was replaced by a commercial for something called Diet Coke. It must be a new product, since she'd never seen it in the stores. But the next commercial, for Ivory Soap, was comfortably familiar. She tore her eyes away from the novelty of actually seeing the blue and white wrapper on a television screen, and began to look around the room again.

Three green plastic chairs were pushed against the wall beneath the television set. And there was a door which was slightly ajar, leading to a small, institutional-looking bathroom.

Where was she? Even though it was difficult, Maura turned her head slightly. The blinds on the window were open, but all she could see beyond the glass was the top of a palm tree. That was no help. Palm trees were common in Southern California.

A table-type cart sat under the window, and it held a massive bouquet of beautiful flowers. There was a small white card attached to a leaf, but it was difficult to read at this distance. She squinted and made out the words, WE LOVE YOU, and then the man's voice spoke again.

"Could you look at me, please?"

Maura tried to turn her head toward the voice, but it was impossible. Something tight was clamped around her neck, restricting her movement. "I can't. My neck won't turn."

"Hold on a minute. I'll take off your brace. You don't need it, now that you're conscious."

She could hear his footsteps behind her. His fingers touched the side of her neck and something ripped. She must have winced, because he held a long white cuff up in front of her eyes.

"I'm sorry if I scared you. It's just a neck brace with a Velcro fastener."

Maura watched as he lapped one end of the cuff over the other. Something made them stick together. Then he pulled them apart and she heard that awful ripping sound again.

"Look this way, please."

It was definitely a command, and Maura turned to look at the voice. It belonged to a handsome man in a white lab coat who seemed vaguely familiar, but that could be explained by the fact that he looked exactly like Paul Newman. She was wild about Paul Newman, and she'd gone to see *The Sting* just last week.

This Paul Newman look-alike was wearing a doctor's stethoscope around his neck, and suddenly everything was clear. She was in a hospital. That explained the bouquet of flowers. And it must be a very expensive hospital if they had color television sets in every room. It was a good thing she'd remembered to send off the premium for her student health insurance!

"What's my name?"

Maura stared at him for a moment and then she began to smile. He was wearing a white plastic identification badge on the front of his lab coat. It read, DR. S. BENNETT, NEUROLOGY. And above his name in small red letters was the name of the hospital, Cedars-Sinai. If this was some kind of test, they should flunk the doctor for failing to take off his name-tag.

"You're Dr. Bennett, Neurologist. And I'm in Cedars-Sinai Hospital."

Her answer seemed to startle him. He stared at her and blinked several times. Then he recovered enough to ask,

"How did you know they took you to Cedars' after the accident?"

"I didn't know . . . ," Maura grinned up at him, ". . . but that's what it says on your badge."

Dr. Bennett glanced down at the front of his lab coat and raised his eyebrows. Then he gave her a sheepish smile. "Okay, my mistake. I forgot I was wearing it. Can you tell me your name?"

"Of course I can." Maura thought about stopping there, but she'd heard that most doctors lacked a sense of humor. He was only asking her a standard set of questions, and it would be smart to cooperate. "It's Maura. I know who I am. But I don't remember why I'm here. You said something about an accident?"

"You were involved in an auto accident three weeks ago. You've had a rough time, but you're going to be just fine."

"I was in a coma for three weeks!?"

Dr. Bennett nodded and turned to head for the door. "Just rest for a minute, Maura. There's somebody here who wants to see you."

The moment the door had clicked shut behind him, Maura struggled to sit up in bed. Her legs moved easily under the sheet. Nothing wrong there. But her arms felt sore, and there was a large, multicolored bruise on her elbow.

Wincing a little, Maura reached up to touch her head. It was bandaged in a turban-like arrangement of gauze and tape that completely covered every inch of her scalp. She must have had some sort of head injury, that much was clear. She just hoped they hadn't shaved off her hair!

The door opened again and Dr. Bennett strode in, followed by a pretty girl with long, blond hair. Was she a classmate? She looked very familiar, but Maura couldn't quite place her.

"I'm so glad you're all right!" The girl rushed to the bed and bent down to kiss Maura's cheek. Even though she was smiling, she was blinking back tears. Who was this girl? And why was she so concerned?

Maura did her best to remember, but she drew a complete blank. Perhaps she was one of the new girls from the dorm. She'd met them all at a get-acquainted dinner, but she hadn't sorted out all the names and faces yet.

"How do you feel?" The girl was staring at her anxiously.

"Not too bad, considering." Maura reached up to touch her turban bandage. "Do you know if they shaved off my hair?"

The girl turned to Dr. Bennett. "Did they? You were here when they brought her in."

"Since there were no skull fractures, they just clipped it short. Don't worry, Maura. You'll look like a punk rocker for a couple of months, but it'll grow back."

A punk rocker? Maura frowned slightly. She'd never heard that particular phrase before. It must be funny, because the girl was laughing.

"Come on, Uncle Steve! That's the last thing she needs to hear!"

Uncle Steve? Maura raised her eyebrows in surprise. The blonde girl and Dr. Bennett were related. But she was almost sure she hadn't met any girls named Bennett. Of course he could be her uncle on her mother's side. Or even . . .

"Sorry, Maura." Dr. Bennett turned to her, interrupting her train of thought. "I know you'd rather visit, but I'm afraid I have to ask a few more questions. What is your address?"

"Room two-thirteen, Andrews Hall. It's a girls' dorm on campus. I'm a sophomore at San Diego State."

Dr. Bennett looked startled and so did his niece. She must

not be a dorm girl after all. But what was so surprising about living on campus?

"You live in San Diego!?"

"Yes, I do." Maura frowned slightly. Of course she lived in San Diego. It was much too far to commute from her parents' home in Brawley. She was about to ask them what was wrong, when a delivery boy came through the door.

"Oh! How lovely!" Maura couldn't help but react as he set the beautiful arrangement of pink roses on the bedside table. "Who sent them?"

"They're from your husband. He ordered them by phone this morning."

"My husband?" Now it was Maura's turn to look startled. It took her a moment to figure it out, but then she realized what had happened. "Sorry. You've got the wrong room."

"You're not Mrs. Thomas? In room five-fourteen?"

"No." Maura shook her head. "I'm Maura Rawlins. And I'm not married."

Dr. Bennett and his niece exchanged a worried look. What was going on? Then the niece reached out and took her hand.

"You really don't know me, do you?"

There was such terrible longing on her pretty face, that Maura was tempted to lie. But something about this girl's level, green-eyed gaze told her she had to tell the truth.

"I'm so terribly sorry." Maura felt tears well up in her own eyes. "I recognize you. And I know that I know you. But I just can't seem to remember."

"Oh!"

It was a cry of pure anguish, and tears spilled over to run down the girl's cheeks. Before Maura had time to think about how inappropriate it might be, she was pulling her close to hug her and stroke her soft, golden hair.

"Don't cry, honey." Maura blinked back her own tears. "I never meant to hurt you. I . . . I love you!"

Dr. Bennett's niece raised her head and gave Maura a tremulous smile. "Everything's going to be all right. I'll help, I promise. And I love you, too, Mom."

Chapter Two

There was a gentle tap on the door, and a nurse stepped into the room. She smiled as she set a small leather suitcase on the bedside table. "Here's your suitcase, Mrs. Thomas."

"Thank you." Maura smiled back, although she felt more like frowning. A full week had passed and she still wasn't used to her married name. Everyone had assured her that she was, indeed, Mrs. Keith Thomas. She'd even met the man she'd supposedly married two years ago. He seemed nice enough, and he was very handsome, but Maura still felt as if she were in a movie, playing the part of his wife. She had absolutely no memory of her husband or the life they'd shared before her accident. Nothing seemed personal, and she couldn't help feeling that the past twenty-three years of her life had happened to someone else.

"Your daughter's in the lobby. Just call the desk when you're ready and she'll come in to take you home."

Maura nodded. She didn't remember her daughter, either, but Janelle seemed much more familiar than Keith Thomas. Jan, as she liked to be called, had come to the hospital every day. And as they had visited, waiting for the day when Maura would be released, Jan had done her best to fill in some of the blanks.

Maura now knew that Keith Thomas was her second husband. Jan's father, Maura's first husband, was dead. Maura had married Paul Bennett right after her senior year of college. Paul had been an lieutenant in the Navy, and they'd lived in an apartment in San Diego until he had been killed in a routine training mission, five months before Jan's birth. Jan had never known her father, and in some strange way, that information had made Maura feel a little better. She had no memory of Paul Bennett, and neither did Jan. They could learn about him together.

After Jan had been born, her Uncle Steve had come into their lives. Steven Bennett was Paul's older brother, and he'd arranged for Maura and Jan to move to Los Angeles. Paul's life insurance benefits had been enough to make a down payment on a condo, and Steve and his wife, Donna, had financed Maura's clothing boutique. The Bennetts had found a wonderful housekeeper to look after Jan while Maura was working, and Nita Ramos was still with Maura, in her new, expensive home in Brentwood.

Maura, Jan, and Nita were part of the Bennetts' extended family. They'd spent every summer at Steve and Donna's cottage in Malibu, learned to ski at their mountain cabin in Big Bear, and attended frequent dinner parties and social functions at the Bennett home in Beverly Hills. Since Steve and Donna had no children, Jan had been like a daughter to them. They'd organized birthday parties for her, gone to all of her school plays and concerts, and even helped her with her homework.

It wasn't just Jan the Bennetts had helped. They'd supported Maura financially, until her boutique had begun to show a profit, and Donna had used her social connections to send high-profile customers to Maura's little shop. Donna had encouraged Maura to market original designs, and some very prominent Beverly Hills women had started to wear Maura's creations. Maura's line of clothing, which she called "Mystique," had grown from a few designer gowns to a full line of high fashion women's clothing. But the Bennetts had given Maura much more than money and encouragement.

Maura had found a loving family to rely on. Uncle Steve and Aunt Donna had never been too busy to baby-sit when Maura had gone on buying trips, or been forced to work late at the boutique. They'd always been there when Maura had needed a shoulder to cry on, or when she'd needed advice. They'd helped her celebrate special occasions, like birthdays and holidays, and Maura, Jan, and Nita had always been included on their vacations. With such a wonderful family, Maura hadn't seemed to need anyone else . . . until Jan had gone away to college and she'd met Keith Thomas.

Jan hadn't told Maura much about her stepfather. She'd dutifully answered questions, but Maura had the uneasy feeling that her daughter didn't really like Keith. It wasn't anything Jan had said; it was what she hadn't said. Jan had shared all sorts of wonderful stories about Nita, and Uncle Steve, and Aunt Donna. She'd even cried when she'd told Maura about Aunt Donna's battle with the cancer that had eventually taken her life. But Jan hadn't volunteered any information at all about Keith, and she'd seemed almost reluctant to talk about him.

"Would you like me to help you, Mrs. Thomas?"

Maura looked up, startled, to see that the nurse was still in the room. "Oh, no, thank you. I'm sure I can manage."

"I'll leave you then." The nurse turned at the door, and gestured toward Maura's suitcase. "That's gorgeous luggage, Mrs. Thomas. Your daughter said it was your favorite."

Maura waited until the door had closed, and then she reached out to touch the soft leather of her suitcase. The nurse was right. It was gorgeous. Although she couldn't remember seeing it before, a name popped into her head. Mario Ammante. This luggage was from the Ammante line, and it came in three colors. This lovely butterscotch, a deep, rich black, and a warm, mahogany brown.

But how did she know that? Did she carry this line of luggage in her boutique? There were so many questions, Maura's head began to pound. She reached out for the bottle of pain pills on her bedside table, but she stopped short of opening it. Although the pills alleviated her pounding headaches, they made her slightly woozy. She'd settle for aspirin, instead. Her headache wasn't that severe, and it was better to have all her wits about her for her return home.

Home. Maura's heart raced in her chest. The last home she remembered was her dorm room at San Diego State, over twenty years ago. When she walked in the door of her house in Brentwood, would it jog her memory? Would she miraculously be cured when she was back in familiar surroundings? Steve had called in an important specialist, and he had told her that it could happen that way. But he'd also warned her that it might take much longer to regain the years of memories that she had lost.

Maura's hands trembled slightly when she unzipped the small leather suitcase and lifted the lid. Nestled inside was a dark green suit. Was this lovely green her favorite color? Had she worn this suit before? Maura blinked and sudden tears came to her eyes. She seemed to remember touching this material before, but that could be wishful thinking.

Under the suit was a frilly, white blouse, and tucked in a

side pocket of the suitcase were silk undergarments. She found fashionable leather shoes in a zippered shoe bag, and a pair of gold earrings and a necklace in a jewelry case. The jewelry was obviously expensive, and that brought up another series of unanswered questions. Had the jewelry been a gift? Or had she purchased it herself? She'd forgotten to ask Jan about her finances. Was she as wealthy as this jewelry seemed to indicate?

Maura felt like a little girl playing dress-up as she slipped into the unfamiliar clothes. The skirt was a bit loose around the waist, but Steve had told her that she'd lost some weight while she'd been in the hospital. That was something else she'd have to ask Jan. Was she one of the incredibly lucky women who could eat anything she wanted without gaining an ounce? Or did she have to watch every calorie to keep her trim figure?

When she was completely dressed, Maura risked a glance in the bathroom mirror. She had short red hair with blonde highlights, green eyes that were the color of the sea on a calm day, high cheekbones that were nicely defined, a generous mouth which seemed to smile naturally, and delicate skin that looked as if it might burn with too much exposure to the sun.

Maura sighed as she gazed at her reflection. The face that stared back at her was almost familiar. She was getting used to her appearance, but she still felt a bit like Rip Van Winkle. Each time she looked at her image in the mirror, she expected to see a young college girl, eager to discover what life was all about. She was always slightly shocked when she encountered this attractive woman in her early forties, who might have been her mother.

There was another tap on the door, and Maura turned away from the mirror. "Come in."

"Hi, Mom!" Jan was smiling as she hurried over to hug her. "You look great!"

Maura smiled back. "Thank you. So do you . . . I think."

"Uh-oh." Jan looked a little guilty as she glanced down at her blue jeans. They were ripped at both knees. "They're fashionable, Mom . . . honest. And I didn't rip them. I bought them this way."

Maura laughed. "That's definitely an example of marketing genius. What's next? Pre-soiled t-shirts?"

"Mom!" Jan's mouth dropped open and she looked completely shocked. "That's what you always say!"

"I do?"

Jan nodded, and then she began to smile. "That's a great sign, Mom! I think your memory's beginning to come back. It's just like Uncle Steve said. Familiar things might jog your memory, and you've seen me wear these jeans about a million times."

"I see." The corners of Maura's mouth began to twitch. "Does that mean you're going to live in those jeans until I remember everything?"

Jan's eyebrows shot up and she giggled. "No, Mom. I'll change when we get home if they bother you. And I promise I won't wear them to any of your fancy family dinners."

"Fancy dinners?" Maura took a deep breath. "I know this is a strange question, Jan . . . but am I a good cook?"

Jan nodded. "Gourmet caliber. Uncle Steve says your *coquilles St. Jacques à la Parisienne* is the best he's ever tasted."

"Oh. I see." Maura smiled at her daughter, but when she turned to pick up the expensive leather purse everyone said belonged to her, there was real worry in her deep green eyes. Not only had she forgotten how to make *coquilles St. Jacques à la Parisienne,* she didn't even know what it was!

* * *

Maura's head was aching by the time Jan pulled her little blue Miata into a driveway off Cliffwood Avenue and stopped before a pair of ornate, wrought-iron gates. Jan had pointed out various sights as they'd driven here from the hospital, and although Maura had tried her best to remember, she hadn't recalled seeing any of them before.

"Do you know where we are, Mom?"

Jan looked hopeful, and Maura didn't have the heart to disappoint her. "Of course I do, honey. We're home."

"Mom!" Jan reached over to squeeze her hand. "You remembered!"

For a moment, Maura almost went through with the deception. But she couldn't start out what she'd begun to think of as her new life by lying to her daughter. She took a deep breath, and shook her head. "No, honey. I don't remember."

"Then how did you know?" Jan looked puzzled.

"I didn't. This is the address on the driver's license I found in my purse, so I assumed it had to be our house."

Jan looked thoughtful for a moment, and then she smiled. "You do a great job faking it, Mom. I think you're going to get along just fine, even if you never get your memory back."

There was a frown on Maura's face, as Jan turned to press some numbers into the keypad mounted on a pole by the side of the driveway. She didn't even want to consider the possibility of not regaining her memory.

"Mom?" Jan turned to her again. "I don't suppose you remember the gate code, do you?"

"No, but it's probably 1984."

"That's right!" Jan looked utterly amazed. "But how did you guess?"

"It wasn't a guess. I started using 1984 for my personal code when I was still in high school. It was the combination of my locker, the last four digits of my phone number, and the number of my personal license plates."

"Why in the world did you ever use . . . ?" Jan stopped suddenly and started to grin. "I get it! You were a big Orwell fan?"

"Right." Maura smiled back. "I didn't really believe Orwell's predictions could happen, but 1984 seemed so far in future, none of us really knew. It was a kind of landmark date. We all wondered what we'd be doing then, where we'd be living, whether we'd be married and have children. And now 1984's come and gone . . . and I don't remember one single thing about it."

Jan looked worried as her mother's smile faded, and she reached over to pat her shoulder. "I've got all those magazines you saved for me. You know . . . the year in retrospect? That sort of thing? We'll look through them together and I'll tell you everything I remember. And if there's something I don't know, we can call it up on the data bank."

"Data bank?"

"It's a service I've got for my computer. You do remember computers, don't you?"

Maura nodded. "Of course. But . . . you actually *own* one?"

"Sure. You bought an Apple for me, my last year in high school."

Maura tried to look as if she understood. Obviously, computers had come down in price. And this "apple" that Jan had referred to, it must be a type of computer. But suddenly, before she could make any comment at all, Jan started to laugh.

"Oh boy, am I a dunce! I keep forgetting where you're

coming from, Mom. For you, it's still the early seventies, when computers were priced out of sight, and no one had ever heard of compact, home models. It's like you're caught in a time warp . . . or don't you know what that is?"

"Star Trek." Maura nodded. "It was my favorite television show. And you're right, Jan. It is a little like a time warp. Is 'Star Trek' still around?"

"Sort of. Now, we've got spin-offs. There's 'Star Trek, The Next Generation,' and 'Deep Space Nine', but nothing beats the originals. They made some movies, too. My favorite is *Star Trek IV*. That's when they come back to earth to . . . no, I won't tell you." Jan turned to grin at her. "I've got it on tape and we'll watch it in the living room tonight, if you're not too tired. Is that okay?"

"Yes. That's fine." Maura nodded.

"Great! Now let's get inside before Nita dies of excitement. She can hardly wait to see you!"

Maura watched while Jan punched in the code. The ornate gates slid smoothly open, and she took a deep breath, preparing for the first sight of the home she didn't remember. As the little blue Miata moved forward through the ornate gates and up the winding driveway, she wondered what "tape" was, and how they could watch a movie in their own living room.

Chapter Three

Maura stood for a moment, staring up at the huge, yellow brick house looming over her. She didn't say a word. She was too stunned. She'd thought she'd seen everything when Jan had led her across the little wooden bridge that spanned a miniature ravine planted with wildflowers, but her first sight of the house she owned left her speechless.

"Well? What do you think, Mom?"

Jan turned to her with hope in her eyes, but Maura shook her head. "I'm sorry, honey. I can't remember ever seeing it before."

"That's okay." Jan's smile was falsely bright. "You're probably sick of being asked, so I'll stop. But you'll tell me if you recognize anything, won't you?"

Maura nodded. Jan was very perceptive. "You'll be the second to know, kiddo, right after me."

"That's another thing you always say!" Jan looked pleased. "Our house is beautiful, isn't it?"

"Very. Actually, it's more than beautiful. It's the home I dreamed I'd have someday."

Jan nodded. "That's what you said when we bought it.

You told me that it was your dream come true. Are you ready to go in and face Nita?"

"I think so." Maura frowned slightly. "Is there something I should know about facing Nita?"

"She always rattles things off in Spanish when she's excited. And she speaks so fast, you have trouble following her."

Maura looked at Jan in surprise. "I speak Spanish?"

"Sure. Nita says you speak like a native. You took intensive Spanish when you were a senior in college, and . . ." Jan stopped suddenly and stared at Maura in alarm. "Uh-oh! You're not a senior yet. You're only a sophomore . . . right, Mom?"

Maura almost laughed. The whole thing seemed so crazy. But she gave a little nod. "I'm afraid you're right. I don't remember anything past the second quarter of my sophomore year. We'll have to tell Nita to speak English until I can take another Spanish class. She does speak English, doesn't she?"

"Oh, sure. Nita's bilingual. That's one of the reasons you . . ."

Jan stopped suddenly as the door was flung open and a short, heavy-set Mexican woman in her late forties came barreling out. She threw her arms around Maura, and kissed her on the cheek. And then she said something in rapid-fire Spanish, ending with the word "Maurita."

Maura was startled for a moment, but then she hugged her housekeeper back. It clear that Nita was genuinely fond of her. And something about the happy tears in Nita's eyes and the genuine warmth of her embrace convinced Maura that she was much more than a paid employee. She had the feeling that she'd shared secrets with Nita in the past, asked for her advice, and relied on her good judgment. And then a picture popped into her mind that made her draw in her breath sharply.

Jan saw the expression on Maura's face, and moved closer to take her hand. "What is it, Mom? Did you remember something?"

"I . . . I'm not sure. This crazy picture popped into my mind, just for a second. I was sitting at a table with Nita, drinking coffee with . . . with cinnamon. Do you make cinnamon coffee, Nita?"

Nita looked delighted as she nodded. "Yes, Miss Maura. Cinnamon and chocolate and chicory. I used to make it for you every night, when you came home from work. But I don't make it much anymore. Mr. Keith doesn't like it."

"You can still make it, can't you, Nita?" Jan's voice was eager.

Nita nodded again. "Yes. I will do it now. Take your mother to her room, Jan. She should change into that pretty blue outfit she likes so much. I moved it to the front of her closet. And then bring her to the kitchen. The coffee will be ready by then."

Maura's head was beginning to pound as she stepped into the house. It was vaguely familiar, but she didn't actually recognize anything as Jan led her up the stairs to her bedroom.

"This is your room." Jan indicated a closed door. "Keith's is right next door, and mine is down there at the end of the hall. Do you want me to help you change?"

Maura turned to her with a smile. "No, honey. I think I could use a little time alone. Give me a few minutes to change, and I'll tap on your door when I'm ready."

Jan nodded, but she seemed reluctant to leave. Maura smiled again as she realized why. "Don't worry, Jan. I'll be fine. And I promise that I'll come and get you right away if anything jogs my memory."

"Okay." Jan walked down the hall to her room, but she stopped, her hand on the doorknob, and turned back to face Maura. "There's a white telephone on your bed table, Mom. It's got an intercom system. Just lift the receiver and press number three if you need me."

Maura watched as Jan went into her room and shut the door. Jan had said that this was her room. And Keith's room was right next door. They were husband and wife, and they'd been married for over two years. Most married couples slept together, in the same room. Why did they have separate bedrooms?

It wasn't a question that she could ask Jan. And she certainly couldn't ask Keith! He'd seemed pleasant enough when he'd come to the hospital to visit, but she remembered absolutely nothing about him. Was she in love with Keith?

Maura shivered slightly as she thought about her husband. Keith had flown to New York last night. He'd been very apologetic when he'd come to the hospital to tell her about the series of business meetings he had scheduled. The meetings were very important. Keith had told her he'd be gone until the end of the week, but he'd offered to cancel if she needed him at home.

Naturally, Maura had told him to go. Jan would take her home, and help her settle in. There was really no reason to cancel his trip. They had the rest of their lives together.

Keith had hugged her, and kissed her lightly on the forehead. He'd told her that she'd always been very understanding. It was one of the reasons he loved her so much. And then he'd left to catch his plane.

Maura had mixed feelings about Keith. She wanted her husband by her side, but she was also relieved that he was gone. Keith represented one more set of problems she wouldn't have to deal with immediately. She had plenty of time to prepare for her husband's return. But even though she tried not to worry, she was naturally concerned about what Keith would expect from her.

Maura's hand was trembling as she grasped the doorknob and turned it. What sort of relationship did she have with Keith? Did he come to her room to make love to her? Did she go to his? Or was their marriage in name only? Nita was their housekeeper. She would certainly know. But how could she ask Nita such a personal question?

Maura took a deep breath and let it out again, gathering the courage to open her door. What secrets would this room hold? Bedrooms were private places. Would her bedroom hold clues to the missing years of her life?

She had to find out. Maura took another deep breath and opened the door. She stepped in quickly, closed the door behind her, and gasped at the lovely furnishings. As a young college girl, she'd stretched out on her inexpensive cotton bedspread and stared up at the perfectly square acoustical ceiling of her dorm room, dreaming about the day when she could have a bedroom exactly like this. It wasn't a square little box, like her dorm room, or the small bedroom she'd had as a child. This was a huge rectangular space, with all sorts of wonderful nooks and crannies. It even had a bay window with a window seat!

As Maura moved further into the room, she began to smile in delight. The colors were perfect; ivory and rose with touches of forest green. The bedspread had printed Victorian lace on an ivory background sprinkled with cabbage roses and scattered rosebuds. Rose clusters and ivory satin piping decorated the draped lace pillow shams, and the sheets and pillowcases had lovely Victorian lace at the hems.

The table by the bed was draped with a cloth of the same design, and a boudoir lamp with a fringed, rose-colored shade sat in the exact center of the table top.

The bed seemed huge, and Maura knew it must be king-sized. She laughed softly as she sat gingerly on the edge of the mattress and stroked the lace border of the pillowcase. She was five feet, nine inches tall and after years of coping with a small, twin-sized bed, she'd promised herself that the first purchase she'd make would be a king-sized bed.

And what a bed it was! Maura's smile grew broader as she noticed the ornate brass headboard. It must have cost her a fortune! Nothing she saw, as she gazed around her, could be found at a bargain basement sale. What she'd thought was wallpaper was actually ivory satin material, covered with lace.

Maura gasped as she noticed the curtains. They were lace and satin, and it was clear they'd been made especially for this room. The floor was hardwood, polished to a dull gleam, and it was partially covered by a large, tapestry-style rug with a design of scattered roses.

There was a wing-backed chair in the corner of the room, covered with mauve velvet. A lamp with a fringed shade stood beside it, and Maura suspected she'd sat there often to read. At the foot of the chair was a mauve and green foot-stool that looked like a genuine antique with its Queen Anne legs and needlepoint roses.

Without knowing why, Maura was drawn to the footstool. As she ran her fingers lightly over the lovely needlepoint design, she began to feel vaguely uneasy. There was something about the footstool she should know, some secret that would provide a clue to her past.

The phone rang suddenly, startling Maura, and she

reached out to answer it without thinking. "Hello. This is Maura."

"Hi, Mom. Are you almost ready?"

"Yes . . . almost." Maura felt slightly guilty. She hadn't even opened the closet. "Could you give me five minutes more, honey? I've been busy, looking at my room."

"Sure, no problem. Did you recognize any . . . uh . . . sorry, Mom. I promised you I wouldn't keep asking."

Maura grinned. It was clear that Jan was trying to be polite in spite of her overwhelming curiosity. "No, honey. But I do think my bedroom's gorgeous. It's exactly what I always wanted. The person who decorated it must have known me very well."

"I guess!" Jan burst into laughter. "You did it yourself, Mom. You said it was silly to hire a decorator when you knew exactly what you wanted."

Maura was amazed. Her bedroom seemed so perfect in every detail, it rivaled the pictures she'd seen in decorator magazines. "Did I furnish any more rooms?"

"You did the whole house." Jan's voice was warm. "And you did such a fantastic job, a photographer from *Home Beautiful* came out to take pictures. There a copy of the magazine around here somewhere. I'll find it and show you."

"But how did I know what to do? Did I take any classes? Or read books on interior decorating?"

"I don't think so. Of course I was only six when we moved in here, and I don't really remember. You could ask Nita. She knows everything about you."

Maura nodded. "I'll ask her. There's another thing, Jan, and I'd really like your opinion. Can I trust Nita enough to ask her some . . . uh . . . personal questions?"

"Of course! Nita's not just our housekeeper, she's your

best friend, and you used to tell her everything. Her feelings would be hurt if you *didn't* ask her lots of questions."

Maura was smiling as she hung up the phone and opened her closet to find the blue lounging outfit. It was a lovely design, and it reminded her of the *ghee* she'd worn when she'd taken karate in college. But her *ghee* had been made of scratchy white cotton, and this one was fashioned from brushed velvet terry cloth in a startling turquoise color that reminded her of the pictures she'd seen of the Aegean Sea.

She examined the pants as she pulled them on. They were a simple cut with elastic around the waist, and a drawstring for added adjustment. They had the comfort of sweat pants, but there was no elastic around the ankles and this made them much dressier.

Maura removed the top from the hanger and smiled as she noticed the wide sleeves. It was robe like, sporting wide lapels that were triple stitched to give it a distinctive ghee style. The cuffs were also triple stitched, and they could be easily shortened by folding them up. A wide belt of the same soft material was attached with loops around the waist. She was about to slip it on when she noticed the tag. It said, "Mystique." This *ghee* must be one of her original designs!

It took only a moment to slip on the top and tie the belt. Maura was pleased as she walked across the room. This was a very comfortable garment. There was no restriction of movement, not even when she bent down to put on the pair of soft leather sandals she found by the side of her bed. Had she sold these fashionable *ghees* in her boutique? She'd have to remember to ask Jan.

There was a notebook on the table next to her bed, and Maura flipped it open. It was blank. No clues to her elusive past here. She chose a pen from the holder next to it, and jotted down several questions to ask Nita. Jan was right. Nita could provide valuable information about the life she'd lived in this house.

Maura sighed and took one last look around her. She wished she could stay here in this lovely room, where she could hide from the unfamiliar world outside. But hiding was the coward's way out, and although Maura knew very little about the person she'd been, she was certain that she'd never been a coward.

"Time to go." Maura picked up the notebook, squared her shoulders, and walked to the door. Then she opened it and stepped out to start living the life she no longer remembered.

Chapter Four

He tried not to show his nervousness as he sat in the straight-backed chair and waited for the inner door to open. He'd shaved so closely this morning, his skin was sore. There was no stubble, not even a hint of a shadow on his rugged cheekbones, and his clothes were carefully chosen. He wore grey slacks, a light blue shirt, and a navy blazer. The image that faced him in the waiting room mirror was that of a highly-paid company executive. It was exactly what they wanted to see. They didn't like to think of him as a hired killer. It offended their sensibilities. And while he was wise enough to know that his appearance probably wouldn't make any difference, it was one less thing for them to criticize.

How long were they going to make him wait? He glanced at his watch and frowned. He'd been here for fifteen minutes, making sure to arrive precisely on time. When he'd knocked on the door, one of them had come out and told him to wait, that they'd call him when they were ready. And even though his ears were finely tuned for any sounds beyond the inner door, he'd heard nothing except faint traffic noises filtering in from the street outside.

While he was waiting, he went over the whole thing again. He'd done his part, rigging the car so the brakes would fail, resulting in a fatal accident. As he'd followed them down the highway, he'd felt an unaccustomed twinge of sympathy for the woman. She was a pretty thing, very classy, the type of woman who'd always been out of his league. But orders were orders, and it couldn't be helped. Both of them had to die.

Everything had gone according to plan. The brakes had gone out, and the car had crashed through the guard rail. There had been only one hitch, one factor that had been impossible for him to calculate. Someone had used a car phone to call for an ambulance.

Just thinking about what had happened next made him shiver. He didn't like to relive the next few minutes, but they would be bound to ask questions. He had to be ready to defend himself, to explain why his plan had failed.

The limo passengers had piled out of the car to stare down the steep embankment. And the girl had been carrying a video camera. There was no way he could have climbed down there to see if he'd been successful. He would have been captured on tape. So he'd rushed to the edge of the embankment and pretended to be just another observer, staring down at the wreck and hoping that the ambulance attendants would bring up two zippered body bags.

He could still remember his relief when they'd carried up the first body bag. But then he'd noticed that a second team of paramedics was still in the ravine, taking a long time with the second victim. Each minute that passed had seemed like an eternity, and he'd begun to shiver in the warm night breeze. The flashing red lights on the ambulance had washed the pale faces of the crowd with what looked like blood, and he'd reached out for the rail to steady himself.

He'd heard a shout from below as a medi-vac helicopter

had appeared on the horizon. It had hovered low over the ravine, the noise of its blades matching the staccato beat of his heart. There had been no reason to stick around for confirmation. If both accident victims had died, they wouldn't have called for air transport.

He'd wanted to leave, to go home and hole up with a bottle of Scotch and the mindless drivel of late-night talk shows on the tube. But he was a pro, and he knew there'd be too many questions if he tried to leave. The lady next to him had been praying, her fleshy cheeks wet with tears. He'd thought about praying, too . . . praying that the helicopter would crash and finish his work, pleading with the God he'd never believed existed for a DOA at the emergency room door. But none of that had happened. She had recovered. And now he was sitting here waiting, preparing for the worst.

This was a new situation for him. He'd never failed on an assignment before, and he stared at the door, willing it to open. He wanted to give his report and leave . . . if they'd let him leave. But the door remained firmly closed.

What decisions were they making in that small room? He had the insane urge to run, but he knew that fleeing would send the wrong message. He'd done nothing wrong. What had happened had been out of his control. He had to stay to convince them that he was blameless.

Just then the door opened, and he was beckoned in. He got up on shaking legs to enter the room, standing in front of the desk, waiting for permission to sit down. After a moment of standing there silently, he realized that permission wasn't forthcoming. They'd make him stand, like a failed errand boy, until they'd made their judgment.

"She's alive."

The voice had a hard edge, even though it was a simple

statement of fact. He took a deep breath, and nodded. "I know. She went home from the hospital today."

"Lucky for you, she's lost her memory."

This time there was a ghost of a smile, and he began to take heart. "She doesn't remember the accident?"

"She doesn't remember anything." The second man spoke. "She's lost total memory of the last twenty years of her life."

The second man was much more frightening than the first. His voice was soft, but it could turn hard at a moment's notice, and he knew that he had to be very careful. "Do you want me to finish the job?"

His question hung in the air for a moment and then faded away as if he'd never spoken. The look in their eyes told him they'd already discussed it and made up their minds.

"Perhaps." The first man shrugged. "We'll let you know. If her amnesia is permanent, there's no need for you."

Their implied meaning was clear and he shivered. If he wasn't needed, he was in big trouble. Guys in his line of work didn't retire to Florida when their services were no longer required.

"But it wouldn't be difficult. I could arrange another accident." He knew he was saying too much, but he couldn't seem to stop. "It could happen at work, or at home, or even at the club. Nobody'll suspect anything. I guarantee it."

The second man shook his head. "No!"

The word was clipped and cold, a definite command. He nodded his acceptance, and looked down at his shoes. No way he wanted to face the ice in their eyes.

"You do nothing unless you hear from us. Is that clear?"

"Yes." He nodded again, and clamped his lips shut to stifle the flow of apologies that threatened to erupt from his throat. He wanted to tell them that he was their man. If they'd just give him a second chance, it was as good as done. There was no way she'd escape him this time. He was good. He was the best. But he said nothing, because nothing was what they wanted to hear.

"Go. We'll be in touch."

He forced his legs to move, to carry him to the door. His hands were shaking as he opened it, and then closed it softly behind him. He hurried across the waiting room to the hallway outside, but he didn't relax, not even when he was in the elevator, riding down to the street level.

When he reached the lobby, he had a sudden urge to stop at the men's room, but he didn't want to take the chance. They'd let him go, and he wanted to get the hell out of the building, out of the area, before they changed their minds.

The moment he got out on the street, he flagged down a cab. His voice was unsteady as he gave the driver an address two blocks from the place where he'd parked his car. As he got out of the cab, he took the time to make sure he wasn't being followed before he walked to his car. And once he got there, he checked it out carefully before he got in, making sure that no one had wired it.

He felt slightly better as he pulled out in traffic, taking a circuitous route toward the freeway entrance. There were no familiar cars behind him, but he checked the rear-view mirror constantly, alert to any surveillance. He didn't relax for an instant, not even when he was on the freeway traveling in the opposite direction. He knew all the tricks and that knowledge might buy him a little time, but it couldn't save him.

When he got home, he double-locked the door and pulled the curtains. Then he got out the bottle, poured himself a drink, and sank down in his favorite chair to think. All his precautions were useless. They knew where he lived. They knew everything about him. There was nowhere to run, no place to hide. He could do nothing to change the inevitable if they decided to take him out. He had to stay on their good side, convince them that his talents were useful, and do exactly what they said. He was merely a pawn in their game, and that made him completely expendable.

"This is wonderful!" Maura smiled at Nita and took another sip of her coffee. "It's the best coffee I've ever tasted!"

"That is what you always say." Nita looked pleased. "I made this for you every night, when you worked late. That was before Jan was old enough to go to school, and sometimes we would wake her up so she could have coffee with us."

"I gave a pre-schooler coffee?!"

"No, Mom." Jan laughed. "You called it coffee, but it wasn't. Nita made hot chocolate for me and I drank it out of a special mug."

"Pigs." Maura winced as her head began to throb. She could almost remember those nights. She turned to Jan, almost afraid to describe the visual image that had come to her. "I'm not sure, but . . . I seem to remember a child's mug. It was green plastic with pink pigs."

"That's right!" Jan jumped up to hug her. "What else do you remember, Mom?"

"I'm not sure . . . but this isn't the table, is it? Our table was . . . blue?"

A broad grin spread over Nita's face. "That is right, Miss Maura. We had a blue kitchen table when we lived in the condo. You still have it, out in the garage. Dr. Steve was right. Now that you are home, your memories are starting to come back."

"Maybe." Maura was a little more skeptical. Regaining her lost memory couldn't be that simple. "Tell me about the table, Nita. Did I buy it here in Los Angeles?"

"No. You brought it with you, from your apartment in San Diego. You said it was the first thing you bought when you moved into your dorm . . ." Nita stopped suddenly and frowned. "Do you think you remember it from before?"

"It's possible." Maura tried not to look as disappointed as she felt.

"But you remembered my baby mug!" Jan was still excited. "How do you explain that?"

"I don't know." Maura turned to Nita. "Do you know anything about it?"

Nita nodded. "I am sorry, Miss Maura. You said it was yours, when you were a baby. You did not take much from your parents' house. All you brought back were some keepsakes . . . family pictures, your mother's jewelry box, the pretty little footstool that is up in your room, and . . . your baby mug. You said you wanted to give it to Jan."

"The pig mug." Maura sighed deeply. And then she realized what Nita had said, and her face turned pale. "My parents . . . are they dead?"

"I am afraid so, Miss Maura. Do you remember how they had always wanted to go to England?"

Maura thought for a moment and then she nodded. "Yes. My father loved Shakespeare. He always talked about going to Stratford-on-Avon. And my mother wanted to see the changing of the guard at Buckingham Palace. Was it . . . a plane crash?"

"No. Your mother was afraid to fly, so they took one of those cruise ships. And the day before they were ready to come home, they both took sick. You got a long-distance call from the hospital in London."

Maura shivered. She'd lived through it all, but she didn't remember. And now, being forced to hear about her parents' deaths from Nita, she felt the pain of loss as clearly as she must have felt it then. "Did I fly over there to see them?"

"There was no time." Nita reached out to pat her shoulder. "You were on your way to the airport when the hospital called to tell you they had died. I paged Dr. Steve and he caught you, just as you were about to get on the plane."

"I didn't go to bring them back?"

Nita shook her head. "You were in no shape to travel. Dr. Steve brought you home, and then he got on the phone. He made all the arrangements to bring them back here."

"What . . . what kind of illness was it?"

"It was a virus." Jan spoke up. "Uncle Steve called the hospital and he talked to the doctor over there."

Nita got up and poured more coffee. When she sat back down at the table, she was frowning. "You were very upset. You thought that if only they had come home, there would have been a way to save them."

"But that wasn't true?"

Jan shook her head. "Uncle Steve found out that it was a new strain of virus. They called it the swine flu, and the doctors over here had never heard of it. They've got a shot for it now, but back then it was usually fatal."

"I see." Maura swallowed the sob that threatened to burst from her throat. Her parents were dead. And she'd lost her last, precious memories of them. She took another sip of coffee and sighed deeply. "Where . . . uh . . . where are they buried?"

"Right here in Forest Lawn." Jan draped a comforting arm around her mother's shoulders. "You wanted them close to you. We go out there sometimes, and you tell me things you remember about them, like the incredible wedding dress Grandma made for you, and the time Grandpa baby-sat with me while you went out shopping with Grandma. He didn't know about disposables, so he used your best pillowcase for a diaper."

Maura winced. She didn't remember any of that. Now, when they went out to visit her parents' graves, Jan would have to tell the stories to her.

Jan exchanged glances with Nita. When she turned back to face Maura, she looked very worried. "You're really pale, Mom. Maybe we shouldn't have told you so much, all at once."

"No. I'm all right." Maura took a deep, steadying breath. "I have to know what happened. Putting off the bad news isn't going to help."

Nita nodded, and exchanged glances with Jan again. "Maybe that is true. But I think we should think of some good news to tell your mother. She does not remember about your scholarship."

"Scholarship?" Maura seized the abrupt change in subject eagerly. Jan looked a little embarrassed, but she was smiling. "Tell me about it, honey."

"Well, it's not *that* great. But I did graduate at the top of my class in high school, and I got a scholarship to Princeton. That's a really good college in . . ."

"I know where it is." Maura interrupted her with a smile. "And I'm very proud of you. Do you like it?"

"I love it! Princeton's got the best psychology department in the nation!"

"And that's your major? Psychology?"

Jan nodded. "Clinical psychology. I've always been interested in why people do what they do. I did a lot of reading when I was in high school. Freud, Jung, Adler . . . anything I could find in the library. And I used to make up psychological profiles of everyone I knew. That's part of the reason I'm going to Princeton. One of the psychology professors read my profiles, and he convinced the college to offer me a scholarship."

"You did profiles of everyone?"

Jan shrugged. "Just about. I had almost fifty."

"How about me?"

"Well . . . actually . . ." Jan stopped, obviously embarrassed. "You don't really want to know, do you, Mom?"

"But I do! If you did a psychological profile of me, I'd like to read it."

"But, Mom!" Bright spots of color rose to Jan's cheeks. "People aren't *supposed* to read their psychological profiles. It could be damaging to their psyches."

"But you let your psychology professor read them. His psyche wasn't damaged, was it?"

Jan began to frown. "No. Of course not. But he didn't know any of the people I profiled."

"Exactly!" Maura began to smile. "And I don't know the me that you profiled, either. I'm a blank slate, Jan. The person I was is a total stranger to me. There's no way the psyche I had could be damaged. It doesn't exist anymore."

Jan looked thoughtful, and then she shook her head. "You're trying to snow me, Mom. And it won't work. Just think about what your profile might say. How would you feel if you found out that you weren't the kind of person you hope you were?"

"I don't have any hope. You have to know yourself to have hope. And I don't know me at all. Look at it like this, Jan. I'm starting over at the age of nineteen. It might help me to know the mistakes I made, so I don't have to make them all over again."

Jan was silent for a long minute. And then she turned to Nita. "What do you think?"

"That is not up to me!" Nita began to frown. "You are the psychologist, Miss Jan. And you are the only one who knows what her profile says. You have to decide."

Jan swallowed hard, and Maura felt a rush of sympathy. She knew she was putting her daughter in a terribly uncomfortable position, but she simply had to read that profile. Something in it might jog her memory. She searched Jan's face for any clue to what she was thinking, but Jan's eyes were cast downward, staring at the table.

"I don't know, Mom." When Jan raised her eyes, at last, she looked very uncertain. "I'd feel a lot better if I could talk to my professor. I don't want to do anything that might hurt you."

Maura nodded. "That's a very good idea. Why don't you call him now?"

As Jan hurried off to make the call, Nita reached out to touch Maura's arm. "Are you really sure you want to read that paper? Jan was still in high school when she wrote it. She was a teenager, and teenagers are very resentful. They are convinced they have all the answers, and that makes them very critical of their parents."

"Are you trying to warn me that Jan's profile might be uncomplimentary?"

"Well . . . yes. It could be." Nita looked very serious. "You two got along just fine, but you did not exactly see eye to eye on everything."

Maura laughed. "That makes sense. Most mothers and daughters disagree on something. But Jan seems to be a very bright young woman. I've got to assume that her profile of me is accurate."

"Maybe. And maybe not. Just remember that she wrote

it three years ago, and she is a much better judge of character now. Back then, she still dreamed about running off with Slash."

"Slash?!"

"He's the lead guitar player with Guns 'N Roses!" Nita noticed Maura's blank expression and she hurried to explain. "Guns 'N Roses is a rock group. And Slash is . . . well . . . he is not the type of boy a mother would like her daughter to date. Perhaps it is a good thing you do not remember."

Maura grinned. "I never thought I'd say it, but there might be some advantages to losing my memory, after all. The last rock group I remember is Guess Who."

'Who?"

"No, Nita. "The Who's a different group."

Nita looked confused. "Yes?"

"Yes is another rock group." Maura started to laugh. "I think we'd better change the subject, Nita . . . unless we want to start our own Abbott and Costello routine."

Chapter Five

Maura sat in her wing-backed chair, tortoise-shell reading glasses perched on her nose. She'd felt strange when she'd put on the glasses; her eyesight had always been a perfect twenty-twenty. But the lenses eliminated the blur she'd noticed when she'd attempted to read without them, and Nita had made her promise to wear them. They'd been prescribed for her a year ago, and Nita said she was prone to headaches if she tried to read for prolonged periods without them.

The glasses weren't the only aid she was forced to use. Nita had also told her that she'd had a problem with leg cramps at night. Her doctor had prescribed some quinine-based capsules that Maura was to take before she went to bed. There was also a special pillow, designed to cushion her neck. If she slept without it, Nita had warned that she'd wake up with a sore, stiff neck.

Maura sighed as she thought about her age. It was hell being suddenly over forty without remembering any of the good times in between. She felt a little like Alice falling down the rabbit hole. Everything was strange and new, and not always pleasant. She was no longer familiar with her own body, much less her own mind.

Maura got up and switched on the stereo. At least the music she'd loved hadn't changed. Recordings were like little time capsules. The music on them was frozen in time to be replayed whenever one wished. Beethoven's *Pastoral* was still comfortingly familiar, and so was Handel's *Water Suite*. Vivaldi's *Four Seasons* was exactly the same, Bessie Smith's voice was still belting out the blues, and Woody Herman and his Thundering Herd were still thrilling audiences with "Early Autumn" and "Caldonia." Compact discs had replaced records in what Maura hoped was her temporary absence, but the music she loved and remembered was still available at the flick of a switch.

Realizing that she was procrastinating, Maura looked down at the thick folder in her hands. Jan's psychology professor had agreed that she should be allowed to read it, but she'd been sitting here for fifteen minutes, clutching the folder like a letter bomb, not daring to open it for fear her life would shatter into a million painful pieces.

With shaking fingers, Maura forced herself to open the folder. Her name was on the first page, Maura Bennett. Of course she wasn't Maura Bennett anymore, not since she'd married Keith almost two years ago. Now she was Maura Thomas.

"Maura Thomas." She said the name out loud. It was totally unfamiliar, a stranger to her lips, so she repeated it. "I am Maura Thomas, Mrs. Keith Thomas."

What would her husband think if she forgot her married name? Just to be sure, Maura repeated it again. And then she looked back down at the folder.

A Psychological Profile by Janelle C. Bennett. Maura blinked back tears are she stared at her daughter's name. What did the "C" stand for. Carole? Candice? Catherine? Charlotte? She had no idea, and that made her very sad.

Suddenly an image popped into Maura's mind. She remembered a sweet grey-haired woman who'd held her on her lap and given her something wonderful to eat. Maura could almost taste it now . . . sweet and crunchy, with a dark, mysterious flavor. Molasses cookies! Maura began to smile as the memory grew. Molasses cookies with crunchy sugar on the top, the way only Granny Kate could make them. Granny Kate . . .

Granny Kate had died when Maura was eight, and she'd lived with them the last three years of her life. Maura could remember the time she'd spent with her grandmother as if it were yesterday. Granny Kate had brought all sorts of wonderful things with her, and Maura had spent many happy hours in her grandmother's room, looking at pictures in the old family album, and going through Granny Kate's wooden trunk that was full of momentos. She still remembered her grandmother's wedding certificate, written in elaborately shaded European script. The bride's name had been the most beautiful, with a graceful loop on the "C," a loop that swirled out and under the rest of the name which was . . . Catherine!

Maura smiled as she realized what her memory meant. She'd loved Granny Kate so much, she was almost sure she would have chosen Catherine for her daughter's middle name.

With one mystery solved, it was back to business. Maura flipped the page on her psychological profile and started to read. The first paragraph was filled with facts. Maura Bennett was an attractive widow of thirty-nine, with a sixteen-year-old daughter. She owned a successful boutique on Rodeo Drive and designed most of the clothing she sold. She was a member of an extended family, including her late husband's brother and his wife, and a housekeeper of American-Spanish descent who had been in her employ for over fifteen years.

A physical description was next. Jan had written that Maura Bennett was five feet, nine inches tall, and she weighed a hundred and twenty pounds. She had auburn hair, green eyes, and a clear complexion that freckled lightly in the sun. Her general health was good, she had no physical abnormalities, and in the interviewer's opinion, she exhibited signs of above-normal intelligence.

So far, so good. Maura found a more comfortable position and settled back to read on. The next section was entitled, "Personal Preferences." Maura Bennett had told the interviewer that she enjoyed most types of music. She'd said that she tried to eat a balanced diet, and she'd claimed to have no self-imposed or medical restrictions on the types of food she ate. Her favorite course of the meal was dessert, and she'd traveled Europe extensively, looking for the ultimate cheesecake.

Maura frowned slightly, and shut her eyes, trying to conjure up a mental picture of cheesecake. Her mother had never served cheesecake; she was almost sure of that. And she'd been on such a tight budget during her college years, she'd seldom gone out to restaurants. She must have learned to like cheesecake later, during those missing years. But Maura had absolutely no idea what it tasted like!

Suddenly, without any warning, the words she'd read hit Maura like a blow. She'd told Jan that she'd traveled Europe extensively. Since Maura had no memory of traveling anywhere, that must also have happened during the missing years.

Maura sighed and did her best to remember. Had she

gone to Europe on some sort of college exchange program?

The memory was there, hovering somewhere behind her eyes. Maura shut them and almost immediately, a scene flashed through her mind. She saw a light blue suitcase traveling down a conveyer belt. It was the baggage room in an airport, and she was reaching for the suitcase. She saw her arm clearly, emerging from the sleeve of a fur-lined parka, but the suitcase was too high, and she couldn't reach it.

She must have said something, because a handsome man, standing beside her, plucked it from the carousel and handed it to her with a flourish. She could hear herself laughing as she raised her eyes to his, and kissed him lightly on the cheek.

Not Keith. Of that she was certain. This man had light blond hair and blue eyes the color of a winter sea. He was deeply tanned, and his face looked vaguely Scandinavian. His lips were moving, and she could see that he was speaking, although she couldn't understand the words. It was some kind of foreign language and she was answering him in his native tongue.

Now they were leaving the baggage area. He picked up his brown, leather bag, slung their ski packs over his shoulder, and tucked her arm in his. They walked past the others, who were also speaking in the same language, and went out through a double glass door. It was dark outside, and snow was falling as they made their way across the street. And then they were entering a parking lot.

Maura felt fear begin to pound through her veins, and she knew that something was wrong. The parking lot wasn't safe, and something horrible was about to happen, something that would change her life forever.

She held her breath, waiting for the awful thing to happen, and there was a noise that made her shiver. It was a loud, frightening noise, and everything began to grow black. She tried to see through the gathering darkness, but her sliver of memory faded away, leaving her with nothing but the lingering sensation of icy tears on her cheeks.

Maura opened her eyes very quickly, and took comfort in her newly familiar surroundings. Her head was throbbing painfully, and she took off her glasses to rub her eyes. She knew her problem wasn't eye strain. The pain was caused by a memory attempting to surface.

Deliberately, Maura shut her eyes again. The hell with the pain. She wanted to remember. But the image was gone, and although she tried her best, it refused to return. Would she ever remember what had happened that night? Or was that part of her life lost to her, forever?

She thought about calling Jan on the intercom. Her daughter would want to know about the strange piece of memory she'd recovered. But some instinct made Maura hesitate, her fingers on the receiver. The memory had been frightening, almost ominous. She was certain that if she'd been able to recall the scene fully, she'd discover that something dreadful had happened. Perhaps it was better to wait, to keep this small sliver of memory to herself and hope that more would resurface.

But would she forget again? Were memories similar to dreams? When she was a child, she'd had vivid dreams. But in the morning, when she'd tried to tell her mother about them, she'd found that she couldn't recall them. Dreams had no substance. They were like smoke in the breeze. The only way to capture things that insubstantial was to write them down, immediately after you'd dreamed them. If you waited too long, they disappeared.

There was a blank notebook on the table, with a pen on top. Maura opened it and wrote down her brief flash of memory, carefully listing all the details. When she was finished, she picked up Jan's portfolio again. Would her psychological profile evoke any more strange memories?

A section on favorite colors was next. Maura learned that her favorite color was dusty pink. When asked by the interviewer if she ever wore clothing of that shade, she'd said no and explained that dusty pink clashed with her hair.

Maura began to smile as she read on. She must have told Jan about the wig, because it was here, in print. Jan had written about the time Maura had borrowed a girlfriend's dark-haired wig, so she could wear a pink dress to a school dance. The wig had slipped, during the festivities, and Maura had been so embarrassed, she'd never attempted to wear pink again.

The next section heading was, "Daily Routine", and Maura read it eagerly. Jan wrote that Maura Bennett was a morning person, not a night person. She did her best creative work in the early morning, and she often got up before daybreak to spend an hour in her design studio.

"Design studio?" Maura reread the words aloud. Where was her design studio? She'd have to ask Jan or Nita.

As Maura read on about her daily schedule, she began to frown. At precisely seven in the morning, she left the house for her morning run. She always took the same route, skirting the perimeter of the country club. When she got home, a few minutes before eight, she showered and joined her daughter and her housekeeper for breakfast. She'd told Jan that she thought a good breakfast was critical, since she was often too busy for lunch.

Maura raised her eyebrows. She must have changed a great deal in those missing years. As a college student, she'd never eaten breakfast. She'd chosen to sleep in late, hurry to her first class, and have a big lunch instead.

There was a frown on Maura's face as she read on. The woman she didn't remember had held daily staff meetings, an hour before her boutique opened. She worked through lunch and left Rodeo Drive at four in the afternoon. She spent the next two hours running errands or relaxing at home. Dinner was at seven, and she retired for the evening at ten P.M.

Maura put down the portfolio and frowned. What she'd read sounded highly organized and very boring. Had she really been that rigid? Of course, this profile had been written while Jan had been living at home. Her schedule might have changed when her daughter had gone off to college.

The next section was entitled, "Social Life", and Maura read it eagerly. She expected to find that she'd rubbed shoulders with the rich and famous, but Jan didn't mention any stellar friends. Maura Bennett attended the annual charity functions that were required by her status as a Beverly Hills business woman, but Jan had written that she didn't seem to enjoy socializing. She hosted one large dinner party over the holiday season, held at a famous Los Angeles restaurant, and she was a frequent guest at her brother-in-law's house in Beverly Hills, but she never held dinner parties at home for anyone other than family.

"How strange!" Maura frowned slightly. Her home was beautiful, and it seemed only natural to invite people in to see it. But Jan had written that she almost never entertained at home. Maura Bennett must have been a very private person, preferring to keep her personal life to herself. But how had that affected her daughter? Was Jan a very private person, too?

Maura read on about her hobbies and recreations. She'd painted what she'd told Jan were "very bad landscapes," and she read an average of six books a month. But these were all solitary pursuits. Hadn't she done anything truly social? Hadn't she made any friends?

The next sentence made Maura feel better, and she began to smile. Maura Bennett loved to dance! Dancing was social, and she must have had a dancing partner. But her hopes were dashed by the next few sentences. She'd told Jan that she'd won several dance contests when she was in high school, but she hadn't pursued it after she'd graduated.

So much for that. Maura sighed deeply. The evidence was mounting up, and she seemed to be a loner. Jan had written that she watched television occasionally, and she preferred dramas to sitcoms. She didn't have any favorite shows, and she never watched the soaps. When asked, she said it just wasn't feasible. She never knew when she'd be home to watch television and she didn't want to get involved in any serial-type story.

The next section was entitled, "Fears and Anxieties," and Maura discovered she was terrified of heights. That made perfect sense. She could remember shaking like a leaf when she'd climbed up on the roof of their family home in Brawley to help her father repair a broken shingle. It was apparent she'd never gotten over that fear, since Jan had mentioned it in her profile.

The subject claims to have no fear of dying, darkness, animals generally or specifically, fire, or drowning. She is not claustrophobic, and exhibits no sign of other common phobias. However, it is the interviewer's personal opinion that she may have deeply-seated anxieties regarding intimate relationships with the opposite sex.

Maura raised her eyebrows and read the sentence again. Then she took off her glasses and rubbed her eyes. How could her daughter write such a thing? She certainly wasn't afraid of men!

Or was she? Maura frowned as she slipped her glasses

back on, and stared down at the sentence in question. If this was accurate, Jan had certainly been in a position to know. But what evidence had caused her to come to this conclusion? She hoped Jan had written more on the subject.

During the past ten years, the subject has not dated nor appeared, publicly or privately, with a male escort. The only male she sees regularly is her brother-in-law, and in this interviewer's opinion, their relationship is strictly platonic.

"Thank God for that!" Maura released her breath in a shuddering sigh. She was very relieved that Jan had no suspicions about her relationship with Steve. But why hadn't she dated? Hadn't she found any men she liked?

Since there is no substantiating evidence, the following is highly speculative: Because the subject's husband, the father of her child, was killed so early in their marriage, this interviewer theorizes that the subject may be suppressing her sexuality, rather than risk losing a second lover.

Maura raised her eyebrows. If she read between the lines, Jan was saying that she was gun-shy. Of course that wasn't true. She'd proved it by marrying Keith, hadn't she?

However, it is also possible that the subject may have limited her intimacy to someone she meets on her frequent business trips.

Immediately after reading this new theory, Maura's head began to pound. Another memory trying to surface? She shut her eyes and tried to make her mind perfectly blank and receptive. And then it started, a series of images so startling she gasped out loud. She knew she was in a hotel room. There was a book of matches in an ashtray and a basket of fruit on the dresser. It was a lovely room, very old-fashioned, with huge oaken furniture and a gold satin bedspread on the bed. She was dressed in a maid's uniform, standing over a brown leather suitcase that was propped open on a low bench at the foot of the bed. Her hands were moving, lifting piles of clothing, looking for something. But the suitcase wasn't hers. It was filled with sweaters and white dress shirts and trousers. Men's clothing, but where was the man?

She heard running water, and her eyes moved toward the door at the far end of the room. He was in the bathroom, taking a shower, singing in a loud, off-key voice. She couldn't hear the lyrics over the sound of the running water, but some instinct told her that he wasn't singing in English.

She stopped abruptly, holding her breath as she heard footsteps coming down the hallway. They were soft footsteps, approaching stealthily, but she was alert to every sound. When they stopped outside the door, she moved like lightning to dive under the bed.

There was the sound of a key in the door and it opened with a click. She felt a draft from the hallway as the footsteps came into the room, and she huddled under the bed, perfectly immobile, inhaling the smell of stale cigarette smoke and slightly damp wool.

The sound of the water was louder now. Someone had opened the bathroom door. There was a gasp, a series of frightening gurgling sounds, and then the footsteps came back to the foot of the bed. She opened her eyes and saw two shoes, a right and a left, supple tan leather moccasins with thick crepe soles. As she watched, items of clothing began to fall to the floor, tossed there by unseen hands. A white dress shirt. A blue and black silk tie. A burgundy, cable-knit sweater. They fell faster and faster, only inches from her face, until there were piles of clothing scattered the length of the bed. Then someone swore in a rough voice, and the shoes moved toward the door.

She stayed there, breathing very quietly, burying her nose in the rug. Too soon to come out, not yet, not yet, but the room was getting very hot. Gradually, she began to detect another odor. It smelled like meat, boiling in a pot, and the room seemed to be filled with vapor. She moved then, rolling out in one fluid motion, until she saw that the room was clear. She dropped something heavy into her pocket and raced to the window, glancing out at the deserted alley five floors below.

Not the stairs. Or the elevator, either. She couldn't use them. But there was a pipe next to the window. She opened the window and climbed out on the ledge. The alley looked small, the galvanized garbage cans mere specks from this height. And then she grabbed the pipe and started to climb down.

"No!" Maura opened her eyes with a snap. This couldn't be her memory. There was no way she could have climbed down five flights, clinging to a pipe. Jan had written that she was terrified of heights.

If it wasn't her memory, whose was it? Maura shivered, her heart beating hard. She was still frightened by the glimpse she'd caught of the alley far below. This must be the memory of a movie she'd seen, or a nightmare she'd dreamed. There was no other reasonable explanation.

Slightly reassured, Maura turned back to Jan's profile again. But she couldn't seem to concentrate on the printed words. The memory lingered, like a persistent fly. It buzzed around in her mind and she couldn't seem to dismiss it.

After several moments of unsuccessfully trying to clear her mind, she sighed and reached for the blank notebook again. It was still a memory, even though it had come from a movie or a dream, and she'd promised herself she'd write down everything she remembered.

Writing it down seemed to help. As she filled the page, the memory began to recede, and when she'd finished, Maura felt much calmer. But she was much too tired to keep on reading. Jan's personality profile would have to wait until morning.

Maura got up and walked to the bed. She took off her robe, folded it neatly, and placed it on the foot of the bed. A glance at the small alarm clock on the night table told her it was almost midnight, and she felt a sharp pang of guilt. It was much later than she usually went to bed.

She set the alarm for five A.M., and pulled out the knob on the back. Then she climbed under the covers and reached out to flick off the light. The specialist at the hospital had recommended that she get back to her normal routine as soon as possible. He'd told her that performing habitual tasks sometimes evoked forgotten memories. It was certainly worth a try, and now that she had a copy of the schedule she'd kept, she'd try to do everything just as she'd done it in the past.

As she closed her eyes, Maura thought about the day to come. She'd get up the moment the alarm went off, and go to her studio before daybreak. From what she'd read in Jan's personality profile, that was her normal habit. Since she didn't know where her studio was, she'd simply walk through the house, opening doors until she found it. Once she got there, she'd sit at her desk and try to remember what she'd been designing before the accident.

Her morning run was at seven. Nita should be up by then, and she could ask her for directions to the country club. Something along the familiar route might jog her memory. It certainly should. According to Jan, she'd been running the same route for over ten years.

The run would take forty-five minutes, longer if she found she was out of shape. When she'd finished, she'd come home to shower and dress in the one of the business suits she'd found in her closet.

The big breakfast. Maura frowned as she thought about eating pancakes and sausage, or eggs and bacon. There was bound to be a big glass of orange juice, and Nita might even make hot cereal. She'd have to force it down somehow. Jan had written that she believed in the value of a large, well-balanced breakfast.

The boutique was next. Since she wasn't sure exactly where it was, she'd ask Jan to drive her there. Instead of her morning meeting, she'd ask her employees questions and try to learn how her business worked. She'd spend most of the day going over her ledgers and receipts, and she'd ask Jan to pick her up at precisely four o'clock.

When she got home, she'd relax until dinner at seven. Nita seemed like a very sweet woman, and she'd probably make all of her favorite foods. Even if she no longer liked them, she'd pretend she did. And after dinner was over, she'd talk to Jan and Nita, or read, or listen to music until ten, when she habitually went to bed.

Maura frowned. Where was the excitement? She'd always craved adventure, but it seemed to be missing from her life. She supposed there must have been a reason why she'd developed such a boring routine, but she couldn't remember what it was. Her schedule seemed totally inconsistent to the life she'd anticipated when she was in college. She didn't want to get up early and work in her studio, her morning run sounded horribly boring, and she certainly didn't want a big breakfast. She'd prefer to sleep in late, and have coffee on a tray in her room, but she couldn't do that. They'd expect her to follow her normal routine.

Maura's eyes snapped open, and she stared up into the darkness. Why did she have to do everything exactly the way she'd always done it? There was no law that said she had to get up at the crack of dawn. The police wouldn't come to arrest her if she didn't go on her morning run, and absolutely no one would stand over her and force-feed her that big breakfast she didn't want to eat.

Should she change her routine? Maura began to smile as the idea told hold. Perhaps it was time for her to live dangerously. She'd sleep until she woke up. And then she'd ask Nita to bring her coffee and toast in bed. Forget the run. She wasn't overweight, and she'd figure out some other way to get her exercise. And she didn't have to go to the boutique tomorrow. Jan had mentioned that she had a capable staff, and her business could get along without her for the next couple of days. She'd go to the boutique when it was closed for the night so she could familiarize herself with her business practices in private. And while she was at it, she'd go over her personnel records. It would be easier to face her employees when she knew more about them.

The moment she'd decided, Maura flicked on the light and reached for the clock. She pressed in the alarm button with a deliberate snap, and flicked off the light again. Until circumstances proved that her routine was useful, she'd indulge herself.

Maura was smiling as she snuggled under the covers and closed her eyes. She felt better than she had all day. Jan's profile had been very helpful, telling her what her schedule had been like, but this was her life and she was taking charge of it again!

Chapter Six

Maura opened her eyes and groaned as she glanced at the clock. The alarm hadn't sounded, but it was five A.M. Perhaps she was a creature of habit, after all. But just because she was awake at this ungodly hour didn't mean she had to actually get out of bed. She could always roll over and go back to sleep.

There was a tall cypress tree outside her window, and Maura smiled as she heard the birds start to twitter and stir. Although it was still dark, a mourning dove anticipated daybreak with its soft, sad song. The eerie notes hung in the pre-dawn stillness, echoing through the ravine. And then, from the distance, a second dove answered, calling out its sorrowful lament.

There was a note of poignancy in the dove's call that made Maura shiver. The melancholy notes brought unwelcome thoughts of death and dying, of grieving and weeping for a loved one who was gone, never to return.

Maura pulled the covers over her head and snuggled up in their warmth. She tried to put such morbid thoughts out of her mind, to think of something pleasant that would lull her back to sleep. But the doves kept calling out mournfully, back and forth, their cries softer now as they were filtered through the blankets, but still perfectly audible.

She had almost dropped off to sleep when another sliver of memory pierced her mind. It was so clear, it made her gasp with intense feelings of loss and desolation. She was standing on a hill of snow, under a large tree. Its branches were bare and she could see a small fire on a level piece of ground in the distance. The firelight cast flickering red shadows against the white surface of the snow. It would have been a pretty picture, if she hadn't known why the fire existed.

They were thawing the ground for his funeral, three men dressed in long, dark coats with fur caps on their heads. The fire would burn for three days, until the ground was soft enough to dig his grave. And then he would be buried. He was gone from her, forever.

It was bitter cold, so cold that she could barely feel her feet, encased in warm, lined boots. She was wearing a parka, black with a fur lining, and her hands were tucked into leather mittens lined with the same fur. There was something warm over her face, to keep out the frozen, night air. It was a woven ski mask with holes for her eyes and her mouth.

In the very back of her mind, Maura protested. This scene was wrong. It couldn't have come from her memory. Steve had told her that her husband had died in the summer. But the images were persistent, pulling her along as they continued with startling clarity.

She was moving now, over the snow with a smooth glide. It was clear that she was on skis. She traveled down the hill another few feet, and stopped by another tree. Now she was close enough to hear them speaking in hushed voices as they placed wood on the fire. The words were foreign, but she understood them perfectly. They were praising him, one of their number they'd lost.

There were tears in her eyes as she listened to their words of praise. He'd been a brave man, a good man, and he'd made them proud. They were glad the woman had escaped, but it was a pity she couldn't attend his funeral to pay her final respects. What kind of world was it when his own wife wasn't allowed at his funeral?

His wife?! Maura gasped, but there was no denying what they'd said. They couldn't be talking about her. She'd only lost one husband, Jan's father. They must be wrong. Or perhaps she wasn't this man's wife. She could be a friend, a very close friend who was grieving his death.

One man seemed to be the leader of the group. He was taller and slightly older than the rest. They listened as he spoke, and then they split up to ski off into the woods. She'd heard him say that they had to gather more firewood. But the older man stayed behind and she saw him beckon to her.

Trees whirled past as she skied rapidly down the hill, and Maura felt doubt grow in the back of her mind. This couldn't be her memory. Jan hadn't mentioned skiing in her profile. As far as she knew, she'd never skied, and the woman in these images was clearly an expert.

His arms opened as she skied up to him. He held her for a moment, patting her back, and then they turned toward a wooden shack at the edge of the clearing. There were tears in her eyes as he took her arm and escorted her there. She slipped off her skis, and opened the door. And then she was inside, alone with . . .

The shack was cold. Ice cold. And there was a bundle on the bench, wrapped in blankets. She pulled off her mittens and folded down the blankets, gazing down through a blur of tears at his dear face.

It was the man from the airport! The man with startling blue eyes, blond hair, and a vaguely Scandinavian face. Even in death, his color hadn't faded. He was deeply tanned, and he looked physically fit. She reached down to touch his lips, the lips that had kissed her only hours ago. Warm lips that were cold now, as cold as death.

There was a tap on the door. It was her signal to hurry. She quickly pulled back the blanket a bit further, and uncovered his hand.

Her fingers were growing numb from the cold, but she slipped off his watch and opened the back. There was something inside, something wrapped in a thin piece of paper, which she took out and tucked into an inner pocket of her parka. And then she reached for his gold ring, turning it so the inscription glittered in the light from the bare bulb hanging from the ceiling. *To Nick. Love forever, Emmy.* Her hands were shaking, and she was blinking back tears as she slipped it from his finger and placed it on her own.

There was another knock, sharp and urgent. Her fingers flew as she wrapped the blankets around him again, and hurried to the door. A nod to the older man, another brief hug, and she was snapping on her skis. And then she was flying over the snow, disappearing into the dense woods that surrounded the small graveyard.

She looked back once, when she'd reached the safety of the trees. The clearing was deserted now. The older man had vanished. And then she saw them, a party of six men coming over the top of the hill. They had come for him. She had arrived just in time, and they would fail to complete their mission.

Faster, faster. She dug her poles into the snow and skied down another steep hill. She seemed to ski for hours, arms and legs moving in a practiced rhythm until she got to familiar terrain.

There was a farmhouse over the next rise, and she zigzagged down to the barn. The hay was piled deep on the lee side, and she slipped off her skis and pushed them into the pile. And then she ran to the house to change into her nightgown and eat the snack the mother had left on the bed-stand for her.

She saw herself cutting off a wedge of cheese and spreading it on a piece of coarse black bread. The cheese tasted like peanut butter and it was delicious. *Gjetost*. The name popped into her mind. *Gjetost* was brown goat cheese, and it was one of the things she loved best about being in this part of the world.

She finished the snack and climbed under the covers. It was cold and she pulled the goose-down comforter up, all the way to her nose. Her dreams were uneasy, but somehow she managed to sleep right through the pounding on the door. And she looked appropriately dazed when they came to question her. Of course she could ski, but not very well. She was trying to learn, but she didn't have much time to practice. She was an exchange student and her class work was very demanding. As a matter of fact, she had a test in calculus this morning. Could they possibly give her a ride to the university? The professor wouldn't accept any excuses for being late.

Maura's eyes opened with a snap. Calculus?! This memory couldn't possibly be hers. She'd always avoided math like the plague, and she'd barely managed to pass the required class in her freshman year.

There was no way she could sleep now. Maura switched on the light and reached for her notebook. She knew this memory wasn't hers. It must be from a book she'd read, or a movie she'd seen, but she'd write it down anyway.

As she faithfully transcribed the images she'd seen, Maura blinked back tears. She had no idea why this dream, or whatever it had been, had affected her so deeply. What she'd seen hadn't actually happened to her. It was impossible that she had been personally involved. She didn't speak any foreign languages except Spanish, she didn't know how to ski, she'd never taken calculus, her name wasn't Emmy, and she'd never been married to anyone named Nick.

Maura put down the pen and got out of bed, trying to shake off the effects of her disquieting dream. She dressed in the forest green jogging outfit Nita had laid out the previous night, and laced up her running shoes. She didn't feel much like exercising, but doing something physical might chase away the sad feeling that still lingered with her.

A glance at the clock told her that it was still early, barely six o'clock. She'd go down to the kitchen and put on the coffee. A good, strong cup of coffee might get her in the mood for her run.

The house was quiet as she tiptoed down the stairs, her footsteps silent on the thick carpeting. She passed through the living room, pausing to touch the lovely grand piano that dominated the room, and hesitated, her fingers on the swinging kitchen door. Nita was up, and she was talking on the phone. Maura could hear her clearly. She was speaking in Spanish, but somehow the words were miraculously translated in her mind.

"It is much too early to tell. She seems to have memory of some things, but not others."

There was a pause. Nita must be listening to the speaker on the other end of the line.

"No. It is very little. A piece of furniture, that is all. And

Jan's baby cup. But the memory for those things might have come from before."

There was another pause and Nita sighed. "Of course I will. You know that she is also my very good friend. I will make her favorite dishes for dinner tonight. You will come, yes?"

All was silent for a moment, and then Nita laughed. "I am not sure she is prepared for my hot salsa, but I will make the sweet tamales with pork and raisins. And pineapple flan for dessert. It is very good for her to have the family with her again, and I will make certain that she is ready before he comes back."

There was another pause, and Maura frowned. Was Nita talking about Keith? And why did she have to get ready for his homecoming?

"Yes, you can count on me. And you can be certain that Jan knows nothing. You should not worry. I will call you immediately if there is concern."

Maura's frown deepened. What was it that Jan didn't know? And who was on the phone with Nita? She had a good notion to barge right in the kitchen and ask, but some instinct stopped her. Nita had sounded very secretive on the phone. And she'd been speaking in Spanish, a language she assumed that Maura no longer remembered. Perhaps it was best to wait and listen, to see if she could learn any more.

Before she had time to really consider her actions, Maura found herself quietly climbing the stairs again. She let herself into the bedroom and then she went out again, closing the door loudly behind her. She hurried down the stairs, making what she considered was a normal amount of noise, and called out as she reached the kitchen door. "Nita? Are you in there?"

"Good morning, Miss Maura!" Nita smiled as Maura came into the kitchen. "Would you like coffee?"

Maura nodded, and observed Nita closely. Nita's smile seemed totally genuine, and she didn't look the least bit guilty about her early morning telephone conversation.

"Are you going to run this morning?" Nita waited until Maura was seated at the table, and then she brought over a mug of coffee.

"I'm not sure. Do you think I should?"

Nita nodded. "You always run, Miss Maura. You never miss a day when you are home, and your body is accustomed to the exercise. Perhaps you should not go too fast or too far, but I think you should try."

"You're probably right." Maura sighed in resignation. "It'd be a pity to get out of condition when it seemed to mean so much to me, before. And who knows? I might just recognize something along my normal route and get my memory back."

Nita nodded. "This is true. You may remember something of great importance to you. I will go with you, if you like."

"You stay here, Nita. I'll go." Jan stood in the doorway, dressed in grey sweats and running shoes. She was grinning as she turned to her mother. "You'd better thank Nita, Mom. You don't know the supreme sacrifice she was willing to make for you. The only exercise Nita ever gets is dancing on *Cinco de Mayo.*"

Nita laughed. "That is not true, Miss Jan. I get plenty of exercise around here. Up the stairs, down the stairs, all day long. But you are right. I do not like to run unless someone is chasing me. It seems wasteful."

"Oh, sure." Jan's eyes were sparkling and Maura could tell that she loved to tease Nita. "It's about as wasteful as making the beds every morning . . . when you know you're just going to unmake them again, at night."

Nita looked amused, but she managed to put on a stern expression. "That is different. I have explained it to you before, Miss Jan. A woman is judged by the house she keeps. Dishes must be washed, beds must be straightened. It is only right."

"Okay, you win." Jan was laughing as she kissed Nita on the cheek. "And I was just teasing. My bed's made. Come on, Mom. Finish your coffee and let's go. If we don't get started now, we'll never get to the boutique on time."

Maura took one last sip of coffee and got to her feet. This wasn't the time to tell Jan about her decision to play hookey from work. They'd discuss it when they were running . . . if she wasn't too out of shape to talk.

When she came out of the bathroom, he was just hanging up the phone. She'd heard him talking and she knew who he'd been calling. He always called to check in, first thing in the morning.

"So what did you find out?" She gave him a quick kiss on the forehead, just enough to tease and tantalize, and then she climbed under the covers again. "Did her memory come back?"

"No. She loves the house, though. Nita says she calls it her dream house."

"Of course it's her dream house. She designed it, and it cost her a bloody fortune!"

"A little bitter, aren't we?"

"Not at all." She fought to keep her expression pleasant. It was impossible not to be bitter, after ten years of living in a dinky apartment with rented furniture, while almost every cent she earned went to pay off the bills her ex-husband had run up. "I'm happy if you're happy. You know that."

"But you'd like to live in a house like that someday . . . wouldn't you?"

"Who wouldn't?" Her fingertips touched his lips, sliding over the generous mouth and down to trail along his bare chest. She was crazy about him, and she was sure he would have married her if things had been different. With her talent and his brains, they could have been the hottest new couple in L.A., giving fancy dinner parties, and making important, social register friends.

"Donny?" She used her pet name for him deliberately. It was short for Adonis, and he reminded her of a Greek God. "That accident she was in. You didn't have anything to do with . . . ?"

"Don't you trust me?!"

There was hurt in his eyes, and she wished she could take back her impulsive words. "I'm sorry, Donny. I didn't mean anything. It's just that . . ."

He silenced her with a kiss and she almost forgot her earlier question. Almost, but not quite. And she was glad he'd stopped her before the fateful words could be spoken. A woman didn't ask her lover a question like that, especially when she didn't really want to know the answer.

"Maybe I should be the one to ask you." He pulled back and stared into her eyes. "You've never liked her that much."

She blinked and stared at him, hard. "Donny! You're joking . . . aren't you?"

"Yes . . . and no. You couldn't stand Grant. Everyone knows that. And you had a lot to gain. You told me you used to run with some pretty rough characters. You could have called one of them, and . . ."

"Don't even say it!" She cut him off before he could go any further. "Look, Donny . . . there's no way I'd ever . . ."

"I know." He cut her off with a kiss. "I trust you. And you trust me. Right?"

She nodded, and then she smiled in pleasure as he moved over to cover her body with his. Their embrace was practiced, but it was still fresh and exciting. She could feel her body begin to respond and she gave a shuddering sigh. Her pulse raced, her breathing quickened, and she felt a tingle of arousal spread from her toes all the way up to the very top of her head. He always had this effect on her. It was why they were so good together. She'd do anything if they could stay like this, locked in each other's arms forever.

"I love you, Donny." She opened her eyes and stared into his, searching for love, and desire, and some kind of wonderful commitment.

"I love you, too. And I'll give you everything you deserve someday. I promise."

He smiled down at her and that was enough. She melted and clung to him, taking him deeply inside her. Their passion drove all thoughts from her mind for a few breathless minutes . . . until it was over and he was stretched out beside her, asleep.

That was when her tears welled up, filling her eyes and spilling over to run down her cheeks. How could he give her what she deserved, when he had nothing? People like the bitch had it all, living in her fancy house, with her fancy family, and her fancy shop, and her fancy clothes. To make matters worse, the bitch wasn't even really a bitch. She was just an ordinary woman who didn't realize how good she had it.

Her pillow was wet, and she flopped it over. And then she

wiped her eyes. She really shouldn't let things get to her this way, but just thinking about all the breaks the bitch had gotten made her feel sorry for herself.

There hadn't been any breaks for her. She'd married early, half-way through her junior year in high school, and she'd picked a real loser. He'd looked good at the time, but he'd almost succeeded in ruining her life. Thank God she'd wised up and divorced him. He was in prison now, where he belonged, but she was still paying the price of her mistake. Things could still turn very nasty for her, if she didn't do exactly what they asked.

Life wasn't fair. Everything would have been so simple if there had been two fatalities. But there hadn't been, and there wasn't a damn thing she could do about it now.

She sighed and rolled over close to him, taking comfort in the fact that they were together, nestled up closely, making their own little world. And then she smiled as she thought of that old phrase her mother used to say: two spoons in a drawer, front to back, fitting perfectly together. It was so comforting to sleep like this, but they only had a few minutes left before they had to get up.

He moved slightly, turning toward her. And she reached out to make sure he was awake to appreciate what she was about to do. They didn't have much time like this anymore, and she had to make every second count.

Chapter Seven

The road past the country club had been very pretty, but not interesting enough to run every day. To her surprise, Maura had managed to keep up with Jan and she hadn't even been breathing hard when they'd finished their run. It was clear that her body was in a lot better shape than her mind. Despite Maura's high hopes, nothing she'd seen along the way had jogged her recalcitrant memory.

There had been another benefit to running, a bonus that Maura hadn't anticipated. She'd been as hungry as a bear when she'd come back to the house, and she'd managed to eat a full stack of Nita's excellent pancakes.

Now that breakfast was over, they were sitting at the table with an uneasy silence between them. Maura had just dropped her bombshell. She'd told Jan and Nita that she wasn't going in to the boutique today.

"But why, Miss Maura?" Nita looked puzzled.

"I thought we'd do something else instead. You said I had a capable staff. Can't they handle it for a few more days?"

"Sure." Jan nodded. "But you always go to the boutique!"

"Then maybe it's time to change my habits. I thought we

could do something else, instead. We could . . . uh . . . drive up to the mountains and go skiing."

"But you don't know how to ski." Jan looked very concerned. "And you always told me you didn't want to learn."

"Oh. I guess skiing's out then." Maura filed that information away for future reference. What she thought she'd remembered last night couldn't possibly have happened if she couldn't ski. "How about the movies? I'd really love to see a film."

"Which film would you like to see, Miss Maura?" Nita stared at her intently.

"Actually . . . anything from the past twenty years will do. It doesn't matter if I've seen it before. I won't remember anyway."

"Mom!" Jan looked shocked. And then she began to laugh. "I guess that's true, but I'm not sure you should joke about it."

Nita didn't seem to find this amusing. She was frowning as she leaned close to peer at Maura. "You are giving excuses, Miss Maura. I think there is some reason you do not want to go to the boutique."

"Is that true, Mom?" Jan looked concerned. "Whatever it is, I think we should talk about it. Maybe I overstepped my authority here, but I told them you were coming and everybody's waiting for you. They're going to be really disappointed if you don't show."

Maura sighed. She wasn't sure she could explain it to Jan and Maura, but she really didn't want to go. Just mentioning the boutique made her nervous, and she had no idea why. "Did I . . . uh . . . *like* to go there, before the accident?"

"Of course you did." Nita looked shocked. "You love the boutique. You told me that your happiest hours are spent there."

Jan nodded. "It's true. I used to have to drag you out of there to keep your tennis appointments."

"Tennis?" Maura was glad to be side-tracked. "I play tennis?"

Nita looked proud as she nodded. "You learned a year ago, Miss Maura. You have a coach at the country club, and he says that you are doing very well."

"Then let's play tennis instead of going to the boutique. I don't remember my tennis lessons, and I want to see if it comes back to me."

"You have to book a court, Mom." Jan shook her head. "And you usually have to call a day in advance. I can call for tomorrow, if you want to play then. But I really think we ought to go to the boutique today. I know you're not looking forward to facing more strangers, but the longer you put it off, the more nervous you're going to be."

Maura sighed, and then she nodded. She'd run out of excuses and she supposed she had to go. But she wasn't going alone. She make Jan go with her. "Jan? You'll come with me, won't you?"

"Of course I will! And I'll introduce you to everyone."

"How many . . . employees do I have?" Maura held her breath. She hoped it wasn't too many.

"Only five. And that's not counting your partner. She's out of town for the week."

"Partner?" Maura swallowed hard. She was beginning to feel nervous again. Perhaps her anxiety about the boutique had something to do with her partner. "I don't understand, Jan. I thought the boutique was mine."

"It is. Liz Webber's only a junior partner. And that's just on paper. She draws a salary as manager of your shop."

The moment Jan said Liz's name, Maura began to feel very uneasy. Was there some secret about Liz Webber that she could no longer remember? "Liz Webber manages my boutique?"

Jan shook her head. "No, she manages your shop. That's where you manufacture your clothes."

"Oh. I see. I design the clothes and Liz sews them?"

"Well . . . yes. At least that's the way it started. Aunt Donna hired Liz as your pattern maker and she worked her way up. And when she wanted to go into business for herself, you convinced her to stay by offering her a junior partnership."

"Do I like her?"

Jan was silent for a moment and then she nodded. "I think so. She's not a close friend or anything like that, but you always say you couldn't get along without her."

"What do you think, Nita? Do I like her?"

Nita shrugged. "Miss Webber is not a friend, no. But you are pleased with her work. You taught her how to choose fabric, and you trust her to go out to buy from the factories."

"Trust is very important." Maura nodded. "And I guess it's not that important whether I like her or not, as long as she does a good job."

As she sipped her coffee, Maura began to feel better. She wasn't sure why, but just knowing that Liz wouldn't be at the boutique was a huge relief. "Jan? Are you sure my employees will be disappointed if I don't come in today?"

"I'm sure, Mom. They're all looking forward to seeing you again. And I made everyone promise that they wouldn't ask questions about your memory."

"Well . . . all right. I'll go." Maura put down her coffee cup and stood up. "But only if Nita promises to go to the market while we're gone. There's something special I'd like to have."

Nita nodded. "Of course, Miss Maura. What is it?"

"Gjetost."

Jan looked startled. *"Gjetost?* What's that?"

"It's a kind of brown goat cheese that tastes like peanut butter. It's usually spread on black bread and eaten as a snack. Do you think you can find it, Nita?"

Nita nodded. "Of course. I will go to the Beverly Hills Cheese Store. They have everything. But you never mentioned that you liked goat cheese before."

"That's because I don't know whether I do, or not." Maura laughed at their puzzled expressions and did her best to explain. "I'm not sure if I just read about it, or actually tasted it, but I seem to remember eating it. And I'd really like to try some when we get home."

Nita looked very determined as she nodded again. "I'll find it, Miss Maura. And I will find black bread, too. We will have it when you get home from the boutique, and perhaps it will help you remember."

As Maura followed Jan out to the car, she couldn't help feeling a bit apprehensive. Would the *Gjetost* and black bread really bring back a part of her memory? And did she really want to recall the painful emotions she'd experienced last night, when she'd relived that scene at the snow-covered graveyard?

The boutique was impressive, no doubt about it. Maura had been almost awestruck when Jan had pulled up in front of the dusty pink covered awning on Rodeo Drive. And she'd smiled when she'd realized that she had named her boutique after Jan. *Fille Janelle* wasn't a large boutique, but it had all the amenities, including valet parking. And the moment Maura had stepped through the door, her employees had rushed up to hug her and welcome her back.

Jan had been as good as her word. There had been no questions about her lost memory, although Maura could tell that Sylvia, her stylish, middle-aged boutique manager, was dying to ask what she remembered and what she didn't. Jan must have been very firm in her instructions to the staff, because the only question Sylvia had asked was whether she felt strong enough to take a tour through the boutique.

Sylvia had reintroduced Maura to Heather, a young, blond U.C.L.A. student who was one of their best saleswomen. She'd told Maura that Heather and Bonnie, a dark-haired senior at Cal Arts, had been very successful in bringing the younger crowd to *Fille Janelle*.

Maura had met Diane, a lovely, brown-haired English woman with a charming accent and impeccable taste in clothing, and Cherise, a stunning black woman in her early thirties, who had spent two years in France studying design. Maura was pleased that her employees seemed to love the boutique, and from their warm smiles and genuine concern for her, she was convinced that she'd been a good boss.

"And this is one of your most successful designs." Sylvia pulled an outfit from the glass closets that lined the walls of the small shop, and turned to Maura with a smile.

Maura was surprised as she examined the outfit, loose-fitting pants made of boldly-printed cotton, with a bib that was attached like overalls. It reminded her of something, but she couldn't quite remember what.

"Sylvia?" Maura was puzzled as she turned to her manager. "Do you know when I designed this outfit?"

"Last year. You were going through some of Jan's old baby clothes, and you . . ."

"Rompers!" Maura gave a delighted smile. "Jan used to have rompers just like this! And when I remembered how she loved them, I decided to dress them up a little, make them more feminine, and do them in adult sizes."

"They're one of your hottest items, Mom. And they still look good on me." Jan was smiling as she took the rompers and held them up to show her mother how they'd look on her. "They're really popular with the college crowd. Heather and Bonnie wore theirs on campus, and all the girls asked where they could buy them."

Sylvia nodded. "They were so popular with the college girls, we couldn't keep up with the demand. When they came in, we gave them a swatch book and asked them to choose the fabric they wanted. The girls really liked the idea of having something made, especially for them."

"We put their names on a waiting list." Heather continued the story. "And then Bonnie came up with the idea of personalizing their rompers."

Maura turned to Bonnie with a smile. "How did we accomplish that?"

Bonnie pointed to the front of the bib. "See this patch? It's made of washable suede, and we embroidered it with the girl's initials, right here in the shop. The girls really loved ordering something that was monogrammed."

"That was a very good idea." Maura smiled at Bonnie. "I hope I gave you a bonus."

Bonnie grinned back. "You did. You always give us bonuses when we come up with an idea you use."

"We have another bonus which no one has mentioned." Diane smiled at Maura. "You choose the particular outfits that will look best on us, and give them to us for our personal use."

Cherise nodded. "It's a great perk and it makes sense. My whole closet is filled with your clothes, and every time I wear a new outfit, people ask me where I bought it. That's one of the ways *Fille Janelle* attracts new customers. You're a very smart businesswoman, Mrs. Bennett."

Maura smiled at the compliment, but she made a mental note. Cherise had called her Mrs. Bennett, not Mrs. Thomas. Did that mean that she didn't use her married name at work? But perhaps Cherise had been working for her before she'd married Keith and she was in the habit of calling her Mrs. Bennett. She'd have to check the personnel file to find out if that was true.

There was just time for a quick tour through the boutique before they opened their doors at eleven. Maura was amazed at how beautifully her boutique was decorated, especially when she found out that she'd done it all herself. The showroom floor was covered with a deep pile carpet in a lovely shade of mauve which matched the color in the thin pin-stripe on the deep grey fabric walls. There were two settees, several cushioned chairs, and a low coffee table, forming a conversational group in the far corner of the room. The furniture was made of light ash and it looked very comfortable, cushioned in the same shade of mauve.

Maura had already seen the closets that lined two of the walls, a section for each size she carried. There was a huge, beveled glass mirror in one of the corners, oval shaped and framed in the same shade of light ash wood. The mirror was on a stand and it tilted, providing a head-to-toe view. And it was flanked by two light ash hat trees, one filled with hats and the other with costume jewelry and scarves.

"Do we sell leather goods?" Maura turned to Sylvia. She was sure she remembered carrying luggage and purses in her boutique.

Sylvia nodded. "Of course. Come with me and I'll show you."

Maura gasped as Sylvia led her through a small archway

and into another, smaller room, lined with light ash shelves. There were leather purses of every conceivable size and shape, the same buttery soft luggage Jan had brought her at the hospital, and a gorgeous array of shoes, especially chosen to compliment the outfits she had designed.

"You do all the buying." Sylvia answered Maura's unspoken question. "A small shoe factory in Italy makes our line of shoes and handbags, and you just contracted with them for our luggage."

"Ammante's?" Maura held her breath until Sylvia nodded. She'd remembered the name of one of their suppliers. "How about the hats? Who makes those?"

"A firm in France. You design some of them. And our costume jewelry comes from Germany. You also buy some from Switzerland, but they only deal in semiprecious stones."

"How about the scarves? They're lovely."

"It took you a while to find a place to make those." Sylvia smiled. "You finalized the contract just last year. There's a wonderful textile firm in Helsinki that does the sheers, and a Swedish plant makes all the woven belts."

"And I travel to all of these places?"

"Yes, you do. You make four or five overseas trips a year. As a matter of fact, that's where you were going when . . . ." Sylvia stopped in mid-sentence, and looked terribly embarrassed. "Oh, dear! I promised Jan I wouldn't mention anything that might be traumatic!"

Maura smiled. Jan had obviously been trying to protect her. "Don't worry, Sylvia. The accident's not traumatic. How could it be, when I don't remember it? *That's* what's traumatic!"

"It must be terrible." Sylvia looked very sympathetic. "I

know I shouldn't ask, but . . . do you remember this place at all?"

"Not really. But that's all right. I'm getting the pleasure of seeing it all over again, for the first time."

"You certainly have a good attitude. Of course you've always had that." Sylvia sighed and patted Maura on the shoulder. "But I want you to know that if there's anything I can do to help, all you have to do is ask."

Maura nodded. Jan had told her that Sylvia had been with the boutique since it had opened. And she certainly seemed to care. "There is something, Sylvia. But I'm not sure exactly how to ask . . ."

"What is it?"

"Actually . . ." Maura faltered. How did you ask someone if they'd been a friend?

"Come on, Maura. You've never been shy around me."

Maura took a deep breath. She'd just have to ask. "Sylvia?"

"Yes?"

"Were we . . . uh . . . friends?"

Sylvia laughed. "Of course we were. We couldn't have worked together for so long, if we hadn't been friends."

"Then you know how I used to feel about people?"

Sylvia eyes narrowed. "Which people?"

"Well . . ." Maura took a deep breath. "I'd like to know about Liz Webber. Did I like her?"

"Liz Webber?" Sylvia looked very uncomfortable. "You never actually *said* anything about Liz, but I know you thought she was a good worker."

"But I didn't like her."

"I think you might have liked her at first." Sylvia swallowed hard. "Look, Maura. I really shouldn't be talking about this. It's not like I really know anything. It's all just speculation."

"What's speculation?"

Sylvia took a deep breath. "Let's just forget it, Maura. There's no reason to bring all this up right now."

"Bring *what* up?" Maura could feel her frustration rise. "You said we were friends, Sylvia. And I really need some answers. Something about Liz Webber makes me very nervous."

"That's understandable!" The moment the words popped out of Sylvia's mouth, she looked embarrassed. "Forget I said that."

"Please, Sylvia . . ." Maura reached out to touch Sylvia's arm. "When I got up this morning, I didn't want to come to down here. It was almost as if there were something or someone I didn't want to face. And then, when Jan told me that Liz was out of town, I completely changed my mind. Then I could hardly wait to see the boutique and meet all of you again."

Sylvia nodded. And then she sighed. "Okay. What do you want to know?"

"I want to know about Liz. Why do I feel anxious every time I hear her name?"

Sylvia sighed again. And then she glanced around to make sure no one was near enough to hear. "Look, Maura. I think the reason you're so nervous about Liz, is because . . ."

Sylvia stopped, and Maura touched her arm, again. "Yes?"

"All right. I'll tell you. You used to like Liz, but you don't anymore."

"Why?" Maura took a deep breath and held it. She knew

she wasn't going to like the answer she was forcing Sylvia to give her.

"Because you're almost sure that Liz Webber is having an affair with your husband!"

Chapter Eight

Maura was in her room when the doorbell rang. It had taken her a while to get over her shock, but she'd thought it all over and realized that there might be no real basis for her former suspicions. Liz was attractive. Everyone she'd asked had told her that. And Sylvia had admitted that she hadn't seen anything improper transpire between Keith and Liz. Perhaps she was just a jealous wife, mistrustful of every attractive woman her husband met.

The intercom buzzed, and Maura took one last look in the mirror. She was wearing a lovely, green silk hostess gown, one of her own creations. It had a high, Mandarin collar, and the front buttoned all the way up to her neck. The waist was elasticized, emphasizing the full skirt that fell to mid calf. From the front, it was a simple, sleeveless gown, but the back was quite a surprise.

There was no back, unless you counted the high collar which held the dress in place and Maura's curly, auburn hair covered that completely. The view from the back was startling, just a swirling skirt that made her look as if she were topless. Of course, that illusion dissolved the moment she turned around.

She'd designed the gown for Jan to wear to a psychology department party last year. Jan had named it her "Sybil" dress, in honor of the famous case of multiple personalities. To Maura's surprise, it had turned out to be a popular design. It seemed everyone wanted to be a prim and proper lady from the front, and a courtesan from the back.

The intercom buzzed again. They were waiting for her. Maura went out the door and paused, wondering how she'd react to their dinner guest. When they'd come back from the boutique, Nita had mentioned that Steve would be joining them for dinner. And that meant Nita's conversation this morning had been with Steve.

As she walked down the stairs, Maura reviewed the telephone conversation she'd overheard. The first part had been understandable, since Steve was a doctor. Naturally, he would ask questions about her memory. But Nita had said, *It is very good for her to have the family with her again, and I will make certain that she is ready before he comes back.* She was sure they'd been talking about Keith. And she wanted to ask Steve why she had to be ready before he came back.

There was another question, one that really puzzled Maura. Nita had said, *Yes, you can count on me. And you can be certain that Jan knows nothing. You should not worry. I will call you immediately if there is concern.* What was that all about? Steve would know, and she had to find the opportunity to ask him.

As she walked down the stairs, Maura thought of another question, one that hadn't occurred to her before. Why had Nita spoken in Spanish? Steve had obviously understood her, or she would have switched to English.

Maura hesitated slightly, as she reached the foot of the stairs. She could hear Jan's voice coming from the living room. Steve must be waiting for her there. She reached up and fluffed her hair, feeling a little like a girl on her first date.

But that was silly. Steve wasn't her date, he was just her brother-in-law.

"Mom!" Jan jumped to her feet as Maura entered the living room. "You look gorgeous . . . doesn't she, Uncle Steve?"

Maura turned to Steve, who was smiling at her, and felt a blush rise to her cheeks. She remembered her first impression of him, and how she'd compared him to her favorite actor, Paul Newman. That resemblance was even more startling tonight, perhaps because he was wearing a blue shirt that was the exact color of his eyes.

"You do look beautiful, Maura."

Steve rose to his feet to give her a hug, and Maura's heart beat wildly. She told herself she shouldn't be feeling this way, and she pulled away at the first opportunity, but she knew her cheeks were bright with color.

"It's good to see you again, Steve. Would you like a drink? Or an appetizer?" Maura hurried to the antique sideboard to pick up the silver tray of appetizers that Nita had arranged. "I asked Nita to pick up some *Gjetost* and black bread."

"*Gjetost?*" Steve looked startled.

"Mom thinks she remembers eating it once." Jan hurried to explain. "But she's not sure whether she actually tasted it, or read about it in a book."

"Why don't you try some and see?" Steve took one of the triangular shaped pieces of black bread and spread it with the cheese. "Open wide, luv."

Maura opened her mouth obediently, but she almost choked on the delicious-tasting cheese as she realized what Steve had said. He'd called her "luv!"

"Do you remember the *Gjetost*, Mom?"

Jan looked curious, but she didn't seem startled by the

term of endearment her Uncle Steve had used. Perhaps it wasn't personal, after all. Jan had mentioned that Steve had studied in London. He might have picked up the term in England and it was possible he called all women "luv."

"Mom?"

Jan looked a little concerned, and Maura quickly responded to her question. "No, honey . . . I don't really remember it, but I certainly like it."

"Are you sure?"

Steve seemed relieved when Maura shook her head, and Maura was puzzled. She turned to him with a frown on her face. "You look relieved that I don't remember. Is there something you'd rather I forgot?"

"Actually . . . yes." Steve nodded. "You see, I remember the first time you tasted *Gjetost*, and it wasn't a pleasant occasion."

Maura walked over to perch on the edge of the couch. "I think you should tell me about it."

"It was the day of Paul's funeral. Donna and I came down to San Diego, and after the service, we offered to take you out to lunch. You wouldn't go. You said you just wanted to go home to be by yourself, but we didn't think that was a good idea, especially in your condition."

"Because she was pregnant with me?" Jan smiled at her uncle.

"That was part of it. The other part was that your mother was having false labor pains at the time. Donna and I weren't sure they were false, so we decided to stay over, just in case."

Maura looked puzzled. "But I didn't have Jan until six weeks later. Isn't that right?"

"That's right." Steve smiled as he nodded. "We just didn't

want to take any chances. Your parents had already left, and you were all alone."

Maura shivered a little. It would have been terrible to be all alone, after her husband's funeral. "So you and Donna stayed at my apartment?"

"Yes. You insisted on giving us your bedroom, and you bedded down on the couch. And then, about three in the morning, you got a terrible craving for peanut butter."

Maura's eyes widened. "I woke you up to go after peanut butter at three in the morning?"

"No." Steve grinned. "None of us could sleep that night. We were all in the living room, watching a dreadful old movie on television. Do you happen to remember what it was?"

Maura shook her head. "Not really."

"Neither do I." Steve laughed. "I went out for the peanut butter, and the first place I found that was open was a Scandinavian deli down the street. They didn't carry peanut butter, but they sold me some *Gjetost* and black bread. And they absolutely guaranteed me that it would satisfy your craving."

"Did it?" Jan was intrigued.

Steve turned to his niece and grinned. "It seemed to. Your mother fell asleep before the end of the movie, and she didn't wake up until eleven the next morning."

"And that's the only time I ever had *Gjetost?*" Maura frowned slightly. Her dream was so clear, it simply had to be a real memory.

"As far as I know." Steve spread some more cheese on a triangle of bread and popped it into his mouth. "It does taste like peanut butter. And I think it would go nicely with that chilled bottle of fume blanc I brought. Shall I open it now?"

"Only if I can have a glass." Jan grinned at her uncle, and

then she turned to her mother to explain. "You let me have wine at home, Mom . . . honest."

Maura nodded. "That sounds reasonable to me . . . but more than half a glass and your wings are clipped for the rest of the night."

"I know, Mom. That's what you always say."

Jan was grinning as she went off to fetch wine glasses, and Maura turned to Steve. "Is that what I always say?"

"Absolutely." Steve nodded. "You told me you thought it was a good idea to introduce Jan to fine wines at home. That way it wouldn't be as much of a temptation to go out with the crowd and drink the cheap stuff that kids usually buy."

"Did it work?"

"It worked perfectly, all through high school." Steve draped a casual arm around her shoulders. "Jan's favorite champagne is Dom Perignon, and there aren't many high school boys who can afford that."

Maura laughed. "Lord! I hope I didn't price her right out of the date market!"

"Not a chance. Jan's always been very popular, but she's also very picky. She's never fallen head over heels in love. The only date you've really objected to was the boy with the triple-pieced ear and the gold nose ring."

"What?!" Maura turned to gaze at Steve in alarm, but then she realized that his eyes were twinkling. "You're kidding, aren't you?"

Steve pulled her a little closer and patted her on the head. "Of course I am, luv. You can be proud of Jan. She's a very level-headed young lady."

"Thanks, Uncle Steve." Jan came into the room just in time to hear his comment. "Nita says it'll be another fifteen minutes, so we have plenty of time for the wine. And she promised to steam off the label for your wine book, Mom."

"My wine book?"

"Right." As Jan passed the wine bottle and corkscrew to her uncle, she looked a little upset. "I'm sorry, Mom. I forgot that you wouldn't remember. You keep scrapbooks with all your favorite wine labels."

"But . . . why?"

"So you can remember your favorites." Steve took the corkscrew and deftly opened the wine.

"That's right." Jan smiled at her mother. "You write a brief description under the label, and list the foods you think would compliment each wine. It's sort of a hobby . . . right, Uncle Steve?"

Steve nodded as he deftly opened the wine and passed the bottle to Jan. "The last time I asked, you were up to ten volumes."

"I drink that much wine?" Maura looked horrified as Jan handed her a glass. It sounded as if she might have a drinking problem. "Tell me the truth, Jan. Am I . . . uh . . . an alcoholic?"

"No way!" Jan started to laugh, but she sobered quickly when she realized that her mother was really worried. "You don't actually drink all that wine, Mom. You taste it. Or you order it at a restaurant and ask to bring home the empty bottle. I've been with you at parties, and I've never ever seen you torqued."

"Torqued?"

Steve laughed. "It's what we used to call 'bombed' in our day. And don't worry, Maura. You don't have a drinking problem. As a matter of fact, you don't have any other sort of problem that I know of. So stop holding that wine glass as if it's an angry dog that's about to snap at you, and take a sip. I want you to tell me what you think of my selection."

Maura laughed, and raised the glass to her lips. She took

a small sip, but instead of swallowing, she swished it in her mouth. She wasn't sure how, but she knew the wine was an excellent vintage.

"Well?"

Steve was gazing at her approvingly, and Maura nodded as she swallowed. And then she said the first thing that came to her mind. "Very nice. It's on the light side with a hint of fruit, but it has enough body to carry."

"When would you serve it?"

Steve leaned forward, and Maura had the uncomfortable feeling he might know she was feeling slightly dizzy, just being this close to him. "I'd serve it with something light."

"Fish?"

Maura shivered. She wanted to move back, away from Steve, but she didn't want to be obvious about it. Actually, that wasn't true. She'd much rather move forward, into his arms, but that would be totally inappropriate. What was wrong with her? She found herself unreasonably attracted to Steve, and she was married to Keith!

"Not fish." Maura took a deep breath and answered his question. "It's not really an entrée wine. It would do best at brunch, and I'd serve it with omelettes, vegetarian with no strongly-flavored cheeses, but what I'd really suggest is . . . blintzes!"

"Perfect!" Steve reached out to touch her forehead with his lips. "I've taught you well, luv."

He moved then, turning to talk to Jan, and Maura attempted to catch her breath. Blintzes? She didn't even know what blintzes were! Steve had obviously been the one to teach her about wine, but under what circumstances? And why did she have trouble breathing every time he was near? But before Maura could ponder any other questions, Nita appeared in the doorway.

"Dinner is served." Nita looked proud. "I hope you like it, Miss Maura. Mr. Steve suggested Mexican food."

"I'm sure it'll be delicious." Maura smiled, and got to her feet. As far as she knew, the closest she'd ever been to Mexican food were Doritos and Fritos, and the limp, taste-less burritos they'd served at the college cafeteria.

"Incredible!" Maura sighed as Nita passed her the platter of tamales. "Which ones are sweet, Nita? You told me before, but I forgot."

"These, Miss Maura." Nita pointed to the far end of the platter where there were smaller tamales, wrapped in corn husks.

Jan grinned as Maura picked up a tamale and put it on her plate. "Don't forget to unwrap it, this time."

"I won't." Maura laughed. When she'd attempted to eat her first tamale, she'd tried to cut through the corn husk. "And don't be so mean to your mother. She's not the type to make the same mistake twice."

Jan grinned back good-naturedly. "Great! At least I won't have to worry about you marrying again!"

"What?!" Maura was so startled, she almost dropped her fork. Was Jan referring to Keith?

"Sorry, Mom." Jan blushed beet red. "I didn't mean it, honest. We always joke about things like that."

Before Maura could ask any questions, Steve jumped in. "No harm done. But there will be if I keep eating. Did you make any Mexican coffee, Nita?"

"I did." Nita nodded and rushed off toward the kitchen, but she stopped at the doorway with a grin. "I know you have eaten much, Mr. Steve . . . but do you have room for my pineapple flan?"

Steve laughed. "You're a devil, Nita. You know I can't resist your pineapple flan. Just cut me a small piece. That way, I can have seconds. And let's have it in the living room where we can be more comfortable."

"Nita makes the best pineapple flan in the world," Jan hurried to explain. "And Uncle Steve always says he's too full for dessert, but he usually has two pieces."

Maura nodded. The time had passed to ask any questions about the strange comment that Jan had made, but she'd add it to her mental list of questions to ask Steve.

"Would it be rude if I took my dessert up to my room?" Jan didn't quite meet her mother's eyes. "There's a movie going on that I really want to watch."

Steve nodded. "Go ahead, honey. Your mother and I'll manage without you. Right, Maura?"

"Oh. Yes . . . of course." Maura frowned slightly. From the emotionally-laden looks that Steve and Jan had exchanged, it was clear they'd worked this out in advance.

"Take your time, Maura." Steve grinned at her. "I love to see you eat. You hardly touched your food when you were in the hospital."

"That's because it wasn't worth touching!" Maura gave him a dirty look. "All I got the first couple of days was Jell-O and broth."

Steve raised his eyebrows, and Maura drew in her breath. One eyebrows was a little higher than the other, giving him a rakish, devil-may-care look.

"Now look, luv. You might not know it, but I was doing you a big favor. There's no way the hospital kitchen can ruin Jell-O and broth. Regular hospital food isn't exactly gourmet fare. It's a lot like airplane food."

"Domestic, yes." Maura nodded. "But have you ever flown on SAS?"

Steve leaned forward to stare at her, and Maura began to feel very uncomfortable, especially when he reached out to touch her arm.

"Have you flown on SAS, luv?"

"I . . . I'm not sure." Maura sighed deeply. "For a second there, I thought I remembered. But I watched a lot of television while I was in the hospital. I could be remembering a commercial."

Steve laughed. "That's probably it. SAS just launched a huge ad campaign. Finish up your tamale, Maura, and we'll have coffee and dessert in the living room."

Chapter Nine

Maura had finished every bite of her tamale, just to prove that she could. And she'd also eaten a full serving of Nita's pineapple flan, accompanied by a cup of strong, Mexican coffee. Nita had cleared away the dishes, and now she and Steve were sitting on the couch, enjoying the blaze he'd made in the river rock fireplace.

"I'm glad you started a fire, Steve." Maura turned to him with a smile. "There's something very comforting about hearth and home."

"I know. Watching a fire makes most people relax. It also encourages intimate conversation."

"Intimate?" Maura felt her heart beat hard. "I don't understand. Are we . . . intimate?"

"Not in the traditional sense of the word. But we *are* good friends."

Maura took a deep gulp of air. She hadn't realized that she'd been holding her breath, waiting for Steve's answer to her question. Thank goodness they weren't intimate! Although she didn't remember any part of her life with Keith, she hoped that she'd been a loyal wife.

"Maura?"

"Yes, Steve?"

"I know you need a friend right now. And I want you to feel free to discuss every aspect of your life with me."

Maura nodded. This was the opportunity she'd been searching for. "All right, then. I'd like to ask you some questions. I'm warning you right now . . . some of them might be personal."

"Go ahead, luv." Steve smiled at her. "I'll tell you everything I know."

Maura took a deep breath and reminded herself that honesty was the best policy. And then she started to speak. "I know that you called Nita this morning. I'm not exactly proud of snooping, but I overheard part of the conversation. That's what I'd like to ask you about."

"Fair enough." Steve nodded. "Ask me."

"Why did Nita speak to you in Spanish?"

"Because I took Spanish in college, and I don't want to lose my skill. Nita helps me brush up, whenever she can."

Maura nodded. That explanation sounded reasonable to her. "Okay. Now tell me who *he* is."

"He?" Steve looked puzzled. "Which *he* are you talking about?"

"The *he* on the phone. Nita said I had to be ready before *he* came home. I assumed she meant Keith, and I want to know what I'm supposed to be ready for."

Steve laughed. "That's easy, luv. There's a benefit dance at the Biltmore next month. Keith was hoping you'd be what he calls 'up to speed' before the big event."

"That's all?"

"Absolutely." Steve grinned at her. "Anything else?"

"What is it that Jan doesn't know?"

This time Steve looked completely bewildered. "Sorry, luv. I don't know what you're talking about."

"Nita said that Jan knew nothing. She told you not to worry, and she promised to call you immediately if there was any concern."

"Oh, *that!*" Steve sighed. "Lord, Maura. I was hoping to break it to you gently, but . . ."

"What is it?" Maura felt her adrenaline race. "Tell me, Steve!"

"We arranged it all before the accident, but it's clear you don't remember. And I didn't want to just spring it on you without any warning."

"Spring *what* on me?"

"The dog."

"What dog?"

"The one I bought for Jan. She's always wanted a dog. You said it was all right with you, so I put down a deposit on a puppy."

"A puppy?" Maura began to smile. "That's wonderful, Steve! I've always loved dogs . . . at least I think I have. What kind of puppy is it?"

"He's an Australian sheep dog. Wait until you see him . . . he's three different colors, and he's got the cutest little face. The breeder says he's very smart, and he'll make an excellent watch dog."

"He sounds wonderful!" Maura clapped her hands in delight. "When can you pick him up?"

"I'll call to arrange it. If the puppy's ready to be adopted, I'll pick him up tomorrow. But don't tell Jan. It's supposed to be a surprise."

"I won't breathe a word." Maura grinned. Having a puppy in the house would be fun. But how would Keith feel about a puppy? Wasn't that something wives were supposed to discuss with their husbands?

"What it is, luv? You look worried." Steve reached out to drape his arm around her shoulders again.

"Did I . . . uh . . . do you know if I discussed this with Keith?"

"I have no idea. But I really don't think it'll be a problem. Bonnie and Clyde were staying here when you married Keith, and he got along just fine with them."

"Bonnie and Clyde? Who are they?"

"The Emmersons' dogs. They're the two black labs that live next door. The Emmersons went to Europe for six months, and Nita agreed to look after their dogs. They were supposed to stay in their own yard, but . . ." Steve shook his head and began to laugh. "Maybe it's a good thing you don't remember."

"Why? What happened?" Maura began to smile.

"Well . . . the first night after the Emmersons left, Bonnie and Clyde got lonesome. They jumped the fence into your back yard, and chewed right through the back door. When you woke up the next morning, you found them both sleeping at the foot of your bed."

"What did I do?"

"You called a carpenter to put in a doggy door, and you bought two outrageously priced dog beds. Bonnie and Clyde lived with you until the Emmersons came home."

"And Keith didn't mind?" Maura still looked a little anxious.

"Not at all. He told me he was glad that Bonnie and Clyde were here to protect you when he was out of town."

Maura nodded. Keith had told her that he ran an import export business, but she really didn't know much about it. "Does Keith have to go out of town very often?"

"Every couple of weeks or so. But you travel frequently,

too. You try to arrange your schedules so you're home at the same time."

Maura began to frown. If they both traveled frequently, it didn't sound like much of a marriage. "Steve?"

"Yes, luv?"

"Do I . . . uh . . . love Keith?"

Steve raised his eyebrows. "I assume you do. After all, you married him."

"Do *you* like him?"

That question seemed to take Steve by surprise. He took a deep breath and winced a little. "To be perfectly honest, he's not exactly the man I would have chosen for you, but I like him well enough. I'd like anyone who made you happy, Maura. You're very important to me."

"Thank you." Maura felt tears come to her eyes, and she turned away quickly, to blink them back. It was clear that Steve loved her . . . as a sister-in-law, of course.

Steve poured a little more coffee from the silver carafe that Nita had left, and leaned back against the couch cushions again. "Any more questions?"

"Yes. I loved your brother, didn't I?"

Steve nodded quickly. "Yes, you did. And his death was a terrible blow to you. I think the only thing that kept you going was the fact that you were pregnant."

"She's wonderful, isn't she?"

It was more of a statement than a question, and Steve grinned as he nodded. "Jan is what we aging hippies like to call 'good people.' You did an excellent job as a mother, luv. And hiring Nita was part of it."

"Jan told me that you and Donna found her for me. I'll always be grateful for that. I don't exactly remember, but I have a strong feeling that Nita was one of the people who kept me sane."

Steve nodded, again. "That's true. And Donna was another. I don't think I'll ever stop missing her."

"I feel the same way." Maura sighed. "I just wish I could really remember her. From the things Jan's told me, she must have been a saint."

Steve started to laugh. "I wouldn't go quite that far. Donna was Irish. Her last name was O'Mally. And she had a temper that could make grown men quake in their boots."

"You?"

"Even me." Steve grinned, and looked a little sheepish. "I'll never forget the day you moved here. I suggested that you put Jan in a good, professional day care center while you started your boutique. The moment the words were out of my mouth, Donna hit the roof."

"Donna didn't approve of day care?"

"Oh, that wasn't it." Steve was still grinning. "She thought I was casting aspersions on her ability as a substitute mother. She was just a little thing, five feet two inches tall, she stood there with her eyes flashing, and she faced me down. She said, 'I'll take care of this dear, sweet baby! And if you don't like it, you can just find another place to hang your hat!' "

Maura was surprised. From the things Jan had told her, she'd assumed that they'd hired Nita immediately. "Donna took care of Jan?"

"For the first six months. Bottles, formula, toys, cribs and playpens, she turned our house into a nursery. And all this from the woman who said she didn't think career women could be good mothers."

Maura frowned slightly. "Donna had a career?"

"Oh, yes. She was a very talented illustrator. Books, magazines, you name it. She worked at home, and you two took turns with the baby. You were living with us at the time."

Maura couldn't help feeling guilty. It sounded as if Steve's life had been severely disrupted. "I'm sorry, Steve. It must have been hard on you."

"Are you kidding? It was one of the happiest times of my life! You see, Donna couldn't have children. This was our one chance to spoil a baby outrageously, and we made the most of it."

Maura giggled. "Well, Jan doesn't seem to be the worse for it. And she certainly loves you. I'd say you did a pretty good job as substitute parents."

"We enjoyed it. And we were pretty upset when you decided to move out to a place of your own. But the boutique was on its feet by then, and we realized that you needed your own life."

Maura nodded. "That's when I hired Nita? After I moved?"

"That's right. Nita was working for a friend of Donna's at the time, but their youngest had just started school. Donna convinced them they didn't need a nanny any longer, and Nita went to work for you."

"But Nita's still here. And Jan's in college. I'm glad she decided to stay with us all these years . . . but why?"

"You wouldn't let her go." Steve started to chuckle. "When Jan was growing up, you worked long hours at the boutique. You really needed Nita to live in. And then, when Jan was old enough to get along without supervision, you convinced Nita to stay on as your housekeeper."

"It sounds as if I manipulated her. Tell me honestly . . . does Nita want to leave?"

Steve shook his head. "I'm sure she doesn't. You've always told her that she's part of your family and this is her home for life."

Maura gave a huge sigh of relief. "Thank goodness! I don't know what I'd do without her . . . especially now. Nita knows more about me than I do!"

"True." Steve began to smile. "Come to think about it, even *I* know more about you than you do."

"Are you sure about that?"

"Positive. Ask me a question about your life, and I'll prove it."

Maura felt her breathing quicken. This was the perfect opportunity to ask about some of the strange inconsistencies in her dreams. "Did I marry again, after Paul was killed?"

Steve frowned slightly. "Of course. You married Keith two years ago."

"I didn't mean Keith. I meant . . . did I marry anyone else in between?"

"Not that I know of." Steve still looked concerned. "Do you think you remember someone else?"

"Not really. Do I know anyone named Nick?"

"Nick?" Steve took a moment to think about it. "I don't think so. Of course, I'm not familiar with all your business contacts. Why do you want to know?"

"I had a weird dream last night, about a man named Nick."

"Oh?" Steve moved closer. "Tell me about it, luv."

Maura swallowed hard. For some strange reason, she was reluctant to tell Steve about her dream. "It's not really that important. I just dreamed I was married to a man named Nick, that's all."

"Have you been having other dreams?"

"A few." Maura hesitated again. She really wanted to describe the scene in the airport, and the way she'd hidden under the hotel room bed and escaped down a pipe, but she didn't want Steve to think she was crazy. It was better if she asked the questions. That way she could control the situation.

"I do have a question." Maura tried to look perfectly innocent. "I know I've worked at the boutique for the past twenty years, but have I ever held any other jobs?"

"I'm sure you have, but I might not know about all of them. You were working as a secretary when Paul met you. And you mentioned being a waitress once at a small café in your home town."

"Was I ever a maid in a big hotel?"

Steve shrugged. "Not that I know of, but I know you worked your way through college. I don't think you would have been a maid, though. With your skills, you would have found something that paid much better."

"How about my education . . . do I speak any foreign languages?"

"Spanish. You remember that, since you understood our telephone conversation this morning. And I think you know enough French to get by on your buying trips."

Maura began to frown. She was sure that the language she'd heard in her dream hadn't been Spanish or French. Perhaps she'd rent some foreign movies, to see if she could identify the language of her dream.

"Anything else you want to know?"

Maura nodded. "Just a couple more things. I want to know more about Grant, and why he was taking me to the airport."

"That's easy." Steve smiled. "Grant was your accountant. He'd been with you from the very beginning, and he handled all the books for *Fille Janelle.* He called you to say he had some business to discuss, and you told him you'd have a few minutes if he took you to the airport."

Maura shivered slightly. She didn't remember Grant at all, but she wished he hadn't offered to give her a ride. "Tell me about him, Steve. Was he married?"

"No. Grant was a confirmed bachelor. He was a really nice guy, but he was married to his work. I met him when he came into my office for what he thought was a heart problem. It wasn't, and he was so relieved he invited me out to lunch."

"And that's how he became my accountant?" Maura was puzzled.

"No, that's how Grant and I became friends. He ran his own firm, and he had the reputation of being the best tax man around. He handled all sorts of big accounts; Lorimar Pictures, the Hilton chain, even some overseas corporations. *Fille Janelle* was really too small for Grant to handle, but he met you at one of our dinner parties, and you impressed him so much, he took you on."

"Did I like him?"

Steve smiled. "He was your friend, luv. You went out to dinner together at least once a month. And he was crazy about Janelle."

"I'm really sorry about what happened." Maura sighed deeply. "Do you happen to know what he wanted to discuss with me?"

"I don't know, but it must have been important. Grant hated the drive to the airport. He usually took a limo when he had to fly out."

"I wonder if I'll ever remember." Maura's voice was wistful. "Not just the thing with Grant, but the rest of those missing years. I was hoping my memory would come back by now, but everything's still a blank."

Steve nodded, and reached out to take her hand. "You're trying too hard, luv. Just relax and let nature take its course. One day, when you least expect it . . ."

"The Spanish Inquisition!" Maura began to laugh. "Remember that old Monty Python sketch? No one expects the Spanish Inquisition?"

"Of course I do. It was one of my favorites, right along with the Dead Parrot sketch."

"And the Albatross, and Mr. Smokes Too Much, and the Lumberjack song!" Maura could feel her excitement grow. "When was that, Steve? It had to be the seventies, didn't it?"

Steve nodded. "The late sixties or the early seventies . . . I'm really not sure, luv."

"I'd better find out, right away! I might be remembering something from my missing years!"

"Take it easy, Maura." Steve took both of her hands and squeezed them. "That's exactly what I was talking about before. You have to relax and stop trying to force your memory to come back. It doesn't matter when Monty Python did those sketches. You remember them, and that's good. Rushing out to research it just puts you under pressure, and that's bad."

Maura sighed and tried to relax, but relaxing was very difficult. She was very conscious of the way Steve was holding her hands. His fingers were strong, and she was sure they could also be gentle. Suddenly, she had the urge to feel those fingers on her bare skin, sliding over her back and . . .

"Maura? Did you hear what I said?"

Maura came out of her daydream with a jolt. "Yes, Steve. I heard you. And I know that you're probably right."

"Of course I'm right. I'm the doctor and doctors are always right."

Maura laughed, and pulled away to reach for the carafe

of coffee. She had to stop thinking about Steve as anything other than a brother-in-law. She willed her hands to be steady as she turned and smiled, holding out the carafe. "Would you like more coffee, Steve?"

"Just a half a cup. And then we'd better think about getting you to bed."

The mention of bed made Maura draw her breath sharply. And even though she tried not to read anything into his words, her hands trembled slightly as she poured the coffee. She was sure that Steve's remark was perfectly innocent, but her cheeks felt warm, and she knew she was blushing. Her reaction to him was completely irrational and she wished it would stop.

As they sat, watching the fire and sipping coffee, Maura did her best to relax. Steve was part of her family, a good friend and nothing more. The accident had played havoc with her emotions, and it was only natural to overreact. She'd have to learn her responses to the people in her life all over again to make sure they were appropriate.

"You're very quiet." Steve slipped his arm around her shoulders again, and gave her a little hug. "Is something wrong, luv?"

"No. Everything's just fine."

Maura smiled, but she felt more like crying. It was a good thing Keith was coming home soon. Once she got back to a normal life with the man she'd married, she could stop imagining Steve's arms around her, and his lips on hers. She'd transfer all her affectionate feelings to her husband, where they rightfully belonged. Everything would be fine when Keith came home. The moment she saw him again, she was sure she'd stop wishing that she'd married her brother-in-law instead.

Chapter Ten

He checked his shoes, to make sure they were properly tied, and stepped into the elevator. It had been a very good week. He'd figured out exactly what to do to save his hide, and they had bought it. Now all he had to do was work out the details with them.

As he rode up to the fourth floor, he grinned at his image in the mirrored wall. His clothing was perfect, purchased especially for this job. With his carefully styled hair, and the special accessories he'd picked up this morning, he was sure he'd fit right in. The necessary social graces were easy. He'd played this part many times before, in the past. He was very convincing, and if he ever got the notion to go legit, he'd probably take up acting.

He tried on a smile and it looked good, but his grin was even better. It made him look younger, and he tried to remember what it had been like back then, back when he was a teenager.

It was a warm fall day with the big homecoming game coming up that weekend. Brightly colored leaves graced the trees, falling in brilliant piles of orange, and red, and yellow. There was a hint of smoke in the crisp afternoon air, and solid thuds from the football field as his friends beat their brains out, tackling the dummy. But he wasn't outside, practicing with the Cardinals, Garrison High's football team. He was sitting in a stuffy schoolroom, with a pull-down map of Europe covering the blackboard, making up an English test for Miss Morrison.

Miss Morrison was a dinosaur. She was a permanent fixture at Garrison High, ranking right up there with the battle-scarred desks, and the old metal lockers that lined the hallways. Miss Morrison was ancient. She'd been around when his father had gone to Garrison High, and even back then she'd been obsessed with the poem, "Invictus." She called it a good character builder, and every one of her students had to memorize it.

He wasn't into poetry, and he'd seriously considered ignoring the assignment, but Miss Morrison had threatened to fail anyone who couldn't recite "Invictus." Since he had to keep up his athletic eligibility, he'd struggled through the damn thing, line by sing-songy line, and phrase by preachy phrase. And since he'd missed class last Friday, he was here, after school, to recite it for her.

"I'm waiting!" Miss Morrison glared at him as he stood in front of the first rows of desks. As the class cut-up, she obviously expected him to fail. But he was prepared to recite the stupid poem perfectly. It would be such a shock, the old bat would probably have a heart attack.

"Out of the night that covers me. Black as a pit from pole to pole. I thank whatever Gods may be. For my unconquerable soul."

For a brief second, Miss Morrison looked impressed. But

then she tapped her pencil on her grade book and glared at him again. "Go on!"

"In the fell clutch of circumstance, I have not winced nor cried aloud. Under the bludgeonings of fate, my head is bloody but unbowed."

As he went on, in his best radio announcer's voice, Miss Morrison lost her severe expression. And by the time he'd reached the last line, she was actually beginning to smile.

"Very nice. Very nice, indeed."

Miss Morrison made a mark in her grade book and snapped it closed. She was still smiling, and he was startled to see that her aging face looked almost pretty.

"Your recitation was the finest I've heard in over thirty years of teaching. Perhaps you should consider going into the field of education. With your gift for the spoken word, you could be an inspiration to your students."

"Thank you, Miss Morrison." He managed to look properly grateful. "Does this mean that I passed?"

Miss Morrison nodded. "Yes, indeed. With honors. You may go now, and join your compatriots on the athletic field."

He still remembered the feeling he'd had, watching Miss Morrison smile. Her unexpected approval had come very close to influencing his life. For several days, he'd actually entertained the notion of teaching. But teachers were nothing but poorly paid servants of the school district, and he'd wanted much more than that. There was a whole world out there for the taking.

He gazed at his reflection in the mirrored wall, and grinned broadly. What would Miss Morrison think of him now? He'd used his gift with words in a way she could never have anticipated. But she might be pleased to know that he'd never forgotten "Invictus." It had given him the idea to take control of his own future. And ever since he'd placed the call that had saved his skin, the last two lines of that silly poem had been running through his mind. *I am the Captain of my fate. I am the Master of my soul.* He was the captain. And he was the master, too. One phone call had convinced them that he was the only one who could pull off the job.

The elevator doors opened and he stepped out. There was a jaunty bounce in his walk as he opened the office door and went inside. He was in character. They were bound to be impressed. Even his knock on the inner office door had the ring of certainty, and they called out for him to enter immediately. It was amazing what a little self-confidence could accomplish.

They were sitting at the conference table. The older man with the piercing eyes sat at the head. He was the leader, and although they never used names, everyone referred to him as the Eagle. The man with the soft voice sat on his right, an underling, but still very powerful.

The Eagle spoke first. "You're certain you can pull this off?"

"I'm positive." He sat down in a chair without being asked, and crossed his legs. "It'll take a while. You'll have to be patient."

"How long?" The man with the soft voice looked concerned.

"A couple of weeks, maybe more. It's tricky and you can't rush an operation like this . . . not if you want it done right."

"Understood." The Eagle nodded slightly. "We have someone we'd like you to talk to. He's waiting for our call."

He watched while the Eagle dialed a number. He spoke a few words in an undertone, and switched to the speaker phone. "Our man's here. You'd better bring us all up to speed."

"Certainly." The specialist's voice was clipped and unemotional. "The subject is suffering from complete traumatic memory loss, for a period spanning the previous twenty-three years and seven months. Her family is attempting intensive therapy."

"What kind of therapy are you talking about?" The Eagle leaned forward with a frown on his face.

"They're using picture books, momentos, familiar activities and surroundings, anything that might evoke a memory. Thus far their efforts have been completely unsuccessful."

Now the man with the soft voice was frowning, too. "What do you think? Is there a chance she'll remember?"

"There's always a chance, especially since the daughter's involved. She's a psychology major at Princeton, and she's following the advice of an expert in the field. Personally, I don't think it'll happen."

"Why?" The Eagle was still frowning.

"Compare memory to a rubber band. When it snaps, it's no longer functional. And it's almost impossible to mend."

"You're saying her memory has snapped?" The soft-voiced man raised his eyebrows. "What about temporary amnesia?"

"That's just it. Temporary amnesia is temporary. Even when the trauma is severe, memory loss seldom lasts this long. It's been over three weeks since the accident. If she were going to regain her memory, I think she would have by now."

"Maybe. And maybe not." His voice was firm as he spoke up. "You're dealing with statistics, and what you're saying is probably true for the average case of memory loss. But there's always an exception, and she might be it."

"Is he right?" The Eagle spoke directly into the speaker, leaning forward to wait for the reply. It came only after long deliberation.

"It's possible. Not probable, but possible."

"Then we'll have to wait and see." He spoke up again. "Is there anything else you can tell me?"

"One thing. She's very bright, and they're giving her what amounts to a crash course on the past twenty-three years of her life. She may answer questions accurately, and this will give you the impression that she remembers. But she may simply be repeating the things that they've taught her."

He nodded, and asked the important question. "How will I know?"

There was another silence. And then the speaker phone crackled into life again. "That's extremely subjective. I would suggest a prolonged period of observation. Take careful notes, and give them to your contact. We will make the final decision."

The Eagle reached out and switched off the speaker phone. He spoke softly into the receiver for a moment or two, and hung up the phone. Then he pushed back his chair and stood up.

"You know what to do. Let us know immediately if there's any change."

"Yes, sir." He rose quickly, like a schoolboy who'd been sent on an errand. His instinctive obedience rankled. After all, he was a seasoned professional. But it was best to treat these men with respect.

"You'll find that everything is in order." The man with the soft voice smiled at him. "Pick up your packet at the usual place."

"Thank you." He turned and took measured steps to the door. He was playing the part of someone who could not be intimidated. His back was straight as he walked across the outer office and out, into the hallway.

Outward appearances were deceiving. He'd built his career around that basic premise. Even though he appeared to be completely calm and self-assured, he held his breath as the elevator arrived. And he didn't begin to breathe normally again until he was back on the freeway, headed in the opposite direction.

"Isn't he the cutest little thing you've ever seen?" Jan held the puppy on her lap, cuddled in a fluffy bath towel.

Maura nodded, and reached out to stroke his silky head. Steve had arrived, shortly after breakfast, with the Australian shepherd puppy. He'd made a stop at the pet store on the way, and he'd also brought them a huge box, filled with all the accessories the salesman had told him were necessary for a ten-week-old puppy.

"Look at this!" Nita's eyes widened as she reached into the box and pulled out a rawhide bone that had to be at least three feet long. "I do not think he is ready to chew on something this big."

"It must be for later," Jan laughed. "What else is in there, Nita?"

"A basket for a bed, four different brands of dog food, and six rubber toys that look like vegetables. There is also a matching leash and collar, and a book on how to train him."

Jan looked confused. "Train him? But I don't really want him to do tricks. I think that would detract from his basic dignity and make him look silly."

"Oh, Jan!" Maura started to laugh. "That's not what training means. He has to be housebroken. That's a part of his training. And he has to learn how to walk on a leash. He should also learn to heel, sit, stay, stop barking, and lie down on command."

"I understand about the housebreaking. But why does he have to learn all those other things?" Jan looked intrigued.

"You don't want a badly behaved dog who'll jump up on your guests when they come in the door. Or a dog who barks at every sound. Dogs need to learn the rules and obey them. A well-trained dog is much happier than a dog who isn't trained at all. He knows what's expected of him and he does it."

Jan frowned slightly. "That sounds like a lot of work."

"It's not that bad." Maura smiled at her. "Training really isn't that difficult. It's just a matter of consistency. Puppies want to please their masters, and you'll be surprised how fast he'll learn."

Both Jan and Nita looked at Maura in surprise. There was a moment of silence, while they exchanged glances, and then Jan asked the question.

"Mom? You sound like an expert. Have you trained many dogs?"

"I . . . I don't know." Maura could feel a headache coming on, and she forced herself to relax. "I don't *remember* training any dogs, but I do seem to know a lot about it."

Jan nodded, and turned to Nita. "We've never had a puppy before, have we, Nita?"

"No. Only Bonnie and Clyde next door. And they were already trained. Perhaps you had a dog when you were a child, Miss Maura?"

"I don't think so."

Maura shut her eyes and tried to remember. She could picture the small frame house where she had grown up, and there were no pets, except . . .

"I had a goldfish!" Maura's eyes snapped open. She'd

seen a glass bowl, sitting on her dresser. It was filled with bright blue gravel, a small ceramic castle with openings for the windows and doors, a green plastic plant, and a very fat goldfish swimming around and around in the water.

Jan frowned. "Think carefully, Mom. Are you sure that's all you had?"

"I'm positive." Maura nodded. "I couldn't have a dog or a cat because my mother was allergic to animal dander."

Nita looked thoughtful. "Perhaps you had no dogs when you were a child, but think about when you went away to college. Did you have a dog then?"

"No. I lived in the dorm, and there were no pets allowed. If I did have a puppy, it had to be when I was married to Jan's father."

"Let's call Uncle Steve and see." Jan looked hopeful as she picked up the phone. "Keep your fingers crossed, Mom. You may have remembered something from those missing years."

Maura watched while Jan punched in a number on the phone. She waited a moment, punched in another number, and hung up without speaking. Then she turned to her mother. "He'll call us back in a minute."

"But . . . how?" Maura was confused. "You didn't leave a message."

"I called his beeper number. Uncle Steve always carries his beeper, and he answers his pages right away."

Beepers? Pages? Maura was confused. She must have looked as puzzled as she felt, because Jan began to smile.

"Sorry, Mom. I forgot that you wouldn't know about beepers. Uncle Steve carries a pager that beeps whenever he gets a call. The first number I dialed was his pager number. When it answered, I punched in our number. His pager has a digital read-out so he knows who to call almost instantly."

Just then the phone rang, and Jan reached out to answer it. "Hi, Uncle Steve. Sorry to bother you, but we need some information. Mom seems to remember training a dog, and we need to know if she had one when she was married to my Dad."

There was a brief silence and Jan frowned. "You're sure? Not even for a little while?"

There was another silence, and Maura began to frown, too. Jan looked very upset.

"It's all right, Uncle Steve. I was just hoping, that's all. Are you coming over to see the puppy tonight?"

There was another silence and Maura found that she was holding her breath. She wasn't sure whether she hoped he'd say yes or no. She wanted to see Steve, but it might be best if she didn't. He seemed to arouse feelings in her that were totally unsuitable for a woman who was married to another man.

"Great! Hold on a second and I'll ask." Jan turned to them with a grin. "Uncle Steve wants all of us to join him for dinner tonight. And he says he'll get reservations at Lawry's!"

Nita shook her head. "Tell him thank you, but I cannot go. I am expecting a call from my brother. But you and your mother should go and not worry. I will stay here and take care of the puppy."

"Mom?" Jan turned to her with a hopeful expression. "Say yes . . . please? Lawry's is my favorite restaurant in the whole world!"

Maura hesitated. She'd already decided that she shouldn't be alone with Steve, but Jan would be with them. And they were going to a restaurant, which was a public place.

"Yes. I'd love to go to Lawry's." Maura nodded quickly.

"Thanks, Mom!" Jan grinned, and turned back to the

phone. "It's all set Uncle Steve. Nita can't go, but Mom and I would love to. Should we meet you there, or what?"

Maura tried to stay calm as Jan made all the arrangements, but her cheeks were flushed and her eyes were sparkling. She wasn't sure why she was so excited. Perhaps Jan's enthusiasm was contagious.

"What sort of place is Lawry's?" Maura asked the question just as soon as Jan had hung up the phone.

"It's super! Prime rib, the best you've ever tasted, and creamed spinach, and creamed corn, and big baked potatoes dripping with butter, and sour cream and chives. And English trifle for dessert. It's massive food coma time, Mom!"

"It sounds wonderful." Maura laughed. "But I wasn't really asking about the cuisine. I was thinking about what to wear."

Jan nodded. "Okay. Well . . . it's a Southern California restaurant, Mom. That means you could go in jeans and a blouse if you wanted to, but most people at Lawry's dress up a little more than that. We can go semi-formal, if you'd like."

"Perfect." Maura smiled at her. "I'd better go over the clothes in my closet. There's no time to shop for something new."

"No time to shop?" Jan poked Nita, and they both started to grin. "I don't believe you said that, Mom!"

"But why? It's true. It takes days to find the perfect outfit."

"You design clothes, Miss Maura." Nita laughed. "If you want something new, you just make a drawing, and they sew it for you."

Jan nodded. "And if you're really in a time crunch, you go down to the boutique and pull something off the rack."

"You're both right." Maura started to laugh. "I forgot all about that."

"Why is it so important, Mom? It's not like this is a big,

important party. We're just going out to dinner with Uncle Steve."

Maura tried to think of an answer. She didn't want Jan to guess the effect that Steve seemed to have on her. But then she thought of the perfect excuse and she grinned as she spoke the words. "There's a perfectly good reason why I want to look gorgeous tonight. This is the first time I've gone out, that I can remember, in over twenty-three years!"

Chapter Eleven

After the first bite of her prime rib, Maura had declared that Jan was right. Lawry's prime rib was the best she'd ever tasted. Dinner had been fun, with lots of laughter, but Maura had felt herself begin to grow tense when they'd climbed into Steve's car and headed back to the house. After such an enjoyable evening, it would have been rude not to invite him in for a drink, or another cup of coffee. So she had. And Steve had declined, pleading an early appointment in the morning. Maura chided herself as she climbed up the stairs to her bedroom. She had spent at least thirty minutes worrying about a problem that had never materialized, and she still wasn't sure if she was relieved, or disappointed.

Now Maura was in her bedroom, preparing for bed. She took one last glance in the mirror and smiled. Her dress was gorgeous, a dark green water silk with a deep vee neckline and a slim-line skirt that hugged her figure. She wore a heavy, gold necklace, shaped like shells, around her neck. It was a lovely piece of jewelry, and she'd found it in a velvet-lined jewelry box on the top shelf of her walk-in closet.

Steve had smiled when he'd seen the necklace. And when she'd asked why, he'd told her its history. The necklace was an engagement present from Steve and Donna. They'd given it to her on the night they'd celebrated her engagement to Paul. Steve had seemed pleased to see it around her neck, and Maura was glad that she'd found the jewelry box and chosen to wear it.

Maura unclasped the necklace and put it back in the jewelry box. The box was lovely and she placed it on the low table next to her bed. It was made of intricately carved teak wood, and it had three wide drawers, divided into compartments. It seemed vaguely familiar, and she hoped that she'd remember more about it if she left it out where she could see it.

It didn't take long to get ready for bed. Maura had just put on her robe and slippers when she heard a scratching at the door. During dinner, they'd decided on a name for the puppy. He was called Cappy, for Captain James Cook, the man who discovered Australia. It was clear that Cappy was living up to his famous name. They'd left him in his basket in the kitchen, but he'd managed to climb out and come upstairs to explore the rest of the house.

Maura smiled as she opened the door and spotted the puppy. Cappy was sitting at the threshold, thumping his tail against the rug. His head was tipped to one side, giving him a quizzical look that Maura couldn't resist. He squirmed and licked her hand as she scooped him up and brought him inside.

"You're a good boy, Cappy." Maura scratched him behind his velvet-soft ears. "Nita told me you're practically housebroken already."

The moment she put Cappy down on the rug again, he started to wander around her room. The footstool caught his attention, and he spent several moments sniffing its carved, lion's paw feet. Then he headed for her walk-in closet and gave the interior a thorough inspection. He seemed especially interested in the racks that held her shoes, and Maura hoped that he wouldn't be a chewer.

After he'd finished with the closet, Cappy explored the bathroom. He seemed especially interested in the towels, but the racks were too high for him to reach. After he'd padded around the tiled shower for a moment, he raced back into the bedroom again, looking very proud of himself.

"What do you think? Do you like my room?" Cappy sat up and tipped his head to the side again, wagging his tail. His comical expression made Maura laugh. "I'm glad you approve. But I think it's time I took you back outside one last time before bed. What do you say about that?"

Cappy stared at her for a moment, and then he raced for the bed. He squirmed under the dust ruffle, and peeked out at her, thumping his tail happily.

"Come here, Cappy." Maura sat down on the edge of her bed, and patted the coverlet. "You're going to get lost under there."

But Cappy just squirmed under further, making little panting noises. It was clear he wanted to play.

"Oh, great!" Maura got down on her knees and reached for him. But Cappy retreated further, staying just out of her reach.

"Come on, Cappy. This isn't a game." Maura reached for him again. But she bumped her bed table with her arm, and the jewelry box fell to the floor, scattering the contents all over the rug.

Maura gave up on the puppy. He'd have to wait. She righted the jewelry box and began to pick up the pieces of jewelry. She thought she'd found it all when she noticed that Cappy had come out from under the bed. He was playing with something that had rolled under the dust ruffle, pawing at it and attacking it when it rolled.

"That's quite enough of that!" Maura tried to sound stern, but there was laughter in her voice. Cappy was really a darling. She scooped him up in one hand, and reached for the object he'd been playing with. It was a ring, and she dropped it into the pocket of her robe.

"Okay. Let's go." Maura held him firmly and headed for the door. "It's time for a quick trip outside, and then you're going to go to bed."

But Cappy didn't seem at all inclined to use the grass for the purpose that Maura desired. He wandered around, sniffing at bushes and attacking shadows, while Maura stretched out on a chaise lounge and watched him, amused.

It was a warm summer night, and the skies were clear. Maura glanced up at the stars and frowned. She'd been expecting to see a night sky filled with brilliant stars, but the ambient light of the city made the stars seem dim. She knew she'd seen them much brighter, almost like diamonds floating on a deep, black velvet backdrop, so close she could almost reach up and touch them. But where? San Diego was also a large city with an ambient light. Was she remembering the night sky in Brawley, when she'd been a child?

Maura smiled as she glanced around her back yard. It was truly lovely. There was a black-bottomed swimming pool, shaped like a grotto, with a jacuzzi on the far end. It was surrounded by river rock, with ledges for sitting and sunning. Maura wondered if she'd spent much time in the pool. She'd have to ask Jan or Nita. She was sure she knew how to swim. If she remembered correctly, she'd learned as a child. But that had been at the community swimming pool, a rectangular, concrete structure filled with tepid water and screaming children. Her own private pool looked much more inviting.

Maura closed her eyes, imagining how it would feel to slip into the midnight back water, shivering a bit as her body adjusted to the change in temperature, and then stroking across the surface to climb up on the rocks and . . .

She saw the man from her dreams, beckoning to her from the trees. His face was dappled with sunlight and he looked very handsome.

"Nick! You're back!" She could feel her body tremble in anticipation, and she knew she was smiling in delight. "We didn't expect you until tomorrow."

"There's a slight problem. We have to leave immediately. I brought your things. It's not safe to go back to the house."

She swam strongly to the rocks and pulled herself from the water. She could feel the fear wash over her body in a giant wave. "Are they . . . all right?"

"Yes. For now." He wrapped her in a towel, and pulled her close, against his strong body. "They're in the cellar, and they'll head for the border as soon as it's dark."

"Peter, too?"

He shook his head, and gathered her a little closer. And then he started speaking in the foreign language she'd heard in her dreams. "No. Peter's staying. He's an old hand at this. He knows what to do. Now get dressed quickly. We're running out of time."

The image jumped then, from the secluded forest glen to a hilly area, covered with trees and long grass. She could feel herself swaying rhythmically, bouncing up and down, and moving over the terrain with remarkable speed. She looked down to see that she was on horseback. Without a saddle! She must be an excellent horsewoman. She hadn't even known that she could ride.

She was wearing loose-fitting black pants with a black jacket buttoned tightly up to the neck. She rode low, close to the neck of her powerful horse, and she held the reins loosely in her hands.

Hooves thundered loudly behind her. Someone was chasing her, but she didn't panic. She smiled instead, sitting up a little straighter as he materialized beside her. It was Nick, the man she loved.

He was smiling, too, and he gave her a jaunty little salute. "We're almost there. It's just over that next rise."

She nodded, too tired to speak. Somehow she knew they'd been riding for hours, pausing only to water their horses and rest them for the briefest time possible.

They rode together, to the crest of the rise, and stopped to stare down at the small little village below. The houses were tiny, with multicolored roofs, and they reminded her of the houses from the Monopoly set she'd played with as a child.

"Here. You'd better take this in case we're separated."

He handed her a packet which she tucked into her pocket. Although she didn't open it, she knew it contained papers, several important names, and a map. "Do you think that'll happen? That we'll be separated?"

"Possibly." He reached out to touch her cheek. "Let's not borrow trouble. It hasn't happened yet."

She nodded, but she felt a little frightened. She'd never been completely on her own before. He'd always been right there, watching her from around the corner, or down the street. Of course she knew what to do. She'd had excellent training. But the thought of being without him made her tremble slightly.

"Hey . . ." He touched her cheek again. And then he gave her a reassuring smile. "Just remember who you are. That's the important thing. And if you start to panic, start crying. No one expects a beautiful, hysterical woman to make sense. It'll gain their sympathy and buy you valuable time."

"I won't panic." She held her head up high. "I've never panicked in my life. I've gone over this whole scenario so often, I could do it in my sleep."

"Good girl!"

His smile was like sunshine, and she basked in it for a moment. And then the scene changed again, so quickly she almost opened her eyes in surprise.

She was sitting on a stool in a small wooden hut, huddled in a scratchy blanket. The hut was made of rough-hewn logs with a stone fireplace in one corner. The night was chilly and she was shivering, even though there was a fire in the hearth. As she watched, the door opened and he came in, arms laden with firewood.

"This should hold us for the night." He dropped the firewood into a wooden box by the hearth, and smiled at her. "Are you still cold?"

She nodded, and spoke past chattering teeth. "I'm absolutely frozen. I don't think I've ever been so cold in my life!"

"I think it's just a case of nerves, and that's not surprising after what happened today." He pulled two straw pallets close to the hearth, and gathered a pile of woolen blankets. "Come over here by the fire. We'll wrap up in these blankets. They'll keep us warm."

Her legs were trembling as she walked to the hearth, and stretched out on one of the pallets. He covered her with a pile of blankets and then he slid under, next to her, and held her in his arms.

"Is that better?"

He looked concerned, and she smiled. "Much better. I wish we could stay here, forever."

"No, you don't." He laughed, and kissed her on the forehead. "The planks in this hut are chalked with a mixture of mud and manure. It smells very ripe on a hot day."

She laughed, a full laugh that bubbled out of her throat and rang merrily around the small space. It felt good to laugh after all that had happened, and she hugged him tightly. "Thanks, Nick. I needed that."

He laughed, too, and held her tighter. Then he leaned close and kissed her lips, claiming them as his own. She sighed as the kiss went on, blotting out the horror, making everything seem normal again. It was an intimate kiss, one she knew she'd never stop craving. It made her forget that they were in danger on this windswept hilltop, hiding like fugitives from the awful fate that had taken their friends.

Now she was warm in the circle of his arms. Fear had left her, pushed away by the delicious sensation of his lips on hers. She was still trembling, but it wasn't from cold or anxiety. Her trembling was caused by his warm fingers, stroking her back, and the way his tongue swept over the sensitive skin on her . . .

Ankle? Maura's eyes snapped open, and she sat up with a jolt. She could still feel a warm, wet tongue on her ankle, and she laughed as she realized that Cappy was licking her, trying to rouse her.

"All right, Cappy. It's time to go in." Maura sat up and gathered him into her arms. He felt good, warm and soft and very cuddly, and when they got inside the kitchen she almost hated to put him down. But his bed was right by the kitchen fireplace, and that was where they'd decided he'd spend his nights. A puppy needed his own place to sleep. She'd been very firm when she'd told Jan and Nita that he shouldn't sleep upstairs in their beds.

Cappy whimpered when she put him in his basket. It was

such a mournful sound that Maura almost cried. And when she tried to leave to go back to her room, he scrambled out of the basket and tried to follow her.

"Okay, Cappy." Maura put him back in the basket again. "I know you're lonely without your mother, but I can fix that."

The bag of supplies was on the kitchen table. Nita had done the shopping Maura had asked her to do earlier. Maura took out the hot water bottle, and filled it with hot tap water. Then she wound the noisy, old-fashioned alarm clock she'd told Nita to buy, and wrapped everything in a big soft bath towel.

"Here you go, Cappy." Maura placed the towel inside the basket, and moved it close to the puppy. "This is nice and warm and it's got a heartbeat, just like your mother."

Cappy cocked his head to the side, and looked up at her almost apprehensively. But he was curious about the strange package, and he nosed it for several moments. Then, as Maura watched with a smile on her face, he nestled right up to the towel-wrapped bundle, gave a little puppy sigh of contentment, and closed his eyes.

Maura tiptoed out of the kitchen, and went softly up the stairs. She tapped on Jan's door to tell her that Cappy was asleep, and then she went back to her own room. She was still upset about the daydream she'd had, but she supposed it was another figment of her imagination. After all, Steve had told her he didn't think she knew anyone named Nick. She must be remembering a scene she'd watched in a movie. There was no other reasonable explanation.

She was about to take off her robe and climb into bed when she remembered the ring in her pocket. She'd almost lost it once, when it had rolled under the bed, and she wasn't about to lose it again.

Maura reached into her pocket, took out the ring, and placed it on her bed table. Then she slipped out of her robe, got under the covers, and reached for the ring to examine it. It was a plain gold ring, and it was sized for a man. It was approximately a quarter inch thick, of good quality, but not terribly expensive. Was this the wedding band she'd given Paul on the day of their marriage? It would certainly explain why she'd hidden it away in the jewelry box on her closet shelf. Although she didn't know Keith that well, she was sure no second husband would approve of a wife who kept her first husband's wedding band in plain sight on her dresser.

She held the ring closer to the light, and tipped it so she could read the inscription.

But what she saw wasn't what she'd expected at all.

The words were faint, written in a spidery, European hand. They said, *"To Nick. Love forever, Emmy."*

Maura shivered as the dreams she'd had came back to her in vivid detail. The way she'd hidden under the bed in her maid's uniform, peeking out at the assassin's shoes. The scene at the airport where something terrible had happened to Nick. The icy slope where she'd watched them thaw the ground for his grave. The sense of utter desolation she'd experienced when she'd slipped the ring from his finger. The party of six men who'd come to look for the paper she'd taken from the compartment in the back of his watch. How she'd fled over the snow to the small farmhouse, hiding her skis in the barn. The *Gjetost* and black bread she'd eaten before falling into an exhausted sleep.

But nothing in her dreams seemed to fit. Steve had explained how she'd known about *Gjetost*, and he'd told her he didn't think she'd ever been a maid. Jan had said she didn't ski, and no one in her family knew of a man in her past named Nick. Everything Steve, Nita and Jan had told her had convinced Maura that the images she'd seen had been nothing but figments of her sleeping mind. But she'd had another dream tonight, a daydream about Nick that had seemed much too real to be merely a fantasy. And now she'd found his ring, and the fact that she had it changed everything.

Maura turned the ring, and reread the inscription. She *had* known Nick. The proof was right here, in front of her eyes. And since she'd found the ring in her own jewelry box, it meant that her dreams weren't dreams after all. The things she'd dreamed about had actually happened.

They were real memories that had surfaced in her own mind.

Chapter Twelve

"Relax, Mom." Jan patted her on the shoulder. "No one's watching, and it doesn't matter if you play well or not. Don't even think about what you're doing. Just let your muscle memory take over."

Maura raised her eyebrows. "Maybe my muscles have amnesia, too."

"No, Mom. That's not possible. Muscle memory is something that's formed by . . ." Jan started to laugh, as she realized that her mother was grinning. "Okay, okay. You were teasing, and I didn't catch it. Now don't worry about the scoring. I'll take care of that. Are you ready?"

Maura nodded, although the last thing she wanted was to run around on a cement court. After she'd found the ring, she hadn't been able to sleep and she'd stayed up late watching television. When she'd tried to cancel her early morning tennis date, Jan had seemed so disappointed Maura had given in and agreed to play.

As they watched, the couple who'd been using the court gathered up their things and left. The moment they were gone, Jan turned to her mother and smiled, "Come on, Mom. Let's get out on the court and have fun . . . okay?"

"Okay." Maura followed Jan through the gate and stepped out on the court. She didn't see how hitting a fuzzy yellow ball with a tennis racquet could be fun, but she was willing to try. Perhaps she would have felt more like playing if she'd been wearing something attractive, but the short white split skirt and loose-fitting blouse with inserts under the arms looked too much like her old high school gym outfit.

"What's the matter, Mom?" Jan noticed her mother's disgruntled expression.

"It's this outfit I'm wearing. It's really ugly! I'm supposed to be a designer. Why haven't I designed a better-looking tennis dress?"

Jan shrugged. "I don't know. Maybe you just didn't get around to it . . . or you might have figured that a new line of tennis clothes wouldn't sell. The outfit you're wearing is a basic style and it's very traditional. Women have been wearing tennis dresses like yours for years."

"That doesn't mean they can't enjoy something new." Maura glanced down at her outfit again. "Why does it have to be white?"

"It doesn't . . . at least I don't think it does. What did you have in mind?"

"I'm not sure, but this short split skirt has got to go. The length's all wrong for a woman past forty, and the blouse is much too utilitarian. Tennis is an active sport, and these inserts under the arms are constricting. There has to be a way to design a sleeve that accommodates arm motion, but doesn't get in the way."

"Go for it, Mom!" Jan looked pleased. "If anyone can do it, you can. And you won't be wasting your time. There's a big market for sports clothing."

Maura nodded. And then she laughed. "Maybe I will . . . if I can remember where my studio is."

"Uh-oh." Jan winced. "I meant to take you up there, yesterday. Did you notice the set of dormer windows on the third floor, right above the entrance to the house?"

Maura shut her eyes for a moment and tried to visualize the front of the house. Then she smiled and nodded.

"That's your studio. Did you notice the doorway at the west end of the second floor hallway?"

"Yes, I did. I assumed it was another guest bedroom."

"It's the door to the staircase that leads to your studio. You've got northern exposure, and you put in two sets of dormer windows so you could place your drawing table between them. Don't you remember your studio at all, Mom?"

Maura sighed deeply as she shook her head. She had a vague memory of climbing stairs in the early morning, a mug of coffee in her hand. But that memory could be from another time or another place, and she didn't want to raise Jan's hopes.

"Oh, well. Maybe you'll remember it when you see it." Jan smiled brightly. "Come on, Mom. We've only got the court for thirty minutes."

Maura stood where Jan told her to stand, and watched as her daughter took the opposite side of the court. Jan picked up a ball, bounced it with her racquet, and grinned. "I'll serve first. Don't worry about your form, Mom. Just try to hit the ball back to me."

Maura nodded, and went into a crouch on the balls of her feet. She wasn't sure why she did it. It just felt right. The moment Jan's racquet connected with the ball, she moved to the left, and reached up to backhand the ball.

Jan gasped as the ball whizzed over her head and hit just inside the foul line. And then she laughed. "So much for your muscle amnesia. That was a wicked return, Mom. Your serve."

Maura caught the ball and bounced it, as Jan had done. And then quickly, before she could think, she served it. Jan managed to return her serve, and they volleyed back and forth a couple of times. Then Maura used her backhand again, spotting the ball just inside the foul line on the right side of the court.

"I guess the first one wasn't just beginner's luck." Jan was shaking her head as she trotted up to the net. "What's going on, Mom? You've never played this well before."

Maura shrugged. "I don't know. When I hit the ball, it just felt right, that's all. Did I do something wrong?"

"No, you did something right."

Maura and Jan turned to see a young man standing outside the fence, watching them. He appeared to be in his late twenties and he was classically handsome, with finely chiseled features and deep, brown eyes. His hair was dark, cut very short, and he wore gold-rimmed glasses that made him look very studious.

"Sorry for interrupting." He gave them an apologetic smile. "I'm not supposed to be here yet, but the traffic was good, and I'm early. I didn't mean to interfere."

"That's okay." Jan smiled at him. "Did you reserve the court after us?"

"Yes, at nine o'clock. Since I don't have a partner, I was planning to hit a few balls from the machine."

"I haven't seen you here before." Jan gave him a friendly smile. "Are you a new member?"

"Not yet. They gave me a guest pass until they can review my application. You're a member, aren't you?"

"Mom is." Jan nodded. "She got an automatic membership when we moved here. It was just for residents then, but they've opened it up to the public since then."

"Maybe I shouldn't ask, but what are my chances of being accepted?"

Jan shrugged. "I don't know. I've never bothered to read their rules. What do you think, Mom?"

Maura frowned slightly. She didn't remember joining the country club in the first place, and she had no idea what criteria the club used to judge potential members. But she didn't want to discuss her memory problem in front of a stranger, so she shook her head. "I really don't know, but I'm sure it can't be that hard to get in."

"I hope not." He smiled and looked very anxious. "This is a nice club, and I'm keeping my fingers crossed. Their courts are great, and I love to play tennis. It's excellent exercise and normally I hate exercise."

Jan nodded, and began to smile. "Maybe you should play with Mom. She seems to have developed a real talent for the game, and she's a whole lot better than I am."

"She's a whole lot better than I am, too. Even if we teamed up, I think she could beat us." He turned to Maura and gave a little bow. "How about it? I know it's against the rules, but there's no one else here and it sounds like fun."

Maura glanced at Jan, who was smiling happily. It was clear her daughter was interested. "It's fine with me. But if I start to lose too badly, one of you has to jump the net to my side."

The young man nodded and stepped through the gate. When he reached them, he offered his hand to Maura first. "I'm David McGraw."

"Maura Rawlins . . . uh . . . actually, I'm Mrs. Keith Thomas now. Glad to meet you, David. This is my daughter, Jan Bennett."

"Hi, Jan."

David reached out to take her hand. He didn't hold it any longer than was proper, but Maura noticed that Jan began to blush. It was odd to see her normally self-confident daughter so tongue-tied, and Maura decided to take the initiative.

"Come on, you two." Maura herded them toward the other side of the court. "I want to see if my luck holds out so I can beat both of you."

Of course she didn't beat both of them, but it turned out to be a close match. They played three full games, and Maura felt hot and sticky by the time they trotted off the court.

"How about coffee, Mom?" Jan looked eager. "We could all meet in the restaurant after we shower."

David nodded. "That's a great idea. I need something to perk me up before I hit the books. What do you say, Mrs. T.?"

"I say . . ." Maura caught the anxious expression on Jan's face and she nodded. "Yes. Coffee would be fine. We'll meet you in the restaurant, David."

Jan beamed as they headed off for the women's locker room. The moment they got inside, she turned to hug her mother. "Thanks, Mom. I know you planned to get to work early, but I really wanted to have coffee with him."

"I know." Maura laughed. "It was written all over your face. He's a very attractive young man."

Jan nodded. "He seems to be nice, too. And he told me he's new in Los Angeles. What do you think he meant when he said he had to hit the books? Do you think he's an accountant or a lawyer, or something boring like that?"

"I don't know honey." Maura shrugged. "But I know how you can find out."

"How?"

"It's very simple. Take your shower and get dressed. And when we get the restaurant, ask him."

But Jan didn't have to ask. David McGraw volunteered his life story over cappuccino and croissants. He was twenty-nine years old, he'd graduated from Yale with a master's in American history, and he was working on his doctorate. The scope of his dissertation was the mapping of the territory between the Mississippi valley and the Pacific during the early 1840s, and his special interest was John Charles Fremont.

"Fremont?" Jan stopped buttering her croissant and began to smile. "I did a paper on him in high school. Some people called him the first governor of California."

David nodded. "There's some basis for that. Fremont got caught up in the struggle with Mexico over California, and he was, at one time, appointed military governor. Unfortunately, he was convicted of mutiny in 1847."

"But his sentence was commuted, wasn't it?"

Jan looked up at him, a question in her eyes, and Maura hid a smile behind her napkin. She could tell that Jan was eager to show that she knew something about David's field.

"That's right." David grinned as he nodded. "By President Polk. Fremont stood as the Republican party's first presidential candidate in 1856, but he was defeated by . . ."

"James Buchanan!" Jan jumped in with a smile.

"Give the lady ten points!" David laughed. "You're a history buff, aren't you?"

Jan shook her head. "Not really. But Fremont's life is fascinating. I did a psychological profile on him once, and I concluded he was an authentic megalomaniac. After that, I could understand why he exceeded his authority and declared martial law."

"Do you still have it?" David leaned forward. "Fremont's psychological profile, I mean?"

"I think so. It's probably in a box in the attic."

"Do you think you could find it? I'd really like to read it."

"Sure." Jan nodded quickly. "I keep all my papers. It's just a matter of finding the right box."

"I could help you look for it . . . if you need help, that is."

Jan turned to look at her mother, and Maura nodded. She knew exactly what Jan was asking. Then she turned to David with a smile. "Why don't you join us for dinner tonight? You can look for the paper, then. But I'm warning you. The attic might be very dusty."

"That's no problem." David grinned. "Historians are used to dust, along with cobwebs, crumbling paper, and musty basements. We just carry a clean handkerchief and sneeze a lot."

Maura laughed. David had a fine sense of humor. She wanted to give them a few minutes alone, so she stood up and smiled at Jan. "I'll be right back. Why don't you give David directions to our house? And set a time for dinner."

After a quick trip to the powder room that wasn't really necessary, and Maura returned to the table. She found Jan sitting alone, with a very subdued expression on her face. "Jan? Where's David?"

"He had to leave. He had an appointment in the valley, and he wasn't sure how long it would take him to get there. He told me to thank you for the invitation, and he said he'd see you tonight. Do you know who he is, Mom?"

"What do you mean, honey?" Maura frowned slightly. Jan looked very upset.

"Well . . . we got to talking after you'd left, and he told me his research wasn't the only thing that brought him to California. His uncle just died, under circumstances he thought were unusual, and he wanted to find out more about it."

"That's too bad." Maura looked properly sympathetic. "How did his uncle die?"

"In an auto accident. *Your* auto accident. David McGraw is Grant's nephew!"

Chapter Thirteen

After another of Nita's excellent dinners, they'd gone into the living room for coffee. David sat on the couch with Jan while Maura took the wing chair across from them. Maura had just finished pouring Nita's chocolate coffee, and David smiled as he took his first sip.

"This is really good, Mrs. Thomas. How does Nita make it?"

"She's got a little wooden thing that she spins to mix up the chocolate." Jan spoke up quickly. "And she gets the coffee and chocolate at an import shop. I'm sure she'll let you watch sometime, if you ask."

David nodded. "I will. The cappuccino at the country club was good, but this is a lot better."

"Yes, it is." Maura took a deep breath. She'd discussed the problem with Jan on the drive home from the country club, and they'd decided that they had to tell David that his Uncle Grant had been a friend of the family. How much more they should tell him was still undecided. Jan had insisted that it was her mother's decision.

"Try one of these butter cookies, David." Jan passed the

tray of cookies Nita had baked for dessert. "They're made from my grandmother's recipe."

David took a cookie and tasted it. And then he smiled at Maura. "These are incredible, Mrs. Thomas. Was it your mother who made them? Or Jan's grandmother on the other side?"

"It was Mom's mom." Jan stepped in quickly. "She was the baker in the family. Cookies, cakes . . . you name it. Her lemon cake was pure heaven."

Maura smiled nervously. She didn't remember the butter cookies at all. Thank goodness Jan had covered for her! And then she took a deep breath and prepared to make her little speech. Jan had asked her to break the ice and bring up the subject of David's uncle. "I have something to tell you, David. Jan might not have mentioned it, but your uncle was my accountant."

"You've got to be kidding!" David looked genuinely surprised. "You actually knew Uncle Grant?"

Maura nodded. "He handled the books for my boutique."

"Tell me about him." David leaned forward eagerly. "My mother couldn't remember him that well. Uncle Grant was fourteen years older, and he left home when she was just a child."

"You never saw him?" Maura frowned slightly. She couldn't imagine having family she'd never visited.

"I think he came to see us once, when I was a baby. But then my mother remarried, and Uncle Grant didn't get along with my stepfather. He never came to see us again, and we never drove out here to visit him. And now . . . it's too late."

Maura felt a tug of sympathy. David looked so sad. "Your poor mother. Was she terribly upset by his death?"

"She didn't know." David frowned slightly. "You see, she

died two years ago. But before she went, she made me promise to come out here and see Uncle Grant."

Jan reached out to take David's hand. She seemed to know what was coming.

"I was all tied up with school, and I just didn't get around to it. You know how it is. I thought I had plenty of time to come out here and get to know him."

"But time ran out." Jan's voice was soft. "And now you feel as if you've let her down?"

David nodded. "That's right. And that's why I want to know everything about him. It's too late to meet him, but I'll feel better if I know what kind of person he was."

Maura nodded. "I understand, David. And I'll tell you what I can. Your uncle was a very good accountant, one of the best. He had an excellent reputation, and a list of important clients. But Jan knows more than I do . . . right, Jan?"

"Yes. Absolutely." Jan took up the story. "Grant was a bachelor, but you probably already know that. And he was great with kids. He always had something in his desk for me whenever Mom had to go to his office. I remember asking him once why he never got married and had children."

"What did he say?" David smiled slightly.

"He said he'd have to find a woman who was in favor of bigamy because he was already married . . . to his work."

"That's great!" David laughed. "I'm glad he had a sense of humor. So did Mom. What else?"

"He said that he was crazy about other people's children because you could send them home to their parents if they gave you any problems."

"I guess that's true." David grinned, and then he turned to Maura. "What else do you remember about him?"

"Well . . . I met him at a party. It was at my brother-in-law's house. Steve's a doctor and Grant was his patient."

"Uncle Grant was sick?" David looked concerned.

"No, he wasn't." Jan stepped in again. "He came in for tests. He really thought he had a serious medical problem. And when the tests came back negative, he was so relieved that he took my Uncle Steve out to lunch."

"What else?"

David turned to Maura again, but Jan stepped in. "Your uncle was very handsome and women used to throw themselves at him all the time. But when they mentioned marriage, he knew it was time to call it off. He always used to say that he was waiting for me to grow up so he could marry me."

Maura looked shocked. Was that true? Had Grant really been interested in her daughter? But Jan was laughing as she continued the story.

"Of course it was just a joke. We all knew that. But some of Grant's dates were sadly lacking in the humor department. I think he used it as sort of a test to see which ones would get bent out of shape."

"I'm not sure it was a fair test." David raised his eyebrows. "I bet you were a knockout at ten."

Jan giggled. "Oh, sure! I was skinny and I had braces on my teeth. And that was before I got my contacts, so I wore these impossibly thick glasses. Any woman who was jealous of me wasn't playing with a full deck!"

"Not necessarily." David was still grinning. "Let me see a picture of you back then. I'll be the judge."

"No way! Besides . . . I don't think we have any pictures. Isn't that right, Mom?"

"I . . . I don't know." Maura began to feel uncomfortable. The one thing she hadn't done yet was to go through the old photograph albums. And with David here, this wasn't really the time.

But David didn't look convinced. "I'm sure you have pictures. Let's get them out and take a look."

"Oh . . . all right." Jan tried to give an exasperated sigh, but she ended up laughing. "I guess it would be all right. What do you say, Mom?"

Maura nodded. What else could she do? And then she stood up. "Go ahead. But I really have some things to do, so if you'll excuse me . . . ?"

"Don't leave, Mrs. Thomas." David reached out to take her arm. "Jan and I were just kidding around. We don't have to look at pictures right now, if you don't want to. I'd really rather talk to you. You're a . . . well . . . you're a fascinating puzzle to me."

Maura frowned slightly. "But . . . why?"

"Maybe I'm getting in deep here, but I've always been the outspoken type." David gave her an engaging grin. "It's your interaction with Jan. You two have been doing it ever since I got here. I'm trying not to be too nosy, but I don't understand. I ask you a question and Jan jumps in to answer. It's almost if she's afraid you'll say the wrong thing."

Maura exchanged looks with Jan. David was right. But before either one of them could think up an explanation, he shook his head.

"It's the strangest thing. If I didn't know better, I'd think that Jan was the mother and you're the child she's trying to protect. I've got a really strong feeling there's something about you Jan doesn't want me to know."

"Don't be silly, David." Jan tried to smile, but her face was red. "You're just . . . uh . . . imagining things, that's all."

David didn't look convinced as he turned to Maura. "Is that true, Mrs. Thomas?"

Maura was about to say it was, when she reconsidered. Did it really matter if David knew she'd lost her memory in the car accident that had killed his uncle? Jan liked David. That much was clear. And if she began dating him, their secret was bound to come out.

"You're not imagining anything, David." Maura sat down, again. "Jan *is* protecting me, and I think it's about time we told you why."

"I had no idea!" David looked embarrassed. "I'm sorry, Mrs. Thomas. I never would have asked all those questions if I'd known. It certainly wasn't my intention to pry into family matters."

Jan nodded. "We know that, David. But Mom made the decision to tell you, so now it's all out in the open. Maybe you didn't notice, but I was shocked when Mom told you how she met Grant. She remembered! And that's a real breakthrough, right, Mom?"

"Not really, honey." Maura sighed. "Steve told me about that party. I'm sorry if I got your hopes up, but I was just telling David what Steve told me."

"Then you don't remember?"

Jan looked disappointed, and David slipped his arm around her shoulders. "Hey, Jan . . . give it time. Memory's not something you can rush. And now that I know about the problem, maybe I can help. How about it, Mrs. Thomas? Let's get out those old photograph albums and see if something comes back."

"Well . . . all right." Maura smiled at him. David really was a nice man. "But if we find any really bad photographs, please don't tell me if they're me."

* * *

David had left after they'd finished going through the third album of photographs, but he'd promised to meet them for tennis in the morning. Jan had said she wasn't sleepy, so they'd carried the old albums up to Maura's room and spread them out on the bed.

"Look at this one, Mom." Jan stretched out on her stomach, a pillow propped up under her arms. "Do you know who this is?"

"I hope not." Maura's eyes widened as she stared down at a photograph of a woman with her hair teased out so far from her head, she looked as if she were wearing a fuzzy basketball for a hat. "I refuse to believe it, honey. That simply *can't* be me!"

"Relax, Mom . . . it's not. It's your college roommate, Rachel."

"Thank God!" Maura breathed a sigh of relief. "But who's this mousy-looking girl with the horrible shapeless dress and braids?"

"That's you!" Jan laughed so hard, tears rolled down her cheeks.

Maura shook her head. "You've got to be wrong. It may look like me, but I'd never wear a bedspread with little elephants printed all over it!"

"It's a granny dress, Mom." Jan was still laughing. "They were the rage back then."

"Back *when?* When was this picture taken?"

"Your junior year in college. You told me that you were into macrobiotics and megavitamins. You wouldn't eat anything except brown rice and organically grown vegetables."

"It's a wonder I didn't starve!" Maura gave the picture one last look, and reached out to flip the page. But what she saw on the next page made her mouth drop open in astonishment. The handsome man from her dreams was staring back at her, a slight smile on his face!

Maura swallowed hard. She was almost afraid to ask. "Is this your . . . father?"

"No. It's just someone you met in college. I don't remember his name. I think you said he was a visiting professor or something like that."

Maura tried to keep perfectly calm as she asked the question. "Think hard, Jan. Did I ever tell you his name was Nick?"

"Nick?" Jan frowned. "No, I don't think that's it. Let's take his picture out and see if anything's written on the back."

Maura clasped her hands to keep them from trembling as Jan slipped out the picture and turned it over. But the back was perfectly blank.

"Sorry, Mom." Jan slipped the picture back into its sleeve. "I just wish I could remember what you . . ."

"Jan? What is it?" Maura watched as Jan began to frown. "Did you remember something?"

Jan sighed, and gave a little shrug. "Not really. There was something about his name, though . . . something weird. When I looked at his picture, I had a mental image of a bottle of Coke."

"Coke?" Maura looked puzzled. "But why?"

"I was probably trying to associate his name with an object. I was really into stuff like that for awhile. You know . . . if a guy's name was Matt Greenfield, you were supposed to think of an exercise mat stretched out on a field of green grass."

"A bottle of Coke . . ." Maura thought hard. "Are you sure it was Coke?"

"Positive. I saw the shape of the bottle. It's very distinctive. But I think there was a blue and white label on it, the kind they put on for generic products. That could mean his name was soft drink, or soda, or . . ."

"Cola!" Maura clapped her hands together. "Think about it, Jan. Someone named Nick might also be called Cola. Both names are short for Nicolas."

Jan nodded as she stared down at picture. She was obviously intrigued. "Cola does sound right. But who is he? He must be important. You remembered his name."

"I . . . don't know." Maura sighed. She wasn't about to tell Jan about strange dreams, not until she knew if they were real or fantasy. "Perhaps I'll remember more about him if I relax and give it some time."

"Good idea, Mom." Jan smiled her approval and flipped the page. But just then the doorbell rang, startling both of them.

"It's after nine." Maura looked puzzled as she glanced at the clock. "Who could it be this time of night?"

"I bet it's Nita." Jan laughed as she hopped off the bed. "She went out to walk Cappy, and she probably forgot her keys. I'll go let her in, Mom."

The moment Jan was gone, Maura flipped back to Nick's picture. She definitely knew him. Just looking at his picture set her emotions in a turmoil. There was a burst of happiness when she first saw his smiling face, and she could almost feel the texture of his hair, and the warmth of his skin. At the same moment, her heart felt heavy with sadness, and tears of grief threatened to spill from her eyes to run down her cheeks. Somehow she knew that he was no longer alive. It wasn't the dream about his funeral that made her come to this unhappy conclusion. It was the hollowness she felt inside when she looked at his face.

Maura closed the album with a sigh. There was enough

sadness in her life without inviting more. Then she glanced at the clock again. Jan had been gone for at least ten minutes, and she could hear her talking to someone in the entry way.

"Mom?" Jan called out from the foot of the stairs. "You'd better come down. There's someone from your past that I know you'll want to meet."

Chapter Fourteen

Maura could see him as she came down the stairs. The young man standing next to Jan was tall and thin, with sandy-colored hair worn slightly long in the back. He looked very determined, and he was dressed in a uniform of some kind. A policeman? Someone from the armed forces?

Jan and the visitor were so engrossed in their own conversation, they didn't look up as Maura paused on the stairs, searching her memory and trying to place the young man. It was no use. He was a complete stranger to her. Of course Jan had been a stranger, too, when Maura had first seen her in the hospital. And so had Keith, and Nita, and Steve. This could be someone she'd known well in what she'd begun to think of as her former life. It was silly to hesitate here on the stairs when the answer was only a few feet away. Jan knew her problem, and Maura was sure that she'd figure out some way of reintroducing her to the young man.

"Hello." Maura smiled, and extended her hand. The young man took it, and shook it formally. And then he smiled.

"Hello, Mrs. Thomas." The smile changed the complete look of his face. He was suddenly very handsome and his deep brown eyes crinkled with warmth. "You look a lot better than you did in the hospital. Of course you probably don't remember me, right?"

"Yes. I mean, no . . . I'm sorry, but I don't remember you." Maura frowned slightly, and picked up on the cue he'd given her. "You came to visit when I was in the hospital?"

The young man nodded. "I drove straight there, and I waited until I was sure you were going to make it. They hadn't contacted your family yet, and I didn't think you should be alone."

"Thank you. That was very kind."

"It was the least I could do. I dropped by a couple of times after that, but you were still in a coma. That's why you don't remember me."

"That's only part of it!" Maura gave a little laugh. She hadn't really discussed her memory loss with anyone other than family, but something about the young man's smile invited confidence. "Did I know you before the accident?"

"Not unless you happened to be looking out the rearview mirror. I'm Hank Jensen, and the limo I was driving was the first car on the scene."

"I'm glad to meet you, Hank." Maura smiled again. "And thank you for calling the ambulance. You probably saved my life."

"It wasn't me, ma'am. I don't have a telephone up front. One of my passengers called."

"Oh. I see." Maura was impressed with his honesty. He could easily have claimed credit for the call. "Well . . . thank you anyway. If you hadn't been driving behind me, I might have lost more than my memory."

Hank nodded, and then he looked uncomfortable. "I guess I shouldn't have come here, but I called the hospital and they told me you'd gone home. And I thought you might want to know what happened that night . . . especially since your friend was . . ."

"Killed." Maura supplied the word he seemed to have difficulty saying. "That was very thoughtful of you, Hank. I don't remember the accident at all."

"Nothing?"

"Absolutely nothing." Maura sighed. "Let's all go into the living room where we can be more comfortable and you can tell me about it."

They were just settling down on the couch when Nita came in the door with Cappy. The moment she took off his leash, he raced for Maura, but he stopped short as she held up her hand.

"Cappy? Sit!"

Cappy looked at her for a second and then he sat down promptly, staring up at her with his tail thumping.

"Good boy!" Maura reached out to scratch his ears. "Now let's see if you remember this one . . . Cappy? Down!"

Cappy stared at her again, for a split second. And then he promptly sank down at her feet.

"Good boy!" Maura laughed and scratched him behind the ears again.

"That's fantastic, Mrs. Thomas!" Hank was clearly impressed. "Have you taught him anything else?"

"Not yet, but I will. We're working on stay tomorrow. And he's doing just fine on a leash."

"That's because you're so good with him." Hank smiled at Cappy and reached out to pet him. "Did you ever train dogs professionally?"

Maura glanced at Jan who gave her a slight nod. Maura knew what the nod meant. It was up to her to take Hank into her confidence. "I could have trained dogs, Hank. I really don't know. You see, I seem to have lost total memory of the last twenty-three years of my life."

"No kidding!" Hank looked every bit as shocked as he sounded. "I don't know what to say Mrs. Thomas . . . except I'm really sorry. It must be hell, trying to pull your life back, if you know what I mean."

"Not exactly." Maura smiled at him. The concept was intriguing. "What *do* you mean exactly?"

"Well . . . it'd probably be a lot easier if you could just start over, fresh. But you can't because of your family. It's almost like going off to camp with a suitcase your mother packed for your twin brother."

"What?!" Jan started to laugh. "Explain that, Hank."

"That's easy. Just picture yourself at Camp Winnemaka, opening your suitcase. Everything fits. You and your brother wear the same size. But they're not your clothes, and you feel strange wearing them. Unfortunately, they're all you have, so you're stuck." Hank turned to Maura with a smile. "Just like you're stuck with the baggage of your former life. It's somebody else's baggage. You don't remember the reasons why you did what you did back then, but you have to carry on with what that other Mrs. Thomas started."

Jan gasped and turned to Hank in surprise. "That's brilliant! And you're absolutely right. I never thought of it before, but Mom's living someone else's life, desperately attempting to make it her own. She's wearing someone else's clothes, doing someone else's job, living in someone else's house, with someone else's family. And we're all expecting her to turn into that someone else, that other Mrs. Thomas she doesn't even remember."

"Come on, Jan. It's not quite *that* bad." Maura started to laugh. "At least the other Mrs. Thomas wasn't a total bitch."

"Mom!" Jan looked shocked for a moment, and then she

laughed, too. "At least you managed to hang onto your sense of humor. Maybe you don't exactly remember, but you laugh at the same things and you make the same jokes."

Hank looked very serious as he nodded. "Just remember . . . 'I hasten to laugh at everything for fear of being obliged to weep at it.' "

"Shakespeare?" Jan raised her eyebrows.

"Pierre de Beaumarchais. He was a French dramatist and he knew that laughing and crying were polar ends of the same emotion."

"Psych major?" Jan was clearly interested.

"No, I'm studying film at Cal Arts. You have to be a student of human emotions if you expect to capture them on film."

"Have you made any films, Hank?" Maura smiled at him.

"Not yet, but I'm almost ready to start my student project. Making a film is very expensive, and that's the reason I drive limos for my uncle. The tips are good and I can work every weekend."

"I made you coffee, Miss Maura." Nita came in with a carafe of coffee and a tray of cookies. "Is there anything else you need?"

"Nothing. Thanks, Nita."

Nita poured the coffee, and passed around the plate of cookies. She seemed pleased as Hank took two.

"I will take this little *bambino* now, and put him to bed." Nita scooped up the puppy and carried him to the door in her arms. "I wrap the hot water bottle in a towel with the alarm clock. Is that right?"

Maura nodded. "That's right. Make sure to wind the clock. The ticking'll remind him of a heartbeat. He'll think he's cuddled up next to his mother, and he'll go right to sleep."

"That's a great trick." Hank looked impressed. "Are you sure you didn't raise dogs, Mrs. Thomas?"

"I don't think so." Maura frowned slightly. "Tell me about the accident, Hank. I'd really like to know what happened that night."

"Well . . . I was following you on the freeway. I thought the license plate was interesting, so I got close enough to read it. It said D-P-R-E-S-H-E-8."

"What does that mean?" Maura was puzzled.

"Depreciate." Jan smiled as she told her. "They have vanity plates now. You can order almost anything you like, as long as it's no more than eight letters or numbers. Uncle Steve got him that license plate for Christmas one year, and he liked it so much he kept it."

"Very clever." Maura nodded. And then she turned to Hank again. "Did you see me in the car?"

Hank looked very uncomfortable. "I noticed you right away. You'd been crying and you were fixing your makeup in the lighted mirror on the visor."

"Crying?" Jan turned to her mother in alarm. "But . . . why?"

Maura shrugged. "I have no idea. I don't remember it, honey."

"Maybe I should ask Keith when he gets back. He probably knows exactly why you were crying." Jan's voice was hard, and Maura frowned slightly. It was clear that her initial impression had been correct. Jan wasn't on the friendliest terms with her stepfather.

"Don't do that, honey." Maura reached out to touch her arm. "Perhaps I wasn't crying at all. I could have gotten a piece of dust in my eye."

"Well . . . all right." Jan nodded. And then she turned to Hank. "Tell me about Uncle Grant. Did he look upset?"

"I don't know. I just saw his face from the side. I noticed his haircut and the expensive suit he was wearing, but that's about it."

"Uncle Grant knew how to dress." Jan nodded. "How was he driving?"

"Very carefully. He obeyed the speed limit and he signalled when he changed lanes. I remember thinking that he was a cautious driver."

"Then what happened?" Maura leaned forward. "I thought we were speeding when we crashed through the guard rail."

"You were. But that was afterwards. He took it nice and slow when he got off at the exit. They're working on the ramp, and there's a blinking caution sign. He was driving perfectly, until he got into the curves. That's when he started to go faster."

"I don't understand." Maura was puzzled. "Why did he speed up then?"

"I don't think he did it intentionally. He was trying to slow down. I saw his brake lights flash. But the car just went faster. I think his brakes went out."

"That must be it. I know Grant would never speed up on a curve. Why, I remember one time when . . ." Maura stopped in midsentence. Her mind was suddenly blank. Whatever she'd been about to say was gone. But Jan was staring at her with a hopeful expression, and she knew she had to try to explain. "Sorry, Jan. I think I was beginning to remember something, but it's gone now."

Jan reached out to take her hand. "That's okay, Mom. Almost remembering is better than drawing a complete and total blank. I'd say it was a step in the right direction, wouldn't you, Hank?"

"Absolutely!" Hank nodded. And then he began to frown.

"Are you sure you want to hear the rest, Mrs. Thomas? It's pretty scary."

"Yes. I want to hear it." Maura nodded. The details of her car crash couldn't be any more frightening than the strange dreams she'd been having.

"Okay. The brake lights were on. I already told you that. He started to brake the moment you crested the top of the ramp. But the car just leaped forward into the curves, picking up speed and swerving all over the road. I heard the tires squeal against the pavement, and I think he was trying to turn back and forth to slow down. But it didn't work. The grade was too steep, and you started to fishtail out of control. That's when I put on my own brakes and stopped."

Hank paused, but Maura motioned him on. She wanted to hear it all.

"I guess I shook up my passengers up pretty good when I stopped, but I wasn't worried about them. We were safe at the side of the road. I jumped out and watched as you side-swiped the guard rail on the right side of the ramp. It held. I don't know how. It was only a temporary wooden rail, but it didn't break. But then your car bounced back and headed for the opposite rail."

"Oh, Mom!" Jan moved closer, and put her arm around Maura's shoulder. "You must have been terrified."

"She was. I heard her scream, and I've never felt so helpless in my life. And then the car plowed through the left barrier and tumbled end over end down the side of the hill."

Maura shivered slightly. What she'd heard had been horrifying, but it almost seemed as if it had happened to another person. She took a deep breath and asked, "How long did it take for help to come?"

"I'm not sure, but I don't think it was more than a minute. They'd just finished treating a broken arm at the airport when the call came in, and they just jumped in their van and high-tailed it out to you. There wasn't anything they could do for your friend, but they hooked you up to some kind of life support and called for a helicopter. They'd just lifted off when the car blew up."

"My God!" Jan turned pale. "It was that close?"

Hank nodded. "Just like in the movies. You could probably sue if the car hadn't blown up. I'm absolutely sure the brakes were faulty, but now there's no way to prove it."

"It doesn't really matter." Maura drew a shaky breath. No one had told her that she'd come quite that close to death. "But why did you follow me to the hospital?"

Hank looked embarrassed for a moment and then he shrugged. "I guess I just felt close to you. When I saw you wiping those tears away, I wanted to do something to make you feel better. And then when your car crashed, I dropped off my passengers and drove straight to the hospital. I know I probably shouldn't have interfered, but I held your hand and talked to you right up until they took you to surgery."

"Thanks, Hank." Jan blinked back tears. "That makes me feel a lot better. All this time, I thought that Mom was there all alone."

Maura nodded. "So did I. But why didn't you visit me later, when I was awake?"

"They caught me." Hank looked very sheepish. "I had to lie to get into the emergency room. It was family only. And I . . . well . . . I said I was your son. I hope you're not mad about that."

Maura laughed. "Of course not! I'm glad you kept me company, even though I didn't know it. But how did you get caught?"

"Your husband told them that you didn't have a son. And

the next time I came, they told me to get lost before they pressed charges."

"That's too bad." Jan frowned. "I wish I'd known. I would have taken you in with me. I could have said that you were my boyfriend. They never would have known the difference."

Maura watched as Hank's face began to color. It was clear he liked Jan.

"It wouldn't have worked." Hank looked down at the rug. "The minute you showed up with your real boyfriend, they would have known that I was a fake."

"*What* real boyfriend?" Jan laughed. "I don't have one."

"You don't? But you're so pretty, and nice, and . . . I don't believe it!"

"Believe it. It's true." Jan laughed, again. "I've never been Miss Popularity. I guess I'm just too serious."

Hank nodded. "Yeah. Me, too. And this film I'm making takes up almost every minute of my time. Say, Jan . . . do you know how to play tennis?"

"Yes." Jan grinned at him. "I'm not very good, though. Do you?"

"No, but I've got to learn. You can't break into film in this town without knowing how to play tennis."

"But . . . why?" Jan looked puzzled.

"Because that's where you make all your important contacts. It used to be golf, and then it was racquetball. And now it's tennis . . . at least that's what my professor says. I know I'm probably out of line here, but I can't afford a tennis coach, and I was thinking that maybe you'd . . ."

"I'd love to." Jan jumped in quickly. "And we've got lots of extra racquets and things like that. When are you free?"

"How about tomorrow afternoon? I get out of class at two,

and I could be here by three. I could even pick you up in the limo so you could impress your friends."

"Great idea!" Jan grinned at him. "I'll call and reserve a court. You don't mind playing at the country club, do you?"

Hank laughed. "Do I mind? You've got to be kidding! I've never been inside a country club in my life!"

"You'd better get used to it. When you're a big important producer, you'll have to join. Isn't that right, Mom?"

"Definitely." Maura smiled at them. "How about an early dinner at the club, after your game? It'll be my treat."

Jan nodded. "Great! That sounds just . . . uh-oh. You can't take us out tomorrow, Mom. Keith's coming home, and Uncle Steve invited both of you for dinner. Did you forget?"

"Yes, I did." Maura sighed. She felt every bit as disappointed as Jan looked. But she could do something about her daughter's disappointment.

"I guess you'll just have to go without me." Maura smiled at both of them. "They'll let you sign for me, won't they, Jan?"

Jan nodded, but Hank still looked upset. "You don't have to buy my dinner, Mrs. Thomas. I can pay my own way."

"I'm sure you can." Maura smiled at him. "But I'd really like this to be my treat. It's my way of saying thank you for visiting me in the hospital."

"But I explained all that. I *wanted* to visit you."

"And I *want* to say thank you by treating you to dinner. Is it a deal?"

"Well . . . okay." Hank still looked a little uncomfortable. "But the next time you need a limo, it's free."

They visited for a few more minutes, and then Maura excused herself. She was still smiling as she went into her room and closed the door. Jan was positively blossoming.

Nita had told her that Jan hadn't gone out much in high school, and Jan had admitted that she hadn't dated anyone during her freshman year at Princeton. Suddenly there were two possible boyfriends on the scene, and Maura wasn't sure which one she liked best. David seemed like a wonderful young man, and so did Hank.

It took only a few minutes to get ready for bed, and Maura sighed as she switched off the light. It had been an exhausting day, and she simply had to get some sleep. She was about to drop off to sleep when she thought of it.

Keith was coming home tomorrow.

Maura shivered slightly, even though her room was warm. She knew nothing about her husband. He was still a stranger to her. Perhaps that was why Steve had extended his dinner invitation. He'd known that this first night with Keith would be awkward for her, and he'd attempted to make things easier.

There was a frown on Maura's face as she went over their schedule. Steve was picking Keith up at the airport, and bringing him back here. And there would barely be time for him to shower and dress before they had to leave for the restaurant. Dinner would be fine. Steve had a date, and they would make a foursome. But how about after dinner, when they came back here and Steve and his date left? Would Keith insist on reinitiating the intimate relationship they must have shared?

Maura shivered again. The prospect of making love with her husband was more than a little disconcerting. It was like sleeping with a man on a first date, something she doubted she'd done in the past. What sorts of things did Keith like in bed? And would she be able to please him? These were all questions that would be answered by this time tomorrow night.

As she dropped off to sleep, Maura was still frowning. But her last conscious thought wasn't about Keith and whether or not he would make love to her. She was trying to imagine what Steve's date would be like, and wishing that they could switch places.

Chapter Fifteen

She had just slipped into one of her favorite dresses, a knee-length, midnight blue silk that hugged her figure like a second skin. The dress was simple, one of her own creations, with a bodice cut low enough to be provocative, held in place by thin spaghetti straps.

He was fixing his collar in front of the mirror and he gave an appreciative whistle as he caught sight of her, entering the room. "You look incredible! But are you sure you want to wear that dress? You're going to attract a lot of attention."

"Why not?" She shrugged and the bodice slipped down slightly. "No one knows us here."

"That's true, but there may be photographers. Some pretty big names hang out at the restaurant. I tell you what . . . let's have dinner at the hotel, instead."

"Oh, Donny!" Her lips formed into a pout. "It's our last night and I want it to be special. And I've never been to the Four Seasons before. No one'll pay any attention to us. We're not celebrities."

He raised his eyebrows and leered at her. "You look like one in that dress. It's one of yours?"

"Of course." She bent over to slip on her shoes, giving

him an excellent glimpse of her breasts. "I designed it last year, but this is the first time I've actually worn it."

"It's really . . . uh . . . I don't know how to describe it."

She laughed and turned around slowly, giving him a full view. "It's fashionable and feminine, and very sexy. That's why she wouldn't buy it for her line. She said it was too revealing, that a woman would need a perfect body to wear it, and most of her clients wouldn't want to take the chance."

"She's right." He chuckled as he walked over to kiss the side of her neck. "Her clients want clothes that hide their faults. That's why she designs all those loose, drapey things."

"But this looks good on me, doesn't it?"

She turned slightly, so he could see her in profile, and he nodded. "It looks great! But it needs something, and I think I know what it is."

"A different hemline?" She frowned slightly. As far as she was concerned, the hemline was perfect.

"No. Think higher."

"A belt?"

"Definitely not, but you're going in the right direction."

"The neckline?" Her frown deepened. "You think it's too low?"

"It's perfect, but you could use something to set it off. Shut your eyes and I'll show you."

She shut her eyes and waited as his footsteps receded. She hoped he wasn't about to give her one of those tacky gold chains everyone in California seemed to wear. Then his footsteps returned and she felt something cold and metallic being placed around her neck. Costume jewelry. She just hoped it wouldn't be something that would ruin the look of her dress.

"Keep your eyes closed and walk to the mirror. I'll guide you."

His voice was filled with anticipation, and she felt a tingle of pleasure. He'd never presented her with a gift before, and even if his choice was a piece of cheap-looking trash, she'd wear it with a smile on her face.

"Okay. You can open your eyes now."

She drew a deep breath and reminded herself that it was the thought that counted. And then she opened her eyes.

"It's . . . it's gorgeous!" Her eyes widened as she stared at the necklace he'd fastened around her neck. If this was costume jewelry, it was a great knock-off. It looked genuinely antique, with heavy gold overlapping circles, each one containing a stone. The stones were gorgeous and they looked to her untrained eye like opals. Of course that wasn't possible, unless . . .

"It's not real . . ." There was fear in her eyes as she turned to face him. "Is it?"

He nodded and grinned like a schoolboy caught with his hand in the milk money. "It's real. I had it made up especially for you."

"But . . . how?" She turned to look at the necklace again, her face a curious mixture of fear and pleasure. She loved the look of its glittering beauty, the solid feel of precious metal resting around her neck, but she knew he couldn't afford to give her something this expensive.

"Don't worry about it." He wrapped his arms around her waist and hugged her. "I found the gold base in a box in the attic, along with some other broken jewelry. It used to be set with pearls, but most of them were missing. I had my jeweler repair it and put in the opals."

"It's gorgeous! But where did you get the stones?"

"They're from the last shipment. I wrote them off. And now that Grant's gone, she'll never find out."

"But Grant told her all about how you were skimming

when he took her to the air . . . oh!" She stopped suddenly, her face mirroring the sudden revelation. "I almost forgot. She doesn't remember anything Grant told her . . . right?"

He grinned and kissed her neck again. "Right. I worked on the books while she was in the hospital. When she turns them over to a new accountant, he'll never suspect a thing. And what she doesn't know can't hurt her . . . or us."

"But what if she remembers? They said her memory could come back."

"It's a long shot. Personally, I don't think it'll ever happen, but if it does I'll think of something."

"Okay." She nodded, and then she turned to kiss him. "You're really brilliant, you know that? And I love my new necklace!"

He grinned. "I knew you would. Just don't wear it when you get home. Somebody might start asking questions."

"I'll be careful, I promise. But I can wear it tonight, can't I?"

"That's why I gave it to you now, instead of saving it for your birthday." He picked up her coat, and held it out. "Let's go. Our reservation's at seven. And then we can come back here and celebrate all night."

She kept the smile on her face as he helped her slip on her coat. But when he turned to open the door, she blinked back tears. If this was her birthday present, it meant they wouldn't be together next week. She'd have to spend another birthday alone. That was the trouble with having a married lover. He had other, more important commitments. And when she'd suggested this whole plan, she hadn't realized how lonely the holidays and birthdays would be.

"What's the matter?" He turned, catching her in the act of wiping away a tear.

"Nothing. I just love you so much. And I wish you could be with me more, that's all."

He frowned slightly. "But you were the one who wanted me to marry her. And you know we have to be careful. If anyone suspects we're more than friends, it could blow everything sky high."

"I know." She forced a smile and took his arm. "And I know I shouldn't ask this, but . . ." She stopped, trying to force the words back. It would serve no purpose to ask. But she simply had to know what to expect. "When you get home . . . will you have to sleep with her?"

He looked at her in surprise. And then he nodded. "Of course. Come on, honey . . . be reasonable. She'll think there's something really strange going on if I don't."

"I guess you're right." She gave a little sigh. "But I wish you didn't have to."

"Hey, don't forget that all this was your idea. There's no backing out now. And there's no reason why a husband shouldn't sleep with his wife, unless . . ." He stopped, and gave her a devilish grin. "Honey! Don't tell me you're jealous at *this* stage of the game?"

"No. Of course I'm not." Her face colored slightly, and she turned away. She didn't want him to know that she was lying. Every night he spent with the bitch was agony, but she had to endure it. The rewards far outweighed any momentary pain.

"Cheer up, babe." He gave her a little squeeze. "It won't be forever. And when it's all over, we'll be together."

"Right." She hugged his arm tightly as they walked out the door. She really had no right to complain. It was her plan, and he'd agreed. And now he was just doing what she'd asked him to do. But she wished he wouldn't play the loving husband quite so convincingly. If she wasn't careful, he might get to like being married to the bitch with all her money, and her fancy house, and her socially prominent friends. He might get to like it so much he'd decide to play the part for real. And where would she be then?

They'd only gone a few steps before she stopped, pulling him to a halt. And then she smiled up at him with a devilish grin of her own. "I've got a great idea. Let's change our plans for tonight. I don't feel like going out to eat after all."

"You don't?" He looked puzzled. "But I thought you were dying to go to the Four Seasons."

"I was. But then I got to thinking that it's our last night. And I don't want to waste a second of it."

He started to smile then, a smile that grew wider with each passing second. "Aren't you hungry?"

"I'm starving." She licked her lips in a way that she knew would turn him on. "Let's go back to our room, Donny. I'm sure I can find something there to fill me up."

He was watching a video tape when the phone rang, and he took time to put it on pause before he answered. He knew better than to answer on the first ring. Guys in his line of work let the phone ring at least three times before answering. If you picked up right away, it gave the impression that you were nervously waiting right there by the phone.

"Yeah?"

"It's me. Did you make contact today?"

"Of course." He grinned into the receiver. They were the anxious ones, not him. "No problem."

"Did you learn anything?"

"Some. You'll get it all in my report."

"Don't play games with me! You know what I want."

He smiled. It was dangerous to make them nervous, but

he couldn't resist. "There's no sign of her memory returning yet, but I plan to help her along a little."

"How?"

"I'll ask her some questions, and see what answers I get. Give me a week. I'll know more then."

"You'll call if something happens before that?"

"Of course."

"But you won't do anything until you check with us. Is that clear?"

"Perfectly." He hung up the phone with a smile on his face. The person who hung up first won. That was another maxim he'd learned.

There was a soft knock on the door. Two taps, evenly spaced, and then a third. He crossed the room in his stock-inged feet and checked the peephole before he opened the door.

"Hi, baby!" The blonde that entered was past her prime, with dark roots and teeth that needed straightening. "Sam said you called in for me?"

"That's right. Do you remember what I want?"

"Sure thing." She grinned and took the envelope he handed her, stuffing it in her purse without opening it. "The same as last time?"

He nodded, the color rising to his cheeks. He hated to associate with someone like her, but it was too risky to pick up someone who wasn't a pro. She knew the drill. He'd taken her through it step by step the last time he'd called for her.

"Where do you wanna do it, baby? On the couch like last time?"

"No." He shook his head. "Let's go in the bedroom. Follow me."

He led the way to the bedroom. Not that she could get lost. It was only a three-room apartment.

"Nice sheets." She sat down on the edge of the bed, and ran her hand over the brightly patterned sheets printed with cars and trucks and buses. "I got ones with flowers up at my place. You wanna come over and see them next time?"

"Sure. Maybe I'll do that." He grinned at her, although he had no intention of setting foot in her apartment. It was bad enough having her here, letting her know where he lived. There was an old quote, something about how desperate men did desperate things. And he was definitely desperate. He always got this way when he was zeroing in on a kill, and he needed some way to defuse the energy that might cause him to act prematurely.

"Hey . . . you're shaking." She reached out and pulled him down to the bed. "Hot to trot, huh, baby?"

He nodded, although that wasn't the truth. He despised what she was about to do, and he was thoroughly repulsed by her. He hated her heavy makeup, and her sickening perfume, and her coarse way of speaking. But he needed her to be exactly the way she was, an older image of his first sexual partner.

"Now?" She gave him what she thought was a sexy smile. And when he nodded, she patted the bed. "Come on, baby. Your mom said you can't stay up past eight, so it's time to put you to bed."

He shuddered, but he felt himself hardening. And his face turned red as she reached out and unzipped his pants, pulling them down with both hands.

"That's a big one for such a little boy!" She giggled, a thoroughly incongruous sound for someone who was at least ten years past her bubble gum-chewing, high school cheerleader stage. But he'd asked her to giggle and play a teenage baby-sitter.

She reached out and flicked at it with her finger, batting it, playfully. "What do you think you're gonna do with that, huh? You're not even old enough to know what you got. Maybe I'd better roll you over and see if it'll go down."

There was a fluffy white bath sheet on the bed table and she flipped it out on the bed. Then she patted the center of the towel, and grinned at him. "Roll over, baby. And put it right there. We don't want any mess on the sheet."

She rolled him over and giggled again, more convincingly this time. But perhaps it was because he couldn't see her. His face was buried in the pillow. "Your mom said I gotta clean you up before I put you to bed."

"No! No bath!" His voice was high and childish, with a hint of petulance. But she just laughed, the way she was supposed to do.

"Come on, baby. You know you can't go to bed without a bath."

"No!" He said it again, and tensed. He knew what was coming next. And her hand smacked hard against his buttocks, making him gasp.

"There's more where that came from, so you better behave. I'm the boss while your mom's away. Now don't move while I get the water, or I'll smack you again!"

The bed springs creaked as she got up, and he heard her go into the bathroom. The water ran for a long time, and he rolled over, grasping the part of him he'd just discovered, and pulling at it with his fingers.

"Stop that!" She came back into the room, carrying a pan of steaming water and a bar of soap. "You're a very bad little boy!"

But he didn't stop. It felt too good to stop. He just moved his hand up and down, smiling at her.

She hit out at his hand, her fingernails grazing the part of him that felt so good. It didn't hurt. It just made him want more. But then she flipped him over again, and he could hear her wring out the washcloth. "If you were older, I'd smack you again. But you're too little to know what you're doing."

The washcloth was hot, much hotter than the one his mother used, and it hurt his bottom where she'd smacked him. At the same time, it felt good and he started to squirm up and down on the towel, rubbing himself against the material.

"Hey!" She sounded exasperated. "Cut that out! You're not supposed to do that!"

But he barely heard her as he squirmed and rubbed, trying to drive himself into the mattress.

"I said, cut it out!" She flipped him over again. And then she stared at the place between his legs. "Jeez! I gotta do something with you. Your mom's gonna fire me if she sees you like this!"

He watched as she squirted some baby lotion on her hands and rubbed them together until they were slippery. Then she grabbed his legs and pulled them apart, and began rubbing him with the lotion.

"No!" He tried to squirm away from the fingers that held him. "No, no!"

"Don't move!" She swatted him with the palm of her slippery hand. "You started this. And now I gotta finish it up before your mom gets home."

He started to cry then, but it didn't do any good. Her fingers were grabbing him, pushing and pulling and making him feel all funny inside. And she was holding him down with her other hand, digging her nails into his leg.

"Noooo!"

He wailed, and she smacked him again. "Do it, baby! Make it happen right now!"

But nothing happened as her hand went up and down. And nothing happened when she grabbed his testicles and squeezed them between her fingers. The thing between his legs was still hard no matter what she did.

"Jeez!" She sighed as she shook her head. "You're lasting longer than my boyfriend, and he's really a stud. I'm gonna go call Rosie. She'll know what to do."

The mention of Rosie's name made him snap. He reached out to grab her and threw her roughly down on the bed, driving into her with so much force the headboard of the bed slammed up against the wall. Once, twice, and it was over in a burst of pure frenzy. But when he came to his senses, he found her staring up at him with fear in her eyes.

He let her go. He'd been gripping her arms so hard there were white marks where his fingers had been.

"Sorry about that." He smiled to put her at ease. He would need her again before this was over. "I really lost control this time. I think it was because you're so fantastic. You should have been an actress."

"Yeah?" She began to smile back. "You really think so?"

"You were perfect, exactly the way I wanted. And I think you deserve a little more than the going rate, don't you?"

"Whatever you say. You're the boss." She smiled at him coyly, her fear washed away by the prospect of money she wouldn't have to turn over to her pimp.

"Just wait a second. I'll get it." He stood up and pulled on his pants. And then he took his wallet out of his pocket. "How about an extra fifty? You're worth it."

"That's sweet." She took the money and tucked it into her bra. Then she got up and headed for the door. "You wanna wave bye-bye to me?"

He laughed. This one had a sense of humor, even though she was stupid. "The game's over. Maybe next time."

"See you soon." She opened the door, and then she turned and stared at him. "How about I get another girl? We could have lots of fun."

He tried not to react, but he couldn't help frowning. Another girl was one more person who'd know about him. But he knew better than to tell her why another girl simply wasn't acceptable, so he forced a grin.

"You're doing just fine on your own. Besides . . . you'd have to split the profits if you brought in another girl, and you don't want to do that, do you?"

"No way!" She shook her head, and turned to go. "Just call Sam when you want me again, and I'll be here with bells on."

He kept the smile on his face until the door had shut behind her, and he crossed the room in three quick strides to lock it securely. Then he poured himself a drink and sat down on the couch, lost in the fantasy she'd started for him.

Of course Rosie had come over, and she'd stared at him, too. And she'd tried to do what the other one had with no result. But Rosie had a boyfriend who'd taught her a lot about kinky sex, and she'd brought a magazine she'd snatched from under her older brother's bed. Between the two of them, they'd subjected him to some things that were very pleasant, things that made him hot just thinking about them. But as the minutes ticked by, they'd grown desperate. And they'd tried other, more drastic things that made him shudder to this day.

It was almost like it had happened yesterday and the

memory of the searing pain was still as fresh as on the night it had happened. The awful soreness had lasted for days, and he hadn't been able to tell anyone what was wrong. They'd almost killed him and no one had ever found out about it.

It hadn't ended with that night. They'd discovered a new toy to play with, and they'd abused him until he was old enough to talk. And when they'd finally tired of him, they'd threatened to kill him if he ever told anyone what they'd done.

"Jesus!" He reached up to wipe the sweat from his forehead with the back of his hand. He'd almost blown it tonight, by showing how he really felt. She'd been just a little too convincing, too much like his abusive baby-sitter. He had to be very careful to exercise perfect control. Girls like her were rare. He'd only found a few in the past. And he wanted to play it all out, work his way through the whole scenario. He couldn't let her know how excited it made him, how he longed for that ultimate release. She'd run for her life if she ever guessed how it would all turn out in the end.

Chapter Sixteen

Maura glanced at the clock in her studio. It was five minutes past one. But hadn't it been five minutes past one the last time she'd looked? And certainly at least an hour had passed since then. Her clock must have stopped. There was no other explanation.

She picked up the telephone to dial the number for the correct time of day. And that was when she noticed that the clock hadn't stopped, after all. The minute hand was moving, creeping around the face of the clock so apathetically it seemed to be in slow motion.

Maura sighed and picked up her sketchbook again. She was working on her design for a new tennis outfit, but it was going very badly. She couldn't seem to concentrate, and all her ideas seemed impossible to implement. Perhaps her talent for design had disappeared, along with her memory.

But her memory hadn't disappeared, not completely. She'd remembered Nick's name. Did that mean that her memory was coming back?

Maura pulled out her desk drawer and stared at the picture she'd taken from the photograph album. Nick. Nicolas. Cola. She wished she could remember more about him. She had his wedding ring, the ring that Emmy had given him. But who was Emmy? And how had Maura met them?

She tried, but she couldn't remember Emmy at all. There was no visual image connected with her name. But Jan had said that Nick was a visiting professor, and that meant she must have known them both in her college years. They could have been very close friends. Perhaps they'd even been neighbors when she'd been married to Paul. She could imagine sitting at her blue kitchen table, pouring coffee and exchanging confidences with Nick's wife, Emmy. It would certainly explain why she knew so much about their lives and why she felt such overwhelming grief when she looked at Nick's picture. But why did Maura have his wedding ring? There must be a reason why Emmy hadn't kept it, but she had no idea what that reason would be. There were just too many pieces missing, and until she remembered them nothing would make any sense.

Maura glanced up at the clock again, but only a few minutes had passed. She felt like screaming for it to speed up and race toward the moment she'd been anticipating all day. Keith was coming home and she might have told him about Nick and Emmy. All she had to do was ask him, and he could clear up the mystery.

Nita had given her Keith's itinerary, and Maura flipped open the airline pamphlet to check the times. Keith was in Denver right now. At one thirty-three, he'd be boarding his connecting flight, and he'd arrive in L.A. less than three hours from now.

There was a knock at the door, and Maura hurried to open it. Nita was standing there, balancing a tray.

"Hello, Miss Maura. Here is your lunch." Nita walked in and placed the tray on Maura's desk. And then she gestured toward the stairwell. "I had to bring Cappy with me. He would not stay behind in the kitchen."

Maura grinned as she saw Cappy coming up the last stair. "You'd better leave him here, Nita. He looks exhausted from all those stairs. I'll bring him down later."

When Nita left, Maura picked up Cappy and cuddled him in her arms. His ears were limp, his tail was down, and he gave a deep, doggy sigh as he looked up at her. "What's the matter, Cappy? Are two flights of stairs too much for a little guy like you?"

Cappy's tail thumped feebly. He was so tired, only the tip moved. And as Maura watched, he gave another deep, doggy sigh and closed his eyes.

"You're so tired, you can't stay awake." Maura smiled as she took him to the daybed in the corner of the room. She put him down, and he snuggled right up to a feather pillow without opening his eyes.

"Some company you are!" Maura laughed, and returned to her desk. Nita had prepared what she claimed was Maura's favorite lunch, a salad *niçoise*. Maura took one bite and frowned slightly. It was delicious, but something was missing.

She stared down at the beautifully arranged salad plate, and mentally reviewed the ingredients; tuna, anchovies, tomatoes, potatoes, green beans, hard-boiled eggs, ripe olives and Boston lettuce, dressed with an herb vinaigrette. It all seemed to be there, but the taste was different, not quite what she remembered. She shut her eyes and tried to recall where she'd had salad *niçoise* before. It had been a long time ago, at an outdoor cafe, on a busy street somewhere in . . .

*   *   *

The waiter was Belgian, and she was amused by his accent. He was also one of them and a friend of Nick's so she tried not to show it. He rolled his r's when he told them the special was "crrrrispy" duck, and he sounded as if he had a terrible cold.

Nick ordered the duck, but she wasn't very hungry. She hadn't known they were stopping to eat, and she'd made herself a snack before Nick had come to pick her up.

"Try the salad *niçoise.*" Nick smiled at her across the table. "They're famous for it here."

The wine was delicious, a dry, white vintage she'd never tasted before. It came from a region that was known for its excellent vineyards, and Nick had promised to take her on a tour of the most prestigious wineries when they had the time. She sipped very slowly, drinking very little, knowing that alcohol and business didn't mix. They had a job to do later, and she needed to keep all her wits about her.

Nick was wearing the ring. She could see it on his finger, brushed gold reflecting the sunlight. And she was wearing a ring, too. It had a cloudy, dark blue stone with a star hidden in its depths. It was very old. She could tell by the antique, filigreed silver mounting. It was very dear to her. Someone she loved had given her the ring.

The waiter appeared with her salad, beautifully arranged on a clear blue glass plate with a fluted edge. Nick smiled, urging her to try it.

The first bite was ambrosia. The vinaigrette was sharp and tasty, liberally sprinkled with fresh herbs. And the tuna was exquisite. When she asked why this salad was so different from any she'd tried before, Nick told her that the tuna was fresh. And then he laughed and said he'd done her a terrible disservice. Now that she'd tasted fresh tuna from the

Baltic Sea, she'd never be able to enjoy the canned variety again.

She finished her salad, every bit of it, and Nick had eaten his duck. And while they were waiting for strong, black coffee to be served, she turned to look around the small patio restaurant.

The floor was bare, decorated only by smooth grey stones, set into concrete. The low walls were made of the same type of stone, and white lattice-work panels at the top lent privacy from the street traffic. Plants set in pots stood against the walls, tall plants with glossy green leaves and bright pink, waxy flowers. The round tables were made of wrought iron painted white, with matching chairs. The seats of the chairs were covered with bright pink fabric and the tablecloths were of the same color. The combination of white, pink and green was very pleasant, and to add to the ambience strains of Mozart played softly in the background.

They were the only customers, sitting across from each other at one of the small tables, their knees almost touching under the tablecloth. Just Nick. And her. There was no other woman who might be Emmy. Where was she? And why wasn't she here with her husband? The Maura who'd been there knew, but this Maura didn't.

As they sipped their coffee, another couple came in to sit at a table nearby. It was clear they were tourists by the cameras that hung around their necks. The man, a tall, dark stranger who looked vaguely Latin, asked Nick a question in a foreign language. Nick answered him in the same language, and took the camera he offered.

Maura smiled as the couple moved closer together, and Nick stood up to take their picture. But then someone whistled a warning, and she turned to see Peter motioning frantically from the kitchen door.

She didn't think, she just lunged forward to knock Nick down behind the low wall. And then they ran, bending down low, to the kitchen door.

There was an explosion somewhere behind them as they passed the gleaming, stainless steel counters. And then they were out in a dark alley, running to a car.

The back doors were open, and she slid in, rolling to the other side. She felt Nick land beside her, and the door closed with a solid thunk.

"Stay down!" The voice was Peter's, and the car barreled forward, screeching down the alley and through the streets. She could see Nick's face as they sped past the street lights, and he looked very different in the strobe-like light. The Nick in the restaurant had been relaxed and happy, smiling as they'd talked about ordinary things. This Nick was tense, poised for action, and she shivered as she realized that he was quite formidable.

"You are okay?" He felt her shiver and he glanced down at her.

"Yes. The explosion . . . what happened?"

"Somebody knew we were there. It's not a safe place anymore. Have we lost them, Peter?"

There was a laugh from the front seat. "Of course. That's why I'm the driver and you're the passenger. But stay down until we get to the house. I want to drive by and check it out before we go in."

The floorboards of the car were far from comfortable, but Nick stretched out and cradled her against him. At first his arm was tense around her shoulders, but as the miles passed he began to relax. "What do you think? Was it Henri?"

"Possibly. But if it was, he got his just rewards. He took a bullet."

She knew she shouldn't, but she couldn't help asking. "Is he . . . dead?"

"Oh, yes." Peter's voice was hard. "I saw him and there's no doubt about that."

"But what if he wasn't the one who . . ."

"Hush." Nick stroked her cheek with his hand. "You've got to remember, life isn't fair. And they don't play by the rules."

They rode several miles in silence, and the motion of the car almost lulled her to sleep. Nick must have thought she was sleeping because he spoke very softly. "This isn't going well, Peter. What do you think about sending her back?"

"I would, at least temporarily. Your concern for her could make you careless, and there are other lives at stake."

"No!" She sat up, and pulled away from Nick's comforting embrace. "I have to stay. They spent months training me, and you can't find a replacement overnight."

Nick pulled her back against his chest again, and sighed very softly. "That's my decision. If I say go, you'll go. This is much more dangerous than we thought it would be."

"But I volunteered." She felt the tears well up in her eyes. "And I want to be here with you and Peter. You can't send me home. Not after everything we've been through. Besides, it would look strange if I left right now when there's only a few more weeks to go."

"But you'd be safe." Peter spoke up from the front seat. "And Nick wouldn't spend valuable time worrying about you. I think you should fly back. You've become a liability."

Nick nodded, and kissed her lightly on the cheek. "Peter's right. You have to leave. We'll make the arrangements tomorrow."

She started to cry then, hot stinging tears running down

her cold cheeks. She didn't want to leave him. Not now. Not ever.

"Don't cry." Nick held her tightly as he whispered the words in her ear. "It's for the best."

She shook her head, and tried to deny it. "No, Nick. I can't leave. It's not fair."

"It's not fair if you stay." His voice was low and intimate, so only she could hear. "Do this for me. It's what I want most in the world. Go back home, and take my baby away from all this. I want both of you to be safe."

Maura's eyes opened with a snap. His baby?! She hadn't known that Nick had a baby. If she'd gone back home with Nick's baby, what had happened to the child?

As she asked herself these questions, a terrible suspicion began to grow in Maura's mind. Was Janelle really her child? Or were Janelle's parents really Nick and Emmy?

"That's ridiculous!" She spoke out loud and Cappy woke up to look at her. He must have sensed her distress because he hopped off the daybed and raced across the floor to paw at her leg.

"It's all right, Cappy." Maura picked him up. "I just had another weird dream, that's all."

It had to be a dream. Maura frowned as she thought it through carefully. Janelle was her child. Steve and Donna had been with her the night she'd gone into labor, and they'd taken her to the hospital and waited until Janelle was born. Nick and Emmy's baby was another child. Somehow, she was reliving Emmy's life, mistaking Emmy's memories for her own.

Maura reached for the notebook she carried with her, and wrote down everything she could remember. It had seemed as if everything had happened to her, but it was Emmy's life she was remembering. Where was Nick and Emmy's child now? Maura frowned deeply. She wished that she could remember.

It wouldn't do any good to ask Janelle. She had barely remembered Nick's name, and she would have mentioned his wife and child if she'd known about them. And Nita hadn't known anything either, when she'd shown her Nick's picture. Steve had claimed no knowledge of Nick, and Maura doubted that Keith had anything to tell her.

Maura sighed, and then she came to a decision. It was a waste of time to question everyone. Nick and Emmy had been involved in something very dangerous, and it was obviously she'd told no one about them and their child. Of course she wanted to know more about them. She had to discover how they fit into her life. But that was a mystery that only she could solve.

And to solve it, she had to get her memory back.

Chapter Seventeen

There were two high, narrow windows by the side of the front door, and Maura gazed out through the curtain. Somehow, she managed to put a smile on her face as she watched Steve's car round the bend in the driveway and pull up in front of the house. Her husband was home.

Steve popped open the trunk and got out of the driver's side to walk around to the back of the car. The passenger's door opened and Keith got out, too, but the body of the car blocked her view of his face.

Maura felt her hands begin to tremble and she clasped them together tightly. There was no way she wanted Keith to know how nervous she was. It might hurt his feelings, and that would be terrible.

She opened the door and stood there waiting, trying to look like a normal wife, happy that her husband was home from his business trip. She must have been convincing because Keith grinned from ear to ear when he saw her.

"Hi, honey!" He came up the steps with a jaunty wave. "Sorry we're late, but the flight was delayed."

Maura nodded. "I know. I called the airport to see if your

flight was on time. They told me you were an hour late on your take-off from O'Hare."

"I brought you a little something from New York." Keith presented her with a department store bag. "I guess I should have had it wrapped, but I was in a rush when I bought it."

Maura was surprised as she took the bag. Did Keith always bring her gifts when he traveled on business? She was about to ask him when she realized that it would be tactless on her part. She'd find out later, from Nita or Jan.

"Go ahead, open it." Keith grinned at her. "It's something I think you'll like."

Maura opened the bag and took out the box inside. It was brown and gold and it said "Opium" on the side in gold embossed letters.

"Why don't you use some tonight?" Keith was smiling as if they had a secret to share. "It might bring back some fond memories."

Maura smiled back, but her mind was reeling in shock. Opium was a drug! "You want me to . . . use this tonight?"

"Absolutely. That's why I bought it. Nita said you were out, and I know you don't like to go anywhere without it."

"Uh . . . thank you." Maura tried not to look as shocked as she felt. Evidently the movement to legalize marijuana had been much more successful than anyone had dreamed back in the seventies! "Tell me, Keith . . . do I . . . uh . . . use opium often?"

Keith nodded. "Every day. You told me you don't feel like yourself without it. You've been using it ever since I met you."

"Then it's a . . . a habit?"

"I guess you could say that." Keith chuckled. "You get really upset when you run out."

"And you don't mind that I use opium?"

"Of course not. I enjoy it, too. What's the matter, honey? Don't you like it anymore?"

"I . . . I'm not sure." Maura's face turned pale. She'd never dreamed she was addicted to drugs! And then she had another thought that made her shudder. "How about Jan? Does she use opium, too?"

Keith shook his head. "You let her try it a couple of times, but she decided it wasn't right for her."

"I . . . I see." Maura tried not to show how horrified she was. She'd given her daughter opium! Thank God Jan hadn't become an addict! "How about Nita? Does she use opium?"

"No. Opium's very expensive, and Nita prefers something that's imported from Mexico. One of your girls went down there last year on vacation, and she brought some back for Nita's Christmas present."

Maura groaned. She couldn't believe she'd asked one of her employees to import drugs for Nita. It had to be illegal. And she certainly wouldn't use opium again, now that she knew about her addiction! Somehow she'd managed to kick her dependency, and now it was time to start her life over, drug-free.

"Maura? What's wrong?"

Keith looked genuinely concerned, and Maura gave a deep sigh. Then she handed him the box and squared her shoulders. "I know you meant well, but I want you to take this back. I haven't had any since I left the hospital, and this is my chance to put it all behind me."

Steve came up, just in time to hear the tail end of their conversation. And he looked just as shocked as Keith did. "What are you talking about, Maura?"

"I don't remember how I got addicted, but I know I don't want to use opium anymore. And I asked Keith to return it."

"Addicted?" Steve started to laugh. "Maura . . . I can't believe you thought . . ."

Keith stared at him for a moment, and then he began to laugh, too. "It all makes sense. Opium didn't come out until the eighties. And Maura doesn't remember the eighties."

"Why are you laughing?" Maura began to frown. "There's absolutely nothing funny about drug addiction, even if it's legal now. It's a horrible . . ."

"Maura . . . wait," Steve interrupted her. "Trust me. You're not addicted to drugs. Let Keith open the package and show you what's inside."

Maura watched while Keith opened the package. And she gasped as he took out a lovely designer bottle in a distinctive shape with a crystal stopper at the top.

"Think hard, Maura. Do you recognize this?" Keith was grinning as he held it up.

Maura started to shake her head. But then she had a sudden vision of opening a similar bottle at her dressing table. She'd pulled out the stopper and dabbed some of the amber liquid inside on the pulse point of her throat, and the inside of her wrists, and . . ."

"Perfume?!" Maura's mouth dropped open. "Opium is a perfume?"

Keith nodded. "That's right. And you've been wearing it ever since I met you. You never went anywhere without it."

"Oh, no!" Maura laughed so hard, tears came to her eyes. "I thought it was *really* opium!"

Steve grinned. "And you thought Keith was bringing you illegal drugs?"

"Not really. I thought drugs were legal now. They were talking about legalizing marijuana when I was in college, and I just assumed that . . ."

"It didn't happen, Maura." Keith was still laughing.

"Drugs are still illegal. Now about the Opium I brought you . . . would you like to try it?"

Maura nodded. "I'd love to! And I'll use it tonight, I promise. I'm sorry I was such an idiot, Keith."

"No problem." Keith gave her a little hug. "I should have thought it through before I gave it to you. Sometimes I forget that you don't remember any of the time we've been together."

Maura hesitated slightly, and then she hugged him back. Keith sounded sad, and she could understand why. He knew she'd forgotten him completely and that had to be a blow to his ego. No husband would enjoy knowing that his wife regarded him as a stranger.

"Well . . . I'd better get dressed if we're going out to dinner." Keith stepped back and picked up his suitcase. "I'll take a quick shower and meet you both down here. Why don't you get Steve a drink, Maura?"

Maura nodded and headed for the liquor cabinet. It was easy to recognize because it had crystal decanters arranged on top. She reached for the unblended Scotch, poured out two fingers in a low tumbler, and filled another, taller glass with bottled water. There were three containers of nuts on the bar: peanuts, cashews, and pistachios. She ignored the peanuts and cashews, and filled a bowl with pistachios.

"Here you are, Steve." Maura carried the glasses over to him, and set them down on the coffee table. Then she went back for the bowl of pistachios and set that out also. "Would you like something else to tide you over? I can ring Nita for some chips and salsa."

"No, this is fine." Steve took a sip, and then he looked up at her. "What is this, Maura?"

"I . . . I'm not sure. I think the decanter said Scotch."

"Why did you give me Scotch, instead of bourbon, or whiskey, or rum?"

"Because . . . I don't know!" Maura stopped, suddenly confused. She'd poured the Scotch without thinking. Her hand had just gone to one of the decanters. "Is that right? Do you usually drink Scotch?"

"Yes. Exactly two fingers with water in a separate glass. And I prefer pistachios to peanuts or cashews. Sit down, Maura. You look faint."

Maura sank down on the couch next to him, and took a deep breath. Then she turned to him with a question in her eyes. "Does this mean I'm beginning to remember?"

"Perhaps." Steve frowned slightly, and slipped his arm around her shoulders. "But it may have been simple motor function memory, without any conscious thought."

"What's motor function memory?"

"Your hand automatically went to the right decanter and poured the proper amount. And you chose the pistachios because they were in the container you used every time you poured me a drink."

"I see." Maura frowned, recalling her tennis game with Jan. "Is motor function memory similar to muscle memory?"

"It's exactly the same. Your central nervous system has a memory of frequently repeated actions. A left-handed person with amnesia doesn't usually make a conscious decision about which hand he should use. He just reaches out with his left hand without thinking, because he's done it that way so many times before."

Maura nodded. "So what you're saying is that my body may remember what my mind doesn't?"

"It's certainly possible. One of my friends runs an Alzheimer's care facility, and she runs into phenomena like this every day. One of her patients, an elderly concert pianist, sat down and played Rachmaninoff's *Piano Concerto Number Two* in its entirety. But when she asked him what piece he'd played, he couldn't tell her. His fingers remembered the moves, but his mind didn't recall anything about it."

"That makes me wish I'd learned to play the piano." Maura sighed deeply. "At least I'd be able to do something."

"The designing isn't going well?"

"It isn't going at all. I know what I want, but I can't seem to get it down on paper. It's like I've forgotten how to draw. I spent two hours this morning trying to design a sleeve before I realized it couldn't be sewn that way."

"Maybe you're getting hung up on the details." Steve smiled at her. "Just let your fingers do the drawing, and make your mind a total blank."

Maura frowned slightly. "That shouldn't be difficult. My mind's a total blank anyway. Just this afternoon I had to ask Nita where we kept the light bulbs. I don't know where anything is anymore!"

"Neither do I . . . especially after my cleaning lady comes. She puts everything away where she can find it, and I don't have a clue. I have to call her at home every time I run out of toilet paper."

"I hope you have a phone in the bathroom." Maura started to laugh, and Steve joined in. It felt good to laugh after the disappointing news that she might not be regaining her memory after all.

"Maura? I'm ready." Keith came into the room. "Is this a private joke?"

"Not at all." Steve grinned at him. "Maura was feeling bad because she forgot where they kept the light bulbs, so I told her I didn't know where the toilet paper was at my house."

Keith nodded, although it was clear he didn't understand the joke. Maura took pity on him and stood up. "Never mind, Keith. I guess you had to be here. Would you like me to fix you a drink?"

"No, thanks. I'll have wine with dinner. Shouldn't you be getting ready, Maura?"

"Yes. I'll do that." Maura excused herself and hurried up the stairs. When she got to her room, she glanced at the clock and frowned. They still had a half hour before they left for the restaurant and she was already dressed. Running a comb through her hair and freshening her lipstick would take only a fraction of that time.

She'd just combed her hair when she thought of it. Perhaps Keith hadn't liked the dress she'd chosen. Unfortunately, there was only one way to find out, and that was to ask him.

She was about to go back down the stairs when she remembered the intercom connected to the telephone. There was a sheet on her bed table giving her the codes, and she punched out twelve for the living room.

"Hello?" Keith answered so promptly she knew he must have been sitting right by the phone.

"It's me, Keith. Did you like the dress I was wearing? Or would you rather I change?"

There was a moment of silence and then Keith laughed. "Sorry, Maura. I forgot that you wouldn't remember. Usually, when we go out to a fancy restaurant, you wear one of your own designs."

"Oh." Maura nodded, even though she knew he couldn't see her. "Is there any dress you prefer?"

"It's really up to you, but I don't think you've worn the black voile to *Champagne Bis*. It looks good on you and it's classy enough. If anyone's there, you might get a mention in the trades."

"The trades?"

"Yes, honey. *Daily Variety, The Hollywood Reporter, L.A. Style,* places like that. It could do you a lot of good."

"Thank you, Keith. I'll be down shortly." Maura winced at the note of formality in her voice. As she hung up the phone, she gave a deep sigh. Life was much more confusing now that Keith had come home. He seemed to expect her to behave in a certain way, and she had no idea how to fulfill his expectations.

Unfortunately, there were three black dresses in her closet, and Maura had no idea which one was made of voile. She certainly didn't want to bother Keith again. He might lose patience with her. And Nita had taken Cappy to her sister's house so her nieces and nephews could play with him. There was no one else to ask except Jan, and she was having dinner at the country club with Hank.

It only took a moment to get the number for the country club from the information operator, and Maura dialed it quickly. She asked for Jan, and a few moments later, Maura had her on the line.

"What's wrong, Mom?" Jan sounded anxious.

"Nothing that you can't fix. Keith wants me to wear my black voile dress tonight, and I don't remember what voile looks like."

Jan laughed. "No problem, Mom. Voile can be made from a lot of materials, but yours is made of silk. You do remember what silk is, don't you?"

"Don't be cute, Janelle!" Maura was grinning as she chided her daughter. "Of course I know what silk is. What does this black voile dress look like?"

"It's got a scoop neck, butterfly sleeves, and a straight skirt that's slit up to mid thigh. And you always wear your black velvet heels with it. They're in your shoe tree, third pair from the left on the second row."

"How do you know where my shoes are?" Maura laughed. "Do we wear the same size?"

There was a brief silence and then Jan laughed. "As a matter of fact, we do. And you've got lots of really neat shoes, Mom."

"And I let you borrow them?"

"Well . . . not exactly. But Nita and I used to try them all on while you were at work."

"I think I'd better put a lock on my closet." Maura tried to sound stern. "Is there anything else I should know about the dress?"

"No, not really. Just don't wear a necklace. It spoils the look. Try a ring. And have a wonderful time."

"Thanks, Jan. I will." Maura hung up the phone and raced to the closet. Now that she knew what to look for, the black voile dress was easy to identify. She slipped it on, found the shoes that Jan had recommended, and grabbed her jewelry box to look for something suitable.

One by one, Maura went through her rings, but nothing seemed right. She was about to give up when she noticed something stuck under the flap of one of the compartments.

"What's this?" Maura pulled it out and gasped as she recognized it. The ring was made of silver and it had an antique, filigreed silver mounting. And inside the mounting was a deep blue stone with a star hidden in its depths.

Maura slipped it on her finger and gave a little sigh. She knew she'd worn it before. It gave her a sense of well-being and it felt very comfortable on her finger. Then she remembered, and her eyes widened in shock. This was the same ring she'd been wearing at the restaurant the night Nick had told her to leave with his baby.

She stared down into the depths of the sapphire and willed it to give up its mystery, to trigger some piece of the puzzle that might explain her strange memories. How had the ring ended up in her jewelry box? And who had given it to her?

The star inside the stone glittered brightly, hinting of a mystical revelation. But absolutely nothing happened. She was still just as confused as she'd been before she'd found it.

Maura sighed as she slipped off the ring and placed it inside her jewelry box. Keith and Steve were waiting for her, and she had to go down. As she left her room, she took a deep breath and made a decision. She wasn't sure how she knew, but it was best not to mention the ring. It had come from her missing years, and it was her personal secret, a clue to the woman she had once been.

Chapter Eighteen

Hank looked anxious as Jan came back to the table. "Is there anything wrong?"

"Not a thing." Jan sat back down and frowned slightly. "It was Mom. Keith wanted her to wear her black, voile dress, but she couldn't remember what it looked like."

"It must be awful, losing your memory like that." Hank still looked very concerned. "I wish there was something I could do to help her."

"Me, too. We're all trying to help her fill in the pieces, but there's still a lot of blanks. She remembers the first nineteen years of her life, but everything past that is gone."

Hank nodded. "How about your housekeeper? You said she'd been with you for years."

"That's true. Nita's helped a lot, but she started working for us after I was born. She doesn't know anything about Mom before that."

"How about your uncle, the doctor? He must have known your mom before then."

"He did." Jan nodded. "But Steve didn't meet her until she got engaged to my dad. He would know, but he's dead."

"I'm sure your mother must have had friends in college."

Hank looked thoughtful. "Is there any way you could contact them?"

"No. Mom talked about her college friends once in awhile, but I don't remember their names."

"How about her college records?" Hank looked thoughtful. "Some of her professors might remember her. And they might know who her friends were."

Jan stared at Hank for a moment, and then she began to grin. "That's a great idea! Why didn't I think of that?"

"Because you're too close to the problem, and you're not thinking clearly. I'm an outsider. She's not my mother, so I can look at the whole thing objectively."

"Thanks, Hank." Jan reached out and patted his hand. "I'll get started on it first thing in the morning."

"You'll have to get some kind of release from your mom. Most colleges won't send any records without that."

"You're right." Jan reached into her canvas tote bag and pulled out her notebook. "I'd better make a note. I think I can do the whole thing by fax, if I get her to . . . oh, great!"

"What's the matter?" Hank reacted to her expression. Jan was staring down at her open notebook with a worried look on her face.

"This isn't my notebook. I must have taken Mom's by mistake. Maybe I should try to call her at the restaurant. She might need a phone number or something. She always keeps a list of the numbers she calls most often on the inside of the back cover."

Hank watched while Jan flipped to the back cover. It was perfectly blank.

"That's funny." Jan was clearly puzzled. "Maybe this isn't Mom's notebook, after all."

"Flip through it. Maybe you'll recognize her handwriting."

Jan flipped through the notebook and shook her head. I can't tell. It's printed and Mom always writes. It could be hers, but maybe it's not."

"Why don't you read a page or two? You might be able to tell that way."

"I guess I could . . ." Jan frowned slightly. "But I hate to do that. It might be personal."

Hank nodded. "I understand. But you don't ever have to tell her that you read it. And you can stop the minute you know it's hers. You'll never know who it belongs to if you don't read it."

"I suppose you're right." Jan sighed deeply. "Okay . . . here goes . . .

" 'I'm standing on a hill of snow, under a large tree. Its branches are bare and I can see a small fire on a level piece of ground in the distance. The firelight is casting flickering red shadows against the white surface of the snow. It would be a pretty picture, if I didn't know why they'd built the fire.

"They're thawing the ground for his funeral, three men dressed in long, dark coats with fur caps on their heads. The fire will burn for three days, until the ground is soft enough to dig his grave. And then he will be buried. He is gone from me, forever.' "

Jan shivered slightly and looked up at Hank. "This can't be Mom's notebook. She never mentioned anything about a funeral in the snow."

"Read a little more." Hank urged her. "Maybe she's writing about something that happened in her childhood."

"That's impossible. Mom's lived in Southern California all her life. And it never snows in the Imperial Valley. I'm almost positive this isn't hers."

"Then it can't hurt to read on." Hank gestured toward the

notebook. "Go ahead. It's really interesting. I'm getting great visuals."

"Well . . . all right." Jan flipped the page and started to read again.

" 'It's bitter cold, so cold that I can barely feel my feet, encased in warm, lined boots. I'm wearing a parka, black with a fur lining, and my hands are tucked into leather mittens lined with the same fur. There's something warm over my face, to keep out the frozen night air. It's a woven ski mask with holes for my eyes and my mouth.' "

"This is great stuff!" Hank looked excited. "Go ahead, Jan."

" 'I'm moving now, over the snow with a smooth glide. I must be on skis. I travel down the hill another few feet and stop by another tree. I'm close enough to hear them speaking in hushed voices as they place wood on the fire. The words are foreign, but I understand them perfectly. They are praising him, the one of their number they've lost.' "

Jan looked up and met Hank's eyes. It was clear that both of them were enthralled with the story that was enfolding. "I know for sure that this isn't Mom's. She doesn't speak any foreign languages except Spanish, and she's forgotten most of that."

"Look at the first page, Jan . . . or on the inside of the front cover. Is there a name?"

Jan flipped through the notebook and shook her head. "There's no name anywhere."

"It reads like a story." Hank looked thoughtful. "Do you think someone was starting a book?"

Jan shrugged. "I don't know. But I agree with you. It definitely reads like fiction. And I think it's very intriguing."

"Me, too. Do you have any idea how you got this notebook?"

"Not really. I take mine with me everywhere. And this is a common type you can buy at any stationery store. I guess someone had one just like it. They got mixed up and took mine, and I ended up with theirs."

"Did yours have your name on it?"

Jan shook her head. "I never got around to stamping it with my name. And there's no way they could tell. The pages are full of things like, 'Call Mom,' and 'Pick up dry-cleaning,' and 'Dentist appointment.' They'd know exactly what I do every day, but they'd have no idea who I was."

The waiter came with their dinner, and they stopped speaking until he'd served them. Then Jan picked up the notebook again. "Do you think I should turn it over to the club's lost and found department?"

"I wouldn't, especially since you don't know when you got it. It could sit here for years without anyone claiming it."

"Okay. I'll keep it." Jan slipped the notebook back into her bag. "But I'm not exactly sure what I should do with it."

"I'm not sure, either. But I think we'd better read it all the way through. Maybe there's a clue to the writer's identity."

"Oh, good!" Jan looked delighted. "I wanted to read it anyway, and that's a perfect excuse. Now I don't have to feel guilty about prying into someone else's personal life."

They were enjoying their dessert, an incredibly rich *crème brulée*, when Keith spotted someone he knew. "Would you two excuse me for a moment? Hugh Carson just came in, and I need to confirm an appointment with him."

Maura smiled, and nodded. Secretly, she was relieved. Dinner had been tense, and she thought she knew why. Steve's date, a very nice female doctor, had been called away on an emergency during the salad course. The moment she'd left, and it had just been the three of them, the tension had started to build.

It was clear that Keith resented her close relationship with Steve, a relationship which seemed to have survived her memory loss. And even though Maura had tried to treat Keith as a loving wife would treat her husband, calling him "honey" and "dear," he must have noticed that there was no real warmth in her voice.

"You're quiet tonight, Maura." Steve turned to her the moment Keith left the table. "Is something wrong?"

"No. Not really. It's just difficult finding myself married to Keith, and not being able to remember why I married him, or whether or not we had a good marriage."

Steve nodded. "You don't feel close to him anymore?"

"He's a stranger. I don't really know him at all. The memories are gone and love is . . . well . . . I'm just not sure. Do you know if I loved him?"

Steve looked vaguely uncomfortable. "I assume you did. You married him."

"You must have seen us together. Did we look as if we were in love?"

Steve took a deep breath and let it out again. "Look, Maura. I'm not the right person to judge something like that."

"But you're the only one I can ask!" Maura tried not to look as upset as she felt. "You spent a lot of time with us, didn't you?"

"No. I did my best to leave you alone."

"But why?" Maura was confused. "I thought you were my friend."

"Let's just say I had some personal problems. And you had your own life as Mrs. Keith Thomas. I didn't want to interfere. That's why I left you alone."

"But you're back in my life now?"

Steve hesitated for a long moment. And then he reached out to take her hand. "Look, Maura . . . I really don't know whether I'm doing you a favor or not, but yes . . . I'm back."

Jan unlocked the door and motioned for Hank to follow her to the kitchen. "Let's get some Cokes and carry them out to the patio. It's warm out tonight, and we can sit by the pool."

"Are you sure that's all right?" Hank looked a little nervous. "I mean, your mother's not home and we're here alone."

"No, we're not." Jan pushed open the kitchen door and reached down to catch the furry ball that hurtled out of his basket. "Cappy's here, and that means Nita's around here somewhere. Besides, Mom's met you and she won't mind. Trust me."

Hank nodded. "Okay. I just didn't want to do anything wrong. I like your Mom and I'd feel bad if she got mad at me."

"She won't." Jan handed Cappy to him and took several cans of Coke from the refrigerator. "Cappy can go outside, too. We can keep an eye on him while we read the rest of the notebook."

It didn't take long to get settled at a table, and Jan lit the lantern she'd brought out with her. "Do you want to read, or shall I?"

"You read, I'll listen." Hank smiled at her. "I like the sound of your voice."

"Thanks. Okay, here goes . . .

" 'There were tears in my eyes as I listened to their words of praise. He'd been a brave man, a good man, and he'd made them proud. They were glad the woman had escaped, but it was a pity she couldn't attend his funeral to pay her final respects. What kind of world was it when his own wife wasn't allowed at his funeral?' "

"His wife?" Hank shivered slightly. "The woman who's watching from the trees . . . is she his wife?"

Jan nodded. "I think so, but I don't know for sure. Maybe she says.

" 'One man is the leader of the group. He is taller and slightly older than the rest. I hear him tell them to gather more firewood and they split up to ski off into the woods. The older man stays behind, and he beckons to me.

"Trees whirl past as I ski rapidly down the hill. And his arms open as I approach. He holds me for a moment, patting my back, and then he gestures toward a wooden shack at the edge of the clearing. There are tears in his eyes as he takes my arm and escorts me there. I slip off my skis, open the door, and then I am inside.

"The shack is cold. Icy cold. And there is a bundle on the bench, wrapped in blankets. I pull off my mittens and fold down the blankets, gazing down through a blur of tears at his dear face. His eyes are open.' "

Jan shuddered and handed the notebook to Hank. Her hands were trembling. "You read. I think I'm going to cry."

Hank cleared his throat, and took up the story. " 'He has startling blue eyes, blond hair, and a rugged face. Even now, his color hasn't faded. He is deeply tanned, and he looks physically fit, my handsome lover.

"I reach down to touch his lips, the lips that kissed me only hours ago. Warm lips that are cold now, as cold as death.' "

Tears began to gather in Jan's eyes, and Hank reached in his pocket to offer her his handkerchief. Jan gave him a tremulous smile of thanks, and he read on.

" 'There is a tap on the door. It is my signal to hurry. I quickly pull back the blanket a bit further, and uncover his hand.

"My fingers are growing numb from the cold, but I slip off his watch and open the back. There is something inside, something wrapped in a thin piece of paper, which I take out and tuck into an inner pocket of my parka. And then I reach for his gold ring, turning it so the inscription glitters in the light from the bare bulb hanging from the ceiling. To Nick. Love forever, Emmy. My hands are shaking, and I am blinking back tears as I slip it from his finger and place it on my own.' "

"Did you say Nick?" Jan's eyes widened as Hank nodded. "That's funny . . . Mom's got a picture of a man named Nick and he looks like the man in this story."

"Relax, Jan. This description's pretty generic. And everyone knows at least one Nick."

"But I don't know any . . ." Jan stopped, and sighed. "I take that back. I do know a Nick. As a matter of fact, I know two. Go on, Hank. It's just a coincidence."

" 'There is another knock, sharp and urgent. My fingers fly as I wrap the blankets around him again, and hurry to the door. A nod to the older man, another brief hug, and I am snapping on my skis. And then I am flying over the snow, disappearing into the dense woods that surround the small graveyard.

" 'I look back once, when I reach the safety of the trees. The clearing is deserted now. The older man has vanished. And then I see them, a party of six men coming over the top of the hill. They have come for him. I have arrived just in time, and they will fail to complete their mission.' "

"What mission?" Jan was enthralled. "Keep on reading, Hank. Maybe she'll tell us."

" 'I dig my poles into the snow and ski down another steep hill. I ski for what seems like hours, until the terrain grows familiar. There is a farmhouse over the next rise, and I zigzag down to the barn. The hay is piled deep on the lee side, and I slip off my skis and push them into the pile. And then I run to the house to change to my nightgown and eat the snack the mother has left on the bed table for me, *Gjetost* and bread, my favorite.' "

"*Gjetost?*" Hank looked puzzled. "What's that?"

"It's a goat cheese that tastes like peanut butter. Mom loves it. We had some just a couple of nights ago. Do you want me to see if there's any left?"

"That's okay. I'll try it some other time. Let's see how this ends."

" 'I finish my snack and climb under the covers. It is bitter cold and I pull the goose-down comforter up, all the way to my nose. My dreams are uneasy, but somehow, I manage to sleep right through the pounding on the door.

"I look dazed when they question me. Of course I can ski, but not very well. I'm trying to learn, but I don't have much time to practice. I'm an exchange student and my class work is very demanding. As a matter of fact, I have a test in calculus this morning. Could they possibly give me a ride to the university? The professor won't accept any excuses for being late, especially from an American.' "

Hank paged through the notebook, scanning the other sections, and then he sighed deeply. "That's it. She doesn't write any more about that. It's almost as if she was interrupted, and never got a chance to finish it."

"But there's more . . . isn't there?"

"Sure. But each one is like a slice of life. They're little self-contained scenes that might make up a unified whole if she'd written them all. And I get the impression that the whole would be much more than these scenes indicate."

Jan nodded. "Like a *Gestalt?*"

"Exactly! I'd really like to do this as my student film. It'd be a great project!"

"I can see it all now . . ." Jan looked just as excited as he did. "Produced and directed by Hank Jensen! Starring . . . who?"

"Jan Bennett, of course. With a cast of total unknowns pulled from one of my Cal Arts film classes. You'll work on it with me, won't you?"

"I'd love to!" Jan began to smile. But then she looked down at the notebook, and her smile faded away. "You can't use this, Hank. We don't know who wrote it. You'd have to find out and get the writer's permission."

Hank sighed, and then he nodded. "You're right. And there's no way we can do that."

"Let's read the rest." Jan picked up the notebook and opened it to the next section. "There might be a name we could trace, or a location where we could go to ask questions."

Just then the patio door opened and Maura stood in the open doorway, silhouetted by the light from the kitchen. "Jan? Are you out here?"

"I'm here, Mom." Jan grabbed the notebook and stuffed it in her bag. "Hank and I were just talking about his student film project."

"That's fine, honey. Hello, Hank."

"Hi, Mrs. Thomas." Hank turned toward the patio and waved.

"Is Cappy out there with you?"

"Hank's got him." Jan glanced at the puppy that had

cuddled up in Hank's lap and gone to sleep. "Did you have a good time at dinner?"

"Yes. It was fine. Will you make sure you lock up when you come inside? And put Cappy in his bed with his clock and his hot water bottle?"

"Of course. We'll probably be up late, so I'll say goodnight now. See you in the morning, Mom."

"Goodnight, honey. I love you."

The patio door slid closed again, and as they watched, the kitchen light flicked off. Then there was only silence and the chirping of crickets.

A long moment passed and then Hank turned to Jan. "Am I wrong, or did your mother seem upset?"

"You're not wrong. She's always upset when Keith's home."

Hank digested that remark in silence, and then he cleared his throat. "Look . . . I know it's none of my business, but I like you. And I get the feeling you don't exactly approve of your stepfather."

"He's not my stepfather. He's just my mother's husband."

"Jan . . ." Hank reached out to take her hand. "I hate to disillusion you, but any man who marries your mother is your stepfather."

"Maybe, but I don't think of him that way. And he doesn't think of me as a daughter. We're strangers who happen to love the same person . . . if he *does* love my mother, that is."

"Is there a reason why you think he doesn't?"

Jan sighed, and then she shook her head. "Nothing I can put my finger on. He's nice to her, but he doesn't really act like a husband. And she's polite to him, but she doesn't really act like a wife."

"What do you think husbands and wives are supposed to act like?"

"There's supposed to be some sort of bond there, some kind of understanding that doesn't need words. My Uncle Steve and my Aunt Donna were like that. They knew each other so well that he'd start a sentence, and she'd finish it. I remember one time, when I was just a kid . . ." Jan began to smile at the memory. "I really believed that they could read each other's minds."

"Tell me about it."

Jan's smile grew wider, and she nodded. "I must have been about eight, because I remember that I was in third grade. And it was a month or so before Christmas. Mom was working late at the boutique, and I'd gone over to Uncle Steve's and Aunt Donna's for dinner. It was dark when they got ready to take me home, and we all got into the car. Uncle Steve was just pulling out of the driveway, when he turned to Aunt Donna and asked, 'Should we . . . ?' And before he could finish his question, she said, 'Oh, yes. Definitely.' And then Uncle Steve asked, 'But do you think . . . ?' And she cut in again, and said, 'I know they have. I saw them this morning.' "

"Wait a minute . . ." Hank started to laugh. "Did you ask them what they meant?"

"Yes. Aunt Donna said, 'He asked me if we should take you past the big Christmas tree the Petersons put up every year in their yard. And I said we should. And then he asked me if I thought they'd decorated it yet. And I told him that I'd seen them working on it this morning.' "

Hank laughed. "They didn't realize they'd finished each other's sentences?"

"No. It was absolutely amazing. They were always on the same wavelength. And you could see how much they loved each other, every time you were in the same room with them. He was always touching her hair or her shoulder when he walked past her chair, and she'd always smile at him in a special way. I guess that's why I grew up thinking that people got married because they were so love, they wanted to spend their whole lives together."

"That's beautiful, Jan. And that's the way it would be in a perfect world. But I think you're being just a little unrealistic. People get married for all sorts of reasons."

"Maybe." Jan shrugged. "But that's the way it'll be for me. And a couple of years ago, when I asked Mom, she said that was exactly the way she felt about my dad."

"But you don't think she feels that way about Keith?"

"I know she doesn't." Jan shook her head. "It's none of my business. I know that. And Keith's never done anything bad to her, or to me. But the whole thing is driving me crazy!"

Hank reached out and took her hand. "Why, Jan?"

"Because I'm studying to be a psychologist. And I'm a pretty good judge of people and their motivations. And I just can't figure out why the hell she married him!"

Chapter Nineteen

Maura took a deep breath for courage as she shut the patio door and turned back toward the living room. She'd much rather join Jan and Hank, but her husband was waiting. She just wished she knew what he'd expect, this first night they were together at home.

Keith smiled at her as she came back into the living room, and Maura smiled back. Then he patted a spot next to him on the couch, and she walked over to sit down. There must be something they could talk about to break the ice. It was even more difficult, now that they were alone, than it had been over dinner with Steve.

"It's good to be home." Keith draped a friendly arm around her shoulder. "What have you been doing since I've been gone?"

"Oh . . . the usual. I played tennis with Jan, and I went to work at the boutique . . . things like that."

"Have you designed any new clothes?"

"No. I tried to do a tennis outfit, but I couldn't get the sleeves right. I really hope I haven't lost my touch."

Keith gave her a little hug. "Don't worry, honey. It'll all come back. It's like Steve says . . . you just have to be patient.

Are you going ahead with the fashion show, or did you decide to cancel?"

"The fashion show?" Maura turned to look at him in alarm. *"What* fashion show?"

"You always have one at the end of the summer, to introduce your new fall line. Your regular customers expect it, but we could figure out some way to get out of it if you really don't want to do the show."

"No. I'll do it." Maura nodded quickly. "Do you know if I've started designing the clothes?"

"Everything's done except the highlight. I ran into Liz a couple of weeks ago and she told me."

"The highlight?" Maura was puzzled. "What's that?"

"It's the special outfit you present at the very end of the show, your grand finale." Keith sighed, and turned to her. "Poor baby! You really *have* forgotten, haven't you? It must be hell!"

"It is. Or maybe it's heaven." Maura eye's narrowed as she remembered what she'd learned about Liz. "There might be some things in my life I'd be better off forgetting."

Keith looked shocked for just a moment, and then he smiled and nodded. "That could be true for anyone, I guess. I know I'd rather forget that last speeding ticket I got. Or the miserable food we had on the plane."

"We?" Maura raised her eyebrows. "I thought you came back from New York alone."

"I did. But there were other passengers on the plane. They served something they called, *filet de boeuf en croute* in first class, but that was a joke. The beef was overdone, they used a liver paste instead of truffles, and it certainly wasn't wrapped in brioche dough. It tasted exactly like those pre-packaged crescent rolls that come in tubes at the grocery store."

Maura nodded and tried to look as if she remembered what *filet de boeuf en croute* was. "Did they serve champagne?"

"You'd have to stretch to call it that. It was domestic and it couldn't have cost them over two dollars a bottle. And speaking of champagne . . . would you like a glass? After all, this is an occasion."

"Oh. Yes, of course it is." Maura put a smile back on her face. "Do I like champagne?"

Keith chuckled. "You love it, especially if it's Dom."

"Dom?"

"Dom Perignon. It's your favorite. Unfortunately, we don't have it on hand. I should have thought to pick up a bottle."

"That's all right." Maura smiled at him. He looked very apologetic.

"We do have a very nice domestic Korbel. Why don't you go up and get ready for bed, and we can have it in your room."

"Yes. Of course." The smile was still on Maura's face, but it felt as if it was frozen there. "That's very thoughtful of you, Keith."

"I have an ulterior motive. I just want you to relax, honey. You're sitting here on the edge of the couch, and you're acting as if I'm about to chew you up and spit you out in little pieces."

"I . . . I'm sorry." Maura got to her feet. "I'll go upstairs then. And I'll see you . . . later."

All the way up the stairs, Maura chided herself. She wasn't a blushing bride. She was a married woman and she shouldn't be embarrassed when her husband told her he was coming to her room. But why *did* she have her own room? She'd decided it wasn't appropriate to ask Jan, and she hadn't worked up the nerve to ask Nita. Could she gather the courage to ask Keith, the husband who was still a stranger to her?

It took longer to get ready for bed than usual, perhaps because her hands were shaking and she kept dropping things on the rug. She'd never felt so unsure of herself, or so incapable of making decisions. Would Keith like the pink negligee, or the white? Or would he expect her to wear nothing at all? Should she dab on a bit more Opium, or would he prefer that she wore no perfume to bed? What would it be like, making love with her husband? It was a totally new experience for her. She had no memory past her sophomore year in college and she'd been a shy virgin back then, afraid to indulge in the wild romantic weekends her classmates had experienced.

At last she was ready, and she slipped a pretty, forest green caftan over her thin silk negligee. And then she went to turn down the bed. But would turning down the bed be too obvious? Perhaps she should wait and let him take the initiative. She was hesitating, trying to make a decision, when she heard a soft tap on her door.

"Come in." Maura tried to sound relaxed and confident, but her voice quavered a bit.

"I can't. Open the door, honey. My hands are full."

Maura rushed to the door and opened it. And then she gasped as she saw what was on the tray he was carrying. There was a bottle of champagne in an ice bucket, two fluted glasses, a basket holding something wrapped in a white linen napkin, and three crystal bowls. One was filled with something that looked like tapioca except that it was black in color, another had grated, hard boiled eggs, and the third held chopped onions.

"I brought us a snack." Keith grinned at her as he walked over and set the tray on the bed table. "When you asked me if you liked champagne, I got to thinking that you probably wouldn't remember caviar, either. So I thought I'd see if you like it."

Maura looked down at the one bowl she couldn't identify. The black tapioca must be caviar. "Did I like caviar in the past?"

"Yes, although this isn't Beluga caviar." Keith looked apologetic. "Beluga's your favorite, but it's very expensive, and we don't usually have it on hand unless we're planning to entertain."

Maura started to laugh. "Maybe it's a good thing I lost my memory. I won't know the difference between Dom Perignon and Korbel. And I won't remember the taste of Beluga caviar. That makes me a cheap date."

Keith looked perplexed for a moment, and then he started to laugh, too. "You're kidding, right?"

"I am." Maura grinned at him, and then she gestured toward the caviar. "How do you eat this anyway?"

"I'll show you, right after I open the champagne."

Maura watched as Keith took the bottle from the ice bucket and opened it deftly. When the cork slid smoothly out of the neck of the bottle with a barely audible pop, she frowned slightly. "This champagne must be different than the bottles I've seen in the movies."

"Why is that?" Keith started to pour.

"Well . . . I thought the cork was supposed to explode. And I expected the champagne to foam up and spill down the sides of the bottle."

"No, honey." Keith grinned as he handed her a glass. "They only do that for effect. That's why you have to be careful not to shake the bottle. If the champagne foamed up, you'd lose a lot."

Maura nodded and looked a little wistful. "I envy you,

Keith. You really seem to know what you're doing. I wonder if I'll ever be able to learn everything, all over again."

"Of course you will. It's just going to take a little while, that's all." Keith raised his glass and smiled at her. "To you, Maura. You're a remarkable woman. Now taste your champagne and tell me what you think."

Maura raised the glass to her lips and took a sip. Then she took another, and smiled. "It's not as sweet as I expected, but I like it."

"Are you ready for the caviar?"

"I'm ready."

Keith was grinning as he folded back the linen napkin and took out what looked like a piece of toast with the crusts cut off. "These are toast tips. Do you remember them?"

"Not really. But I can see what they are. What do you do with them?"

"First you spread one with caviar." Keith picked up the small silver spoon and scooped out some caviar. He spread it on the toast tip and motioned to the other two bowls. "Egg or onion? Or both?"

"Both." Maura nodded. "I like eggs and I like onions. I remember that."

"Sour cream?" Keith uncovered a small dish Maura hadn't noticed before.

"I . . . I don't know. I don't remember if I like it."

"Then let's try the first one without." Keith handed her the triangle of toasted bread, and watched her expectantly as she took a bite. "Well? What do you think?"

Maura was smiling as she swallowed. "I think I have expensive tastes. I love it, Keith! Can I try a little sour cream now?"

"Of course you can." Keith handed her the spoon. "Just put a little dollop on the top. I think you're going to like it,

Maura. You used to want your caviar with everything on it."

Maura did exactly as he instructed, and tasted it eagerly. Then she nodded. "It's delicious, and it's even better with the sour cream."

"Let's sit over here, where we can relax." Keith carried the tray over to the bed table, and sat down on the bed. "Come on, Maura . . . bring your champagne glass and get comfortable. I'll fix you another toast tip."

"But . . . aren't you going to have any?"

"I will. But I'll wait a bit. Right now, I'm having too much fun watching you."

Maura took the second toast tip he prepared for her, and smiled at him. "This makes me curious. I wonder what other marvelous things I've forgotten."

"I don't know, but we'll discover them." Keith poured more champagne in her glass. "I'll ask and you'll tell me if you remember them. And if you don't, we'll try them together."

"Give me an example." Maura popped the toast tip into her mouth and chewed.

"How about chocolate souffle?"

"Chocolate souffle . . ." Maura looked thoughtful. "I don't remember that, but I know I'll like it. Jan brought me a box of See's chocolates when I was in the hospital and they were delicious."

Keith took a sip of champagne and smiled at her. "How about lox and bagels? You used to love them."

"Lox . . ." Maura began to smile. "Is that the same as *gravlax?*"

"I don't know. I've never had *gravlax*. It's Scandinavian, isn't it?"

Maura nodded. "It's salmon marinated in dill, and they usually serve it with a mustard sauce as an appetizer. If it's eaten as a main course, they garnish it with lemon wedges and serve it with toast and a cucumber salad."

"How do you know that?"

"I . . . I'm not sure." Maura shook her head. "But I can remember eating it. And I'm sure I watched when it was prepared. I just don't remember where that was."

"Maybe you had a Scandinavian friend in high school or college."

"That's possible." Maura nodded. "I think I remember opening a refrigerator and basting the *gravlax* with the marinade. It must have been a friend's house, because my parents weren't fond of fish."

"Do you remember any other foods?"

Maura paused for a moment, and then she nodded. "Yes, but not at my parents' house. My father was strictly a meat and potatoes man. He called vegetables 'rabbit food,' and my mother used to have to sneak them in by mashing them up with the potatoes. We never had anything the least bit unusual. But I do remember going somewhere else to eat smoked bacon with onions and apple rings. And sour cream waffles. And little brown cakes with brown sugar and cardamom. And the very best thing I ever tasted was herring salad with apples!"

"You definitely had a Scandinavian friend." Keith smiled at her. "What else do you remember?"

"Thin sugar cookies that were rolled into cones when they came out of the oven and stuck in a water glass to harden. They were filled with sweetened whipped cream and berries and served for dessert."

"That sounds wonderful." Keith nodded. "What else?"

Maura thought for a moment and then she laughed. "*Lutefisk.* But I won't tell you about that right now. It'll make you lose your appetite."

"Do you remember the dessert board at the Beaumont Hotel? It ran the length of the dining room."

"No." Maura shook her head. "I don't remember that."

"How about the short little waiter with the strange voice? You called him Mr. Foghorn."

Maura shook her head, again, and Keith looked very disappointed. "You don't remember Paris at all?"

"Paris? No . . . I really don't remember a thing about it. Is it important?"

"It seemed so at the time." Keith shrugged and tried to make light of it, but Maura could tell his feelings were hurt.

"Tell me about it. Maybe I'll remember."

"Well . . . we got there in the morning and we did some sightseeing. The Eiffel Tower, things like that. And then we had a fabulous dinner in the hotel dining room where we sampled the dessert board. Mr. Foghorn was our waiter. And when we finished dinner, we went up to our suite."

"Our suite?" Maura raised her eyebrows. "That sounds expensive."

"It was, but it was worth it. The honeymoon suite at the Beaumont Hotel has the best view of the city."

"The honeymoon suite?" Maura began to blush. "I'm sorry, Keith. I didn't realize we went to Paris on our honeymoon."

Keith nodded. "I figured you wouldn't remember. I guess I was just hoping, that's all."

"Try not to feel bad, Keith." Maura reached out and touched his arm. "I really wish I could remember, but everything's a blank from the day I finished my finals in my sophomore year in college to the morning I woke up in the hospital. It's not just our honeymoon. It's everything. You do understand that, don't you?"

"I understand." Keith managed a smile. "It's just a blow

to my ego, that's all. No man likes to think that his wife has forgotten their honeymoon."

Maura nodded. "I can understand that. But it's not like I forgot. It's more like it never happened. You saw my reaction when I tasted the caviar. I knew I'd eaten it before, but I was experiencing it all over again, for the very first time."

"That's true." Keith reached out to pull her closer. "Thanks, honey. It makes me feel a lot better to know that you want to experience our honeymoon all over again."

Maura thought about trying to explain. That wasn't what she'd meant at all! But then Keith was taking her into his arms, and silencing any protest she might have made with his kiss.

Chapter Twenty

Maura's mind floated free as Keith kissed her. It was a pleasurable kiss, a nice kiss, but there was nothing breathless or exciting about it. The phrase "familiar strangers" popped into her mind. Jan had explained it, several days ago. Familiar strangers were the people you saw every day, usually in a certain spot or at a certain time. A familiar stranger was the man who filled your car with gas at your favorite service station. You saw him every time you drove up to the pumps, but you might not even know his name, or recognize him if he was out of uniform. Another familiar stranger could be the person who delivered your groceries, or parked your car, or rode on the same bus with you every morning. Taken out of context, you might not recognize these people because you expected to see them in a certain place, doing a specific thing. Keith was a familiar stranger to her. She'd adjusted to sitting next to him in a restaurant, and having him in the house. But his presence in her bedroom, and his role as her lover, was completely out of context.

"Maura?" Keith pulled back to look at her and there was sadness in his eyes. Even though she'd tried not to let him know, he must have sensed that she was permitting, rather than enjoying, his kiss. "Do you want me to go?"

Maura shook her head quickly. She didn't want to hurt his feelings. "No. Of course not. I'm just a little nervous, that's all."

"I understand." Keith put his arms around her again. "Don't worry. We'll take it slow. And anytime you want me to stop, I will."

Maura nodded. Her mind was in turmoil. What was the matter with her? The desire she must have felt for Keith in the past had disappeared along with her memory.

And then he was kissing her again, and she did her best to respond. She'd seen enough romantic movies, and she knew what to do. But it was all a pretense. She was playing the part of a woman in love without feeling any of the emotions. She was hoping that if she played her part convincingly enough, it might become real.

And now he was turning down the covers, pushing her down on the bed, and arranging a pillow under her head. He was kind and sweet, and she really should appreciate the time he was taking to set her at ease.

"Is this better?" Keith propped himself up on one elbow to look at her.

"Yes. Perfect." Maura did her best to sound breathless and eager as she held out her arms. "Kiss me again, Keith."

He did, and Maura trembled in his arms. It wasn't a response to his kiss. It was simply a reaction to the lie she was living. But Keith must have thought it was a shiver of delight, because he pulled back to smile at her.

"That's better. Now you're just like the Maura I love. I knew you'd remember how good we were together. You do remember, don't you?"

"Yes. I do." Maura nodded, and did her best to smile. She

didn't want to shatter his illusions. "Could we turn out the light?"

"That's what you always say. And that's why I call you my shy little bride." Keith chuckled and reached out to flick off the light. "Is that better, darling?"

"Yes. It's much better." Maura sighed deeply. It was much easier to pretend in the dark. Now he couldn't see how she winced when he slipped off her robe and nightgown. And he couldn't notice her expression of dismay when she heard him take off his clothes.

"It's going to be wonderful, honey. You'll see."

His voice was low and intimate as he climbed back into bed with her, and she shivered again. He seemed to interpret that as a compliment to his skill as a lover, because he gave a chuckle, deep in his throat, and reached out to run his fingers over her body.

She shivered again, more violently this time. And her nipples began to harden under his fingers. She didn't feel any passion in her mind, but her body was responding to his touch.

"I think you're going to like this." His lips slid across her body, nibbling and licking at her sensitive flesh. "And I'm sure you'll remember all the times we did this before. It's just too good to forget."

But she didn't remember. And although the sensations he created were very pleasant, her mind was not involved. She had no feelings of warmth or love. It was quite the opposite. What she really wanted was for him to stop. He seemed to sense her uninvolvment then, and he leaned over to whisper in her ear.

"Come on, honey. Show me how much you love me."

Her mind spun in crazy circles. What did that mean? She *didn't* love him. She was sure of that now. But she must have loved him in the past. It wasn't fair of her punish him for her memory loss. She had to respond to his urgent need. But how?

Then something occurred to her, a phrase she'd heard from a song. *If you can't be with the one you love, love the one you're with.* Jan had tuned her radio to an oldies station on the way to the boutique, and they'd been playing Crosby, Stills and Nash.

Maura reached up and put her hand on the back of Keith's neck. That seemed to please him, because he gave a little groan and began to breathe faster.

What next? Maura tried to think of something else to do, but nothing occurred to her. She wouldn't have to think if she truly loved Keith. Then everything would happen naturally. Perhaps she should think of someone else, someone she'd really loved. It wasn't right, but all she really cared about was sparing Keith's feelings.

But who could she think of? Maura's mind spun in crazy circles. Nick. The handsome man from her dreams. But thinking of Nick wouldn't do any good. She'd imagined making love with him in the goat-herders shack, but she hadn't dreamed any of the details.

Maura moved her fingers slightly, and Keith groaned again. He seemed very grateful for any loving response she made, and she simply had to convince him that things hadn't changed between them. After all, it wasn't his fault she couldn't remember how much she'd loved him.

Who else had she loved? Maura knew she must have loved her first husband, but she had no memory of him at all, and the details of their sex life were a complete mystery. It wouldn't do any good to pretend she was with Paul Bennett when she didn't even know what he'd looked like. It had to be someone else, someone she knew right now. And the only other man she knew and liked was Steve.

Although she really didn't want to think of Steve, she saw his image as she stared up into the darkness. And although she knew it wasn't right to think of him this way, her cheeks turned warm and a soft sigh of passion escaped her lips. It was Steve's face she saw as she reached up with both arms and wound them around Keith's neck.

Keith groaned again, a little louder this time. His voice was shaking with desire as he whispered in her ear. "I knew you'd remember, darling. I can tell by the way you're touching me."

For a moment Maura was confused. Touching him? How? And then she realized that she was caressing his neck with her left hand and running her fingers through his hair with her right.

"I love you, honey."

His voice was low and intimate. But it wasn't Keith saying the words that evoked a rush of pleasurable sensations that flowed through her body. It was Steve. And Maura felt a flood of desire so intense it made her tremble and a delicious weakness stole over her.

"Make love to me, darling." Maura sighed and reached out to caress his shoulders. And then his back. And every part of his body she could reach, with a trembling eagerness that was completely new to her.

He moved over her then, straddling her body, and drove into her with a glad cry of passion. And Maura let her mind float free as she sighed and whimpered in pleasure. Steve was making love to her, and it was wonderful. The sensations she felt were new and familiar, both at the same time, and comforting as well as frightening in their intensity. Her body seemed to act of its own accord, welcoming him into her quivering depths. Their bodies moved as one, searching for that ultimate release.

And then there was a blinding rush of sensation that left her breathless, crying out for more. And more. And more. And then a sense of marvelous completion that drove every thought from her mind.

When she was capable of thought again, it was impossible to tell how much time had passed. She sighed and stretched, feeling more alive than she had at any time since her accident. She turned to him, to tell him how marvelous it had been. And in the dim light from the street light outside, she saw his smiling face.

Maura drew in her breath sharply, and began to tremble again. But this time it wasn't from pleasure. The man who was holding her in his arms wasn't the man she'd expected to see.

"What's the matter, darling?" Keith reached out to pull her closer. And then he chuckled, thinking he understood her reaction. "There's nothing to be embarrassed about. You were wonderful. It was the best ever!"

Maura nodded and let him hold her. What else could she do? He was her husband and she could never let him know that every sigh, and moan, and rush of intense desire had been for Steve, not for him.

"Have you learned anything?"

The voice had the hard edge he'd come to expect, and he scowled down at the receiver. "Not yet, but it's early. I'll let you know when I do."

"We don't have forever. We want results, and we want them fast."

He was reminded of a phrase he'd heard once, "people in

hell want ice water," but he managed to keep himself from blurting out the words. That wouldn't be wise when they held most of the cards.

"Did you hear me? I said we want results!"

He gripped the receiver tightly, fighting for control. "It's all up to you. If you want her taken out, I'll do it now. But if you're after information, you'll give me some time. Just let me know."

There was a long silence, and he tapped his foot nervously on the carpet. Had he blown it with his boldness? But then the voice laughed, a humorless chuckle. "Okay. We'll play it your way. I'll call you again tomorrow."

He sighed as he broke the connection and placed the receiver back in its cradle. They were putting on the pressure, and so far there'd been no results.

He walked over to the counter to retrieve the drink he'd fixed himself earlier, but the ice had melted and he poured it down the drain. He mixed a fresh one and carried it over to the coffee table where a bulky scrapbook lay open to the page he'd been reading. Mounted in the center was an old newspaper article with the heading, LOCAL STUDENT WINS FOREIGN SCHOLARSHIP.

He took a sip of his drink and stared down at the picture that took up a full two columns. She was about Jan's age, and their similarity was striking. He gazed at the picture for a moment or two, and then he began reading the article.

The winner of the prestigious Humanatis Scholarship was announced today, and Miss Maura Rawlins, a senior at San Diego State College, was awarded top honors. The Humanatis Scholarship is given to a promising young man or woman who wishes to pursue further study at a foreign university or college. The applicant must pass a proficiency test in four foreign languages, and be in the top five percent of his or her class. Miss Rawlins was nominated by professors from three different departments: mathematics, science, and foreign languages. She has been accepted at the University of Helsinki in Finland and she will fly overseas at the end of August to enroll for the fall semester.

There was a knock on the door and he shut the scrapbook, shoving it out of sight under the couch. "Hold on. I'm coming."

"I hope not." The voice carried through the thin, wooden door, along with an accompanying giggle. "If you come now, you don't need me. I might as well turn around and leave."

He was laughing as he opened the door. Whores usually didn't have a sense of humor.

"Hi, baby!"

He smiled as he noticed her appearance. She was wearing a plaid jumper with a white blouse, and her hair was in a ponytail. It was a perfect outfit. It reminded him of the girls' school uniforms they'd worn in his old home town.

She grinned at him and whirled around, making the skirt flare out. Then she chomped on her gum and blew a bubble that snapped neatly. "How do I look, baby?"

"Perfect. Where did you get it?"

"From my school. It's a real drag, but we have to wear them. You get detention if you don't."

He grinned and nodded. She was perfect. "You're good, you know that?"

"Of course I'm good. That's why your mommy pays me to baby-sit. I know exactly what to do with a horny little boy like you."

He began to grin. She'd been in character since the moment she'd stepped in the door. She was really marvelous.

"It's late and it's past your bedtime." She frowned at him. "Let's go, baby. You need your bath and then we'll put your jammies on."

She tossed her purse in the chair, and grabbed him by the hand. "I said, come on! You have to behave yourself tonight, baby. And don't you dare get that thing up again, after all the trouble we had the last time!"

He nodded, and followed behind her as she tugged him into the bedroom. He was almost into the fantasy. Almost, but not quite. He had time for one last clear thought before the excitement carried him away. Too bad he'd have to kill her soon. She was the best he'd ever had.

Chapter Twenty-One

She was watching a parade of some sort. There were tall men in fur hats with flaps over their ears, marching in a straggling formation while children cheered and waved flags. It wasn't a military parade. It was a celebration. And then they were all in a clearing next to a wooden enclosure. Nick took her hand and pulled her through the boisterous crowd so they could see.

The animals had antlers and she asked if they were deer. Nick laughed and hugged her. He wouldn't really expect a California girl to know, but didn't she remember *The Night Before Christmas*? Reindeer? She was astounded. She'd never seen a reindeer except in pictures, and these animals were much bigger than the ones that pulled Santa's sleigh. But why were they here? And what did reindeer have to do with the celebration?

This was something the Laps did every year, Nick told her. It was time for the reindeer races, and today was like a holiday. The men in the parade were competitors. They would harness the reindeer to a sleigh, and ride on it to the finish line.

She stared at the herd of reindeer. Several big males were

pawing at the frozen ground, and they had wickedly pointed antlers. Was this dangerous?

Not really, Nick laughed. The Laps had domesticated these reindeer. It would be a lot like harnessing milk cows to a wagon. The only trick was to drive them to the finish line without falling off. They had a few minutes to wait until the races started. Would she like a hot drink?

Maura nodded. Even though she was wearing a full-length parka, and warm boots on her feet, she was chilled. It was winter, and although the weak winter sun did its best to warm the frozen ground, the air was frigid and little clouds of puffy white steam escaped from their lips when they spoke.

A young couple was standing next to them, and Maura noticed the girl's coat. It seemed to be handmade, with brightly colored strips of cloth sewn together like a patch-work quilt. She smiled at Maura and Maura smiled back. And then she spoke to the girl in her native language, to ask about her lovely coat.

The girl seemed proud as she told her that her mother had sewn the coat by hand. She'd taken an existing parka that was so badly worn it was almost falling apart, and she'd patched it with strips of material that she'd saved from other clothes. The girl smiled as she told Maura that it was the only coat like it in the whole village, and all the other girls envied it.

While she was talking to the girl, Nick motioned to a nearby child and gave him some coins. The boy raced off and came back in a few moments with two steaming cups. He tried to give back the change, but Nick shook his head, and the boy ran off with a happy smile on his face.

Maura stared down at the reddish-colored liquid, and took a tentative sip. It was delicious and it was filled with a combination of spices, some of which she could identify. There were cardamom, clove and ginger, with a whole stick of cinnamon. The liquid was sweet and strong and it had the taste of berries and citrus. She took another sip, larger this time, and smiled.

Nick asked if she liked it, and she nodded quickly. It was wonderful! What was it called? Reindeer blood, he told her. And she came very close to dropping the cup on the snow in shock. Reindeer blood?!

Nick laughed and reassured her. It wasn't really reindeer blood. It was a glogg made of crushed berries, liquor and spices, and it was similar to mulled wine. And then he leaned down to kiss her on the tip of her nose. The kiss was wet. Very wet. It felt as if he were licking her nose. Over and over, until she opened her eyes and . . .

"Cappy!" Maura laughed and reached out for the little puppy. "How did you get in here?"

And then she noticed that her door was open. Keith must have failed to close it all the way when he'd left her room.

"I guess I'd better walk you." Maura got up and blushed as she realized she hadn't bothered to put on her nightgown after Keith had gone. She slipped into a sweat suit, pulled her hair back into a ponytail, and smiled at Cappy. "Wait just a minute. I have to write down my latest dream."

Maura reached out for the notebook she usually kept by her bedside, but it wasn't there. She remembered using it in her studio to write down her last dream, but she was sure she'd carried it down with her. She could remember hurrying down the stairs, in a rush to get dressed for Keith's arrival. But the phone had rung as she passed the table in the hallway, and she'd stopped to answer it. She must have set it down and left it there by the phone.

"Come on, Cappy. We'll pick it up on our way down."

Maura scooped him up and carried him out into the hall. But the notebook wasn't on the table where she'd left it. Perhaps Nita had picked it up. She'd have to remember to ask at breakfast.

Jan poked her head out the door as Maura passed by. "Good morning, Mom. I'm glad you're up. I need your advice about something."

"What is it?" Maura tried to hold Cappy still, but the little puppy was squirming frantically.

"What's wrong with Cappy?" Jan frowned slightly as she noticed how Cappy was struggling.

"I think he needs to go outside. Why don't you get dressed and join me? Bring out some coffee and we can talk on the patio."

The moment Maura got Cappy outside, he raced for the nearest bush. When he was through, he ran back to her side and sat down, staring up at her expectantly.

"Good boy, Cappy!" Maura reached down to scratch his ears. "You're catching on very fast. I think we'll have you housebroken in another day or two."

A butterfly fluttered past them, and Cappy ran off to chase it. Maura sat down on a patio chair, and gave a deep sigh. She had so much to do and so little time to do it. Somehow, she had to come up with the perfect design for the highlight of her fashion show, and she had absolutely no idea what it should be, or even how she should start.

As she sat there in the early morning sun, Maura thought about her latest dream. She remembered the coat the girl had been wearing, and she began to smile. The girl's coat had been a parka, but the one she designed would be much lighter. It would be a cotton coat, cut along the lines of the dusters that the early automobile drivers had worn, and it would be a random patchwork design. Each coat would have the same pattern, but the material would be randomly selected so that no two would be exactly the same.

"You look happy this morning." Jan came out, carrying a tray with two coffee cups and an insulated carafe. "I suppose that's because Keith's home."

Maura reacted to the disapproving tone in Jan's voice. This was a perfect time for Jan to get her feelings about Keith out in the open. "Isn't it normal for a wife to be happy when her husband comes home?"

"I guess so." Jan's cheeks began to color, and Maura could tell she wished she hadn't brought up the subject of Keith.

"I think we should talk about Keith." Maura took the cup of coffee that Jan had poured for her and set it down on the glass table top. "I know you don't like him. And I think you should tell me why."

"Because I think he's cheating on you! And I don't want you to be hurt!" Jan couldn't meet Maura's eyes, and she looked down at the table instead.

Maura nodded. "Okay. Fair enough. What makes you think he's cheating on me?"

"I told you." Jan sighed deeply. "We've been over it all before."

"You're forgetting, Jan . . . there isn't any *before*. I don't remember anything that happened before the accident."

"Oh, God!" Jan's face turned pale and she looked stricken. "I forgot that you wouldn't remember. I just thought that you were ignoring everything I told you."

"I can't ignore something I don't remember. You'd better tell me again, honey. You may be right and if you are, I want to know about it."

Maura reached out to take Jan's hand, and Jan gave her a shaky smile. "Okay. But you got so upset the last time I told you. I don't want that to happen again."

"It won't. Now spill it. I need to know everything."

"It happened about four months ago. You were gone on a business trip, and Uncle Steve invited me to lunch. I was sitting in a booth at Marie Callender's. That's the place we went on Monday, remember?"

Maura nodded. "I remember. Go on."

"Well . . . they have these high-backed booths so you can't see the people sitting next to you. And I was just waiting, with no one to talk to, so I listened to the conversation from the booth in back of mine."

"Okay." Maura nodded. "Tell me what you heard."

"I didn't recognize their voices, but it was a man and a woman. She was complaining about how they never had any time together, and he told her to be patient, that everything would be over very soon, and then he'd be free to be with her."

"A divorce?"

Jan nodded. "That's what I assumed. And then he told her that his wife was leaving on a business trip soon, and he promised to spend every night with her."

"I see." Maura began to frown.

Jan looked very upset and she took a deep breath. "Are you really sure you want to hear this?"

"I'm positive. Go on."

"That's when she kissed him, right there in the booth. I could see their shadows through that frosted glass at the top. And then she asked him how he was going to explain that to the kid."

Jan faltered, and Maura squeezed her hand. "What did he say?"

"He said the kid was no problem. He'd just tell her that he was going on another business trip. She'd never know the difference, and he didn't spend much time with her anyway. That was the housekeeper's job."

Maura nodded. "And you didn't know who they were?"

"Not then. But I remember thinking what a louse he was, that his wife probably trusted him and didn't have a clue that he was having an affair. I felt sorry for his wife, and sorry for the daughter, too. And then the woman kissed him again and asked him if he had to go back to work right away. And he said no, he'd told his secretary that he had a long lunch meeting, and she didn't expect him back before three."

"That's when they left?"

Jan shook her head. "No. There's more. He said he wanted her to take the rest of the day off because he'd booked a suite at the Beverly Hills Hotel. She threw her arms around him and kissed him again. And she told him that she'd always wanted to stay there, but was he sure they could afford it?"

"It's expensive?" Maura frowned slightly.

"Very expensive. And he told her not to worry, that he wasn't picking up the tab. He said he'd charged it to his wife's credit card and her accountant never checked up on the receipts."

Maura sighed deeply. "That figures! What else?"

"Not much. The woman just laughed and said it would be that much better, knowing that the bitch had paid for the room. And then the waitress brought their bill and they left."

"And that's when you saw them?"

Jan nodded. "They passed right by my booth, but they didn't see me. They were too busy laughing, and hugging, and fawning all over each other to notice anyone else."

"Keith and Liz Webber?"

Jan looked shocked. "How did you know?"

"Sylvia told me she suspected they were having an affair. I managed to convince myself that it was just gossip, but now I know it was true."

"I'm sorry, Mom." Jan looked close to tears. "I really didn't want to upset you, but I had to tell you."

Maura nodded. "I'm glad you did. But you said you told me before. What was my reaction then?"

"You cried. And then you got mad at me for telling you. Keith was gone, and I thought you'd have it out with him when he came back. But he was still out of town when you left for the airport, and . . . that's when you had your accident. When Hank told us he saw you crying in Uncle Grant's car, I figured it was because of Keith's affair."

"Maybe that's the reason why I don't love him anymore." Maura didn't realize she'd spoken aloud until she saw Jan's face. Her daughter looked hopeful and upset at the same time.

"Are you sure you don't love him?"

"As sure as I can be." Maura shrugged slightly. "I know this may sound strange, but do you have any idea why I married Keith in the first place?"

Jan started to laugh, and then she clamped her hand over her mouth. "Sorry, Mom. I know it's not funny, but you don't know how many times I've asked myself that question in the past."

"And what did you decide?"

Jan shook her head. "I don't know. You never really confided in me before the accident."

"Well . . . that was a mistake." Maura sighed deeply. "How about Nita? Did I tell her?"

"No. I asked her, and she said you'd never discussed it.

You just told her that you were getting married to Keith, and you did."

"I didn't say I loved him?"

"Never." Jan shook her head. "I asked you once, and you said that was a private matter between you and Keith and it was rude to ask such a personal question."

Maura frowned. "It's sounds like I had a blind spot when it came to Keith. Was I always so secretive?"

"Not always. And only about certain things. Keith was one. And your business trips were another. I learned not to ask questions about where you'd been or what you'd done. For a long time I thought you had a lover that you met when you went out of town."

Maura looked thoughtful. "You could be right. Unfortunately, we'll never know unless my memory comes back."

"I can see it all now." Jan laughed. "Some incredibly handsome Frenchman will knock on our door. And when you answer it, he'll pull you into his arms, and tell you that he's managed to track you down at last."

Maura began to laugh, too. "And I'll call the police because I won't know him from Adam!"

It felt good to laugh, and every time they were about to stop, the image of the Frenchman sent them off into a new gale of laughter. Finally Maura managed to gain some control over her mirth. "Okay. Let's get serious. What do you think I should do about Keith?"

"You're asking me?" Jan's eyes widened.

"You know me better than anyone else. What would you do under circumstances like this?"

"I . . . I'm not sure." Jan began to frown. "I'd be dying to fire Liz and send Keith packing, but I think I'd wait until I had all the facts. I'd keep my eyes open until I knew exactly what was going on. Don't forget, I heard him say it would be over soon. And people who are anxious to get out of a marriage can turn nasty. He must be planning to file for divorce and take you for every cent you're worth."

"That's impossible." Maura shook her head. "I found a copy of our prenuptial agreement. If Keith divorces me, he gets only a small settlement."

"That was really smart, Mom. I'm glad you had that agreement drawn up. It means Keith couldn't gain anything by divorcing you. The only way he could get any money is to . . ." Jan stopped suddenly, and her face turned pale.

"Jan? What is it?" Maura stared at her daughter.

"I just remembered what Hank told us about the accident. He said the brakes went out all of a sudden. But David talked to his uncle's mechanic, and he said that Grant had the Mercedes in for servicing just a couple of days before the accident. They checked everything out, and the car was in perfect running order."

"No, Jan." Maura shook her head. "I know what you're thinking, but there's no way that Keith could have had anything to do with Grant's brakes. He was out of town at the time."

"But he could have asked someone else to do it. Maybe you don't remember, but you can hire people to do horrible things like that. And Keith had a motive. If he wanted to be with Liz, he had to get you out of the picture."

"Believe me, honey . . . that didn't happen." Maura reached out to take her hand. "I read over my will. When I die, Keith inherits half of the profits I made after our marriage, and that's not a lot. Most of the money was poured back into the boutique and his gem business. Any assets I had before our marriage are set up in a trust fund for you."

"Does Keith know that?"

"Absolutely. A copy of the will was stapled to the prenuptial agreement he signed. Keith had to initial that he'd read it."

Jan didn't look convinced. "All the same, I think you should watch your back. Desperate people do desperate things, and they don't always think rationally."

"That's good advice, honey. I'll be careful." Maura nodded. And then she remembered that Jan had originally asked for advice from her. "You said you needed to ask me for advice. Was it about Keith?"

"No. It's about Hank and the movie he wants to make."

"He told me he was searching for a good plot. Did he find it?" Maura smiled at Jan's obvious excitement. It was clear that she really liked Hank.

"Actually, the plot found him." Jan began to grin. "I'm not exactly sure how it happened, but my notebook got switched with somebody else's. We had to look through it to find the name of the owner, and it's filled with these incredible stories!"

"And Keith's going to use them for his movie?"

"Not exactly." Jan gave a little sigh. "There weren't any names inside the notebook, so we don't know who owns it. That's why I wanted to ask for your advice. We have to get the author of the stories to sign a release, and we don't know how to find her."

"Her?"

Jan reached into her pocket and pulled out a notebook. She flipped it open and shoved it across the table to her mother. "I think it's got to be a woman, and so does Hank. Just read it, Mom. And tell me if you think we're right."

Maura's eyes widened as she stared down at the notebook. It was hers! She knew that Jan and Hank hadn't meant to pry into her personal life, but they had read all about her puzzling dreams!

Jan stared at her mother in amazement. Maura's face had gone white with shock. "Mom? What's wrong?"

"This notebook . . . it's mine."

"Yours?" Jan looked puzzled. "But, Mom . . . what were you writing? A book?"

"That's right." Maura seized the suggestion eagerly, and a little color began to come back to her face. She didn't like to lie to Jan, but it really couldn't be helped. If she admitted that the incidents in the notebook came from her dreams, Jan would think that they might be actual memories trying to surface. And then Jan would ask her all sorts of questions that she couldn't answer.

"I can't believe this!" Jan began to smile. "These stories are really good, Mom. They're romantic, and scary, and joyful, and tragic, all at the same time. That's just what Hank needs for his movie. You'll let him use them, won't you?"

"I . . . well . . . I don't know." Maura struggled for words. "I never even considered showing this notebook to anyone. I just had the urge to write, and I did."

"But it's wonderful! And Hank promised that I could play the female lead. Please, Mom . . . it's only a student film, and you don't have to have your name on it if you're embarrassed."

Maura's mind spun in crazy circles. If these were only dreams, no harm would be done if Hank turned them into a student film. And if they were actual memories, she might remember more if she saw them on the screen.

"You could help us write the screenplay, Mom." Jan reached out to take her hand. "Please say yes. It'll be fun."

"Well . . . all right." Maura gave in reluctantly.

"You're an angel, Mom!" Jan jumped up and ran around the table to her hug her mother. "I'm going to call Hank! He'll be so excited!"

As she watched her daughter run into the house, Maura felt a sense of foreboding. Would this be like Pandora's box? Once her dreams were turned into a movie, would they fly out of hiding to cause all sorts of grief for the ones she loved?

Chapter Twenty-Two

Jan was frowning slightly as she walked off the court. Playing tennis with David was a real challenge. They were evenly matched, and he was fiercely competitive. She'd seen how he had reacted when she'd won the first game. David didn't like to lose. So she'd deliberately made a couple of bonehead mistakes in the second game and he had won. That seemed to make him happy, but Jan didn't like to lose just to save his ego. They had two entirely different viewpoints. David thought of tennis as a battle between two opposing forces, while she felt that it was only a game. David's objective was to win, and hers was to play a good game and have fun.

"That last game was great!" David smiled at her as he picked up his sports bag to make room for the next couple who'd reserved the court. "I was a little off in the first game, but next time we play, you won't stand a chance."

"You're probably right." Jan forced a smile. She was glad he was happy, but she wished she hadn't felt obligated to let him win.

"Let's go dancing tonight. I found this great little club, and I made reservations."

Jan sighed and shook her head. "I can't, David. I'm working with Hank, tonight."

I don't understand why you had to get involved in this project with him." David looked very disgruntled. "You've been so busy working with him, I hardly ever get to see you."

"I know. I didn't realize it would take up this much time, but I can't back out now. I promised I'd help."

David nodded, but he still looked annoyed. "I guess I'd better call to cancel our reservations."

"I guess so." Jan decided it was time to lay down some ground rules. She wanted a good relationship with David and he had to know how she felt. "I'm sorry I can't go out with you, David, but you should have asked me earlier, before you made plans. If you had, I would have told them that I had a date. They could have gotten along without me tonight."

David looked surprised. "They? I didn't realize you were working with a group."

"It's not really a group . . . yet. It's just Hank, and Mom, and me. We're still in the early stages, but we'll be bringing in other people soon."

"You didn't tell me your mom was working on this project. I thought it was Hank's student film."

"It is, but Mom's helping us with the script." Jan began to smile. "She wrote these fabulous stories. And when Hank read them, he decided to use them for his film."

"That sounds interesting." David gave her an engaging grin. "I'm sorry about the reservations, Jan. I shouldn't have made them without asking you first. I guess I'm not really cut out for this dating stuff."

Jan laughed. "You're doing fine. And I'm sorry I can't go dancing. It really sounded like fun."

"Do you have time for coffee?" David glanced at his watch. "I'm free for the rest of the afternoon."

"Me, too." Jan nodded. "Mom's busy designing something for her fashion show, and Hank's not coming over until six."

"Great! Let's go change and I'll meet you in the restaurant. I want to hear all about this film Hank's doing. If he needs someone to research for historical accuracy, maybe I could help."

"That's a great idea!" Jan grinned at him. "Nita's making pot roast for dinner, and there's always enough for one more. Why don't you join us and we can talk about it then?"

As she walked toward the ladies' locker room, Jan tried to figure out how she felt. David seemed jealous of the time she was spending with Hank, and that was a good sign. It proved that he liked her a lot. But she'd known David less than two weeks, and it was much too soon to think of a commitment. She wanted to be free to date other men, primarily Hank. She liked him a lot, too.

It didn't take long to shower and change. Jan ran a brush through her hair, and checked her appearance in the mirror. Her cheeks were flushed and her eyes were sparkling. She hadn't really been interested in any of the college boys she'd met, but David and Hank were different. They seemed more mature, and she liked both of them. A lot.

As she picked up her sports bag, and left the locker room, Jan began to grin. She had two boyfriends now, and she wasn't sure which one she liked best. Perhaps it had been a mistake to invite them both for dinner, but the evening certainly wouldn't be dull!

* * *

Maura smiled as she glanced down at the drawings that were spread out on her worktable. She knew they were good. She'd shown them to Sylvia and the girls, and they had been full of praise for what they would call her Joseph's coat. The name had been Cherise's idea. The coat had reminded her of the multicolored coat that the biblical Joseph had worn. And since Liz had been out of town, Cherise had taken the drawings home with her and made up the pattern with pieces of material they'd hand-picked from existing bolts at their shop.

The first Joseph's coat was ready, and it hung on the dress dummy in the corner of Maura's office. Now all that remained was to see if it could be manufactured at a reasonable cost. And that meant Maura had to meet with Liz Webber.

Sylvia tapped softly on the open door, and stepped into Maura's small office. "Liz just returned my call. She'll be here at three-thirty."

"Thank you, Sylvia." Maura began to frown. She really didn't want to have anything to do with Liz, but she'd decided to follow Jan's advice. She wouldn't let Liz know that she knew about her affair with Keith until she was sure that she had all the facts.

"Do you want me to sit in on your meeting?" Sylvia looked concerned.

"I don't know. Do you usually sit in on the meetings I have with Liz?"

Sylvia shook her head. "No. You usually meet alone, just the two of you. I bring you coffee and shut the door. And you buzz me if there's anything you need."

"Then that's what I'll do this time. Thanks, Sylvia." Maura sighed as Sylvia left the room. She wasn't looking forward to her meeting with Liz, but it was necessary. She couldn't put a new item of clothing on the market without checking with her junior partner. Liz was her production manager, and she handled all the factory details. She was the only person who could tell her if the coat was practical.

Maura remembered what Sylvia had told her. The cost of manufacturing had to be small enough to allow for their profit margin. Liz would figure the cost, add on profit, and come up with the lowest price they could charge and still make money on the garment. They had to be careful that production wasn't too costly, or it would drive the price tag up too high for their clientele. Since Liz was the expert at setting prices and researching costs, they had to coordinate their efforts. There were only a few days left before the fashion show, and the Joseph's coat had to be ready for sale shortly after it was introduced.

Thinking of Liz brought a dull pounding to her temples, and Maura reached for her bottle of aspirin. She had forty-five minutes before Liz came in, and she needed to relax. She washed down the aspirin with a cup of water, and sat down behind her desk again. Then she closed her eyes and tried the trick that Steve had taught her, concentrating on something pleasant to make the headache go away . . .

She was in a field of long-stemmed green grass, sitting on a rough-hewn bench. Brightly colored flowers on long stalks were waving softly in the breeze. The day was warm, and the sun peeked through the tall branches of the trees, dappling the grass with bright spots of shifting gold.

It was very peaceful, and very quiet. The only sound was the far-away barking of the dogs as they played in their kennel. And then he was at the edge of the field, accompanied by two large dogs, one walking on either side of him.

The dogs saw her and their tails began to wag. The one on the left made a joyful whining noise, and looked up at

Nick, waiting for permission. Nick laughed and called out to her. "Shall I let them go?"

She nodded, and Nick gave a hand signal to the dogs. They both sat down obediently, staring up at him, waiting for his next move. He gave them another hand signal and they jumped up, bounding toward her.

"Hi, Natasha. Hi, Boris." She laughed and sat down on the grass so they could lick her face. The dogs were huge, but she wasn't afraid of them. "Have you been good today?"

Nick walked up and sat down beside her. "You did a good job with them. They passed with flying colors."

"I'm glad." She reached out and gave both dogs a hug. "When will you use them?"

"This weekend."

She hugged the dogs again, and frowned slightly. "Are you sure they're ready?"

"I'm sure. Don't worry, they'll be fine. Dogs like Boris and Natasha are common to the area, and no one pays attention to a dog running loose. It's a lot less dangerous for them than it is for us."

"I know, but . . ." She took a deep breath and let it out again. "It's not professional, but I really love them. They're like . . . family to me."

Nick nodded and slipped an arm around her shoulders. "They feel the same way about you. And that's why they'll get back here as fast as they can with the message."

They played with the dogs then, throwing sticks and letting them retrieve until they'd had their fill. Nick poured out water from his canteen, and the dogs drank eagerly. And then they were ready to lie quietly at their feet, panting in the warm sun.

"See what she sent for you?" Nick unzipped his backpack

and handed her a package wrapped in a clean, white piece of cloth. "She baked *kermakakku* today, especially for you."

She smiled as she unwrapped the package and took out a piece of cake. It was still slightly warm, and it was golden brown on top.

"It smells heavenly!" Her mouth began to water as she smelled the scents of cinnamon, cardamom and vanilla. She took a bite, and smiled at the rich sour cream and spice taste. "It's just as good as it smells!"

"I don't suppose you'd share a slice with me?" Nick grinned at her.

"Oh! Sorry!" She laughed and handed the rest of the package to Nick. "She's a dear. She's always making something for me."

"She gave me something else for you." Nick reached into his pocket and pulled out a velvet packet. "Go ahead. Open it."

She opened the packet and gasped as she saw the ring. It had a filigreed silver mounting and a stone with a star glittering brightly in its dark, blue depths. "It's beautiful! But . . . why would she give this to me?"

"It was my grandmother's. She saved it for the woman who would be my bride."

"Oh, Nick!" She threw her arms around his neck and hugged him tightly. She knew she'd never been this happy before.

Nick smiled at her. "You'll marry me then?"

"Yes!" She nodded quickly. "I love you, Nick."

"And I love you, too, my lovely Emmy."

Emmy?! Maura's eyes snapped open, and she began to tremble. Nick had called her Emmy. She'd heard him very plainly. But she wasn't Emmy!

Before she could think about this puzzling development

any further, the intercom on her desk buzzed. Maura took a deep breath and reached out to answer. "Yes, Sylvia?"

"Your husband's on line two. He says it's urgent."

Maura took another deep breath and pressed the button for line two. She'd been very uncomfortable around Keith ever since the night that they'd made love, and she was actually relieved when he'd left the next evening on another business trip. "Hello, Keith."

"Hi, honey. Listen . . . I really need to talk to Liz. I called the factory, and they said she was on her way there."

Maura frowned and bit her tongue. She really wanted to ask why Keith needed to talk to Liz, but it was best not to make that sort of inquiry. "Sorry, Keith. She's not here yet. Shall I have her call you when she gets in?"

"Uh . . . no. That won't work. I'll be in and out for the rest of the day. But you can have her call me tonight at the hotel."

"Does she have the number?"

"Uh . . . no. She doesn't. Hold on a second and I'll get it."

There was a frown on Maura's face as she reached for a pad and a pen. Keith hadn't bothered to give her the number of his hotel, but he wanted to give it to Liz.

Keith was back on the line a moment later, and Maura dutifully wrote down the number. "Is there any message you want me to give her?"

"Yeah . . . uh . . . tell her I managed to match the stones her friend needed for the necklace. I just need to know how many she wants."

"Okay. I'll tell her." Maura wrote down the message. "You matched the stones for the necklace, but you need to know how many to buy. Is that right?"

"Perfect. I'll try to give you a ring later tonight. Goodbye, honey."

After she'd hung up the phone, Maura stared down at the note pad thoughtfully. She was almost sure the message Keith had given her was a lie. But how could she prove that?

The moment she thought of it, Maura began to smile. She wasn't nervous about her meeting with Liz anymore. Now she was eager to see her, to find out if Liz would fall into her trap.

Less than five minutes later, Maura's intercom buzzed again. It was Sylvia to tell her that Liz had arrived.

"Send her in, Sylvia. And you can bring us coffee in five minutes or so."

"Maura. Hello!" There was a welcoming smile on Liz's face as she walked in and extended her hand. "You really gave us all a scare. I'm so glad you're all right!"

"Thank you, Liz." Maura gave a brief nod. Liz should have been an actress. If she hadn't known differently, she would have been sure that Liz was one of her good friends. Rather than comment on her phony sincerity, Maura gestured toward the mannequin. "I designed the highlight of the show while you were gone. What do you think of it?"

Liz moved closer to look at the Joseph's coat. She cocked her head and walked slowly around it, frowning slightly. And then she turned to Maura and smiled. "It's very good. I like it a lot."

"Then I have some drawings I want you to see." Maura led her over to the table.

As Liz studied the drawings of the Joseph's coat, Maura studied Liz. She was a strikingly beautiful woman with the figure of a super model. That was clear, even under the severe grey business suit she was wearing. Her dark black hair gleamed under the lights, her deep blue eyes sparkled, and her complexion was a flawless peaches and cream. No wonder Keith was having an affair with her. Liz was gorgeous!

Why was she so dispassionate about her husband's affair? Maura knew that most wives who'd had occasion to face their husband's mistresses would be torn by feelings of rage and jealousy. But she was strangely calm and almost clinical as she assessed Liz. Of course, she wasn't in love with Keith, and that might be the reason why she could be so objective.

Liz seemed to feel Maura's eyes on her, and she turned around with a smile. "Your drawings are perfect, Maura. And I love the look of the coat. I don't see any reason why we can't put it into production. Just give me a minute to do a few calculations, and I'll figure our cost."

Maura nodded and got up. "Use my desk. It'll be easier."

"Thank you." Liz placed her briefcase on Maura's desk, and opened it. She took out a pad of paper and a calculator, and began to jot down notes.

There was a tap at the door, and Sylvia came in, carrying a tray of coffee. She set one mug down in front of Liz and brought the other to Maura. "Do you need me for anything else?"

"Not right now, thank you, Sylvia." Maura smiled at her. "I'll buzz if we need you."

"Thanks for the coffee, Sylvia." Liz took a sip, and started to add up numbers. As she grew more involved with her calculations, she slipped off her jacket and rolled up the sleeves on her white silk blouse.

As Liz turned toward her again, Maura drew in her breath sharply. Liz was wearing a gorgeous necklace. It was antique, with heavy gold overlapping circles, each one containing an opal in its center. Something about the necklace was very familiar and Maura began to frown. She seemed to remember it, but it had looked very different in the past. The stones were new. She was sure of that. Something else had been in their place.

Maura shut her eyes and tried to concentrate. And as she searched her mind, she saw the necklace again, in startling detail. The opals were gone, and in their place were lovely pearls.

"Maura? Are you all right?"

Maura opened her eyes. Liz looked worried, so she shook her head. "I'm fine. I was just resting my eyes. That's a lovely necklace, Liz. I think I saw one that was very similar, except it was done with pearls. Is it an antique?"

Liz's face turned white. And then little blotches of red appeared on her cheeks, spreading into a full blush. "You're right, Maura. It's an antique. It was a gift from my . . . my boyfriend. I usually don't wear anything this ornate to the office, but I forgot I had it on."

"If I had a necklace like that, I'd wear it every chance I had. It's really lovely."

Liz nodded, and she seemed to relax a little. "I was thrilled when he gave it to me. It's one of a kind and it belonged to his grandmother."

"He must be very serious about you, to give you a family heirloom."

"Yes . . . I think he is."

Maura smiled, and tried to look perfectly innocent. She wasn't sure how she knew, but she was almost certain that Keith had given Liz the necklace. "Are there wedding bells in your future, Liz?"

"Perhaps. But not for a while. We have a few problems to work out first."

Maura nodded. She knew perfectly well what those problems were. Keith was married to her! But she didn't want to tip her hand and let Liz know that she'd guessed. "Oh, Liz? I almost forgot to tell you. Keith called for you."

"Keith called here?" Liz blushed again. "What did he want?"

"He left his phone number and asked you to call him at his hotel tonight. And he said to tell you he managed to match the stones for your friend's ring. He just needs to know how many to buy."

"Oh . . . good!" Liz nodded quickly. "One of my friends has a dinner ring with some missing stones. It's a . . . ruby ring. With uh . . . I think they're little chips of topaz around it. Some are missing, and Keith was going to try to match them for her. She'll be absolutely delighted!"

"I'm glad he was successful. Would you like to call your friend now, and tell her the good news?"

"No. She . . . uh . . . I don't have her work number. I'll phone her at home, tonight."

Maura nodded. "Don't forget to ask her how many stones she needs."

"I won't. And then I'll call Keith right back to tell him."

Maura watched Liz carefully, as she went back to work with her pad and calculator. She hadn't asked for Keith's phone number. That meant he had already given it to her. And Liz had been lying about her friend's ring, since the piece of jewelry that Keith had mentioned was a necklace.

"Just a second and I'll have the figures for you." Liz scribbled something on her pad. "It looks really good. I think we can turn a nice profit on your Joseph's coat."

"Wonderful." Maura nodded, but her mind wasn't on her new design. It was on the proof she'd just gathered. She'd hoped that Keith had broken off with Liz, after the night she'd spent with him. But it was clear that Liz and Keith were still involved. Unfortunately, Maura wasn't quite sure what she wanted to do about it.

Chapter Twenty-Three

"That was gruesome, wasn't it, Mom?" Jan sat on the corner of the bed and giggled. "I should have known better than to get Hank and David together."

Maura nodded, and stroked Cappy's head. After David and Hank had left, they'd taken Cappy upstairs with them, and he'd fallen asleep on Maura's bed. "Perhaps you shouldn't have told David about the project. Now that he's volunteered to help, they'll be together at every meeting."

"Oh, God!" Jan sighed deeply. "I should have my head examined. And to make matters worse, I invited them both to the fashion show tomorrow night. I just hope they won't be at each other's throats."

"They seemed fine, tonight."

"That's true." Jan nodded. "But this temporary peace might not last for long. Jealousy is very destructive, and it's an extremely volatile emotion."

Her daughter's words reminded Maura of the meeting she'd had today, and she nodded. "Speaking of jealousy, I met with Liz Webber today."

"You didn't!" Jan threw herself back on the pillows. "I'll say one thing for you, Mom. You've got a lot of nerve!"

Maura shrugged. "It didn't take nerve. She's still my production manager and I had to consult with her on my new design."

"Were you jealous, Mom?"

"No. Not really." Maura shook her head. "At first I was angry at being deceived, but I took your advice and I decided not to take any action until I had all the facts. After that, it was interesting to see how far they'd go to keep things from me."

"But you weren't jealous?"

Maura shook her head. "No. I guess you have to be in love to feel jealous."

"Tell me about it." Jan rolled over on her stomach and propped her head on her elbow.

"Well . . . Keith called to speak to Liz. But she wasn't there yet. He said he'd matched the stones for her friend's necklace, and asked her to call him at his hotel tonight. I figured the stones for the necklace were just an excuse to get in touch with her, so I asked him for his number."

"Let me guess." Jan raised her eyebrows. "Liz already knew his number."

"She must have. She didn't ask me for it. But that's just part of it. I gave Liz the wrong message, and she didn't know the difference."

Jan looked puzzled. "How did you do that?"

"I told her the whole story about the matching stones, but I said it was for her friend's ring. And she couldn't wait to give me a detailed description of this lovely ring her friend had inherited."

"Very smart, Mom." Jan looked impressed. "Did you discover anything else?"

"I'm not sure. Liz was wearing a beautiful necklace she

said she got from her boyfriend. And I had a very strange feeling I'd seen it before."

"On Liz?"

Maura shook her head. "I don't think so."

"What did the necklace look like?"

"It was antique." Maura began to smile. "And it was made of heavy gold overlapping circles, almost like coins except they were a dull, hammered finish, not shiny. Each circle had an opal in its center."

"Are you sure they were opals?" Jan seemed surprised when Maura nodded. "I remember seeing a necklace like that when I was a little girl, but the stones were white and glossy."

"Were they pearls?"

"Maybe. I wish I could remember, but . . . oh, wait a minute, Mom. I know exactly where I saw it. I'll be right back, okay?"

Maura watched as Jan raced from the room. Cappy whimpered and Maura reached out to pet him. "Don't worry, little guy. She's coming back."

It only took Jan a moment to return with a picture frame clutched in her hand. "I had this hanging in my room. It's a picture of your grandmother."

"Granny Kate." Maura smiled and reached for the gold oval frame, but when she looked at her grandmother's likeness, she gasped in shock. It was an old studio portrait of her grandmother and grandfather on their wedding day, and Granny Kate was wearing the necklace!

"You were right about the pearls. But how did Liz get the necklace? It was up in the attic in a box with all the other antique family jewelry."

"Keith." Maura's lips tightened in anger. "He must have taken it and reworked it for Liz. No wonder I remembered that necklace! I wore it on my wedding day. And I told you that you could have it to wear when you got married!"

Jan nodded. "That's right. You called it the family wedding necklace, and you told me that it practically guaranteed a happy . . . Mom!"

"What is it?" Maura frowned. Jan had stopped in midsentence and she was staring at her in shock.

"You remembered!"

Maura wasn't sure exactly why Jan was so excited. "Of course I did. That necklace has been in the family for four generations."

"But you remembered that you'd promised it to me. And that was before your accident. You remembered something from your missing years!"

Maura looked thoughtful, and then she nodded. "You're right, Jan. I couldn't have promised you that necklace before you were born. I *did* remember!"

"I'm calling Uncle Steve!" Jan reached out for the phone.

Maura felt a rush of excitement at the mention of Steve's name. "But it's late, honey. He might be in bed."

"He made me promise to call if you had a breakthrough, any time of the day or night. And it's only ten o'clock. Uncle Steve never goes to bed before midnight."

"Well . . . all right." The corners of Maura's lips turned up in a delighted smile. She felt happy, and very excited. It wasn't just that her memory was coming back, although that was wonderful news. Most of her excitement was caused by the prospect of seeing Steve again.

"I knew you were going to be upset with me." Liz sighed deeply as she paced the floor in front of the kitchen wall phone. "But it wasn't my fault, Donny . . . honest! I was rattled when she called me in, and I forgot I was wearing the necklace."

"And you think she remembered it?"

The voice that came over the receiver was icy, and Liz shivered. She'd known Keith for over five years, and she'd never heard him this angry before.

"No . . . she didn't actually remember it." Liz took a deep breath, and tried to explain. "She just kept staring at it with this funny expression on her face. She said it was gorgeous, and then she asked me a lot of questions about where I got it."

There was a long silence, and the line hummed with long-distance noises. Then Keith spoke again, and his voice was much warmer. "Okay. I don't think we have anything to worry about. You made up a pretty good story, and she probably bought it. But don't ever wear it in front of her again. We don't want to do anything to jog her memory."

"I won't. I really did forget I had it on. It's just that I love it so much, I hate to take it off."

Keith chuckled. "You like it that much?"

"I adore it. It's the best present you've ever given me! I'm wearing it right now."

"What else are you wearing?"

Liz looked down at her jeans and sweatshirt. They weren't very romantic, and he deserved a little touch of fantasy for not yelling at her about the necklace. "I'm not wearing anything except my robe. And that's only because it's cold in the apartment. I'm getting ready to go to bed."

"And you're going to keep the necklace on?"

"Yes, I am." Liz smiled. The necklace was in her jewelry box, but he didn't have to know that. "Remember our last night in the hotel? That's what I'll look like when I go to bed."

"Cut it out, babe. We're over four hundred miles apart."

His voice was strained, and Liz grinned. She knew exactly what she was doing. "You have to fly back here tomorrow anyway. I'm supposed to pick you up at the airport at three. Why don't you come back early?"

There was another long silence, and then Keith chuckled. "You know I hate midnight flights. Are you sure it'll be worth it?"

"I know it will, but make up your own mind." Liz put just the right note of seduction in her voice. She knew it would drive him crazy. "Do you remember that long, black coat I designed?"

"The one that looks like a trench coat?"

"That's the one." Liz laughed, low in her throat. "I don't think I'll bother to wear anything else to the airport . . . just my beautiful necklace and the coat."

There was another silence and she heard the sound of paper rustling. Then he came back on the line.

"There's an Air West shuttle leaving here at eleven. I can make that if I hustle. It lands at LAX at twelve-seventeen."

"I'll be waiting at the gate." Liz smiled into the receiver. "Hurry, darling . . . or I'll just have to start without you."

Keith hung up the phone with a smile on his face. Liz was really something. There wasn't a doubt in his mind that she would actually meet him in her coat and necklace and nothing else. She was wild and impulsive, the sexiest woman he'd ever known. But there were times when her impulsiveness led to problems.

All it took was one call to the hotel switchboard, and they'd made all the arrangements. It cost a fortune to stay in a first-class hotel, but it was worth it for the service.

The woman at the switchboard had promised to ring his room when the limo arrived, and he packed his bag, thinking of Liz. It didn't take long to fill his small suitcase. He'd traveled light. When he was ready, he sat down in front of the window that looked out over the city and thought about what Liz had told him. She could be right. It was possible that Maura's memory was coming back.

Although the room was an even seventy degrees, he shivered. He didn't like to think of what would happen if Maura remembered. She'd cut him off. That was for certain. And then she'd hire someone to investigate all those expenditures he'd told her were business related. He was almost sure he'd managed to cover his tracks, but what if he was wrong?

He got up to pace the floor, back and forth in front of the expensive view. If Maura discovered how he'd tapped into her profits from the boutique and channeled them into his own accounts, his gravy train would go off the tracks. And if she found out about his affair with Liz, he'd be in even deeper trouble. She'd fire Liz. That was certain. And then she'd divorce him. He shouldn't have signed that prenuptial agreement. All Liz's plans would go up in smoke, and they would be left with nothing.

What could he do? Keith's hands started to tremble and sweat popped out on his forehead. He had bills to pay, and the type of people he owed wouldn't accept any excuses.

A bank sign with the time and temperature flashed on and off several blocks away. Ten-thirteen. Seventy-two degrees. Security Investments.

He watched the sign for a moment or two, and then he began to smile. He needed a security investment, and the answer was right at his fingertips. They'd approached him several weeks ago, but he'd told them he wasn't interested.

The number was in his wallet, and his fingers trembled as

he fished it out. They'd promised him a hundred thousand dollars for one lousy phone call. All he had to do was tell them when her memory returned, and they'd make a deposit in the Swiss account they'd set up for him.

He stared down at the number and frowned. One phone call and he'd be free and clear, but he was almost certain that these men played rough. They hadn't actually told him what they'd do. They were much too sophisticated for that. But he had his suspicions, and he didn't think he was wrong.

He knew exactly what would happen if Maura died. He'd been thinking about it ever since the man had approached him. He would inherit her share of the boutique. That was spelled out in the prenuptial agreement. And since Liz was her junior partner, she would get the other half. Jan was secure. Maura had set up a trust fund for her that was generous enough to keep her on easy street for the rest of her life. No one would lose if Maura died . . . except Maura.

His hand reached out for the phone and hesitated. Could he do this to his wife? She'd always been fair with him, and even though they weren't in love, he'd come to like and respect her. Making the call would be signing her death warrant. He was almost certain of that. Could he do that to the woman who'd been so good to him?

The phone rang, and he jerked his hand away. And then he took a deep breath and answered it. His limo was here and he told them he'd be right down.

On his way out of the room, he turned back once to look at the phone. He'd done the right thing. He hadn't called. Any calls he made from the hotel would be listed on his bill. The air phone on the plane was out, too. Those calls would be listed on his phone card. But there were pay phones at the airport.

Keith was frowning as he got into the elevator and rode

down to the lobby. He still hadn't decided what to do. He'd talk it over with Liz when she met him at the airport, and they'd decide then.

Steve must have broken the speed limit, because he was knocking on the door in less than ten minutes. When Maura opened it, he handed her a bottle wrapped in a foil sack with a bow at the top, and gathered her into his arms.

The hug seemed much too brief to Maura, and her face was flushed when he pulled back to look at her. "Congratulations, luv. This calls for a celebration and I brought the champagne. Where's Nita? She should be in on this, too."

"I'm here, Dr. Steve." Nita came in from the kitchen, carrying a tray filled with something that smelled heavenly. "I made your favorite appetizer."

"Nita . . . you shouldn't have." Steve whisked a cracker from the tray as Nita passed by, and popped it into his mouth. "Crab and cream cheese on Ritz crackers. And they're perfect, as usual."

Nita giggled, and set the tray down on the table. "Will you let Miss Maura and Miss Jan have some, or shall I make another batch?"

"I'll let them have one apiece, maybe two if I'm feeling generous."

"I have the little *brie en croûte,* also." Nita smiled at him proudly. "They will come out of the oven in three more minutes. I have made something for everyone tonight."

"Brie en croûte?" Maura clapped her hands together. "They're mine! Did you make deviled eggs with mustard for Jan?"

Nita nodded. "I did."

"How about your favorite, Nita? The thin slices of Black

Forest ham spread with cream cheese, and rolled around white asparagus?"

Nita nodded, and she wiped a tear from her eye with the corner of her apron. "Oh, Miss Maura! You remembered every one. It is so good to have you back!"

"I did, didn't I?" Maura began to grin. "It's happening! And it's not just a one-time thing. I'm really beginning to remember!"

Steve opened the champagne and poured four glasses while Nita went to get the rest of the appetizers. Then they all sat around the low round table to enjoy this moment of celebration.

"To Mom and her memories." Jan raised her glass in a toast. "I feel like the little girl in *Poltergeist* because I can say, 'They're back!' "

Maura laughed. "I'm not sure I like that comparison. She was referring to the spirits from the cemetery they paved over when they built the housing development, wasn't she?"

"Uh . . . right." Jan stared at her mother. "Do you really remember that movie?"

"Of course. You were young, third grade or so, and you begged and pleaded to see it. I thought it was a little too scary for an impressionable young girl, but you wore me down until I finally agreed to take you, against my better judgment. It turned out that I was the one who was scared, while you just sat there very calmly, analyzing the characters' reactions."

"Chalk up another memory!" Jan grinned at her. "And it's definitely from the missing years. Isn't that right, Uncle Steve?"

Steve nodded. "You're definitely experiencing a rush of memory, Maura. But so far your memories have been entirely benign."

"Benign?" Maura turned to face him, and a blush rose to her cheeks as she saw the fondness in his eyes. "What do you mean?"

"You don't remember any emotionally charged incidents, do you?"

Maura thought hard. She didn't remember her first husband's funeral, and she had no memory of Keith. There were still large gaps in the life she'd lived before the accident.

"You're right, Steve. I don't." Maura frowned slightly. "Is that bad?"

"No. It's a very natural pattern. When memory returns, most people recall the benign incidents first. When they're comfortable with those incidents, they begin to remember the other, unpleasant things they've buried a little deeper in their subconscious."

"That makes a lot of sense." Jan nodded. "Mom's experiencing some very weird dreams about unpleasant things, and some of them are really traumatic. Of course we know they never happened, but her subconscious memories could be the basis of her dreams."

"That could be true." Steve gave Jan an approving smile, and then he turned to Maura. "Did you record those dreams in writing?"

"Yes. I did exactly as you told me. I listed every detail that I could remember."

"And now Hank is making them into a movie!" Jan looked pleased. "Do you want to read the script, Uncle Steve? Mom's helping us with it, and it's really good."

"Yes! Definitely! Do you have it here?"

"Sure." Jan nodded. "I'll get it for you, but it's our only copy. You can read it tonight, or you can wait and I'll have it photocopied for you."

"I'd like to read it tonight, after our celebration. And that reminds me . . . have you told anyone else about the return of your mother's memory?"

"No." Jan shook her head. "We haven't had a chance. You told me to call you right away and that's what I did."

Steve nodded, and then he smiled at them. "I want you all to promise to keep this a secret. Trust me on this. Don't mention it to anyone else."

Jan nodded, and so did Nita. But Maura looked puzzled. "Why do we have to keep it a secret?"

"Memory's a tricky thing, luv." Steve slipped his arm around Maura's shoulders. "If everybody and their cousin starts asking you questions, it could slow your progress. And I don't care how well-meaning your friends are, they won't be able to keep from quizzing you on what you remember and what you don't."

Jan nodded. "That makes sense. If someone questions Mom, it'll cause her anxiety and that'll slow her progress. I promise I won't tell anyone, Uncle Steve."

"And I will not tell anyone else." Nita nodded solemnly.

"Anyone *else?*" Steve turned to Nita. "Did you mention it already?"

"Only to Mr. Hank. And he was so glad! He called a few minutes ago, and this was before I knew that it was a secret."

"I'll call Hank and tell him not to mention it." Jan turned to her uncle. "He's crazy about Mom, and he'll do whatever's best for her."

"Are you sure? He could hurt your mother's progress if he asks questions."

"You can depend on Mr. Hank." Nita looked very serious. "He is a fine young man."

Maura nodded. "Yes, he is. You don't have to worry about Hank. I trust him completely."

"All right, then." Steve smiled at Maura. "Just remember . . . don't tell anyone else about your memory."

They all nodded, but Nita looked concerned, and she turned to Maura with a frown. "But you must tell Mr. Keith, yes? He is your husband."

"He's the last one I'd tell!" Maura answered abruptly and then she blushed when everyone turned to stare at her. "I wasn't going to tell you quite so soon, but I've made a decision and I'm filing for divorce."

"But . . . why?" Steve looked puzzled.

"I shouldn't have married Keith in the first place. And I'm sure he wants to be free just as much as I do. But that's got to be a secret, too. I don't want anyone to know about it until I check with a lawyer."

"Of course." Steve nodded. "But are you sure you're not making a rash decision? Perhaps you should wait until your memory fully returns."

"No. I'm positive I'm doing the right thing. I just have to work out the details. You won't mention this, will you?"

Jan and Nita looked very solemn as they shook their heads, and Maura noticed that they didn't seem upset. The only one who looked at all surprised by the news was Steve, and he turned to her with a question in his eyes. "Do you remember anything at all about your marriage to Keith?"

"No. Not yet. But nothing I might remember will change my mind. Even if things were right between us before, it doesn't really matter now."

"You're very sure?" Steve still looked a little doubtful.

"Very. I know that our marriage is over, and it's senseless to keep up the pretext."

Steve nodded. "All right then. I can see how determined

you are, and I won't try to talk you out of it. But I wish you'd tell me what prompted your decision."

"I will . . . later." Maura gave him a small smile. "But right now, let's celebrate!"

Chapter Twenty-Four

Jan was sleeping when her phone rang, and she woke up enough to glance at the clock. After midnight. Who could be calling her private number at this hour? It was probably a wrong number, but she reached out to pick up the phone anyway. If she didn't answer, the caller might try every five minutes or so for the rest of the night.

"Hello?" Jan's voice was fogged with sleep.

"Hi, Jan. I'm sorry to wake you. You were sleeping, weren't you."

It was a statement rather than a question, and Jan nodded. And then, realizing that her caller couldn't see the nod, she said it out loud. "Yes, I was. Who is this?"

"It's David. I was doing some research for the film, and I discovered something very interesting. But I dialed your number before I realized it was so late. Should I call back in the morning?"

"No. I'm awake now." Jan smiled into the receiver. She liked the warm feeling it gave her to talk to David when it was late, and everyone else was sleeping. "What did you discover, David?"

"The location. I checked out all the foods your mother

remembered from her dreams, and they're definitely Scandinavian. And I did a rough drawing of the terrain she described. I think we should set the film in Finland."

Jan began to frown. There was no way they could afford to go overseas. "You mean . . . we should go there?"

"No." David laughed. "I just mean that we should find a location here that looks like Helsinki, Finland."

"Why Helsinki?" Jan was intrigued.

"I did some research and it ties in with the scene where our main character goes off to the university. The one in Helsinki has quite a few American students."

Jan began to smile. "That sounds fine to me. How far is Helsinki from the Russian border?"

"Russia?" David sounded surprised. "I'll look it up, but I know it's not far. Why do you need to know?"

"Hank thought we should set the funeral scene just outside of St. Petersburg. The girl has to ski all the way to the farmhouse, so it can't be too far."

"I see." There was a silence and then David spoke again. "That should be all right, especially since it's winter. She could ski across the ice. But why did Hank want to use a location in Russia?"

"The dogs' names were part of it. Boris and Natasha. And Hank said that if we mention Russia, it would explain our main character's motivation. Our audience'll think she's some sort of spy."

"I guess that makes sense." David seemed a bit dubious. "But is she really a spy?"

"We don't know. And neither does the audience. It depends on how you perceive the film, and every time you go to see it, you might come to a different conclusion."

"Okay . . ." David chuckled. "Far be it from me to criticize an artist, since I have absolutely no artistic talent.

Whatever Hank decides is fine with me. And that reminds me . . . do you have his phone number? I need to ask him something."

Jan rattled off the number from memory, and David wrote it down. And then he spoke again. "Where were you? I tried to call a while ago, but no one answered."

"Sorry." Jan smiled. "Mom and I were having a family celebration with Nita and Uncle Steve."

"Was it someone's birthday?"

"No. Nothing like that." Jan began to frown. She didn't want to lie to David, but it was becoming difficult to avoid a direct answer. "It was just a family thing. Some good news, that's all."

"What good news?" David was insistent. "Can't you tell me?"

"Not really. I promised Uncle Steve that I wouldn't tell anyone."

"I'm not anyone, I'm the man who loves you."

Jan gripped the phone so tightly her hand began to shake. This was the moment she'd been waiting for. No man had ever said he loved her before.

"What's the matter, Jan? Did I shock you?"

"Yes. You did." Jan tried to keep her voice calm. "I . . . I'm glad you love me, David."

David chuckled. "That's not the answer I was hoping to hear. I thought you might say you loved me, too."

"I . . . I can't say that, David. It wouldn't be honest. I like you a lot, but I haven't really known you long enough to love you."

"You will." David sounded very confident. "We'll give it some time, Jan. I'm not trying to rush you into a commitment or anything like that. I just want to be with you. Now tell me about your family celebration. Did your mother's memory start to come back?"

Jan was so shocked she almost dropped the phone. How did he guess that? But she couldn't tell him. She'd promised not to tell anyone. "I . . . I'm sorry, David. But I can't talk about it."

"All right, I won't force you. But if that's what happened, I'm really glad. And I promise not to let on that I know. Is that fair enough for you?"

"Yes." Jan smiled. David was really very understanding.

"I'll see you in the morning then." David's voice was warm. "Don't forget, we have a tennis date at ten."

Jan smiled. "I won't forget. Are you going to pick me up?"

"Of course. Is nine all right? We could catch a quick cup of coffee before we get out on the court."

"Wonderful!" Jan's smile grew wider. She could tell that David was eager to see her.

"Goodnight, honey. Now go back to sleep. And dream that you love me. Maybe, when you wake up, it'll be true."

Jan said goodnight and placed the receiver gently in the cradle. David loved her! She snuggled back under the covers, and smiled up into the darkness. She'd been perfectly honest with him when she'd told him that she wasn't sure she loved him back. And he was adult enough not to be disappointed.

Jan's eyes closed and she thought of David. She certainly liked him a lot, even though they had some differences they had to work out. David was reasonable and fair, and Jan was sure that once she explained how his competitive behavior spoiled the fun of tennis with him, he'd change his attitude toward the game. Of course he'd been a bit jealous, but that was understandable, now that she knew he loved her.

Jan thought about the meeting they'd had, and she began to smile. David had handled his jealousy very well. Instead of resenting the time she spent with Hank, he'd asked to become part of the project. And now that he was helping them, he seemed to get along just fine with Hank.

She clicked off the light and sighed in contentment. David loved her, and he was willing to wait patiently until she returned his love. It was entirely possible she loved him already. She'd never been in love before, and she wasn't quite sure how she'd feel if she was. When she'd entered high school, she'd asked Nita how she could tell if she was in love. And Nita had told her not to worry, she'd definitely know when the time came.

What would it be like if she married David? Jan knew it was a Hollywood illusion, but her thoughts turned to a little frame house in the valley with a white picket fence and climbing roses, always in bloom. There she was in a pretty dress, serving dinner to her husband and their happy, well-adjusted children. After dinner, she could imagine him holding the baby, rocking him gently while she read stories to the older children in their small, comfortable living room. When it was time to put the children to bed, they'd come back downstairs to sit by the fire and enjoy each other's company. And later, when they went up to bed, he would turn to her and look deeply into her eyes, and he'd tell her how happy he was to have her as his wife. And then they'd kiss, holding each other tightly under the warm blankets. And he would say, "I love you, Jan." And she would say, "I love you too, Hank."

Hank?! Jan's eyes flew open in shock. She was supposed to be thinking of David, not Hank!

Quickly, she ran through the fantasy again, but she knew it was Hank's face she'd seen. Hank had been holding the baby, smiling at her as she'd read to the older children. And it had been Hank who'd looked deeply into her eyes, and kissed her as he held her tightly under the warm blankets.

Jan frowned and rolled over, trying to find a comfortable position. But her thoughts were in turmoil, and she gave a sigh of pure frustration. This really didn't make sense. If she was supposed to love David, why was she thinking about Hank?

Maura felt her heart rate jump as Steve finished reading the last page of the script, and put it down on the coffee table. She told herself that there was no reason to be nervous. Steve wasn't the type to judge what she'd written on its literary merit, but she couldn't seem to quell her feelings of anxiety.

"These are your dreams?"

Steve's voice was soft, and Maura felt a little better. "Yes. I started having them right after I came home from the hospital."

"Do they wake you up at night?"

Maura shook her head. "Not always. Most of them are more like daydreams. I get a terrible headache and I close my eyes to try to relax. And that's when I start dreaming these strange things."

"Do you think there's a basis for any of this?" Steve tapped the script with his finger.

"I . . . I don't know. It seems very real, and then I found . . ." Maura stopped and visibly winced. She really didn't want to tell Steve about the picture of Nick she'd found in her album. Or his wedding band with the inscription. Or the lovely sapphire ring in the hidden compartment of her jewelry box. If she told him that she was beginning to suspect her dreams were actual memories, he'd think that she was crazy.

"What is it, Maura? Please tell me."

"There's nothing to tell. I . . . I'm just very confused, that's all."

Steve slipped his arm around her shoulders and pulled her against her chest. "Don't be afraid, luv. Just tell me what you found."

She could feel herself start to waver as she nestled into the warmth of his embrace. She could tell Steve, and he'd understand. Steve was her friend. He'd been her friend for years. He knew everything about her, all the things that she'd forgotten.

"Maura?" Steve reached out and caressed the back of her neck. "I really need to know what you're thinking."

"Just . . . that you were my friend. You're the only friend I've got. And you've known me longer than anyone else. Actually, you've known me longer than I have."

"That's true."

He chuckled and Maura felt his muscles quiver. It was nice being so close to him, and she cuddled up a little more. She was safe from harm as long as Steve was here.

"So why can't you tell me?" Steve's voice was low, and he sounded very serious. "You used to confide in me. Don't you trust me anymore?"

Maura sat up with a sudden movement and stared at him. "I used to *confide* in you?"

"Yes. You told me everything, right up until the time you married Keith. That's when things changed between us. I guess that's why I'm not really upset that you're divorcing him. I've wanted my Maura back for a long time now."

Maura nodded. And then she moved close again. She

rested her cheek on his chest and sighed in contentment. "I'm back, Steve. And I promise I'll never go away again."

He'd managed to catch a little sleep after she'd left. She'd been particularly good tonight, pulling him into the fantasy the moment she'd stepped in the door. And she'd maintained his fine edge of arousal through the whole scenario. But the contentment he'd felt had faded, and now he was awake again. He'd spent some time thinking about the assignment, and planning out his moves. And then he'd switched on the television and stretched out on the lumpy couch.

He was watching a dull horror movie on the tube when the telephone rang, and he knew immediately who it was. No one else would call him at this hour. He let it ring three times, and then he reached out to answer it.

"Hello?"

"Yes." The voice that carried across the phone line was low and gruff. "We've decided that it's time. You're to go ahead with phase two."

"You're sure?" He gripped the phone tightly, and a smile spread across his face.

"Very sure. Are our terms acceptable to you?"

He thought about asking for more. He really had them over a barrel. But that would have been foolish and he'd never been a foolish man. If he performed well, as he knew he would, there would be other assignments. They would learn that they couldn't get along without him.

"The terms we discussed are more than adequate. I accept the assignment."

"Good." The voice sounded a little warmer. "Can you make it look like an accident? We don't want any inquiries."

"No problem. Accidents are my specialty." He chuckled, relishing the moment. He'd earned their respect with his excellent surveillance, and they'd called on him to finish the job. "You want this to happen immediately?"

"Any time in the next two days will do. Just make sure nothing comes back to us. And call us the moment you've succeeded in eliminating our problem."

He nodded, barely containing his excitement. He truly loved this part of the game. Killing gave him a high he'd never been able to duplicate. He'd tried to achieve that lofty plateau with drugs, sex, and any other vice he could think of, common or uncommon. But he'd found that nothing else would do. Of course it was best if he could see the terror in their eyes, and watch the life fade from their bodies, but this time he would restrain himself. They wanted an accident that no one could trace, and that was exactly what they'd get.

"We have an understanding then?"

The voice prompted him out of his lovely anticipation, and he gathered himself to reply. "Just leave everything to me. I guarantee that you won't be disappointed."

Chapter Twenty-Five

It was the morning of the fashion show, and Maura was on pins and needles. Although Nita had made her favorite French pancakes with strawberries and whipped cream, she hadn't been able to eat more than a bite before she was up, dialing Sylvia at home to make sure she'd remembered to arrange for the caterers and the musicians.

"Relax, Mom." Jan grinned at her across the table. "You're always nervous before a show. Everything'll go just fine."

Maura shook her head. "No, it won't. Some sort of disaster happens every year, but somehow we manage to muddle through."

"Remember two years ago, when you forgot to order the folding chairs?" Jan stared to laugh.

"Of course I do. Steve rented a U-Haul and you raced down to your high school to borrow their folding bleachers."

"You remembered, Miss Maura!" Nita smiled broadly. "Do you remember what you forgot the year before that?"

Maura shook her head. "We didn't forget anything, Nita. It wasn't our fault that the caterers brought chili dogs and beer instead of salmon rolls and chardonnay."

"That was a mistake?" Jan's eyes widened. "I thought you planned it that way!"

"So did everyone else. It was lucky we were featuring our line of sports clothes. Will you excuse me for a minute? I need to check with the florist."

Nita and Jan exchanged smiles as Maura rushed off to the phone again. It was clear she was nervous. Her fall fashion show was covered in all the papers, and invitations to the event were prized by those lucky enough to receive them.

"The florist says his shipment of azaleas came in on time." Maura was smiling as she came back to the table. "We'll use those along the runway."

"Which color?" Jan was curious.

"White. Anything else will detract from the clothes. We'll use the pink and fuchsia in the reception tent."

"You are right." Nita nodded. "They must think the clothes are very beautiful, not the flowers. Tell me about the reception, Miss Maura. Will it be fancy, with linen table-cloths and silverware and crystal?"

"Not this year. The tent is decorated to look like a patio garden with areas of real grass and trees in tubs. We're using white wrought iron tables and chairs and picnic ware."

"Plastic silverware?" Jan looked dismayed.

"No, honey. But the silverware has white handles, and the plates are white china. Everything will be white and green, with the exception of the flowers." Maura took one more bite of her breakfast, and then she put down her fork. "This is wonderful, Nita, but I'm not very hungry. I think I'll get down to the boutique early, to make sure everything happens on schedule."

"Good idea." Jan put down her fork, too. "Do you want me to drive you?"

"No, honey. Steve's picking me up in twenty minutes. I

asked him to come early, and he offered to stay with me for the whole day. What time are you and Nita coming?"

"Around two. That'll give us a chance to help you a bit before the show starts. I told David and Hank to be there at three-thirty sharp."

"How about Mr. Keith?" Nita frowned slightly. "Will he be there?"

Maura nodded. "He called Sylvia to tell her that his flight arrives at three. That'll give him plenty of time to get there before the show starts."

"Do you want me to drive to the airport to pick him up?" Jan didn't look happy about the prospect.

"That's not necessary, honey. I've already asked Liz to do it."

"Liz?!" Jan looked horrified. "Why did you ask her?"

"She's the only one I can spare. I told her to take the morning off, and pick up Keith at three. It'll keep her out of my hair, and I won't have to deal with her."

Nita looked very worried. "You are not going to tell Mr. Keith today, are you?"

"No. I have to check with a lawyer first, to see where I stand financially. When I have all the facts, I'll talk to Keith."

"It sounds like you've got everything under control." Jan grinned and picked up her fork again. "Relax, Mom. Today's your day. It'll be wonderful, you'll see."

Maura nodded, but she wasn't as sure as Jan seemed to be. She'd been nervous and edgy from the moment she'd opened her eyes this morning, and she didn't think her attack of jitters was entirely due to the fashion show. She'd awakened with the feeling that some sort of crisis would occur today, some event that would shape her life for years to come. But she had absolutely no clue as to when it would happen, or what it would be.

He didn't like being in the building, but it was the perfect spot. She owned the three-story warehouse in Santa Monica, and it was where she kept all her records. The building had been red-tagged, right after the last earthquake, and it was locked and entirely surrounded by yellow caution tape. The structure would eventually be demolished. It had been weakened beyond repair. But she had petitioned to delay the demolition, until a team of specialists could go in to remove her property.

Her business records were kept in a room on the third floor, and that was where he was. There was no power. They'd shut it off for fear of fire from the twisted and exposed wiring, but that didn't present a problem for him. He had packed in battery-operated tools, and he'd weakened several floor joists so that they would snap under her weight. When she stepped inside the room, she would crash through to the floor below where the floor joists had been weakened in a similar manner. She would fall through two floors and land on the concrete slab that made up the first floor. No one could survive such a fall.

He stepped around the dangerous spot and moved several file boxes to the edge for bait. They contained the business records she'd need. Then he backed out carefully and closed the door, knowing that the hours he'd spent in preparation would be well worth the effort.

As he let himself out of the warehouse, he began to frown. For the first time in his career, he didn't want to stay to see the expression of terror on her face when she fell. The enjoyment wasn't there, and the twinge of pity he'd felt for her when the car had crashed through the barrier was back in full force. He liked her, and that was a real problem. He'd never gotten this close to his target before, and he actually felt sorry that she had to die. Unfortunately, business was business and it couldn't be helped.

The car he'd stolen was parked on a side street. He got in and began to drive toward the airport where he'd return it to long-term parking. The owner would never know that it had been used, and even if someone had spotted it, there would be no way to trace it to anyone other than the owner. It was a foolproof plan. All of his plans were foolproof. But he didn't have the high he usually felt when he'd set one of his death traps.

After he'd returned the car, he stopped for breakfast at the airport restaurant. The waitress who brought his bacon and eggs was young, with her hair in a ponytail. He flirted with her, and she flirted back. That made him feel a little better. And then he remembered the baby-sitter, and he knew what he had to do to feel that exhilarating high again.

"More coffee?" Maura smiled as Steve nodded, and reached across her desk to pour him another cup. The morning had been hectic, and Sylvia had insisted she take a coffee break in her office with Steve.

Maura felt the change in their relationship. It had happened right after she'd announced that she was divorcing Keith. Neither one of them had said anything, or made any references to what would happen once Maura was single again, but Maura felt much more comfortable around Steve. Now there was the sense of something wonderful waiting to happen, rather than something they both had to fight to keep suppressed.

"I think Sylvia's idea was a good one." Steve captured her hand and held it. "You look much more relaxed now."

"Having you here helps a lot. Jan says I'm always a bundle of nerves before a show, but I don't ever remember being this nervous . . ." Maura stopped in mid-sentence as her intercom buzzed. "Just a second, Steve. I'd better get that. Sylvia wouldn't buzz me if it wasn't important."

Maura pressed the intercom button and picked up the phone. "Yes, Sylvia?"

She listened for a moment, and then she frowned. She made a little gesture of dismay, and then she nodded.

"Okay. I'll take care of it. Tell him to hold and I'll pick up in a second."

"Problems?" Steve raised his eyebrows. Maura looked upset.

"Yes. It's Agent Richards from the I.R.S. He wants to talk to me personally, and he says it's important."

Steve nodded. "You'd better speak to him. It's probably just a routine question, and you can refer him to your new accountant."

"I hope you're right. Grant used to take care of everything, and I don't know a thing about my corporate taxes."

Maura was still frowning when she picked up the phone again. "Hello. This is Maura Thomas."

"Agent Richards from the Internal Bureau of Revenue."

The voice on the other end of the line was muffled, and Maura strained to make out the words. Either Agent Richards had a bad connection, or he was coming down with a terrible cold.

"I'm sorry to bother you, Mrs. Thomas, but we have a problem with your tax liability. Could you please verify some figures for us?"

"Certainly." Maura frowned. She had no idea what he

wanted, but her new accountant could take care of that. "I've hired a new accountant and he has all the paperwork. Would you like his number?"

"We have it, and I called him this morning. But our problem concerns your return for the tax year nineteen ninety-one. That was prepared by a Mr. Grant Adams, and I understand he is deceased."

"That's correct." Maura winced. She still didn't like to think about Grant's death. "Did you say you needed the paperwork for nineteen ninety-one?"

"I did. In addition, we'd like to see your receipts and ledgers for the year preceding, and the year following. That would be tax year nineteen ninety, and tax year nineteen ninety-two. If you can get this information to us by Monday morning, we may be able to avoid an audit."

"I'll have it for you." Maura promised. She certainly didn't want to go through an audit with a new accountant who was unfamiliar with her past returns. "Shall I bring it in to your office?"

"That's not necessary. I'll have a man in the area, and he can pick it up. Shall we say nine o'clock Monday morning? And thank you for being so cooperative, Mrs. Thomas."

Maura was frowning as she hung up the phone, and Steve looked concerned. "What is it?"

"A tax audit. But I might be able to avoid it if I provide them with all the paperwork."

"I'm sure you have it. Grant was very thorough."

Maura nodded, and picked up the phone again. "Sylvia? Where do we keep our corporate tax records?"

Steve watched as Maura's frown deepened. When she hung up the phone again, she sighed. "The records are on the third floor of our warehouse in Santa Monica. But the building's red-tagged from the earthquake. Sylvia says I've been in there before, but I always go at night because it's strictly illegal to enter."

"That's really foolish, luv." Steve looked very serious. "If the inspectors put a red tag on your warehouse, it means it's not structurally sound. Call Agent Richards back and tell him your records are inaccessible. They'll just have delay until someone can go in to retrieve them."

"Good idea." Maura nodded. "I'll call him right now."

But Agent Richards wasn't in. The office was closed and a recorded message told Maura that they wouldn't return until ten o'clock Monday morning.

"What now?" Maura bit her lip in frustration. "Agent Richards is sending a man to collect the paperwork at nine o'clock Monday morning, and I can't cancel because he won't be in his office until ten. They're going to be upset with me, Steve. And the I.R.S. isn't known for being terribly understanding, are they?"

Steve laughed. "Not really. Grant used to say they all had hearts of stone."

"Then there's only one thing to do." Maura looked very determined. "I'm going to have to get my hands on those file boxes, one way or the other."

Steve looked as if he were about to object, but then he sighed. "I'm afraid you're right. Okay, Maura. If Sylvia says you've gone in there before, I guess one more time won't hurt. But I'll go after the show, when we're not so rushed."

"You?" Maura turned to him with a question in her eyes.

"I won't let you do something that dangerous. Just tell me where everything is, and I'll bring it out."

"But I don't remember!" Maura tried to look perfectly honest, even though she remembered exactly where the file boxes were. She didn't like to lie to Steve, but entering the red-tagged building might be dangerous, and she didn't want him to go alone. "Sylvia said we keep our records in a room on the third floor to the right of the staircase, but I have no idea where the file boxes are stacked. It's really sweet of you to offer to play Sir Galahad, but we'll just have to go in together."

"I shouldn't have done it." Keith's hands were shaking as he got behind the wheel of Liz's car. "Maybe I should warn her."

Liz reached out to grip his arm. "Don't be a fool! If you warn her, you'll get both of us in trouble!"

"I could do it anonymously. At least she'd have a chance that way. She could hire a bodyguard or something."

"It won't do any good . . . not if they're really out to get her. Just leave it alone, Donny. It's what we wanted, isn't it?"

"Well . . . yes. But it seems so cold."

"Does this seem cold?" Liz reached out to wrap her arms around his neck.

"Come on, Liz . . . this really isn't the time to . . ."

"Or this?" She nibbled at his lips with her teeth and made little darting moves with her tongue.

Keith groaned. It was impossible to resist her. Liz was his salvation and also his destruction. He didn't like the kinds of things she urged him to do, but he couldn't get along without her.

"Let's hurry and get this done." Liz settled back in the passenger's seat, but she kept her hand on his thigh. The tips of her fingers were touching him in a way she knew was very erotic. "If we finish and get back here early enough, we'll have time to play. What do you say, Donny?"

"I . . . sure, why not?" Keith began to smile. He was putty in Liz's hands when she got like this. She always had some incredible new trick to show him, some unique pleasure he'd never dreamed existed.

It didn't take long to get to the warehouse, and he pulled the car around to the side. "I really don't like this, Liz. Are you sure we have to go inside?"

"I'm positive. I need those designs she did last year. After she's gone, I can claim them. And you need to get your hands on those ledgers, don't you?"

Keith nodded. "I guess so. But going in a red-tagged building . . . isn't that kind of . . . uh . . . risky?"

"Not at all. I've been in here six or seven times since they tagged it. The only tricky part is on the third floor, and I had a builder friend show me exactly where to walk. You don't have to worry about a thing, Donny. Trust me."

Keith began to feel better the moment he was inside. This was the first time he'd been in the warehouse since the earthquake, and it wasn't the disaster he'd expected. He could see quite well by the light filtering in through the high, glass block windows, and the first floor looked almost normal with its crates of supplies and equipment stacked against the walls.

"This looks okay to me." Keith began to smile. "Why did they give it a red tag?"

"The main beam is cracked. That's the one that holds up the roof and supports the walls. But I brought in my builder friend to inspect it and he told me there's really no danger. It would take another big earthquake to knock it down."

Keith swallowed hard. "Let's just hope we don't have one while we're in here."

"We won't." Liz laughed. "You're a hell of a lot safer in here than you are on the street outside. The gangs are moving into this area, and we've had a couple of drive-by shootings on the corner."

Keith frowned. "I don't know if that makes me feel better or worse. Let's get what we came for and leave, okay?"

"Right. Follow me, Donny. The staircase is right over here."

Liz flicked on a flashlight and Keith was puzzled. "Why do we need that?"

"The power's out. And there aren't any windows on the second and third floors. You don't want to fumble around in the dark, do you?"

"Not really." Keith followed her across the floor. He still didn't like the feeling he got, knowing there was a cracked main beam over his head, but she'd think he was a coward if he told her that he was still a little apprehensive.

"The staircase is perfectly safe." She turned back to reassure him. "I had my friend check that out, too."

"Good." He knew he sounded breathless, and he hoped she wouldn't realize that it was a symptom of his anxiety. But the stairs felt solid under his feet, and he began to feel a bit more confident as they climbed up to the second floor. When they reached the landing, Liz stopped and waited for him to join her.

"We had some damage in here."

She let the beam of her flashlight play over the expanse of the second floor and Keith gasped. Bolts of cloth were strewn over the huge floor, like toothpicks scattered from a fallen dispenser.

"This is incredible!" Keith felt awed by the power it must have taken to send the heavy bolts of material crashing to the floor. "Maura didn't tell me there was this much damage!"

"There isn't, not really. The bolts were stacked on those shelves against the wall, and they toppled. It's just a matter of picking them up and restacking them."

Keith frowned. "Why don't you just hire someone to do it?"

"We can't. The building's red-tagged, remember? That means we're not supposed to let anyone in. The city wants this building demolished with everything inside, but her lawyer's fighting it in court. I think she'll win. There's no reason why we can't hire a special crew to get our things out. But her hearing's been delayed, and it'll take time to get permission from the judge."

"How about all this cloth? Don't you need it?"

"Of course we do!" Liz sighed. "But she's willing to take a loss for the cloth. All she really cares about are the files on the third floor."

Keith turned to look at Liz. In the reflected light from the beam of the flashlight, she looked angry. "Those bolts of cloth in your back bedroom . . . are they from here?"

"Of course! If her insurance is going to pay for it anyway, there's no reason why I can't have it. I handpicked all this material, and I can use it later, when I own the business."

"That makes sense." Keith nodded quickly. "Do you want to take a couple of bolts today? I could help you."

"Thanks, but not in the daylight. Someone might spot us. I need her drawings more than I need the cloth. Come on, Donny. Let's get going."

He nodded and they started up the stairs again, to the third floor. As they moved along the stairwell, her flashlight picked up several cracks in the wall.

"Those are big cracks."

Liz laughed. "It's just dry wall, Donny. That stuff cracks at the drop of a hat. It's not structural, so you can relax."

"I'm fine." Keith tried to keep his voice steady. The cracks bothered him more than he was willing to admit.

Perhaps it was easy to crack dry wall, but he'd seen several cracks in the exposed wooden beams, as well.

"Step over this board, Donny." Liz aimed the flashlight at one of the boards on the third floor landing. "My friend says it's ready to go."

Keith nodded, and stepped over the board. It had a jagged crack running through it and it was splintered on one end. "Are there any more spots like this?"

"A couple. I'll warn you." Liz turned around to smile at him. "You wouldn't fall through. It's not that bad. But you might break your ankle, and that would be hard to explain to her."

"Right." Keith's eyes widened as he surveyed the damage on the third floor. It was much worse than the second. Several doors were hanging by one hinge, and one wall looked skewed, even to his untrained eye.

"How about that wall?" Keith pointed. "It looks like it's ready to collapse."

Liz nodded. "It wasn't that way the last time I was up here. I guess the aftershocks caused more damage."

"Liz?" Keith took her arm, and pull her close. "Let's get out of here, huh? I don't want to take any chances and this looks pretty dangerous to me."

Liz seemed to waver for a moment, but then she shook her head. "It'd be stupid to leave now. We're here."

"I guess you're right." Keith gave in. He still felt terribly uncomfortable, but she had a point. They'd already climbed up to the third floor, and it would be stupid to turn around and leave without getting the files and the drawings. "Where's the file room?"

"Right here."

Liz let the beam from her flashlight illuminate the room to the right of the stairwell, and Keith laughed. The door was partially open, hanging by the bottom hinge, and the padlock had pulled out of its hasp. "At least we won't have to worry about picking the lock."

Liz laughed, too, but then she turned to take his hand. "You're really nervous, aren't you, Donny?"

"Yeah. Let's hurry, Liz. I'll feel a lot better when this is over."

Liz gripped his hand tightly. "Me, too. This is a lot worse than the last time I looked. The door wasn't hanging like this. And the padlock was still there. I thought we'd have to smash it open."

"Well . . . this is your lucky day." Keith tried to keep his voice light. "After you, ma'am."

Liz hesitated, and then she shivered. "Let's go in together. Or better yet, let's just get the hell out of here. I've got a bad feeling about this."

"Oh, no you don't!" Keith laughed. He'd never seen Liz exhibit any sign of nervousness before. She'd always been supremely self-confident, and this new aspect of her personality was very appealing. It made him feel strong and virile, and he turned to grin at her. "You were the one who talked me into this crazy stunt, and I'm not leaving without the ledgers. Come on, Liz. Let's go get them. Everything'll be just fine."

"All right . . . if you're sure." Liz let him pull her toward the open door. "I guess I was just being silly. And I really do need those drawings. The bitch won't be able to use them after she's dead."

"Right. Just keep thinking of the great life we'll have when all this is over." He took a step toward the open door, with Liz at his side.

Liz began to smile. "We'll have that gorgeous house!"

"No, honey. She bought that before we were married. The house goes to the kid. But we'll get the business, and all the profits from the past two years. We'll have plenty of money to build our own house, and you can have anything you want. That's even better, isn't it?"

Liz was stopped, right outside the doorway, and turned to look at him. And then she threw her arms around his neck and kissed him. "You're right, Donny. I just never thought it through before. The bitch designed that house, and it would always remind us of her. We'll have a brand new house. Our house. For our new life together. And when it's all built, it'll be all ours."

"Of course it will." Keith nodded. "We'll wait a few months, until all the speculation dies down, and then we'll get married. You'll marry me, won't you, Liz?"

"Yes!" Liz kissed him again. He'd finally asked her to marry him! This was the happiest day of her life!

"We'll go to Vegas . . . or maybe Reno. You can choose any place you want, as long as we keep it small and quiet."

The smile fled from Liz's face. It wouldn't be the big wedding she'd dreamed of when she was a girl. But then she nodded. What he'd said made sense. "You're right, Donny. I always wanted a big wedding, but it wouldn't be smart under the circumstances. We'll slip away and go to one of those wedding chapels in Vegas. That way nobody'll raise any ugly questions. And then we'll come home to our brand new house with no more bitch to keep us apart!"

Liz smiled up at him, and Keith smiled back. "That's right, darling. No more bitch. She'll be gone, forever."

"You'll carry me over the threshold, won't you, Donny?"

"Of course I will. Just like this!"

Keith lifted her up in his arms, and Liz wrapped her arms tightly around his neck. And then he stepped across the threshold of the file room, and they fell together, shocked into eternal silence, to meet the end of all their dreams.

Chapter Twenty-Six

"I called the airport, and they said his flight landed two hours ago." Sylvia gave an exasperated sigh. "You never should have sent Liz to pick him up. They couldn't be stuck in traffic for this long!"

Maura shrugged. "It really doesn't matter, Sylvia. If they get here, that's fine. And if they don't, that's fine, too."

"We have to regard this whole thing as a blessing in disguise." Steve nodded. "We don't have to deal with them if they're not here. And that frees our minds for other, more pressing problems . . . like what happened to those missing shoes."

"Oh, God! I almost forgot!" Maura turned to Sylvia. "Did you locate them yet?"

Sylvia nodded. "The boxes are right where they're supposed to be, all labeled with the models' names and coordinated with their outfits. But Mrs. Durham didn't see them. She decided she looked better without her glasses, and she's as blind as a bat without them."

"Poor Amelia." Maura smiled. "She's so excited about this fashion show. I hope I didn't make a mistake when I asked my customers to model the clothes."

Steve shook his head. "It wasn't a mistake. The advance publicity those ladies gave you is worth its weight in gold. Mrs. Durham told me she's bringing all her friends to the boutique on Monday, to show them the outfit she modeled."

"That's the general idea." Maura smiled at him. "Now if we can just figure out some way to get Amelia to put on her glasses, we won't have any accidents on the runway."

Sylvia looked smug. "I already did that. I told her you'd designed her dress with her glasses in mind, and she'd spoil the whole illusion if she modeled it without them."

"So she's wearing her glasses?"

"You bet! And she was really impressed. She called her husband from the dressing room, to ask him if she could put down a deposit on the dress."

Maura frowned slightly. "But we didn't set a price . . . did we?"

"Yes, we did. You never charge enough for your designer originals so I upped the price a bit. And to make matters even better, Mrs. Durham thinks she's getting a steal. She's paying twenty-five hundred for the dress she's wearing in the show today, and that's half off the ticket price."

"Oh, my Lord!" Maura gasped. "But Sylvia . . . these really aren't originals, not in the true sense of the word. We're planning on mass producing these designs. What will Mrs. Durham think when she sees someone else wearing a dress just like hers?"

"But it won't be just like hers. I told her we'd be selling knock-offs, but she said that didn't matter. She's the only one who'll have the original from the show."

"That's true, I guess." Maura started to laugh. "All right, Sylvia. You've just been promoted to business manager, but I'm not going to ask what you think your increase in salary should be. How about an extra five hundred a week?"

Sylvia nodded quickly. "I accept. I think I'll go back to the dressing rooms and talk to the other models. Maybe they'll all want to buy their designer originals. At half off, they're a real bargain."

Steve waited until Sylvia had rushed off, and then he turned to Maura. "You've worried about Keith and Liz, aren't you?"

"Yes . . . a little." Maura was surprised. Steve had seen right through her casual act. "I just don't understand what could be keeping them. I know Keith's not that interested, but Liz has never missed a show before, and we're including one of her original designs."

"Does she know?"

"Of course. And she was very excited about it. She told Sylvia she could hardly wait to judge the crowd reaction."

"Then she'll be here." Steve walked over to give Maura a little hug. "Don't worry. They probably got delayed somehow, but I'm sure they'll be here by the time the show starts."

But they weren't, and Maura grew more and more worried as the minutes passed. The models did an excellent job, and Diane was impressive as she introduced the designs. The Joseph's coat, modeled by Cherise, was a show-stopper. Everyone wanted to order it, and Sylvia had deposits on over thirty during the first ten minutes of the reception.

"It was a great show, luv." Steve held Maura's arm and escorted her to the reception tent. "The fashion editor from the *Times* told me that it was the best fashion show you've ever done."

Maura nodded. "Yes . . . it did go well. Do we really have to go to the reception, Steve?"

"It'll look very strange if you don't show up. After all, you're the hostess." Steve put his arm around her waist and propelled her toward the tent. "Come on, Maura. You don't want everyone to know you're upset, do you?"

"No, of course I don't." Maura turned around to face him. "You feel it, too . . . don't you, Steve?"

Steve nodded. And then he bent down to place a kiss on her forehead. "Whatever it is, I promise you that we'll face it together."

"That was a really great show, Mrs. Thomas." Hank grinned at Maura. "Of course, I don't know beans about fashion, but I thought your designs were beautiful."

Maura smiled. "Thank you, Hank. I'm glad you enjoyed it."

"I really liked the lines in that long green dress." David spoke up. "It reminded me of the gown Elizabeth the First wore in her coronation painting. Is that where you got the idea?"

"I really don't remember."

Maura turned to grin at him, and David grinned back. "Sorry. I knew that. But it was beautiful and I wanted to tell you. Jan would look gorgeous in something like that."

"Not on a bet!" Jan laughed. "I never go to places where you have to get that dressed up. Mom's Joseph's coat is more my style. I could wear that on campus with jeans and a tee shirt."

Maura nodded. "You're right. I'll have Liz make one up for you."

"Mom?" Jan leaned close so she could speak to her mother privately. "What happened to Liz and Keith? I've been watching for them and they're not here."

"I don't know. No one's heard from them."

"Are you worried?" Jan looked very concerned.

"I'm not sure worried is the right word. I'm angry with Liz. She had a responsibility to be here to help with the show. I counted on her to model her gown, and Heather had to fill in for her. And Keith should have made an appearance. He knew how important this show was to me, and it's awkward to explain his absence. I just hope no one notices that they're both missing, and brings up questions that I can't answer."

"I understand." Jan nodded. And then she pointed to the table where David and Hank were waiting. "I'll be right over there. If you need me, just give me the high sign. I'm really good at fielding embarrassing questions."

"Okay, honey." Maura smiled as Jan walked over to the table and sat down. She wasn't sure how she'd done it, but she'd managed to raise a wonderfully sensitive and helpful daughter.

After Jan left, several more people came up to congratulate Maura. She managed to keep a smile on her face, but with each minute that passed, she grew more and more anxious. She was about to ask Steve if he'd run to the office to see if Keith or Liz had called in, when a dark-haired woman in a business suit headed her way.

"Who's that?" Maura turned to Steve quickly. "She looks important."

"She is. She's the fashion editor from L.A. Style. It's one of the big fashion magazines. Sorry, luv, but I don't remember her name."

"Excuse me . . . Maura?" The fashion editor waved to get Maura's attention and made her way through the crowd. She reached out to shake Maura's hand and smiled. "Fabulous show, darling! This was your best ever!"

"Thank you. It's very nice of you to say so." Maura put

on her best smile, and wished that she could remember the woman's name.

"Have you seen Liz Webber? I wanted to compliment her on her design. Of course it wasn't as sophisticated as yours, but she does show some promise."

"She certainly does." Maura managed to keep the smile on her face. "I'm sorry, but I haven't seen Liz."

With the sixth sense so many reporters seemed to possess, the editor caught the scent of a story in the making. Her eyes narrowed, and she leaned closer. "I noticed that she didn't model her own design. Liz is here, isn't she?"

"She should be, but with a crowd this large, the Pope could be here and you'd never spot him." Steve laughed and extended his hand. "Steve Bennett. I'm Maura's brother-in-law. And you're . . . ?"

"Constance Grafton from *L.A. Style*. What's Liz wearing? Maybe I can spot her?"

"The last time I saw her, she had on a grey business suit with a totally gorgeous necklace." Maura answered the question truthfully. "But she may have changed by now."

"Oh." The woman nodded, and it was clear she was disappointed. But then she brightened as she noticed that Keith was missing. "How about your husband, Maura. Is he here?"

Maura caught Steve's cue and she shook her head. "I'm afraid not. He was supposed to fly in this afternoon, but he must have been delayed. My daughter's here, though. Jan? Come over here a moment, honey."

"Hi, Mrs. Grafton." Jan rushed over to Maura's side. "I haven't seen you since last year, but I've enjoyed your articles in the magazine. Wasn't the show just wonderful?"

"Fabulous. I heard you'd gone away to college, Jan. Are you studying design?"

"No way!" Jan laughed gaily. "Mom has all the artistic talent in the family. I decided to go into a totally unrelated field. I'm majoring in psychology."

Just then Sylvia came rushing up. She looked upset, but the moment she saw Mrs. Grafton, she put on a charming smile. "I'm sorry to interrupt you, Maura, but you have an important call in the office. You'd better go, too, Steve. Your service needs to talk to you. I'll introduce Mrs. Grafton to some of the models while you're gone."

"I need to make a call, too." Jan caught the unspoken urgency in Sylvia's voice, and turned to her mother. "I'll just tell David and Hank where I'm going, and I'll meet you there."

Maura watched as Sylvia walked away, Mrs. Grafton in tow. Thank goodness for Sylvia! Maura could hear her telling the editor all about how they'd used customers as models, and Constance Grafton seemed fascinated. At least one problem was off her back.

"Come on, Maura." Steve sensed that she was hesitant about going to the office, and he took her arm. "Let's go see why Sylvia looked so upset."

Maura sat in the passenger's seat and trembled as Steve followed the police car to the warehouse. She knew that something awful had happened. The officers who'd been waiting for them in the office had told them that they'd found Liz's car parked by the side of the warehouse. A janitor in the building across the street had seen two people, a man and a woman, go inside the red-tagged warehouse. He'd watched and when they hadn't come out again, he'd hammered on the locked door to warn them that the building was dangerous. When he got no response, he'd called the police, fearing for their safety.

"What are they doing in the warehouse?" Steve frowned as he pulled up behind the police car.

"I don't know. Liz knows we're not supposed to go inside. She said she had several bolts of the perfect material for my Joseph's coat, but I told her we couldn't go in to get it."

Steve shook his head. "I doubt that would have stopped her. Does she have a key?"

"Yes." Maura nodded. "I have one and she has the other."

The officers motioned to them, and Maura and Steve got out of the car. Maura handed them her key, and the older officer turned to her. "You folks better stay out here. The building's not safe."

"I know that, officer. But my husband's in there. I really want to go in with you."

"I'd like to come, too." Steve spoke up. "I'm a doctor, and they could be injured. You may need some emergency medical help."

The older officer hesitated, and then he nodded. "We talked to the structural engineer. It should be safe enough if you don't touch anything. But if you come in, it's at your own risk."

"Of course." Steve nodded. "Hold on a second. I'll grab my bag."

Steve was back in a moment, and the older office opened the door. "Is the electricity on?"

"No." Maura shook her head. "The main line snapped during the earthquake."

"Stick close behind us, then. We don't want any more accidents."

The words the officer had chosen contributed to Maura's

anxiety. He thought that Liz and Keith had been in an accident, too. She was shaking as she followed them into the darkened building. The light was fading fast, and the warehouse looked eerie under the beams of their powerful flashlights.

"Hello! Anyone here?" the older officer called out, but there was no answer. It was perfectly quiet, so quiet that Maura could hear her own heart beating hard in her chest. "Hello! This is the police! Call out if you can hear us!"

Maura held her breath as long as she could, and then she let it out in a ragged sigh. No answer. Nothing to mar the perfect silence. If Keith and Liz were here, they weren't able to call out for help.

"The staircase is to your right." Maura was surprised that her voice was steady. "They might have gone up to the second or third floor."

"What's up there?" the younger officer asked.

"We store our cloth and thread on the second floor, and Liz mentioned that she wanted to come in to get some bolts of cloth. Of course I reminded her that we weren't allowed to enter the building, but it's possible that she ignored my warning."

"And your husband might have come along to help her?"

Maura nodded. "Yes. She picked him up at the airport this afternoon, and they may have stopped here on their way to the boutique."

"How about the third floor?"

Maura shook her head. "They wouldn't have any reason to go up there. We don't use it for anything except files and records."

"Okay." The older officer nodded. "You two stand right here and wait while we check out the ground floor. If we don't find them, we'll work our way up."

Steve reached out to wrap his arms around Maura as they watched the two officers search the ground floor. They walked in a clockwise fashion, shining their flashlights into every corner and behind every box and crate. They were approaching the staircase when the younger officer shouted out. "Over here!"

Maura frowned as both of the officers trained their flashlights on what looked like a pile of fallen lumber near the staircase. "What is it, Steve? I don't see anything."

Just then one of the officers pointed his flashlight at the ceiling, and Maura saw a jagged hole where a section of the second floor had been.

"Oh, my God!" She shuddered violently. "You don't suppose they were up there and . . . ?"

"Help me with this board, will you?" The older officer motioned to his partner, and together they lifted off several heavy beams. And then Maura saw it, the arm that was sticking up through the debris. Something gold was reflected in the beam from the officer's flashlight and she shuddered as she recognized Keith's watch.

Chapter Twenty-Seven

Maura took another sip of the cognac Steve had poured for her. She wasn't sure she liked the taste, but it was doing an excellent job of warming her insides. "But Steve . . . are you sure?"

"I'm sure, luv. I went upstairs with them, after Jan came to take you home. There was a hole in the third floor, too, just inside the file room."

Maura frowned. "But I don't understand, Steve. What were they doing up there?"

"We may never know for sure, but the police let me remove all your records. I dropped them off at your accountant's office before I came back here. I think you'll find that Keith was making some unauthorized entries in your books."

"Do you think he was embezzling money from me?" Maura shivered. She felt oddly detached. It didn't really matter what Keith had done. He was dead.

"That's my guess. Your new accountant is very good. And since he used to work in Grant's office, he has access to all his computer records. He told me he should have a report for you in a week or so."

"And you dropped off the tax records I needed for Agent Richards?"

Steve took a deep breath, and then he pulled Maura close so he could look into her eyes. "There is no Agent Richards. I had the police check with the I.R.S."

"But . . . but he called me!"

"*Someone* called you. And that someone identified himself as Agent Richards. But he wasn't."

"But why would someone pretend to be an I.R.S. agent? That's not exactly a ticket to popularity!" Maura started to laugh, but she sobered quickly when she saw how serious Steve looked. "What is it, Steve?"

"Just think about it for a minute, Maura. What did this Agent Richards want you to do?"

"He wanted me to go get my tax records for the year . . . oh, my God! If I'd gone up to the third floor of the warehouse, I would have been . . ."

"That's right." Steve nodded gravely. "It was a setup, Maura. The tax records you needed were right next to the section of floor that collapsed. And I'm willing to bet that those floor joists suffered a lot more than simple earthquake damage."

"But . . . why would someone want to kill me?"

"For something you knew. Or something they thought you were about to remember. Someone knew your memory was coming back. Who did you tell?"

"No one. Just you, and Jan, and Nita. And Nita told Hank."

"Then one of them told someone. Or someone noticed. How about Liz? Did she know?"

Maura started to shake her head, but then she looked thoughtful. "It's possible. She was wearing a necklace and I commented on how beautiful it was. She knew I was fascinated by the design, and I told her I thought I'd seen one like it before with pearls instead of opals."

"And you had?"

Maura nodded. "When I got home, I described it for Jan, and she showed me my grandmother's wedding picture. Granny Kate was wearing the necklace."

"Keith gave your grandmother's necklace to Liz?"

"Yes. He must have taken it from the box in the attic. He took out the pearls. There were some missing. And he put opals in their place. I'm sure Liz mentioned it to Keith, and that means Keith would have known that my memory was coming back."

Steve nodded. "Okay. We'll add Keith and Liz to the list. And they might have told any number of people. How about Jan? Do you think she told anybody?"

"Not exactly." Maura sighed. "But she told me that David guessed, and she didn't deny it. She felt terribly guilty, but she said she just couldn't lie to him."

"I'll add David to the list. This is getting us nowhere, Maura. Too many people are involved already. I think we'd better approach it from another angle."

"What other angle?"

"It's time for you to remember everything. Think back, Maura. There's a reason someone's trying to kill you. Try to remember that reason for me."

"But I can't!" Maura shook her head. "You told me yourself, Steve . . . it's just not possible to turn my memory on and off like a water faucet!"

"Of course not." Steve slipped his arm around her shoulders and gave her a little hug. "But memories can be prodded a little. They can even be kicked right out of hiding. How about it, luv? Are you willing to try a little experiment for me?"

Maura hesitated. "But I thought you didn't want to rush me."

"I said that because I didn't want your memory to come back."

"You didn't? But why?"

Steve looked very serious. "You were safer if you didn't remember, and I was trying to delay the process. I side-tracked you every way I could, including convincing you that your dreams were just a figment of your imagination."

"Because you knew that if I remembered, they'd try to kill me?"

"That's right. But now the game's changed. They think you remember, and you won't be safe unless you do. How about it, luv? Are you ready to remember everything?"

"I'm ready." Maura nodded quickly. "And I'm willing to try almost anything. Are you going to hypnotize me?"

"No. I've got something even better than hypnosis." Steve reached in his pocket and pulled out a videotape. "It's Hank's rough cut of his student film. I want you to watch it, Maura . . . and just let your mind float free."

"All right." Maura nodded. "I'd like to see it anyway. But I don't see how watching Hank's film could possibly . . ."

Steve stopped her protest with a kiss. It wasn't just a peck on the forehead this time. It was a kiss on the lips that left her breathless and wanting more.

Maura sighed as Steve got up to put the tape in the machine. And then she blushed. Did he know how she felt about him? Or was he simply being kind to a sister-in-law who was terribly upset?

"Here we go, luv." Steve took a seat on the couch next to her. "Just watch, and we'll see what happens."

* * *

The scenes rolled by, one by one. Hank had put them in chronological order, and Maura was amazed at how it all fit together. The story was no longer a series of disjointed dreams. It was a plot that she seemed to know. She trembled as she saw the interior of the hotel room, exactly as she'd described it from her dream. And she gasped as she heard the assassin approach the door. As she scrambled under the bed, she felt the rough texture of the rug on her legs and arms, and she felt like sneezing as the loose fibers from the carpet tickled her nose.

Maura held her breath, just as she'd done that day in the hotel room. And she watched his shoes, praying that he wouldn't lift the edge of the bedspread and discover her. And when he'd left, and she climbed out on the ledge to try to get down to the alley below, she felt a jolt of terror that made her gasp and clutch Steve's hand in dizzy fright.

"I was there, Steve." Maura's voice was shaking. "I remember now! This actually happened to me!"

Steve nodded. "You're right. Just watch, Maura. Watch and remember. It's very important."

As the other scenes rolled by, Maura sat there, watching and reliving what she now knew was her own past. It was Jan in Hank's movie, but Jan was just acting out the story of her mother's life. Maura's emotions were in constant turmoil, changing as each moment on the screen passed by. There was joyful anticipation as Nick gave her the ring. She'd loved him so much. And there was fear as he came to get her in the forest pool, and they raced for the safety of the sheepherder's shack. The scene in the restaurant was full of terror. She felt her body tense as Peter signaled to her, and she bolted from her chair to push Nick down, out of range. And then there was fear mixed with exhaustion as Peter drove them away on that long trip to the farmhouse where the others were waiting.

She saw Peter's face in the light from the dashboard, but he wasn't the actor who was playing the part in the movie. He was someone she'd known for years, someone who had traveled back to the States many years later and assumed an important role in her life . . .

Maura gasped and grabbed Steve's hand. "Peter! Peter is . . . Grant!"

"Yes, luv." Steve held her hand tightly. "Just watch . . . and remember."

Maura saw herself huddled in the back seat of the car, traveling over the bumpy road. And she cried with deep, heart-wrenching sobs as Nick and Peter decided she had to leave. And then she heard Nick's words, and they sent her mind reeling.

Do this for me. It's what I want most in the world. Go back home and take my baby away from all this. I want both of you to be safe.

"Jan." Maura's voice was no more than a whisper. "Jan is Nick's child. I remember everything now."

Steve nodded. "Yes. Hush, luv . . . just watch and listen."

Now they were at the airport in Helsinki, and Nick was reaching up to retrieve her bag. They'd just come back from a weekend ski trip, with two wonderful nights in a mountain lodge. She'd managed to talk Peter and Nick into letting her finish out the semester. They'd finally agreed that it would look suspicious if she left before her finals. That meant she had two more weeks to make them change their minds, and she was confident that she could persuade them to let her stay.

Nick smiled at her as he retrieved her light blue suitcase from the conveyer belt and presented it to her with the flourish. She laughed and stood on tiptoes to kiss his cheek.

Then he picked up his brown, leather bag, slung their skis over his shoulder and they walked, arm in arm, out of the baggage area.

"No!" Maura started to tremble violently as they went through the double glass doors and out into the street. She could still remember how the night had felt, cold and frigid, with lightly falling snow that had stung her cheeks. The parking lot loomed in front of them, and she put her hand to her mouth to keep herself from screaming.

Maura closed her eyes, but the scene continued behind her eyelids. It wasn't a movie, it was real. As they started to get into their car, the lights went out in the parking lot, plunging them into darkness. Something was very wrong!

"Easy, luv." Steve slipped his arm around her shoulders, but Maura couldn't stop shivering. And she couldn't stop the images that flashed behind her closed eyelids. She was back there, reliving what had happened that awful night.

"Run!" The word was a command, and Maura obeyed it instantly. She rolled from the open door, and raced across the parking lot toward the safety of the airport. She heard an explosion, a loud booming noise that drowned out the sounds of the busy airport, but she didn't turn around. He'd taught her that turning to look would only slow her speed.

And then she was inside, clutching her blue suitcase as she mingled with the crowd. Her mind was a terrified blank, but her training carried her straight to the ladies room, where she locked herself in a stall and changed to another outfit, complete with a brown wig and horn-rimmed glasses. The light blue soft-sided suitcase was reversible, and she took out her things and zipped it back up so the brown side was showing. She took a chance then, tucking her lovely ring into her pocket. It was against the rules, but she couldn't give it up. Not now. Not ever. Nick had given it to her.

The clothes she'd been wearing went into the bottom of the trash container, wrapped in a department store bag. And then she was walking out of the ladies room, glancing at the plain silver watch she'd slipped on her wrist, and frowning.

She went straight to the restaurant and ordered a cup of coffee. She took a sip, glanced at her watch again, and went to the pay phone against the wall.

The number the international operator dialed was answered on the second ring. The operator repeated her Russian words in English. "Will you accept a collect, person-to-person call for Mr. Phoenix from the Leningrad Airport?"

There was a moment of silence as the line crackled with the weather, and then Peter's voice came back on the line. He sounded very grave and his voice shook slightly. "I'm sorry, operator. Mr. Phoenix just stepped out. Could you have your party call again in fifteen minutes?"

"I'll do that, operator. Thank you." She spoke the words in Russian and hung up the phone, knowing that Peter had heard her voice. And then she went back to her booth and ordered a sandwich she couldn't force down. And watched the reflection of the police cars in the mirror behind the counter. And waited for the man who would come to collect her in fifteen minutes.

Maura's eyes opened with a snap. Steve had put the tape on pause, but she already knew the ending. There were tears on her cheeks as she turned to him and spoke the words he was waiting to hear. "You can stop now, Steve. I remember everything. And I know why they want me dead."

Chapter Twenty-Eight

Maura hurried up the staircase to her room. Her thoughts were filled with memories of Nick . . . memories she knew were real now, of the love they'd shared together.

She'd met Nick on a warm fall day in her junior year of college. She'd been listed on his class roster as Rawlins, first initial "M." He hadn't known her first name back then, but he'd thought of her as "Em," or "Emmy." Even after he'd found out that her name was Maura, he'd continued to think of her as Emmy. It had become his pet name for her, the name he used when they were alone together. She'd loved it so much, she'd had it inscribed on the wedding ring she'd given him in the simple ceremony at the farmhouse.

Now they were gone, Nick's whole family, including his best friend, Grant. They'd died for a cause, but it made their deaths no easier to bear.

Nick had explained it all, right after she'd climbed to the top of the class in his Russian language seminar. The handsome visiting professor had been in most of the female students' dreams, but he hadn't been interested in anyone except Maura. He'd been very impressed with her gift for languages, so impressed that he'd personally recruited her into their select group.

Maura's senior year had involved intensive seminars in four different foreign languages. She'd passed proficiency tests in all four with flying colors. Because of Nick's recommendations and her outstanding grade point average, she'd won a full scholarship to the University of Helsinki. And that was where it had all begun.

The University of Helsinki had an exchange program with the one in Leningrad, and she'd applied to take several classes. Nick's contacts at the Leningrad University had approved her application, and Maura's life was divided between the two cities, one in Finland, the other in the Soviet Union. Her studies as a graduate student were perfect cover for her real work. She brought coded messages from the Soviet Union to Finland, where they were sent on to the United States. Steve had been their stateside contact, and a good friend of Nick's. Maura had flown to meet him several times, carrying important documents that couldn't be trusted to their usual pipeline.

Nick and Maura had been full of plans and dreams, just like any other young couple, and they'd been very much in love. But three months after their small family wedding, things had turned very ugly.

Someone had discovered what they were doing. The scene in the restaurant had been the first attempt on Nick's life, and there had been several more after that, ending in his death at the Leningrad airport. Maura had escaped, but their whole operation was in jeopardy, and it had to be closed down.

Somehow, Maura had managed to take her finals and fly home. She'd been two months pregnant with Nick's baby, and she'd been planning to get a good job and raise the baby alone. She hadn't even considered terminating her pregnancy. Her child was Nick's legacy, and it was a tangible way of keeping their love alive.

Steve had met her at the airport. He knew about the baby. Nick had told him. And he had a perfect solution to Maura's problem. His brother, Paul, needed a wife. There was no reason why they couldn't help each other and gain the benefits from such a marriage.

Maura had listened carefully as Steve had explained the situation. Paul was a gay naval officer, and his superiors had begun to raise questions about his sexual orientation. There was no way Paul would earn a promotion if the Navy found out he was gay, and he might even be drummed out of the service. Paul needed a wife just as much as Maura needed a husband.

Steve had explained that, as Paul's wife, Maura would receive excellent medical benefits. And he'd promised that Paul wouldn't infringe in any way on her life. It was the perfect solution to both sets of problems, and after Maura had met Paul and liked him, she had agreed to the marriage.

Paul had been an wonderful husband, kind and considerate with a marvelous sense of humor. As the months had passed, he'd grown very fond of Maura, and she'd felt the same about him. Both of them had been looking forward to the baby's birth. And then tragedy had struck when Maura had entered her eighth month. Paul had been killed on a routine training mission, and Maura had been left alone again.

Steve had come to the rescue, and he and Maura had been the only ones to know that Jan was not Paul's child. Not even Donna had suspected that her niece wasn't really a Bennett. Steve and Donna had set Maura up in business, and life had gone on rather smoothly. And then Maura had found out that Steve was involved in another assignment for the government, and she'd begged to become part of the old group again.

Steve had resisted. It was too dangerous. This time they were dealing with a drug cartel. But Maura had insisted that Nick would want her to carry on his work.

It had taken months of argument, but finally Steve had given in. Because Maura traveled so much on business, she was a perfect courier. Nita had known what Maura was doing. It had been impossible to keep the secret from her. But Nita had been sworn to secrecy, and she'd agreed to keep Jan completely in the dark. The less Jan knew of her mother's actions, the safer she'd be.

Everything had gone very smoothly for a long period of time. And then, just as they were about to close in on the leaders of the cartel, everything had gone sour.

Grant had given her a message when he'd come to take her to the airport, a message he'd told her was vitally important. She'd run back upstairs to hide it in the usual place, and she'd planned to call Steve from the airport to tell him where to retrieve it. But she'd never reached the airport. And she hadn't remembered the message until now.

Maura's legs were trembling as she entered her room and hurried straight to the footstool. As she smoothed her hand over the lovely needlepoint design, she felt for the catch that was hidden under the material. She squeezed the two metal parts together and there was a sharp click. She lifted the top and exposed the small hollow space that was carved into one leg.

The message was there, rolled up in a tube, and Maura hurried down the stairs again. When she entered the living room, she found Steve pacing the floor anxiously, and she smiled. "Here it is. Grant told me it was vitally important. I was planning to call you from the airport to tell you where it was."

Steve nodded and reached out to take the message. He unrolled it, and then he started to frown. "Do you know what this is?"

"No." Maura shook her head. "Grant didn't tell me. He said I'd be safer if I didn't know."

"He was right. These are the names of the four kingpins in the drug cartel. And one of them is a U.S. senator."

Maura's eyes widened. "Will you have them arrested?"

"Of course. But that might not call off the hit on you. They know that Grant passed you their names. And now that they suspect your memory's returned, they won't take any chances."

"Then I'm still in danger?"

Maura shivered and Steve reached out to hug her. "I want you to stay right here in this house until I get back. Don't let anyone in or out. Have you got that?"

"How about Jan? She went out with Hank, and she's not back yet."

"You can let them in. How about Nita? Is she coming back tonight?"

"No." Maura looked a little worried. "I gave her the night off so she could baby-sit for her sister's children. Do you think I should call her and warn her?"

Steve shook his head. "That's not necessary. She's not in any danger. Here. You'd better take this, just in case."

"A gun?" Maura looked down at the revolver Steve placed on the table. She picked it up and her fingers automatically snapped open the cylinder to check for bullets.

"You remember how to use it?"

Maura nodded quickly. "Yes. Can you leave me a speed loader, just in case?"

"No problem." Steve was grinning as he reached in his other pocket and handed her a speed loader. "You were pretty good with this the last time we went out to the range. Now remember, don't let anyone in except Jan and Hank. Got it?"

Maura nodded solemnly. "I promise."

"I'll be back just as soon as I can." Steve stood up and pulled her into his arms. Then he walked to the door with her and leaned down to kiss her. "Lock up tight after I leave. And turn on the security system. I love you, Maura."

"I love you, too." Maura's voice was shaking as she spoke the words that had been in her heart since that first morning in the hospital. And then he was gone, standing for a moment outside the door, to make sure she slid home the dead bolt and activated the keypad for the security system.

As she walked back to the living room, she felt very lonely and she called for Cappy. The little puppy came running and jumped up on the couch, crawling into her lap when she sat down. Maura held him for a moment, running her fingers through his silky fur, and then she set him down on the floor at her feet. "Guard, Cappy."

Cappy's body tensed at the command, and he looked very alert as he listened for any sound outside. It was clear he knew the command that Maura had taught him. He would growl, low in his throat, if he heard anyone approaching a door or window. A well-trained dog was more effective than any security system, and Maura had taught him the necessary commands.

As she sat there, revolver at the ready, Maura thought about Keith and their hasty marriage. When she'd realized that she loved Steve, she'd married Keith in a desperate attempt to separate herself from Steve and Donna. Her marriage had been a mistake. She'd realized that from the very beginning, but she'd done her best to make it work. She might have been successful, if Keith hadn't had an agenda of his own.

Keith had married Maura for her money, and he'd managed to skim a small fortune from her boutique business to funnel into Liz's accounts. But Liz had gotten too greedy. She'd wanted it all, and she'd talked Keith into taking foolish risks with the books. Grant had caught Keith red-handed, and he'd told Maura about it on the way to the airport.

The accident hadn't really been an accident. Maura knew that now. She remembered how Grant's brakes had gone out, and she knew it hadn't been a simple mechanical failure. Someone had tried to assassinate both of them, but she had survived. And now that she remembered what had happened, they were after her again.

Cappy growled, and Maura got up, gun in hand, to look out through the drapes. A car was coming up the driveway, but it wasn't Hank's limo.

"Hush, Cappy." Maura turned to smile at him. She'd recognized the car and it was no threat. "It's okay. I know who it is."

The doorbell rang, and Maura hesitated, her hand on the knob. Steve had told her not to let anyone in, but this was an exception. She could use some company, and they could talk until Jan and Hank got home. Cappy was still growling and Maura turned to frown at him. "I said it's okay, Cappy. You can stop now."

Maura flicked off the security system and opened the door with a smile on her face. "Hi, David. I'm glad you're here. Please come in."

Chapter Twenty-Nine

Jan's face was flushed and her eyes were sparkling as she wrapped her arms around Hank's neck and returned his kiss. She'd never felt so wonderful in her entire life!

"Is that a yes?" Hank pulled back to grin at her.

"Yes!" Jan shivered slightly, and grinned back. "Nita was right, and now I know exactly what she meant!"

Hank looked puzzled. "Nita?"

Jan nodded, and then she laughed. "Nita told me I'd know if I ever fell in love, and she was absolutely right. I love you, Hank."

"You're sure it's not just tradition?"

Jan stared at him in confusion. "What do you mean . . . tradition?"

"Ingrid Bergman fell in love with Roberto Rossellini, Sophia Loren married Carlo Ponti, and Judy Garland was Vincente Minnelli's wife. Actresses tend to fall in love with their directors."

Jan laughed. "I'm not an actress. I just did that for fun. I'm going to be a psychologist, remember?"

"Right." Hank nodded. "Maybe I'll become your patient. Patients always fall in love with their shrinks, don't they?"

"Sometimes, but that's just transference. It doesn't last. We're going to last, aren't we, Hank?"

"I'm betting on it." Hank pulled her close and kissed her again. "Are you sure you won't want to date other guys when you go back to Princeton?"

"I'm sure. How about you? Won't you get lonely?"

"Of course I will. But I've got my work, and you'll be home on vacations. We'll make it, Jan. I know we will."

"Isn't love wonderful?" Jan turned to him with shining eyes. "Love's so different than I thought it would be. I can't believe I even thought I might be in love with . . . uh-oh!"

An expression of alarm crossed Jan's face, and Hank frowned. "What is it?"

"David. I have to tell him. He told me he thought he was falling in love with me. And when I said I didn't feel the same way, he promised to wait until I did."

Hank's frown grew deeper. "What are you going to tell him?"

"I'm going to be honest, and say I'm in love with you. I owe him that much. I don't want him to think he's got a chance, when he doesn't."

"Okay." Hank nodded. "Do you think he'll be very upset?"

"I don't think so . . . not if I tell him right away. But he will be, if I wait. I think I'll call him tonight. It's only fair."

Hank pulled over to the curb, and opened the door of the limo. "There's no time like the present. Go ahead, Jan. Climb in the back and use the phone."

She'd managed to roll from the bed to the floor, but there was no way she could get free. He'd tied her knees, and her ankles, and her wrists, and then he'd tethered them together.

She knew she had to do something to try to get free now, while she had the chance. The baby-sitter game had gone too far, and when she'd tried to run out of the apartment, he'd caught her and shackled her as his captive.

"Wait right here." He'd laughed as he'd seen the tears of fright in her eyes. "I've got to do a job for some friends of mine. And when I come back, we'll pick up right where we left off."

She'd stared up at him, hardly daring to breathe, hoping he wouldn't kill her right then and there. And he'd knelt down next to her on the bed, and smiled a terrible smile.

"She has to die, but it won't be any fun for me. It has to look like an accident so I can't stick around to see it. But you, my pretty little baby-sitter, will make up for all that when I get back. I'm going to watch you die and I'll make it happen very slowly. Bye-bye for now. I'll be back."

He was evil, and totally insane, and she doubled her efforts. The wool rug scratched her skin as she rolled and inched her way into the living room. She had to try to get out somehow. And then she heard it. The phone was ringing, and it was right by the couch.

With a desperate motion, she crashed into the table, knocking the phone to the floor. And she heard a woman's voice coming out of the receiver. "Hello, David? Hello?"

She couldn't talk. He'd taped her mouth. But she tried to make as much noise as she could, groaning and grunting, and attempting to scream through the tape that covered her lips.

"Hello? Are you all right? David? Answer me!" There was a moment of silence and then a man's voice came on the line. "David? We know you're in trouble. Hold on, guy . . . we're on our way over there right now!"

* * *

"Would you like a drink while we're waiting for Jan to get home?" Maura scooped up Cappy and held him under one arm. For some strange reason, he was nervous around David tonight, and he was still growling, low in his throat.

"Thanks, Mrs. Thomas." David gave her a boyish grin. "Do you have any red wine?"

"It's in the wine rack. And the corkscrew is in the little drawer behind the bar. Choose whatever you like, David. I'll take Cappy outside for a minute, and then I'll put him to bed. I'm afraid he's not being very sociable tonight."

David nodded. "Okay, Mrs. Thomas. Would you like me to pour you a glass?"

"No, thanks. I had some cognac earlier, and that's enough for me."

The moment they got outside, Cappy stopped growling. But when Maura tried to coax him back inside again, he refused to budge. "All right, then. I'm going in without you."

Maura took a step toward the house, and Cappy raced around in front of her to stand in her way. He made the growling sound again, and blocked her way when she tried to step around him.

"What's with you tonight?" Maura tried to pick him up, but Cappy darted away. She'd never seen him act so strangely. And then she remembered how Boris and Natasha had reacted when the authorities had come to the farmhouse the morning after she'd taken the ring and the message from Nick's body. The low growl was a warning. Cappy was telling her that it was dangerous to go back in the house.

"It's all right, Cappy." Maura reached for him again. "There's nobody inside except David."

But Cappy wouldn't let her touch him. And he wouldn't

let her enter the house again, either. His strange reaction made Maura think. What did she really know about David?

David had said that he was Grant's nephew, but was he really? And had their chance meeting at the club's tennis court been planned? Cappy hadn't reacted to anyone else the way he reacted to David. He adored Hank, and Steve, and the gardener, and the pool man. David was the only one he didn't seem to like. Cappy was naturally protective of her because she was his trainer and his mistress. Some dogs had a sixth sense about danger, and Cappy was a very intelligent puppy. It was possible that his instincts were better than hers.

"Are you all right, Mrs. Thomas?"

David appeared in the doorway, and Cappy growled again. Maura glanced down at the puppy and then she made up her mind. It was better to err on the side of caution.

"I'm fine. I'm just waiting for Cappy to finish up. Help yourself to a snack, David. There's a plate of cheeses in the refrigerator."

The yard lights were out, and Maura could see him hesitate in the doorway. And then he turned and went back inside. Now was the time, and she had to hurry.

"Come, Cappy!" Maura whispered the words and the little dog trotted quickly to her side. There was no way she could get to the panic button on the security system, but the circuit box for the lights was on the outside wall of the garage.

Cappy seemed to recognize the urgency, because he didn't make a sound as they ran across the lawn to the garage. Maura opened the box and shoved up on the handle of the master circuit. It made a slight popping sound and all the lights in the house went off.

There was the sound of glass shattering and she heard David's voice. "Son of a bitch!"

He sounded mean, not like the nice college man at all, and Maura shivered. And then he called out again, in the voice she usually heard.

"Mrs. Thomas? Are you all right, Mrs. Thomas?"

Cappy gave a barely audible growl, and Maura reached down to put her hand on his collar. He seemed to know that her gesture meant silence and he stood there trembling, pressed up against her leg.

Maura could hear David walk across the room to the patio door. It slid open and she heard his footsteps on the bricks outside, searching the patio for her.

"Now." Maura whispered the word and they moved to the kitchen door, slipping inside and hurrying to the living room where she'd left the gun under a couch pillow.

But the gun wasn't there, where she'd left it.

And then she heard footsteps behind her and she whirled to run. But he was standing there, holding a flashlight, her gun in his hand.

"Looking for this, Mrs. T.?" He smiled a chilling smile, one that made Maura's blood run cold. There was no pity, or even a hint of humanity in his expression. Cappy had been right. David was the hit man, and she had just provided him with the weapon that he would use to kill her.

"Oh, my God!" Jan's face turned white as she saw the woman on the floor. "Help me, Hank!"

Hank grabbed a knife from the kitchen, and cut through the cords that were binding the woman's wrists and legs. The moment they removed the tape from the woman's mouth, she started to cry.

"I gotta get out of here! He's gonna kill me!"

"Who?" Hank helped her to her feet.

"The guy that rents this place! He's crazy, and he told me he was gonna go do a job. And then he said he'd come back to kill me!"

"A job?" Jan steadied herself on the edge of the couch. "What does that mean?"

"He's gonna kill some lady. I don't know who, but he said he's gotta make it look like an accident. And then he's coming back for me! You guys better get outta here!"

The woman rushed for the door, but Hank caught her by the wrist. "Hold on. What does this guy look like?"

"Tall, dark hair, glasses . . . a real clean-cut guy. Looks like a teacher or something like that. I never guessed that he was such a wacko!"

"She just described David." Hank looked shocked. "I think we'd better call the police."

Jan nodded, and sank down on the couch. "Go ahead. But I can't believe that . . . Hank! Look at this!"

Hank walked over to look at the scrapbook on the coffee table. "Maura Rawlins? Is that . . ."

"Yes!" Jan snatched up the book and grabbed Hank's hand. "Hurry, Hank! That lady he's going to kill . . . I think it's Mom!"

Steve frowned as he squealed around the corner, and got on the freeway. He'd been trying to call Maura from his car phone for the past ten minutes, but the line was still busy. It wasn't like her to tie up her phone line, especially when he'd promised to call to check in.

"I'm sorry, sir." The operator sounded very official. "We listened in, but all we heard was a dog barking in the distance. Your party must have the receiver off the hook."

"Thank you, operator." Steve's hand was shaking as he

clicked off the phone. Something was very wrong, and he had to get to Brentwood as fast as he could!

At first she thought she was out in the rain because her face was so wet. It was a warm rain, and it tickled as it brushed against her nose. She tried to roll away, to hide her face, but the rain kept on falling, brushing against her cheeks. And then it wasn't rain any longer. It was a warm, wet tongue. And she remembered what had happened and tried to sit up.

"Cappy?" Her voice was thick, and she swallowed past the lump in her throat. Her head throbbed painfully, and she remembered how David had hit her with the gun butt. It was dark, but she could see shapes in the dim moonlight that flickered in the windows. She was in the living room, behind the bar, tied up to the edge of the brass rail that ran along its length.

Something glittered under the coffee table, and it drew her attention. The cheese knife. He'd dropped the cheese plate when the lights had gone out, and the knife had landed there. He hadn't bothered to pick it up, but there was no way she could get it, unless . . .

"Cappy? Fetch!" Maura stared at the cheese knife, but Cappy just tilted his head and looked puzzled. She'd been teaching him to fetch toys, but the knife didn't look like a toy. "Fetch, Cappy! Bring me the knife!"

It was no use. Cappy just looked puzzled, but then Maura noticed a little squeak toy on the table above the knife. It was his favorite, a little mouse, and she motioned toward it with her head. "Fetch the toy, Cappy! Bring me the toy!"

Cappy spotted the toy and trotted over to it. But just as he was about to grab it, Maura gave him another command.

"Sit, Cappy!" Cappy sat obediently, his tail thumping the floor. And then she gave him another command. "Down, Cappy!"

Cappy lowered his body to the floor. His nose was only about twelve inches from the cheese knife.

"Crawl, Cappy! That's it. That's a good boy! Now stay!"

Cappy's tail thumped against the rug. David had used the knife to cut a piece of cheese and the scent was still on it. Maura took a deep breath and issued another command. "Fetch the knife, Cappy. Bring me the knife!"

Cappy hesitated a moment and then his teeth closed around the wooden handle. He turned to look at her, and Maura smiled.

"Good boy! Bring it to me, Cappy! Bring it!"

Cappy got up and trotted to her. But she couldn't reach out to pick it up because her hands were tied behind her back.

"Drop it, Cappy." Maura smiled as Cappy dropped the knife only inches from her head. She twisted to the side and managed to grab it in her teeth. It would take a while, but she might be able to saw through the bonds that held her hands. With her hands free, she could untie her feet and then she'd be free.

Maura's mind was whirling as she moved her head back and forth, sawing away at the cords that bound her wrists. He'd told her exactly how she was going to die. It had seemed to give him satisfaction to torture her with the knowledge.

David had weakened the gas line, so it would leak at the slightest jolt. And then he'd rigged an explosive to the security system, and armed it when he'd left. He'd watched Jan open it one night, and he'd memorized the code. When Jan came in, she'd punch in the code and the charge would activate.

And when she opened the door, the house would blow up, supposedly from a gas leak, killing them all.

"Hurry, Hank!" Jan twisted her hands nervously in her lap as the limo barreled down the freeway. She'd tried to call the house to warn her mother, but the line was busy. And although the police were on their way, Jan knew it would take them time to get through the security gates.

"Hold on, Jan." Hank took the off-ramp at a speed that wasn't recommended in the driver's manual, but the heavy car hugged the road and they managed to make the turn. "We're almost there."

Jan nodded, but she didn't trust her voice. She was much too close to tears. She was the one who'd brought David into their home, and she'd told him that her mother's memory was coming back. She had to save her mother's life! If something happened to Mom, it was all her fault. And she knew she'd never be able to forgive herself!

Her first instinct was to go to the front door to warn them, but she quickly discarded that idea. There was a motion sensor trained on the door that would activate the system if they came close enough to hear her voice. There were only two windows that weren't part of the alarm system, the windows that they'd added later for her studio. It was the only way in or out that was safe.

Maura ran up the staircase, Cappy at her heels, and flicked on the lights in the studio. And then she saw it, a car driving up to the gates. It was Hank and Jan in the limo and she had to climb down to warn them. If they touched the security panel, none of them would live to tell about it.

There was a heavy brass lamp on her desk, and Maura pulled the plug out of the wall. She swung it like a baseball bat and smashed the glass out of the window. The heavy canvas tote she used to carry her drawings was hanging over the edge of her easel and she grabbed Cappy and put him inside.

"Stay, Cappy!" Maura shushed him when he whimpered. "There's no way I'm going to leave you behind. We're going for a little climb that'll save our lives."

Maura shivered as she looked down at the driveway below. It was a long way down. She didn't have a rope, and there was no time to get one, but there was an ivy-covered trellis that came all the way up to her windows. Would it hold her weight? Maura wasn't sure, but it was her only hope.

She took a deep breath and backed out of the window, finding a foothold on the trellis. The light strips of wood creaked and pulled away from the wall slightly, and she knew she had to be very careful. A fall from this height would kill them both, but the farther down she was able to climb, the better their chances of survival would be.

The gates were opening now. She could hear them in the distance. She climbed down another foot, and the trellis creaked again. The faster she went, the safer she'd be, and she forced herself to climb down, clinging to the rough, painted wood, and scrambling for footholds on the slippery leaves.

She had reached the second floor by the time the car pulled up in front. It was Jan and Hank, and Steve was just behind them. She took another step, and then another, praying that she'd get down in time. And then she thought of it, and she almost broke into hysterical laughter. Raglan sleeves. She was wearing raglan sleeves, and they didn't restrict her movement. It was the perfect sleeve for her tennis outfit!

Maura turned to look over her shoulder. Jan was getting out of the car. She stopped and stared up at the front of the house. Jan had spotted her, clinging to the trellis.

"Get back! All of you!" Maura shouted out, praying they'd hear her. "The house is wired! If you set off the motion lights, it'll blow!"

The next few moments were a nightmare. No one could get close enough to help her for fear of setting off the motion lights. And Maura knew she had to be very careful not to touch a window on her way down. The middle of the trellis was very close to the glass, and that forced her to stay at the very edge, where the wood jutted out in a diamond shape, held only by glue and tiny decorative nails.

Cappy wiggled once and almost threw her off balance, but she told him to stay quiet and he obeyed her instantly. And then she was down, racing over the lawn toward the waiting cars, crying and laughing at the same time.

"Mom!" Jan hugged her tightly. And then she took Cappy out of the bag and gave him a hug, too. "I couldn't believe it when I saw you up there. I thought you were afraid of heights."

Maura nodded, and gave her a trembling smile. "I am. But I think I'm getting used to it. Maybe I'll try mountain climbing next year. And while I was climbing down, I thought of the perfect sleeve for my tennis outfit."

"Calm down, Mom." Jan turned to Steve. "I think she's a little hysterical. Maybe you'd better give her something, Uncle Steve."

Maura shook her head. "I'm fine. Did they get David? He tried to kill me!"

"I know." Steve wrapped his arms around her. "They picked him up at his apartment. Jan and Hank figured it out, and they called the police."

Maura nodded, and then she reached up to kiss him, in front of Jan, and Hank, and the police. And then she pulled him away from the others, so she could speak to him privately. "Do you think we can retire now?"

"That's a very good idea. We've closed the books on the drug cartel." Steve smiled, and hugged her a little tighter. "Will you miss the excitement? Or did you have another career in mind?"

"I know exactly which career I want to try next, but I need your cooperation. Will you marry me?"

"I thought you'd never ask." Steve laughed, and kissed her. "But what about your new career?"

Maura smiled. It was a smile full of promise and contentment, a smile that she hadn't felt like smiling for a long, long, time. "Wife sounds exciting enough to me."

*"MIND-BOGGLING . . . THE SUSPENSE IS UNBEARABLE . . .
DORIS MILES DISNEY WILL KEEP YOU
ON THE EDGE OF YOUR SEAT . . ."*

THE MYSTERIES OF DORIS MILES DISNEY

THE DAY MISS BESSIE LEWIS DISAPPEARED (2080-5, $2.95/$4.50)

THE HOSPITALITY OF THE HOUSE   (2738-9, $3.50/$4.50)

THE LAST STRAW   (2286-7, $2.95/$3.95)

THE MAGIC GRANDFATHER   (2584-X, $2.95/$3.95)

MRS. MEEKER'S MONEY   (2212-3, $2.95/$3.95)

NO NEXT OF KIN   (2969-1, $3.50/$4.50)

ONLY COUPLES NEED APPLY   (2438-X, $2.95/$3.95)

SHADOW OF A MAN   (3077-0, $3.50/$4.50)

THAT WHICH IS CROOKED   (2848-2, $3.50/$4.50)

THREE'S A CROWD   (2079-1, $2.95/$3.95)

WHO RIDES A TIGER   (2799-0, $3.50/$4.50)

*Available wherever paperbacks are sold, or order direct from the
Publisher. Send cover price plus 50¢ per copy for mailing and
handling to Penguin USA, P.O. Box 999, c/o Dept. 17109,
Bergenfield, NJ 07621. Residents of New York and Tennessee
must include sales tax. DO NOT SEND CASH.*

WHO DUNNIT? JUST TRY AND FIGURE IT OUT!

THE MYSTERIES OF MARY ROBERTS RINEHART

THE AFTER HOUSE	(2821-0, $3.50/$4.50)
THE ALBUM	(2334-0, $3.50/$4.50)
ALIBI FOR ISRAEL AND OTHER STORIES	(2764-8, $3.50/$4.50)
THE BAT	(2627-7, $3.50/$4.50)
THE CASE OF JENNIE BRICE	(2193-3, $2.95/$3.95)
THE CIRCULAR STAIRCASE	(3528-4, $3.95/$4.95)
THE CONFESSION AND SIGHT UNSEEN	(2707-9, $3.50/$4.50)
THE DOOR	(1895-5, $3.50/$4.50)
EPISODE OF THE WANDERING KNIFE	(2874-1, $3.50/$4.50)
THE FRIGHTENED WIFE	(3494-6, $3.95/$4.95)
THE GREAT MISTAKE	(2122-4, $3.50/$4.50)
THE HAUNTED LADY	(3680-9, $3.95/$4.95)
A LIGHT IN THE WINDOW	(1952-1, $3.50/$4.50)
LOST ECSTASY	(1791-X, $3.50/$4.50)
THE MAN IN LOWER TEN	(3104-1, $3.50/$4.50)
MISS PINKERTON	(1847-9, $3.50/$4.50)
THE RED LAMP	(2017-1, $3.50/$4.95)
THE STATE V. ELINOR NORTON	(2412-6, $3.50/$4.50)
THE SWIMMING POOL	(3679-5, $3.95/$4.95)
THE WALL	(2560-2, $3.50/$4.50)
THE YELLOW ROOM	(3493-8, $3.95/$4.95)

Available wherever paperbacks are sold, or order direct from the Publisher. Send cover price plus 50¢ per copy for mailing and handling to Penguin USA, P.O. Box 999, c/o Dept. 17109, Bergenfield, NJ 07621.Residents of New York and Tennessee must include sales tax. DO NOT SEND CASH.

WHODUNIT?... ZEBRA DUNIT!
FOR ARMCHAIR DETECTIVES — TWO DELIGHTFUL
NEW MYSTERY SERIES

AN ANGELA BIAWABAN MYSTERY: TARGET FOR MURDER   (4069, $3.99)
by J.F. Trainor

Anishinabe princess Angie is on parole from a correctional facility, courtesy of an embezzling charge. But when an old friend shows up on her doorstep crying bloody murder, Angie skips parole to track down the creep who killed Mary Beth's husband and stole her land. When she digs up the dirt on a big-time developer and his corrupt construction outfit, she becomes a sitting duck for a cunning killer who never misses the mark!

AN ANGELA BIAWABAN MYSTERY: DYNAMITE PASS   (4227, $3.99)
by J.F. Trainor

When Angie — a native American detective on the wrong side of the law and the right side of justice — attends a family *powwow,* her forest ranger cousin is killed in a suspicious accident. The sleuth finds herself in deadly danger from a sleazy lumber king when she investigates his death. Now, she must beat the bad guys and stop the killer before the case blows up in her face and explodes in one more fatality — hers!

A CLIVELY CLOSE MYSTERY: DEAD AS DEAD CAN BE   (4099, $3.99)
by Ann Crowleigh

Twin sisters Miranda and Clare Clively are stunned when a corpse falls from their carriage house chimney. Against the back drop of Victorian London, they must defend their family name from a damning scandal — and a thirty-year-old murder. But just as they are narrowing down their list of suspects, they get another dead body on their hands — and now Miranda and Clare wonder if they will be next . . .

A CLIVELY CLOSE MYSTERY: WAIT FOR THE DARK   (4298, $3.99)
by Ann Crowleigh

Clare Clively is taken by surprise when she discovers a corpse while walking through the park. She and her twin sister, Miranda are immediately on the case . . . yet the closer they come to solving the crime, the closer they come to a murderous villain who has no intention of allowing the two snooping sisters to unmask the truth!

LOOK FOR THESE OTHER BOOKS IN ZEBRA'S NEW *PARTNERS IN CRIME*
SERIES FEATURING APPEALING WOMEN AMATEUR-SLEUTHS:
   LAURA FLEMING MYSTERIES
   MARGARET BARLOW MYSTERIES
   AMANDA HAZARD MYSTERIES
   TEAL STEWART MYSTERIES
   DR. AMY PRESCOTT MYSTERIES

Available wherever paperbacks are sold, or order direct from the Publisher. Send cover price plus 50¢ per copy for mailing and handling to Penguin USA, P.O. Box 999, c/o Dept. 17109, Bergenfield, NJ 07621. Residents of New York and Tennessee must include sales tax. DO NOT SEND CASH.